The Confidential Casebook of Sherlock Holmes

The Confidential Casebook of Sherlock Holmes

EDITED BY

Marvin Kaye

ST. MARTIN'S PRESS NEW YORK

Additional copyrights on pgs. 355–356

Library of Congress Cataloging-in-Publication Data

The confidential casebook of Sherlock Holmes / Marvin Kaye,
    editor.—1st ed.
             p. cm.
      ISBN 0-312-18071-3
        1. Dectective and mystery stories, American.   2. Holmes,
Sherlock (Fictitious character)—Fiction.   3. Private
investigators—England—Fiction.   I. Kaye, Marvin.
PS648.D4C68   1998
813'.087208351—dc21   97-38389
                                      CIP

First Edition: February 1998

10 9 8 7 6 5 4 3 2 1

To the memory
of a dear friend and fine writer
William L. DeAndrea

Contents

*The Confidential
Casebook of
Sherlock Holmes*

Introduction

The Startling Discovery of Dr. Watson's Confidential Papers

If you love the Sherlock Holmes adventures . . . you have sorely lamented the fact that The Great Detective's best friend, coadventurer and erstwhile roommate John H. Watson, M.D., only wrote sixty of them.

Like me, you have . . . surely dreamed about visiting the bank vaults of Cox & Company, London, to peep into the battered tin dispatch-box that Dr. Watson stored there. This legendary container was crammed full of notes for over sixty additional Sherlock Holmes cases that, for various reasons, Watson never got around to writing. For the past half-century, this seemed to be a forlorn dream, for Cox & Company was destroyed during a World War II Nazi bombing raid.

But now, fifty years later, the truth can at last be told—Dr. Watson's unpublished records have survived!

—from the Introduction to
The Resurrected Holmes
by Professor J. Adrian Fillmore,
Gadshill Adjunct, Parker College (Pa.)

Imagine the thrill when Dr. R., the wealthy Philadelphia scholar and book collector who bought the fabled dispatch-box, first opened his trove of unpublished Holmesiana. The box actually contained a variety of documents: daily memoranda and anecdota that the author did not choose to write up for *The Strand,* the British magazine that first reported the principal adventures of England's remarkable consulting detective, Mr. Sherlock Holmes.

Careful examination of the box's contents revealed a number of tales that Watson never afforded that final professional polish that would have qualified them for publication. Some were cases too mundane or inconclusive to work up as dramatic narrative; some were too sensitive in nature to be made public at the time.

A selection of the latter cases—which Dr. R. arranged to have "ghost-written" from Watson's notes by such renowned authors as H. G. Wells, Theodore Dreiser, H. P. Lovecraft, Dashiell Hammett, etc.—appeared in print for the first time last year in the St. Martin's Press collection *The Resurrected Holmes,* a volume prepared in association with the distinguished Parker College teacher J. Adrian Fillmore, who helped review and choose its contents, and who wrote its introduction.

One evening while examining the Watsonian archives, the professor reflectively stroked his chin and observed to me that the tin dispatch-box was ever so much larger than most Holmesian buffs probably realized.

"Well, it would have to be," I said sardonically, "considering how many 'authentic' manuscripts have come out of it since 1930."*

"Yes," Fillmore mused, resting his hand on the lid of the

---

*The year that Watson's literary agent, Arthur Conan Doyle, died.

box, "but isn't it odd that no one has ever reported the precise dimensions of this fabled repository? Or do you recall any such paper?"

"I do not." I quickly consulted the entries under the heading "Untold Tales and Dr. Watson's Tin Dispatch-Box," in my copy of Ronald Burt DeWaal's *The World Bibliography of Sherlock Holmes and Dr. Watson,* but their titles suggested that their authors (quite properly) were more concerned with the contents of Watson's box than the container itself. Still, the true aficionado thirsts for all possible knowledge concerning his field of specialization.

The professor agreed. Forthwith and posthaste, he fetched a tailor's tape measure and with great exactitude recorded the width, breadth and height of the tin dispatch-box. I wrote them on a slip of paper as he announced them to me. Next, the pedagogue aligned the tip of the tape with the top of the inner lid, plumbed the container's depths with the measuring device, and read off the results.

"No, that must be wrong," I said, comparing the figure with the exterior height. Fillmore carefully remeasured the box's depth, but the answer was the same: four inches shorter than seemed likely. We inspected the workmanship, looking for evidence of layered reinforcement. We lifted the heavy container. Fillmore rested a palm on the lower surface, stuck his other hand in the box and rapped smartly on what should have been the upper side of its bottom. The dull sound produced by this action mutually widened our eyes . . .

"Eureka!" the professor exclaimed. For we had discovered the snug false bottom that partitions Watson's dispatch-box into an upper and a secret lower compartment.

In this nether recess we found two thick stacks of manuscripts whose existence till now has been unknown to Holmesians. Needless to say, Professor Fillmore and I set aside the fascinating contents of the box's upper chamber, and voraciously pored over the new material.

It was apparent to us that these manuscripts differed in character from those that rested so many years in the "B," or upper apartment, of the dispatch-box. Most of the new discoveries appeared to have been written by Dr. Watson himself.

Then why had they never been published? The first few that the professor and I read that evening were too sensitive for publication during Queen Victoria's heyday, yet might have been offered to a Holmes-hungry public during Edward's reign. But then we read further.

I forget whose breath first hissed through clenched teeth.

Before the abrupt and unexplained disappearance of Professor Fillmore from the academic, or for that matter, all scenes, he made preliminary notes for an introduction to the volume you hold in your hand. Here is the final paragraph of that composition:

"As you read through these tales★," Fillmore wrote, "you will see why Watson and Holmes kept these narratives from all eyes. The fact that they were written at all, or, having been penned, had not been subsequently consigned to some working fireplace, attests, I think, to the psychology of our favorite medical amanuensis. Watson was, after all, an author, subject to the generous vanity of that breed of being who collectively set down experience for the edification of some hypothetical future generation."

Fortunately, that's us.

—MARVIN KAYE
New York City
May 1997

★Copyedited by contributors who, for legal purposes, we have "credited" with by-lines.—MK

Delicate Business

Nowadays, tact and delicacy are too often patronized as anachronisms of bygone morality, but Sherlock Holmes and his faithful scribe were gentlemen who valued prudency, especially if the truth ran the risk of injuring their fellows, singly or collectively. The first three cases chronicled in this section deal with delicate business of this character. Perhaps Dr. Watson might have delivered them for publication one day, but I suspect that the fourth narrative never would have been released, inasmuch as the reputation it chiefly affects is that of Sherlock Holmes himself.

*W*atson mentions *"The Darlington Substitution Scandal"* in *"A Scandal in Bohemia,"* which suggests that he might have eventually sent this manuscript to The Strand, but this is purely speculative. Still, one cannot help wondering why, in the case of such a delicate matter, he mentioned Darlington at all. Perhaps Watson was so offended by that individual's beastly behaviour that in spite of Holmes's high moral character, he just could not bear to let the scoundrel escape without some trace of censure attached to his name.

The Darlington Substitution Scandal

BY HENRY SLESAR

O n certain days, my friend Sherlock Holmes would invariably wear a scowl, which further lengthened his saturnine face. These were the days when *The Strand* magazine appeared, its garish cover boasting of yet another "Sherlock Holmes Adventure." As the author of these chronicles I received the brunt of his displeasure, yet it troubled me less and less as I became aware that Holmes wasn't entirely displeased by this celebration of his deductive powers. He would scold me about an excess of melodrama; he would carp about the syntax of the words I put into his mouth; yet by the end of the day, the scowl was erased, and a certain mellowness overtook him. To be perfectly candid, I believe he enjoyed reading *The Adventures of Sherlock Holmes* almost as much as he enjoyed living them.

However, as I have noted before, there were cases which

Holmes forbade me to dramatize for reasons that were usually quite apparent. He would not give grist to the London gossip mills. He would not have reputations ruined, families victimized, and more often than anyone knew, royal titles debased. But this last cause of reticence is not the reason why I have never published the shocking story of Lord Rufus Darlington. It is simply because no charges were ever brought against the man for his horrific actions, and Holmes forbade any accusations which had never been confirmed in a court of law.

Whether this tale reaches the general public is questionable, since I have stipulated that if any surviving member of the Darlington family can prove slander by its publication it is to be returned to the vault where it will reside until the next century.* History has a way of making harmless fable of even the most heinous crimes, but writing as I do now, only days after the Darlington case was resolved, I can scarcely believe that such horror can ever be transformed or forgiven.

Of course, I cannot conceive what the laws of slander may be like in that distant time. I hope they will still protect the weak and innocent. I also hope, fervently, that the laws of the coming years will afford more protection to married women against the brutality of their husbands, cruelty far too easily shrugged off in the age in which we live. In such a time, the Darlington affair might never have happened.

One aspect of the case which made it unlike any other was the part played by Inspector Lestrade, surely one of the most misunderstood figures in the Sherlock Holmes gallery. It is astonishing how many admirers of The Great Detective have relegated poor Lestrade to the role of the hapless professional constantly forced to defer to a gifted amateur who bested him at every turn. In fact,

---

*A descendant of Lord Darlington, Palmer Leeds of Manchester, did solicit the courts to prevent the publication of this story, but his petition was denied.

Holmes admired and respected Lestrade, and cherished his friend-ship, but outside of their professional encounters these two devotees of Justice rarely spent time together. The exception was that bitterly cold day in late January, 1895, when the Inspector, hearing that Holmes was confined to our flat due to a bronchial condition, de-cided to pay a social call.

As a physician, let me declare that Sherlock Holmes was the worst possible patient. The words "bed rest" were anathema to him. All medicines were "quack nostrums," all medical advisories were "incantations." His remedy for all ills was self-prescribed: the seven and a half percent cocaine solution which gave him a false sense of well-being. That was why Lestrade was surprised to enter our quar-ters that snowy evening and find Sherlock Holmes by the fireplace, sucking at his empty meerschaum (tobacco tasted foul in his present state), and giving all the appearance of a healthy man ready to enjoy the company of his peer.

They conversed for a good hour, managing to ignore every contribution I attempted to make. I began to feel a bit nettled, and drank more brandy-and-splash than I was accustomed to having, even on a holiday occasion. I was just beginning to doze off in my chair when the Inspector revealed that he had more than one reason for his visit. He wasn't seeking advice on a case; the crime on his mind had been swiftly and easily solved one year be-fore.

"One year to the day," he sighed, lighting a cigar. "A cold night like this one. But perhaps you don't recall it, Mr. Holmes. It wasn't a case to challenge your skills."

Holmes merely nodded, watching Lestrade with narrowed eyes, waiting for him to speak the name that seemed to float be-tween them like the smoke from his cheroot. For some reason, I felt obliged to supply it.

"Carlton Paige," I said, clearing my throat. "Strange, isn't it? Such a commotion then. Now, hardly anyone recalls the case."

"Except," Holmes said pointedly, "Mrs. Paige."

"Yes," Lestrade said. "I'm sure Mrs. Paige is not very happy tonight. On the anniversary of that terrible event."

"How can she be?" I snorted. "In Bristol Prison for Women? Confined for life?"

"No," Lestrade said quietly. "She is no longer there. She has been transferred."

But when I asked him where, the Inspector ignored my question, and looked at Holmes.

"Do you remember the protesters?" he asked. "When she was first incarcerated? Did they really expect us to free a murderer on 'moral' grounds?"

"Still, she had them," I said, feeling perverse. "Carlton Paige was a vicious wife-beater! He drove that poor women to the limit of her endurance. And when she reached that limit—she shot him!"

Holmes smiled thinly. "I've often heard you claim to be at the end of your patience with someone or other, Watson. Did you decide to shoot them through the heart?"

"This was different," I said stiffly. "It was impulsive. The woman had been brutalized for years, and that night, she snapped!"

"Yes," Holmes said, winking at Lestrade. "She snapped a trigger. Of a gun she had 'impulsively' purchased several days before."

"Well, I'll say this much for Mrs. Paige," the Inspector said. "She didn't deny her crime, didn't try to justify it. Called the police herself, and gave us a full confession on the spot. Took her punishment like—"

"Like a man?" Holmes smiled.

"I can't help but feel compassion for her," Lestrade admitted gloomily. "Especially now that she's gone mad."

"Good Lord!" I said. "Do you mean she's lost her mind?"

"The place to which she was transferred is the Institute for the Criminal Insane. I learned of it only recently. But when her symptoms were described to me, my first thought was—wouldn't Mr. Sherlock Holmes find that fascinating!"

The empty pipe came out of Holmes's mouth and his eyes brightened. "For what reason, Inspector?"

"Well, you like strange stories, Mr. Holmes, and here's one for your notebook. Mrs. Paige is suffering from the delusion that her real name is Emma Jane Darlington. Better known as Lady Darlington."

"Is that really so strange?" I said. "How many Napoleons and Lord Nelsons are in Bedlam this very minute?"

"But you miss the point, Watson," Holmes said. "One can understand a madman believing himself to be a famous personage, even a god. But why this rather obscure wife of a relatively obscure patrician?"

"I can tell you that," Lestrade said. "She *looks* like the woman."

"You mean there's a physical resemblance?"

"How would she know?" I asked. "Being behind bars for the past twelve months?"

"Because of the Rotogravure," the Inspector said. He pulled a folded newspaper clipping out of his pocket, revealing that his interest in this matter ran deep. He handed it to Holmes, and I was forced to look over his shoulder.

"It's a wedding photo," Holmes said.

"Of course," I replied. "Now I remember. This Lord Darlington was something of a roué, but he finally decided to marry. Probably because his father was threatening him with disinheritance if he didn't settle down, produce an heir or two!" I chuckled, but my companions didn't seem amused. I took the clipping from Holmes's hand and studied the sweet, simple face of the bride. The clipping was dated October 1.

"It caused a bit of a stir, this marriage," Lestrade said. "Not that I follow the gossip columns. Mainly because the bride's father is a tea and coffee importer. Hardly blue blood."

"Lovely girl just the same," I said in her defence.

"Yes," Holmes said, "And Mrs. Paige saw this lovely girl in the newspaper, noted the resemblance, and decided that *she* was the happy bride."

"Exactly," Lestrade said gravely. "And that's when the trouble began. She started shrieking night and day that her husband, Lord

Darlington, had betrayed her. That he had put her into this prison in order to continue his abandoned life. She begged and pleaded with her guards to help her, to call her family, her friends, even Darlington himself. She was uncontrollable, Mr. Holmes, totally and completely insane."

"How terrible," I said. "But of course, the woman found her life unbearable. Therefore, she invented a new one."

"Bravo," Holmes said, smiling at me without irony for a change. "Dr. Watson has diagnosed the case with accuracy. Don't you agree, Inspector?"

"Yes," Lestrade said grudgingly. "It has to be the truth." He pulled a large repeater out of his watch pocket and shook his head. "Almost midnight," he said. "I suppose I should be on my way home."

"One more to toast the new year," I said, pouring him a largish brandy. He took it readily enough, lifted it in the air, and we all wished ourselves a Happy 1895. His glass was almost empty when he said, "But I didn't tell you about Lord Darlington's visit to the Institute."

Once again, Holmes brightened.

"Are you saying that Lord Darlington actually visited this woman?"

"Yes," Lestrade said. "Somehow, the story of Mrs. Paige's delusion reached his ear, and he got in touch with one of the physicians in charge. He wondered if perhaps the woman might be helped by a personal visit from Darlington and his wife."

"A reasonable notion," I said. "If she was rational enough to believe her own eyes . . ."

"A very kind offer," Holmes said, his mouth twisting cynically. "But not one would expect from a man of Darlington's reputation. He was hardly an altruistic type."

"It was his wife's idea, I believe. She convinced him that it would be an act of charity. They went to see her together, but with unfortunate consequences. Not only did they fail to convince her, but Mrs. Paige took revenge on the institution by trying to burn it down!"

"Good Lord!" I said.

"Tell me exactly what happened," Holmes said, his gaze as intense as an eagle's.

"The details are still a bit cloudy. When the couple arrived, the Institute directors naturally wanted to protect their safety, and assigned a guard to supervise their meeting. Mrs. Paige objected violently; she would only talk to the Darlingtons alone. Rufus Darlington convinced them to allow this departure from precedent. He was confident he could handle any situation."

I glanced at the wedding photograph again. "He looks capable enough. Rather gigantic physically."

"A collegiate boxing champion," Lestrade grunted. "Obviously, he had little to fear from the madwoman. But he was wrong. While they were alone in Mrs. Paige's room, he made the mistake of lighting his pipe. She suddenly seized his matches, and quickly set her mattress on fire. By the time they obtained help, the whole room was ablaze!"

"Yes," I said. "I recall some small news story about that."

"It wasn't worthy of large headlines," Lestrade said. "But it did have a tragic consequence. Mrs. Paige was badly burned on most of her upper body. And worst of all, the visit failed to rid her of her delusion. If anything, her condition worsened."

Holmes had not said a word for the last few minutes. His eyes were closed, and he was breathing shallowly. I had a moment of alarm, knowing his medical condition. I touched him on the shoulder, but when he opened his eyes they were mere slits.

"I think Mr. Holmes should be in bed," I told the Inspector sternly. "He has not been well for the past three days, and I'm afraid this visit has tired him to the point of exhaustion."

Lestrade rose quickly. "I'm sorry," he said. "I had no idea . . ."

"Of course not," I said. "Because Mr. Holmes was indulging in one of his favorite pastimes—pretending to be someone else. In this case, a person in good health!"

A flustered Inspector Lestrade left a few minutes later, with many apologies for his lack of insight. I accepted them cordially. But when I returned to Holmes, insisting on his immediate retirement, he looked at me so strangely that I wondered if the fever which had taken two days to subside had returned.

Then he spoke. "I would like to see a doctor."

I reminded him that I still bore the title.

"I want to see a very specific doctor, Watson. Tomorrow."

"But why?"

"Because," he said, his voice as sonorous as a church bell, "it's a matter of life and death. Not my own, dear fellow," he added, seeing my expression.

I woke the next morning a good hour and forty minutes past my usual waking time, surely the result of the surplus brandy I had ingested the night before.

I had an uneasy feeling that Holmes was no longer in his sickbed. I heard the distinct rattle of a cup and saucer, and poking my feet into a pair of slippers, I padded out into the parlour, to see a fully dressed Holmes making himself a cup of tea.

"It's all right," he said in a strained voice. "I'm quite well, Watson, I assure you. I tested my temperature this morning, and it was a smidgeon below normal. I did not cough all night, and my head is clear."

"Surely you don't mean to leave the house?"

"It wasn't easy to obtain the addresses I needed, but as it happens, one of the butlers who serves in Lord Darlington's household is an avid reader of your stories in *The Strand*. He was thrilled to talk to me, once I convinced him that I was not merely a fictional character."

"But what addresses did you want?"

"For one thing, the present location of Lord Darlington and his bride . . . It seems that they've gone off on still another honeymoon, this time around the world, a trip bound to last a year or two. Then Lord Darlington reports to a diplomatic post on the island of Anguilla, a rather smallish outpost in the Caribbean."

I was becoming irritated. "What does all that matter, Holmes?"

"It matters a great deal," he answered. "But what matters even more is the name of Lord Darlington's personal physician. It's Blevin. Dr. Hugo Blevin. Do you know him, Watson?"

"Well, yes," I said. "I've met Blevin a few times, at medical conventions. I wouldn't say we were friends, but we are definitely acquaintances."

Holmes smiled broadly. "Then I can use your name as a reference," he said cheerfully, and sailed towards the door, scooping up his greatcoat as he went. He paused in the open doorway, and his lightheartedness vanished like melted snow.

"And when I return, Watson," he said, in a voice flattened by serious purpose, "you and I are going to visit the Institute for the Criminal Insane."

It was some six hours later that I heard the voice of Sherlock Holmes in the downstairs hallway, consulting Mrs. Hudson about some domestic matter. I had spent the day studying my notes on the Musgrave Ritual affair, but my mind kept wandering back to Inspector Lestrade's visit and Holmes's curious reaction to the story he had related. I simply could not understand my friend's interest in a case whose central mystery was only in the mind of a deranged woman.

When he appeared in the doorway, my first thought was for his well-being. There was indeed a feverish look in his eyes, and I was prepared to insist on an examination, but Holmes quickly quashed the idea.

"We must leave at once, Watson," he said. "We must not let this helpless victim suffer another minute more than necessary!"

"Victim? Suffer? What are you talking about, Holmes?"

"My carriage is downstairs. Take your medical bag; it might be necessary. And dress warmly. The air is frigid, and I don't want you to risk your health."

Considering who had been ill these past few days, the remark seemed highly inappropriate. But then I realized that Holmes was pulling my leg, an indirect sign of his affection.

When we reached the Institute, the first guardian of its portals proved to be a stout Welshman with fierce moustaches. For once, Holmes let me do the talking. I gave him my credentials, and asked to see the highest possible authority on a matter of grave importance. This proved to be a thin, ascetic gentleman named Stokes, who heard our names and began to wheeze with excitement.

"Mr. Holmes!" he said. "What a pleasure to meet you in the flesh! Only yesterday I read of your exploits with that nefarious Red-Headed League!" He ruffled his own reddish crown and grinned toothily. "I might well have been victimized myself."

"Speaking of victims," Holmes said cordially, "we were wondering if we could spend some time with your patient, Mrs. Paige. It's a matter of some importance, but I'm sure you'll understand that I cannot reveal its confidential nature."

Stokes looked dismayed at this, but I could see that he was in such awe of The Great Detective that he would not be denied. After a stream of warnings concerning her uncontrollable state, he led us to a door with a small glass panel through which we could discern nothing.

"Her sedative is not scheduled for another hour," Stokes said, "but I'll arrange to have it administered at once, so that your encounter will be less troublesome."

He was about to instruct a matron, but Holmes swiftly intervened.

"No," he said. "We need to speak to the woman with her mind alert."

"Her mind, Mr. Holmes?" Stokes shook his head ruefully. "But her mind is a disordered place, full of wild imaginings."

"Nevertheless," Holmes said firmly.

Of course, he won the point, and after careful unlocking, we were admitted into the room of the pitiful Mrs. Paige.

It was a small chamber, with its walls padded with a vile pinkish cloth. There were only three items of furniture: a narrow bed without either foot or headboard, a table with rounded corners, and a rocking chair drawn up to the barred window.

The woman in the chair turned to stare at us as we entered, and I tried to stifle the sound that came to my throat. I am a physician, after all, and I have seen many disfigured patients. Actually, it wasn't the dirty facial bandages, the unkempt hair, or the healing wounds which shocked me; it was the haunted look in her eyes, as if she had been allowed a glimpse of Hell.

"What do you want?" she croaked, her voice hoarse from endless bouts of shouts and screams. "When will you stop bothering me?"

"My name is Sherlock Holmes, madam; I am a Consulting Detective. This is my associate, Dr. John Watson."

"Another doctor come to poke at me!"

"We are not here to trouble you," Holmes said evenly. "We have come on an important mission—to give you an opportunity to prove the truth of your outlandish claim. Will you answer one question for us?"

"No!" she cried. "I've had enough questions! None of you care about my answers! Get out, out!"

"This might be the most important question you have ever heard. Your life, your future, your freedom may depend upon your reply. Will you listen?"

The rigidity of Holmes's posture, his emotionless tone, the absence of neither indulgence nor pity seemed to startle the woman. She nodded, her unkempt black hair falling in a dirty tangle over her bandaged face.

"Very well," she said, "What is it?"

"I would like to know," Holmes said, "if this phrase holds any significance for you: *the Ace of Spades.*"

She stared at him vacantly, and I'm sure her surprised expression was a mirror of my own.

"The Ace of Spades?" she said scornfully. "I thought I was the one supposed to be mad!"

"Think carefully, madam," Holmes said.

She rose from the rocking chair and turned her face to the window, so thick with grime that the only view it afforded was pale winter sunlight. Then her narrow shoulders lifted slightly, and she turned.

"The Ace of Spades," she repeated slowly. "The birthmark. On his upper right thigh."

If there was even a flicker of acknowledgment on the face of Sherlock Holmes, I missed it by staring open-mouthed at the woman by the viewless window. By the time I turned my attention back to him, that face was wholly transformed. Instead of the carved, stony countenance he could adopt so easily, his features had melted into a look of mingled triumph and—what would be the right word? Compassion.

A smile flickered across his lips, and Holmes said, "I will promise you this, Lady Darlington. I will obtain your release within the next few days. But I cannot predict how long it will take to bring your monstrous husband to justice."

I now understood why Holmes had insisted upon my bringing my black bag. No sooner did he speak these last two sentences than the woman's legs gave out and she crumpled to the floor in a dead faint. It was almost an hour before she was fully recovered, and during that waiting period, I learned the rest of the story as deduced by that astonishing convoluted organ that was the brain of Sherlock Holmes.

It wasn't one fact alone that Inspector Lestrade offered which made me suspicious," Holmes said. "It was the odd combination of events. The fact that Rufus Darlington, for all his aristocratic pretensions, married the daughter of a tea merchant. The fact that he learned 'somehow'—to use Inspector Lestrade's word—about Mrs. Paige's odd delusion, and allowed his wife to convince him to make a mercy mission to a madhouse. The fact that Mrs. Paige insisted on being alone with the couple. The fire that succeeded in maiming her. And then, the quick departure of Darlington and his bride on a long cruise and a distant address . . . Do you see the pattern, Watson?"

"No," I had to admit. "I do not!"

"Rufus Darlington was a murderer," Holmes said. "A murderer who escaped the law, behind the skirts of a woman."

"Good heavens, Holmes! Do you mean Darlington shot Carlton Paige?"

"Mr. Paige discovered the *affaire* between Darlington and his wife. And being a brutal husband, he punished her with a beating that enraged His Lordship enough to make him take a gun to the Paige household. He may have meant only to threaten Paige, but as often happens in such cases, the gun was fired."

"But—Mrs. Paige took the blame!"

"A very noble woman, in her own way," Holmes said drily. "But I suspect that Darlington himself suggested it, promising her that a beaten wife would receive sympathetic treatment in the courts of law. As you know, there was no leniency. Mrs. Paige was sentenced for life.

"It was then that Darlington vowed she would be free, that he would find some way of gaining her release, to repay her for shielding him. It was a daring scheme he concocted, but Rufus Darlington was a daring man . . . It took him many months of 'scouting the field' until he spotted a young woman who sufficiently resembled the new inmate of the Women's Prison. He wooed her passionately, and won her easily. She was beneath his station, of course, but that did not matter. All that mattered was—the resemblance."

Now the light began to dawn in my own mind. "Her 'delusion'! It was all play-acting, wasn't it? She was only pretending that she believed herself to be Lady Darlington."

"It was preparation," Holmes said gravely. "Establishing the mental madness that would precede the *real* Mrs. Darlington's mental condition when the two women traded places."

"So that was the purpose of their visit—to effect the trade."

"Of course. They overpowered the innocent Mrs. Darlington, switched clothing, and started the fire they hoped might destroy all possible evidence."

"You mean they would not have been concerned if the poor girl burned to death!"

"No," Holmes said grimly. "But it hardly mattered when she survived. She was still recognized as a prisoner, with the very same delusion of grandeur . . . And Lord and 'Lady' Darlington were free to travel the world and then live on an idyllic island where no one would ever question her identity . . ."

"And that's why you visited Dr. Blevin. To determine if there were identifying marks or scars which only his wife would know."

"The Ace of Spades," Holmes said. "I wonder if Lord Darlington ever considered his birthmark an evil omen, a harbinger of early doom." He picked up the evening paper, and handed it to me without another word. In the first column was the account of a British steamer called the *Craithie* that had collided with a German ship in the North Sea. Among the listed dead were the names of Lord and Lady Darlington. I tried to evoke a feeling of pity within myself, but failed. As for Sherlock Holmes, he was only concerned with the lighting of his pipe, the pleasures of tobacco once again restored by his return to health.

T he Adventure of the Old Russian Woman" is a case-to-be-told that Watson referred to in "The Musgrave Ritual." His suppression of this narrative probably stemmed from Holmes's reluctance to discomfit those erstwhile artistic "superstars" concerned in the case, JOHN SINGER SARGENT (1856–1925) and JAMES MCNEILL WHISTLER (1834–1903).

The Adventure of the Old Russian Woman

Composed from Notes in the Files
of Dr. John H. Watson

BY H. PAUL JEFFERS

In the two years which passed since I entered into an arrangement to share rooms at 221 Baker Street with Sherlock Holmes, I had through diligent effort accommodated myself to the many singular, even peculiar, traits of character and habits which had brought him increasing respect and work in his unique occupation—private consulting detective. I had grown used to his brooding silences, smelly chemical experiments, many unsavoury-looking callers in the parlour that he insisted on referring to as his "consulting room," and an array of Scotland Yard detectives who appeared to be incapable of solving crimes without his keen guidance. Like Mrs. Hudson, our patient landlady, I accepted the unusual hours he kept and no longer felt astonished or affronted by his abrupt arrivals and departures, which frequently stretched into lengthy, unexplained absences.

I had also become adjusted to being ordered to drop whatever I was doing and accompany him on investigations. "Come, Watson," he would bellow into my room, "the game's afoot!"

With very little to otherwise occupy me in my retirement, I was excited at the prospect of what might lie ahead on occasions such as that which had taken us to Stoke Moran in April of 1883. It was the notes of this singular case, which I had tentatively titled "The Adventure of the Speckled Band," that I was reviewing a few days after our return to Baker Street when Holmes came into my room carrying the afternoon post.

"These items are for you," he said as he dropped a pair of envelopes on my desk.

Until that moment I had accepted without uttering a protest his proprietary attitude toward every envelope and parcel that was delivered to our mutual address by postmen, telegram delivery boys and messengers. Not an item addressed to me passed into my hands without first having been subjected to examination of its exterior by him without remonstrance from me. Consequently, the afternoon following our return from Stoke Moran as I was still feeling unsettled by that horrifying experience, I at last marshalled the nerve to vent my long-simmering irritation at his noisome behaviour.

"Why, Watson," he declared in a wounded tone as he fixed me with a look of bewilderment, "I had no idea you could become so upset over such a trifling matter. You know my methods. I simply presumed that you, a man of science, instinctively appreciated I was simply honing my powers of reasoning based on observation. I assure you that there is nothing so instructive and potentially valuable to the criminal investigator as handwriting, postage stamps and inks employed for postmarks. Have you any concept of all that may be detected about senders of items in the way in which they address their correspondence? Was it addressed in a hurry? What of the stationery? Volumes of information may be unearthed from a simple letter without opening it!"

Only partly assuaged, I grumbled, "I have no doubt you'll be writing a monograph on the subject!"

Taking a pipe from the rack atop the mantle, he exclaimed, "I shall indeed. To date I have catalogued no fewer than fourteen kinds of ink used by the Royal Mail and nearly a hundred watermarks of paper manufacturers in England, as well as more than a score from the United States. For example, in the past year you have received eight letters on stationery made in San Francisco. This led me to deduce that a very close relative of yours is a resident of that city and, I am sorry to say, may recently have suffered a serious setback, probably in relation to his health."

"You are right about the nature of the letters. They concern my brother. He is very ill and the sickness has left him and his wife nearly penniless."

He placed a consoling hand upon my shoulder. "I am deeply sorry, my friend. If there is anything I can do to help, you need only ask."

"Thank you. I'm sorry for losing my temper."

"You did warn me at the time we were discussing our sharing lodgings that you kept a bull pup. Were I you, my friend, I'd have lost my temper over me and my methods long ago. It's I who should be apologetic."

"But how could you have known any of this about my brother without opening the letters? I don't believe I ever mentioned to you that I have a brother."

"No, you didn't. As to my deductions, the writing on the first five envelopes was obviously masculine. They were addressed 'John Watson,' neither a 'Mister' nor a 'Dr. John H. Watson," a familiarity suggesting a family connection. The latter missives were from the same city in the United States but in a feminine hand which addressed you as 'Dr.' From this I deduced that your female correspondent had to be your brother's wife. A sister would also have written to John, not Dr. Watson."

"You always make it seem so simple. But how could you deduce that my brother is ill?"

"That your sister-in-law wrote to you indicates your brother was probably unable to do so himself, evidently because of some incapacitation. Were he dead, you would have received a cable."

"He suffers from a nervous disorder that makes him increasingly palsied in the extremities."

"My deduction was reinforced by the arrival of the woman's letters only two weeks apart. This suggested increasing urgency, for your brother's letters came over a period of several months. Addressing you as 'Dr.' suggested to me that as she wrote to you she had her mind focussed on medical concerns. Evidently, the situation has now become so troubling that you are contemplating rushing to your brother's side in your capacity as physician, as well as concerned sibling." He tapped a bony finger on the longer of the two envelopes he had dropped upon my desk. "A Cunard envelope of that dimension can only be a schedule of sailings. Because Cunard is primarily engaged in trans-Atlantic service, you are at least contemplating going to the United States. The small envelope from Prince's Hall in Piccadilly contains a ticket for a lecture being advertised on behalf of Oscar Wilde on the subject of the playwright's impressions of the United States, formulated during his recent visit over there. A further indication of your contemplation of an American odyssey!"

Taking up the small Prince's Hall envelope, I said, "You are wrong on one point, Holmes."

"Indeed?"

"It is not one ticket," I said, tearing open the envelope. "In view of your own interest in America since your visit there a few years ago, I took the liberty of booking a seat for you, too."

On the following Sunday afternoon it was not without a deep feeling of melancholy that I crossed Piccadilly with Holmes at my side, for it had been there, at the Criterion Bar, that my young friend Stamford had informed me of the existence of a man whom I might find acceptable for sharing lodgings. Now, two years later, sadly mindful that in a few days I would be leaving Baker Street for what might well be a prolonged absence from England and, even more importantly, a lengthy separation from the most fascinating man I ever knew, I approached the lecture hall with both a sense of regret and an eagerness to hear Mr. Wilde's impressions of the country I soon would be seeing for myself.

Alas, the English theatre's most celebrated author since the Bard of Avon proved to be far less interested in enlightening his audience about his impressions of America than in proving to us how greatly he had impressed America. The lecture was witty and charming but lacking in facts that might be of value to one such as I for whom America was not an intellectual abstraction.

I was about to declare this disappointment to Holmes as we were leaving the hall when I heard behind us, *sotto voce,* "The trouble with Oscar, Mr. Holmes, is that he truly cares about only one subject: Oscar! He has many virtues but modesty isn't among them, I'm afraid."

Turning, Holmes faced a man with a trim moustache, dark flowing hair and a rather flamboyant style of dress (for a Sunday afternoon) that suggested a Bohemian nature.

"I cannot agree that modesty is one of the virtues," Holmes said as he shook hands with the fellow. "For Mr. Oscar Wilde to so underestimate his talent as a wit and his place in society as a celebrity would be as much a departure from the truth as to exaggerate those characteristics. Mr. Wilde is a man who knows what his audience expects of him. With one exception that I know of, these people did not come to be informed about America. They came for Mr. Wilde."

"And the exception, Mr. Holmes? Surely not yourself!"

"My friend Dr. John H. Watson," Holmes said, turning to me. "He is away to America in the next few days. Dr. Watson, may I present Mr. James Whistler."

"I've heard of you, sir," I said. "You're an artist!"

That Holmes should know a painter came as no surprise to me. He claimed to be related to the French artist Vernet and boasted often that he might have become a respected painter himself.

"Mr. Whistler is not *an* artist, Watson," said Holmes. "This is the man whom Oscar Wilde recently praised in the press as the first artist not just of England but all Europe. If you want to know about America, Watson, here is your man, for James McNeill Whistler is a native son of that country."

"I'll be delighted to answer all your questions, Doctor. What about dinner tomorrow evening? Come to my studio in Tite Street. You're invited, as well, Mr. Holmes. Perhaps you can use your powers of detection to sort out what has to be the dumbest robbery in British history. A thief broke into my studio a few days ago and, faced with a choice of several paintings by the first artist of England and Europe, as well as those of my friend and house guest, the renowned portraitist John Singer Sargent, made off, instead, with a valueless portrait of an old woman by an unknown painter. Do you think you could make anything of that, Mr. Holmes?"

"I've already made of it that your thief took what he came for. If I had more data I might tell you why. Therefore, I'll be pleased to dine with you tomorrow. After you have satisfied Dr. Watson's curiosity about America, you can tell me more about the purloined painting, which was evidently more valuable than you believed when you acquired it."

"Tomorrow evening it is, Mr. Holmes," Whistler said with a laugh. "Now, if you'll excuse me, I'm invited to a party that Oscar is giving himself, at which all his friends are expected to crown him with laurels for his triumph of this afternoon."

"Two questions before you leave, Mr. Whistler. Where did you obtain the painting? And, if it was of no value, why?"

"I bought it at the weekly art auction of the Gordon Gallery in Sloane Street. It was to be a gift for Sargent. I thought he'd find its primitiveness amusing."

"Thank you. Till tomorrow evening, then."

"Shall we say eight o'clock?"

Because I had affairs to attend to the next day, having to do with the likelihood of my going to America, I did not return to Baker Street until an hour before we were expected to present ourselves at Whistler's studio in Chelsea. Not until the cab was making the turn into Tite Street did Holmes bring up the subject of the painting. "What do you make of it, Watson?" he asked. "Is it not a fascinating problem?"

"Candidly, Holmes, I believe you're making too much of it. I agree with Mr. Whistler. It was simply the work of a very stupid thief who undoubtedly feared being detected and grabbed the nearest object at hand. Your theory that he went there purposely to get that one painting seems to me preposterous on its face. How on earth could he have known Whistler had it?"

"Watson, that is an excellent question. It goes to the very heart of the mystery."

The cab drew up in front of a high and narrow building with a white stucco façade interrupted in the topmost story by a tall north-facing window. Greeted by Whistler, we followed the artist up four flights of steps to a studio that afforded us through the large window a panoramic view of the rooftops of the surrounding low houses of Chelsea to the north and east and the broad sweep of the mighty Thames to the west. Taking in the view as we entered the roomy space was an older man for whom the purloined painting had been intended. He introduced himself: "John Singer Sargent."

As he advanced towards us, his eyes fixed upon Holmes.

"So at last I meet the great detective."

"This is my associate, Dr. Watson," said Holmes.

"Compared to murder, this business of the purloined painting seems a very trivial thing," Sargent said with a wink and a smile in Whistler's direction. "I'm afraid Jimmy has weighted the theft far beyond its importance."

Further discussion of the subject that interested Holmes waited until after dinner, which was devoted for my benefit by

Whistler and Sargent to a far more enlightening and useful discussion of their native country than had been afforded the audience at Oscar Wilde's lecture.

Only after we withdrew from the dining table and ensconced ourselves in comfortable armchairs by an inviting fireplace did the conversation return to the subject of the missing painting and the circumstances of the theft.

"It was a rather amateurishly executed portrait," Whistler said while his friend sat apart from us, drawing pad in one hand and the other clutching a stick of charcoal as his intense eyes darted back and forth between the pad and Holmes. "I found it fascinating from my point of view," Whistler continued, "because it had been executed in tones of grey and black."

"In the style of your famous portrait of your mother that you called 'An Arrangement in Grey and Black,' " said Holmes.

"Yes, but the figure in this case was an old Russian woman."

"I see," Holmes muttered as he leaned forward slightly, the sharp point of his chin resting on the knuckles of his upraised and clenched hands.

"Wonderful," exclaimed Sargent. "Can you hold that pose, Mr. Holmes? You are a natural model!"

"Really, Sargent," snapped Whistler. "Mr. Holmes is not here to pose. If you must sketch him, don't interrupt us."

"I take it that the painting of this woman had been titled by the artist," said Holmes, maintaining the posture.

"It had not. I merely assumed from the look of the old woman that she was Russian. Judging by the rural scene depicted in the background and by her costume—a plain black dress, a tight black babushka—and a sorrowful expression, she *looked* Russian to me."

"You said you bought it at auction at the Gordon Gallery," Holmes said, lowering his hands. "Were there other bidders?"

"A young woman started the bidding at one pound. I thought Mr. Gordon was on the verge of an apoplectic fit. The gilt frame was worth half a pound at least! I raised the bid to two pounds, the young woman dropped out and the painting was mine. Three days later, in spite of the presence of several of my paintings, two portraits that Sargent left in my care, and three or four others that would fetch a tidy sum if auctioned at Gordon's, only that crude and worthless object was taken from this very room."

"Where were you at the time?"

"That afternoon I was paying a call on Oscar Wilde at his mother's house in Charles Street."

"When did you notice the painting was missing?"

"The next day. Because Sargent was expected that afternoon, I wanted to display the painting on an easel, drape it and have an un-veiling. My little joke, you see."

"Did you notify the police?"

"It really was not worth the trouble. I mentioned it to you only because I assumed you would regard the theft as ironic and amusing, as I did. It never occurred to me that the thief came to my studio purposely to obtain that painting, and I still find it difficult to believe."

"It is an axiom of mine that when you have eliminated the impossible, whatever remains, however difficult it may be for you to believe, is the truth. The theft of the painting was not the ironic and amusing error by an ignorant intruder into your world of art. There is something about that painting that in the mind of the thief made it far more valuable than any James Whistler or John Singer Sargent."

With that, the famed portraitist arose from his chair and crossed the studio to present Sherlock Holmes with the product of his efforts. Taking the sketch pad, Holmes studied the charcoal rendering of his hawkish profile and came as close as I had ever seen to a blush.

"It's magnificent, sir," he said, handing back the drawing. "I'm only sorry I did not present you a more suitable subject for your magnificent talent."

"Nonsense, Mr. Holmes," Sargent protested. "You are an ideal subject. You must permit me to do you in oil. Full length. I see you in the regalia of a hunter. Inverness cloak. Deerstalker cap. A magnifying glass in hand. What do you say, sir? Will you sit?"

Whistler bristled. "Sargent, we are not here for your benefit. We are engaged in the solving of a crime. If Mr. Holmes wishes to sit for you, the two of you can discuss the details on your time."

More amused than chastened, Sargent returned to his chair. Unfortunately for Whistler, Holmes promptly demonstrated that he had derived all available data regarding the missing painting and turned the conversation into what I could only describe as cross-examination of the two artists on their varying styles in particular and on the state of art in general that lasted well past midnight and left the painters and me exhausted and eager to call it a night.

The next morning, arising late, I learned from Mrs. Hudson that Holmes had been up and away hours earlier without informing her as to where he was going or when he could be expected back. This left me free to continue preparations for my American journey by calling at the Foreign Office to arrange my travel documents, to take care of paperwork at the American embassy and to consult with an official of my banking firm, Cox & Company, regarding my financial situation, including drawing up a letter of credit to allow me to open banking accounts in the United States. I also provided instructions to Cox & Company concerning what was to be done, should anything untoward happen to me while in America, with a box I kept in the firm's vault which contained certain valuable documents and other papers of a most sensitive nature involving myself and Sherlock Holmes.

Many hours after I returned to Baker Street and long after Mrs. Hudson had wearied of keeping Holmes's dinner warm and edible did Holmes return, announcing his arrival by barging into the sitting room and blaring, "The mystery is nearly resolved, Watson! And a fancy little problem it has been. There remains but one loose end, and that will be neatly knotted at one o'clock in the afternoon tomorrow."

With that, he bounded into his bedroom and closed the door, a signal that I had quickly learned, soon after moving in with him, meant that I was not to disturb him under any circumstances. However, he did take me into his confidence in the morning to this extent. Over breakfast he whispered, "I can tell you this, Watson. The old woman in the picture is not a Russian. She is Serbian. More than that I cannot share with you at this time, except to say that Mr. Whistler's amusing and ironic little theft could have resulted in one of the gravest crises in the already troubled situation on the European continent. Be here at two o'clock and I will explain it all!"

Promptly at that hour, he entered the sitting room to find me as eagerly intent on hearing him as I had been to listen to Oscar Wilde speak about America.

"I began, as you would have imagined, I'm sure," he said, "by paying a visit to the Gordon Gallery in Sloane Street. Mr. Gordon had a vivid memory of the sale of the painting, not only because it nearly went for a paltry one pound and not because it had been bought at two by the renowned James McNeill Whistler. He remembered the event because another buyer for the work showed up at the gallery some three hours after Whistler carried it away to Tite Street."

"So that's how the thief knew Whistler had the painting! Mr. Gordon told him."

"No, Watson. Although Mr. Gordon was offered a great deal of money to reveal the identity of the purchaser, he refused to give out that information. He is a businessman of deservedly high reputation. The person who stole the painting knew it had come into Whistler's possession because the thief's own agent was present when Whistler bought it. That the picture was stolen from Tite Street was pure chance. It would have been stolen from whoever had bought it at the auction. Everything had been organized in a manner to ensure that the individual who had been ordered to buy the painting—the man who showed up late—could not do so. He was late because he had been interfered with. I now know who is the mastermind behind this charade because I confronted him with what I knew at one o'clock. He admitted everything."

"Excuse me, Holmes, but you've lost me. *Mastermind?*"

"I do not choose my words lightly. The man who arranged this theft is one of the most brilliant minds in England, perhaps the world. Little happens of importance in which his presence cannot be detected behind the scenes, manipulating!"

"And you know this man's name?"

"As well as I know my own, Watson. But don't ask me to divulge it. The time may come when I may feel I may safely take you into my confidence concerning him. But not now. As to any idea you might be entertaining about writing about this adventure, I must insist you reveal nothing of it so long as I am breathing under the sun. You may make notes and store them in that box at Cox and Company, but you must not publish any of this for years to come— if ever. As to the painting itself, it was produced by a pedestrian artist who specializes in what may be charitably called folk art."

"How on earth did you learn that?"

"Mr. Gordon is quite knowledgeable. He recognized the brush of a man called Vukcic, who primarily paints rural scenes in the Balkans. I located that man late yesterday and interviewed him. In this instance, his subject was a farm woman in Montenegro. Are you up on the recent history of that region?"

"Certainly, Holmes. Even out in Afghanistan we were keenly aware of the war between Serbia and rebels in Bosnia and Herzegovina. Prince Nicholas of Montenegro intervened on the side of the rebels, declared war on the Turks and, allied with Russia, came out of the crisis by seeing Montenegro's size tripled under the terms of the Treaty of San Stefano in 1878. It is a widely held view among my friends at the War Office that the treaty is not the end of the troubles in the Balkans. Some of the generals are convinced that the treaty has planted seeds of trouble in the near future. They believe the area is destined to explode into a European war of immense, possibly catastrophic, proportions."

"Bravo, my friend. That's it exactly!"

"But what has all this to do with Whistler's painting?"

"It's what's *beneath* the painting that is the crux of it."

"Beneath it? What do you mean?"

"Before Mr. Vukcic rendered the likeness of the old woman, he inscribed on the canvas nothing less than a detailed map of the deployments of Serbian and Montenegran armies in the region."

"The man is a spy! The scoundrel!"

"Exactly."

"For whom does he work?"

"His services are available to the highest bidder. In this instance, it was a representative of imperial Germany. It was an agent of the Kaiser who was to have purchased the painting at the auction at the Gordon Gallery. He surely would have succeeded had not our nameless mastermind learned all this through his own agents and taken steps to delay the Kaiser's man from arriving in time to outbid all others at Gordon's auction."

"Then it was simply a matter of this mysterious, all-knowing individual following whoever bought the painting and making off with it himself. What a clever boots!"

Holmes chuckled. "I assure you this wily fellow did not perpetrate the theft himself. This man hardly ever leaves the comfortable surroundings of his headquarters in Pall Mall. No, it was one of his agents who carried out the theft."

"But what's to be done, Holmes? Surely, Scotland Yard must be brought in on this. The Foreign Office must be informed. The War Office! The fate of Europe—of England—is at stake!"

"I expect that they have been fully informed, Watson. All, that is, save Scotland Yard. This is not the sort of thing that the man at the Diogenes Club would ever entrust to the likes of an Inspector Lestrade! As to the fate of England and Europe, you needn't worry yourself. They are in such competent hands that I'm confident in predicting that upon your return from America you will find both intact. And I do hope you will return soon, old man. I'll be lost without my Boswell!"

Historical Notes: Oscar Wilde's lecture tour of America took place in the latter months of 1882 and early 1883. At that time, Whistler resided in Tite Street and Sargent spent most of his time in Paris, as Watson correctly reported. He was also accurate in relating the events in the Balkans, as were his unnamed sources in the War Office in predicting that the Treaty of San Stefano planted seeds for a monumental war. It began with an assassin's bullet, fired in 1914, in the city of Sarajevo. Students of the Holmesian Canon will note that many years would go by before Holmes finally let Watson know that the secretive fellow who frequented the Diogenes Club was his brother Mycroft, although in this adventure he gives a slight hint of him when he tells Watson that he knows the name of the story's mystery man "as well as I know my own."

Scholars of Nero Wolfe will note that the artist who painted the picture at the heart of this case has the same surname as the best friend of Rex Stout's immortal sleuth.

Whether John Singer Sargent painted Sherlock Holmes's portrait is not recorded either by Dr. Watson or Sargent's biographers.

*S*candal still sells newspapers, but nowadays reputations are more likely to be made than broken by the tongues of rumour. Not so, however, in Victorian and Edwardian England. Imagine, therefore, Watson's diffidence in making public certain details concerning his own literary agent, Arthur Conan Doyle (1859–1930). Doyle was himself a renowned and masterful author of historical novels (The White Company), fantastic tales such as "The Captain of the Pole Star" and that classic novel about living dinosaurs and other prehistoric beasties called, guess what? The Lost World.

The Adventure of the Noble Husband

BY PETER CANNON

In surveying the many cases of Mr. Sherlock Holmes in which I had the privilege to participate, I confess that I have often been torn whether or not to publish the results. More than once in my eagerness to set a stirring story before the public I have, to my shame, shown scant regard for the privacy of Holmes's more illustrious clients. Still, I am confident I know where to draw the veil. I doubt that I shall ever release the full facts regarding Ackerley, the bigamous banana king, who for years maintained a household in Richmond and a "secret orchard" in Castlenau, with neither family the wiser. Tawdry affairs such as this one are best left to moulder in their year-books on the shelves. And yet there are a few cases in this sensitive category which beg for disclosure, if only long after the eminent parties involved have passed on. Such was the adventure of the noble husband, a matter that threatened to destroy not only the good name of one of Britain's most revered authors but also my relationship with my literary agent.

One summer afternoon in the year 1900, finding myself in the vicinity of our old Baker Street lodgings after a professional call, I decided to drop by 221B. Mrs. Hudson informed me that a client had just arrived, but as Holmes customarily welcomed my presence at these interviews I did not hesitate to mount the stairs. In the sitting room I discovered Sherlock Holmes listening to a small, respectably dressed woman with a plain, pale face—an utterly unprepossessing type such as one might pass on the street with scarcely a glance.

"Ah, Watson. I would like you to meet Mrs. Hawkins," said my friend. "I trust you won't mind, Mrs. Hawkins, but Dr. Watson often does me the courtesy—"

"Oh, Mr. Holmes, I'm afraid I . . ." The stranger rose from her chair, her wan cheeks suddenly flushed. She pressed a handkerchief to her mouth to conceal a cough. Then it struck me; I knew this woman, though not under the name of Mrs. Hawkins. As soon as she recovered her composure, she spared us both further embarrassment by introducing, or rather I should say, reintroducing herself.

"It's Mrs. Doyle, Dr. Watson," she said, extending a tiny hand. "We met once years ago, through my husband, who I believe still acts as your literary agent."

"Oh, yes. Quite so," I answered. Her palm trembled in mine. "I regret, however, that it has been ages since he and I last met. How is Mr. Doyle, if I may ask?"

During the silence that ensued, only the sound of Holmes thrumming his fingers against his chair could be heard.

"I am very sorry, madam," the detective said at last, "but if you are indeed the wife of Arthur Conan Doyle, the historical novelist and, more to the point, my colleague Dr. Watson's literary agent, you present me with a potential conflict of interest. I cannot help you."

The woman gave a little gasp.

"I could refer you, if you wish. A Mr. Adrian Mulliner—"

"Oh no, Mr. Holmes, only you can help! Forgive me. Hawkins is my maiden name. I feared you would dismiss me without a hearing if I had revealed my identity immediately. You must understand. I've come all the way from Hindhead. For months I've been in agony over whether or not to seek you out. Please, Mr. Holmes, allow me at least to finish my story."

With these words the woman sank back in her chair and began to cry quietly into her handkerchief. Again she coughed, in a manner that suggested some serious lesion of the lungs. I hardly dared look Holmes in the eye. One would have to be a heartless fiend to ignore her distress.

"Very well, madam," Sherlock Holmes said gently. "As I had barely time to note that you are fond of animals and devoted to your children, a girl and a boy if I am not mistaken, before Watson here arrived, you might as well repeat for him what you have already confided to me."

"Thank you, Mr. Holmes," she answered, her tears now dried. "You are truly a gentleman. As I said before, we met fifteen years ago in Southsea, Portsmouth, on account of my brother Jack, one of Arthur's resident patients. Alas, poor Jack proved to have cerebral meningitis and succumbed within weeks. In my bereavement I naturally turned to Arthur for consolation, and he responded with a warmth that betrayed a deeper sympathy. We married that summer, and a kinder, more protective husband no woman could dare dream for, Mr. Holmes. If you have read my husband's book *The Stark Munro Letters,* you may have gained some notion of the sweet, affectionate home life that was ours in those early days."

Holmes's hooded eyes flickered in acknowledgment, though I was certain he had never opened *The Stark Munro Letters,* let alone any of the popular works penned by my literary agent. For my own part I was doing my best to stifle a smile, despite the gravity of the woman's narrative, as it was not every day that a client failed to express instant astonishment at one of my friend's personal deductions. Mrs. Doyle was either very simple—or very clever.

"This idyll, like all perfect things, could not last, I regret to say," our visitor continued. "First, in '93, I was diagnosed with consumption. My quiet life became enforced. In the autumn of '96 we moved from London to Surrey, for the sake of my health. That first spring in the country, Arthur started to behave oddly. At the time of our engagement he warned me that he tended to long silences and that I mustn't mind, but thoughtful contemplation soon all but gave way to mournful brooding. Of late, when not withdrawn in silence, Arthur has been full of restless energy. He has taken up the banjo, practicing for hours, despite an obvious lack of musical aptitude. As for golf and cricket, games at which he excels, he now plays them with an enthusiasm more befitting a youth half his age."

"Pardon me, madam," interrupted the detective, "but just how old is your husband?"

"Arthur turned forty-one in May."

"Pray go on."

"He has grown increasingly irritable, too. While patient and paternal as always with me and the children, he has allowed himself to get drawn into silly literary feuding."

"A pity, madam, but perhaps not so surprising for a man who has advanced in his career from provincial doctor to world-renowned author."

"You may be right, Mr. Holmes, but there's more." The woman coughed into her knotted handkerchief, then took a deep breath. "In March, just before he left for South Africa—"

"South Africa?" interjected Holmes.

"Yes, to join a field hospital as unofficial supervisor."

"Most admirable. Pray continue."

"As I was saying, this past March I observed Arthur unawares in the garden at Undershaw, our house in Hindhead. He picked a snowdrop and carried it into the library. After his departure I examined his shelves and found pressed between the leaves of a volume of romantic verses three snowdrop flowers—one fresh, the other two dried and withered."

My friend leaned forward, eyes glinting. This was the kind of curious detail he relished.

"Oh, Mr. Holmes, a man does not do such a sentimental thing unless he is in love—in love with another woman!" With this the woman broke into sobs.

"What do you propose I do, madam?" said Sherlock Holmes after a decent interval.

"Please determine whether or not my Arthur remains true."

"And if I confirm your worst fears?"

"Oh, I do not know, Mr. Holmes, I do not know. I am ill, sir, gravely ill. My time draws short in this world. You must believe that Arthur's happiness matters more to me than my own. That he has found room for another in that great heart of his I can accept. But, as long as I live, I shall not abide his being unfaithful!"

Our visitor resumed her sorry weeping. I was deeply moved, and despite the mask of the perfect reasoner he affected, I knew my friend could not be untouched by such pure and intense emotion.

"Where is your husband now, madam?"

"On his way back from South Africa. His ship, the *Briton,* is due to dock next week in Plymouth."

"Ah, then we have some time."

"Oh, my dear Mr. Holmes!"

"Please, Mrs. Doyle. Before I can give my assent, I must first consult Dr. Watson on the ethics of my taking you on as a client. If you wouldn't mind waiting downstairs, I dare say Mrs. Hudson should already have the water on the hob for tea."

After further expressions of gratitude, the woman put on her shawl, which was covered with cat hair, and gathered a shopping bag marked with the emblem of Hamley's toy emporium, containing, I saw as I held the door for her, a doll and a set of tin soldiers. "Thank you, Dr. Watson. Since I so rarely travel to London these days," she said, smiling at her purchases, "I feel obliged to bring home something for Mary and Kingsley to show my expedition has not been unfruitful."

We stood listening to her dainty tread fade down the steps. Then the detective collapsed into his chair, his features unfathomable. A minute passed before he spoke:

"Well, Watson, as I have said to you in the past, the fair sex is your department. What is your assessment?"

"To be blunt, Holmes, if we are to credit what Mrs. Doyle tells us, her husband is suffering from acute . . . frustration. The overindulgence in sport, the banjo playing, the literary feuding, for a healthy male in his prime—"

"Enough, Watson," said Holmes. "Like you, I have concluded that the man is in dire danger of violating his marital vows. The real issue for me, my dear fellow, is your role here. It has never been my policy to pry into your affairs, but just how well do you know your literary agent?"

"Not well, Holmes, though our relations have always been cordial and correct. As fellow medical men we have traded a tale or two of the dissecting room, and Doyle did present me with an inscribed copy of his story collection *Round the Red Lamp*, but there all confidences end. I am grateful that he continues in his capacity as my agent, despite his rising fame as an author, though again it has been some while since I have put any work his way."

After believing Holmes had fallen to his death in '91 in the grasp of his archfoe Professor Moriarty, I was too grief-stricken to publish any adventures beyond that of "The Final Problem." My friend's abrupt resurrection three years later provided an additional jolt which reinforced my silence.

"Tell me, Watson. I confess I am ignorant of literary practices," said Sherlock Holmes, "but why on earth have you not submitted your fanciful melodramas directly to *The Strand* magazine?"

"Well, Holmes, if you can keep a secret, this chap Doyle has done more than act as middle-man. He has touched up my prose here and there, checked details, consistency of names and dates, that sort of thing. After all, he's a professional, I a mere amateur."

I was not about to admit that in many instances my agent had been a virtual co-author. Indeed, to safeguard my posthumous reputation, the extent of Doyle's hand in my own writings must forever remain in mystery.

"Do you, then, have any objections to my assuming Mrs. Doyle's case?"

"None at all, Holmes."

"I am sure Mulliner could handle this affair ably enough in my stead."

"No, Holmes. A lady's honour is at stake. She trusts only you. If a scandal ensues from your investigation, I am prepared to risk the loss of her husband's services—of which I may have no real need in future anyway."

"Good old Watson! How fortunate for your wives to have a man of your loyalty."

"Thank you, Holmes."

For a few moments we sat in a silence that was almost comfortable.

"The old queen cannot live forever," my friend resumed. "Her son, the heir, has already set the moral tone for the new century that looms. With her will pass an age that for all its cant and hypocrisy still upholds the gentlemanly virtues. I suspect, dear fellow, that you and I shall find ourselves increasingly out of step with the laxer times ahead. In the meanwhile, let us put Mrs. Doyle out of her suspense, then join her in a cup of tea."

Later that month the newspapers heralded Arthur Conan Doyle's return from South Africa, on holiday from his exertions in the Boer War. He was badly in need of rest, so a clandestine message from his wife informed Holmes; though that would not prevent him from coming up to London to play for Surrey at Lord's. The detective determined that it might be interesting to learn who might be watching among the crowd. "For now I prefer to theorize in the background," he said before I set off alone for St. John's Wood. "Besides, Watson, you instinctively appreciate the nuances of a game, like the subtleties of women, which I with my logical mind find completely baffling."

In truth I was fond of cricket, if more as a casual peruser of the box scores in the pink sheet than as a spectator on the grounds. In the event I welcomed the chance to visit Lord's, though by the time I entered the gate the teams had adjourned for lunch. I headed for the pavilion, where I nodded to more than a few former patients and consumed strawberries and cream. It was while I was so engaged that I heard a familiar voice at my side.

"Watson, old chap!"

I turned and there stood the tall, athletic figure of my literary agent, Arthur Conan Doyle, wearing whites. He looked a bit gaunt but otherwise exuded robust good cheer.

"My dear Doyle," I said, dropping my spoon. We clasped hands.

"I say, this is a stroke of luck," my companion began in that solid, precise way of his. "I've been meaning to get in touch with you since my return from South Africa—a frightful situation there, you know; it's all in my forthcoming book, *The Great Boer War*. At any rate, on board the ship home I met a journalist named Fletcher Robinson. Told me the most wonderful West Country legend about a spectral hound." Conan Doyle winked. "Back in the eighties, I understand, a crime connected with this hound brought a certain private consulting detective—"

"Sounds promising, Doyle," I interrupted hastily, "but I'd rather we—"

I disliked discussing business in so public a place, but fortunately the arrival of a third party put an end to this line of conversation.

"Ah, Jean," said the author, addressing a young woman dressed in a summer frock that showed to advantage her long, slender neck and beautifully sloped shoulders. "I'd like you to meet my client, Dr. John Watson. Watson, may I present Miss Jean Leckie."

"I'm delighted to meet you, Dr. Watson," said the woman in a Scots accent like a melody. "I used so much to enjoy the adventures of your friend Mr. Sherlock Holmes in *The Strand*. Pray, is there any hope of his return?"

Usually when confronted with this question, as I had been all too often since the appearance of "The Final Problem," my answer was curt. On this occasion, I have to admit, I was no proof against the charm of my lovely interlocutor's smile and went so far as to say that I had not ruled out the possibility.

We were shortly joined by a fourth individual, a balding young fellow in the colours of the opposing Middlesex team. As tall and strapping as Doyle himself, he was carrying a book.

"Good day, Mr. Doyle," said the youth, who despite his imposing build had a shy, quiet manner about him. "I hope I'm not imposing. My name is Wodehouse. You may recall you bowled me out for six this morning."

"Ah, yes, Wodehouse," replied Conan Doyle with a grin. "One of the stars of the Dulwich eleven your final term, I hear."

"My friend Fletcher Robinson tells me the two of you met aboard the *Briton*, Mr. Doyle."

"Indeed, a capital chap. Spoke highly of you as a cricketer— and as an aspiring journalist."

"I confess that for the moment I work in a bank, but literature is my great love. I'm a particular fan of yours, Mr. Doyle." A faint blush mantled the young man's cheek. "Would you be so good as to sign my copy of your latest book?" Here Wodehouse produced the volume he had under his arm, *The Green Flag and Other Stories of War and Sport,* by A. Conan Doyle. The author scribbled on the title page with a pen supplied by his admirer.

"Thank you very much, Mr. Doyle."

"Always glad to oblige a fellow cricketer, my lad. Oh, pardon me, my manners suffered somewhat on the veldt. Allow me to introduce Miss Leckie"—Wodehouse bowed—"and Dr. Watson."

"Pleased to meet you, Dr. Watson. Yet another literary man,

are you not? Author of *The Adventures* and *The Memoirs of Sherlock Holmes*?"

I acknowledged the compliment, though mindful of the fact that if you failed to publish, after a while the public tended to forget you, no matter how keenly they may have received you at first.

Attention soon shifted back to Doyle and his recent writings, then to his musical efforts. "It was I who encouraged Arthur to take up the banjo, to accompany my singing," said Miss Leckie. "He hasn't told me yet whether he had the chance to practice in South Africa, though I gather his butler was threatening to resign until his timely departure from England." She laughed, and we all joined in, no one more heartily than the banjo-playing author himself.

"Maybe Mr. Doyle should consider trying the banjolele instead," suggested the young cricketer.

This sparked more laughter, leading to talk between Miss Leckie and Wodehouse of notable stringed-instrument performers that season on the London music-hall stage. Doyle drew me aside.

"Isn't she a peach, Watson?"

"Miss Leckie is most congenial."

"An excellent horsewoman, rides to hounds, trained as an opera singer in Dresden." The man gave a huge sigh. "I won't pretend with you, old boy. I've already confided in a number of my close friends, as well as my mother. To my immense relief 'the Ma'am,' as I call her, has given her blessing. I know how it must seem. But I can assure you—"

That my literary agent should be sharing such a confidence was more than a little disconcerting, even though of course he was confirming the very information I most vitally sought. Perhaps the strain of attending the wounded in South Africa, combined with his excitement at seeing Miss Leckie after so long an absence, explained his lack of reserve. Fortunately, at this juncture Wodehouse interrupted to say he needed to go grab a bite before returning to the pitch. Shortly after he left we were joined by a couple who greeted Doyle like a long-lost brother, which in a real sense he was.

"Ah, Connie, Willie, I'd like you to meet a friend of mine, Miss Jean Leckie. And this is my client, Dr. John Watson."

I had never met Ernest William Hornung, better known as E. W. Hornung, chronicler of Raffles, the "amateur cracksman," and Conan Doyle's brother-in-law, but I certainly knew him by reputation. While his wife, Constance, caught up with her celebrity brother, I exchanged a few words with my fellow detective-story writer.

"Can we look forward to any new adventures of Mr. Sherlock Holmes, Dr. Watson?" asked the man in a facetious tone I found irritating.

"I think not, Mr. Hornung."

"Come, come, sir. Everyone knows Mr. Holmes has resumed his London practice. It's been years now. When are you going to reveal how he survived that plunge into the Reichenbach Falls?"

"Some things are best left in mystery, Mr. Hornung."

"Dear me, Dr. Watson, you are obstinate. If you refuse to honour us with further tales of your detective friend, then I suppose we lesser authors will just have to do our humble best to fill the gap."

While the exploits of Raffles were all very amusing in their way, they were thin stuff compared with my own. Listening to this man prate, I began to think that perhaps it was time, after all, to "resurrect" Holmes, not that I was about to give my rival the satisfaction of saying so. I made a mental note to talk to Doyle later about that spectral hound legend, assuming we were still on speaking terms after the resolution of the present case.

With relief I turned to the conversation between the ladies, while Doyle reviewed for Hornung some of the finer points of that morning's match. Mrs. Hornung queried Miss Leckie politely about her family, but it soon became clear that she was more interested in a topic closer to home.

"Where did you say you and my brother met, Miss Leckie?"

"At a party, Mrs. Hornung. My parents were entertaining at the Glebe House, in Blackheath."

"You say this was in March, Miss Leckie?"

"March three years ago, Mrs. Hornung."

"To be precise, March fifteenth," Doyle chipped in, giving Miss Leckie's hand a quick squeeze. For an instant both Hornungs frowned.

"I see," said his sister. "Well, we must all have lunch together sometime."

"Right now you must all excuse me," said Doyle, looking at his watch. "Play resumes promptly on the hour."

"Good-bye, then, Arthur. Shall we be seeing you at Undershaw?"

"On the morrow, Connie."

The Hornungs made their farewells to Miss Leckie. Their frozen smiles, if I am any judge, left behind a distinct air of disapproval. But Miss Leckie, with whom I found myself suddenly alone, seemed not to mind if she even noticed.

"Oh, Dr. Watson, isn't Arthur the best and wisest man you have ever known!"

That evening I returned to Baker Street and gave Holmes my report.

"I must congratulate you, Watson," said the detective, "for all your discovery has fallen to you like ripe fruit from a tree. Your literary agent proclaims his attachment to this Miss Leckie as nothing less than an open secret!"

"Yes, Holmes, but I am certain it is no liaison, at least not yet."

"Ah, there lies the nub of the matter. That Doyle has managed to resist temptation for more than three years shows the utmost chivalry. But for how many more years can he or any man in his position hold out? Especially if he must face censorious relatives who could provoke him into doing something rash."

"One has to sympathize with the poor fellow, Holmes."

"Sympathy is all very well, Watson, but one has also to act. The situation is in real danger of coming to a crisis. Tomorrow I shall catch the first train for Hindhead, where I think a little undercover work will be in order."

"Must you go alone, Holmes?"

"Yes, Watson. Were you to accompany me to Surrey and Doyle learned of your presence, he might view your popping up so soon again as rather more than coincidence."

Over the next few days, in between my rounds, I had ample opportunity to reflect on this complex business. Who was in the wrong and who in the right became less and less obvious the more I considered my literary agent's predicament, and I could not help wishing that his wife had spared Holmes and me her problem in the first place. I had no word from Holmes. Then, four days after his departure from London, the wire came urging me to meet him at Paddington in time for an early afternoon train to Gloucester.

I arrived on the platform just as the final whistle was sounding.

"Quick, Watson!" shouted Sherlock Holmes from a carriage window. Moments later I was sitting opposite my friend in an otherwise unoccupied compartment.

"Watson, I only pray that we are not too late."

"Too late for what?"

"Let me start at the beginning. Once settled at an hotel in Hindhead, I sought to gain the confidence of one of the staff at Undershaw. This proved difficult, as the Doyles employ no women susceptible to the charms of the rakish alias I had chosen to assume. Then yesterday, by great good fortune, I was out for a stroll on the road to Undershaw when I ran into a tall, husky chap with a widow's peak. In his hand he had a book, *The Green Flag*. I struck up a conversation and soon ascertained that he was indeed young Wodehouse, as you had described in such telling detail, down for the weekend at the invitation of his new friend and fellow cricket enthusiast.

"Sensing that here was a young man of character, I decided to take him into my confidence. At first he was hesitant, but in the end he agreed to act as my agent-in-place. Like you, he regards a woman's honour as paramount. He told me he was aware that Mrs. Hornung had scheduled and then, at the last minute, cancelled a luncheon in the town for herself, her husband, her brother, and an unknown fourth party. I instructed Wodehouse to keep his ears open and report anything of significance.

"Early today Wodehouse rang me at my hotel. Over the billiard table late the night before, Hornung confronted Doyle on the matter of Miss Leckie. His taunts apparently hit home, for Doyle lost his temper and stormed out of the room. Wodehouse, who witnessed the entire ugly exchange, feared for his host's sanity. He and I agreed to rendezvous within the hour at the same spot as our encounter the previous day.

"Wodehouse had more news by the time we met. Doyle was still in a temper and announced that he had to go away on unspecified business. His guests were welcome to stay at Undershaw. After his departure Wodehouse went into the garden, where he was accosted by Mason, the Doyles' butler, who also serves as his master's valet. Mason was extremely agitated and in a mood to talk to someone. Just as I had, Mason must have instinctively recognized Wodehouse as trustworthy. He informed Wodehouse of a phone conversation he overheard his master make shortly before he left—in which Doyle reserved a room at the Everson Arms in Gloucester, under the name of Mr. and Mrs. Arthur Parker. The man evidently wanted to discuss possible courses of action, but Wodehouse said not to worry and rushed out to meet me."

"I say, Holmes, where was Mrs. Doyle during all this?"

"Too weak to leave her room, conveniently enough for everyone, so Wodehouse gathered. He never saw her, nor did I attempt to communicate with her. I immediately headed for the train station, while Wodehouse returned to Undershaw, vowing that if he ever became an author of fiction he would be sure to leave physical passion out of it. As soon as I got back to London I wired you and went straight to Paddington; hence here we both are, en route in a possibly futile effort to save a gentleman's honour and a lady's virtue."

Any discussion of how we might thwart the designs of the two lovers we agreed to postpone until we got to Gloucester. Upon arrival we discovered the Everson Arms across the street from the terminal, the sort of down-at-heel establishment that catered to commercial travellers and less reputable patrons. In the shabby lobby we decided that Holmes would inquire at the desk, while I would survey the public room, through a side door by the entrance. There, so as to seem an ordinary customer, I ordered a pint of bitter at the bar. I barely touched the glass to my lips when I heard a hearty voice behind me.

"I say, Watson old chap, this is a coincidence!"

I turned my head and there, beaming over my shoulder, was my literary agent.

"Doyle! My goodness, what a surprise," I replied, trying to sound as if I meant it.

"What on earth are you doing in Gloucester?"

I took a long sip of my bitter.

"By Jove, I've got it. You must be helping your friend Mr. Sherlock Holmes on a case. Well, I know better not to ask any further. If you aren't too busy, old boy, might you join us for a little supper?"

Doyle gestured toward a corner table, where I could see two women sitting—one the fair Miss Leckie, the other an elderly woman in black.

"I'll have to ask Holmes first."

"It's quite all right, Watson," said Holmes, who had suddenly materialized on my other side. "We would be delighted to join Mr. Doyle and . . . company."

The two men regarded each other warily and respectfully, as I imagined two gunfighters might have done on first meeting in a Wild West saloon.

"I don't believe I've had the pleasure, Mr. Holmes."

"The pleasure is entirely mine, sir," answered the detective mildly. They gripped hands. Sherlock Holmes was evidently willing to give my literary agent the benefit of the doubt, at least for the moment.

Doyle led us to the table, where he made the appropriate introductions—to Miss Leckie and to Mrs. Charles Altamont Doyle, his mother.

"The Ma'am was good enough to join our party at the last minute," the author explained. "The more the merrier I always say," he added with a laugh, which may have been a bit forced.

While there was undeniably a certain strain in the air, I have to say that supper passed agreeably. Holmes for one appeared wholly at his ease, discussing prospects in the prize ring with Doyle and the careers of various well-known sopranos with Miss Leckie. The senior Mrs. Doyle said little, presiding over the scene with quiet strength and dignity. As the public area filled up with voluble diners, conversation became increasingly an effort and we all focussed on polishing our plates.

Afterwards, as everyone rose and said their farewells, Doyle drew me aside. "I say, Watson," he whispered. "I almost did a foolish thing tonight. A very foolish thing. Fortunately, the Ma'am arrived when she did, though the devil knows how she found out to intercept us here. An amazingly omniscient woman, the Ma'am. After her lecture on fidelity and chastity, I assured her that Miss Leckie and I would never, as long as Louie . . . Well, I trust I can rely on your discretion—and that of Mr. Holmes."

"You can indeed, Doyle," I promised.

Since we had to maintain our pretence that we had come to Gloucester on other business, Holmes and I lingered at the Everson Arms public bar while the lovers and their chaperone proceeded to the railway terminal, to catch a late train to London. Over a final pint of bitter I recounted Conan Doyle's parting comments to me.

"A noble husband, Watson," said Sherlock Holmes. "After this recent test of his mettle, I have no doubt the man will keep his word. The question now becomes what, if anything, we tell that saintly soul, his wife." We finished our pints in silence.

"It has been a long day, old fellow," announced my friend at last. "I am weary and in no mood to hurry back to London. While Gloucester may boast many respectable inns, I am sure the Everson Arms offers as comfortable a bed as any. They should have at least one available room, following the unexpected departure of 'Mr. and Mrs. Parker.'"

The next day, after a short sightseeing excursion to the Forest of Dean, we rode the train back to Paddington. I accompanied Holmes to Baker Street, where two missives awaited him. The first, a wire dated the previous afternoon, was from Wodehouse, stating that Doyle's man Mason had cabled Doyle's mother to alert her to the impending assignation. Mason was confident Mrs. Doyle would do what was necessary. The second was a letter written in a feeble female hand. Holmes read it aloud:

> *My dear Mr. Holmes,*
> *I hope you will not think too badly of me, but I no longer re-*
> *quire your services. While I shall always wonder about the other*
> *woman, I now realize that it is quite the best and wisest course*
> *not to risk disrupting things as they are. Ignorance is bliss, as*
> *they say.*
>
> > *Since his return from South Africa, Arthur has been so*
> *kind and attentive to me, while I, confined to my room, have*
> *been no use to anyone. This past weekend I was too ill even to*
> *receive house guests.*
>
> > *Forgive me my foolishness! With apologies for any un-*
> *necessary trouble I may have caused you and Dr. Watson, I am*
> > > *Sincerely yours,*
> > > *Louise Hawkins Doyle*

"I say, Holmes," I said, unable on this occasion to suppress a smile. "Like Lady Chiltern in *An Ideal Husband,* Mrs. Doyle seems now content to await the perfect partner in the next world."

"Indeed, Watson," my friend replied, with only a hint of testiness, "though let us not forget the tragic example of the author of

An Ideal Husband, who unlike the worthy Mr. Doyle permitted passion to overrule his better judgement."

EPILOGUE

The following year I resumed publication of these memoirs of mine with *The Hound of the Baskervilles,* while P. G. Wodehouse made his first professional magazine sale. In 1902, for his efforts in presenting the British position in the Boer War, Arthur Conan Doyle received his knighthood, though he accepted only reluctantly, at the insistence of his mother. Sherlock Holmes refused a knighthood the same year. Louise Hawkins Doyle died of tuberculosis in 1907. The year after, Sir Arthur married Jean Leckie, who bore him three children. According to his son Adrian, a few months before his death, Conan Doyle left his sickbed unseen to go out into the garden. A few minutes later the butler found him, collapsed in a passage with a heart attack. In his hand he clutched a snowdrop. It had been his custom to observe the anniversary of his meeting Jean Leckie, on the fifteenth of March, 1897, by picking the first snowdrop of the season.

The dating of Watson's manuscripts is often problematic, but "The Case of the Woman in the Cellar" clearly occurred during the so-called Great Hiatus (1891–1894), when the world believed that Sherlock Holmes was dead. It will be abundantly clear to the reader why Dr. Watson quashed this nasty aftermath to The Great Detective's most famous case, The Hound of the Baskervilles.

The Case of the
Woman in the Cellar

BY PAT MULLEN

May 1, 1893

Lestrade was attacked by an unknown assailant near the theatre last night. The shot went off right beside my ear; I am still half deaf. L. had the temerity to suggest that the passing of time has rendered Holmes less than his reputation. I might have killed him myself.

May 5, 1893

It is two years and one day since Holmes's death.

May 6, 1893

Sir Henry Baskerville is to be married. I hope this means he has completely recuperated from his ghastly experience. It does make it a little easier when I see the good that Holmes did in his lifetime, especially the good that lives on in such things as B.'s recovery and happiness.

May 12, 1893

Dear Dr. Watson—

It was with great rejoicing that I received your note. Thank you for your good wishes on behalf of my future wife as well as myself. I met her while I was ill, and we corresponded throughout this past year. Now, after a visit (very proper and quite terrifying) to meet her parents, she has accepted the offer of my hand in marriage. The deed will be done on the 29th of October, and you would make me very happy if you and Mrs. Watson would attend as my guests.

I will be travelling down to London in a few days, and I would enjoy seeing you if you have a free evening.

Yours affectionately,
Henry Baskerville

May 17, 1893

Saw B., who's besotted over his fiancée. Pleasant evening.

May 21, 1893

Dreadful evening. B. should be ashamed of himself.

May 22, 1893

The events of the past few days have been so disturbing that I must set them down. Were Holmes still living, he would listen patiently with that intensity of thought that was unique to him, ask me unexpected questions and then explain clearly and logically what has happened. But he is dead, and it falls upon me to struggle to make sense of all that has transpired.

On Thursday night I met Sir Henry Baskerville at The Continental Club, his residence when he is in London. We had not seen each other since before Holmes's death, and I was glad to see him looking well. He has gained some weight since I last saw him, and lost that ruddy, weather-beaten appearance. He is a short man and he looked directly up into my eyes as he heartily shook my hand and took pains to let me know how grateful he is to Holmes for having saved his life.

He showed me around the club, which was quite grand and once the home of a member of the Royal Household. I had been there years ago with Holmes, and was pleased to see that not much had changed. The service is the best that I've ever experienced, one barely has time to recognize a desire than to find it instantly fulfilled. The staff is so discreet that they are almost invisible.

After a search, we found the suite that I remembered, The India Room. Enjoying myself fully, I admired the dark woodwork and comfortable atmosphere of the place. As I paused to admire the stuffed head of an immense water buffalo mounted on the wall, a chair upholstered in red Moroccan leather was placed behind my knees. Moments later a cigar materialized from out of nowhere and was lit without my having to so much as turn my head. Throughout the evening brandy never seemed to disappear from my glass.

All this magic was performed by an army of servants who lurk silently in corners, quite invisible until they sense the faintest hint that they are needed. A few seem to have been with the place all their lives, as they are quite ancient. One fine old fellow called Warrington was especially attentive to us.

Sir Henry has completely recovered from the trauma of his cousin Roger's—whom I still think of as "Stapleton"—attempts on his life, and I quite enjoyed his quick wit and amusing company. He is in love. The lady in question, Abigail Ferncliffe, is a young woman from an old and wealthy family. The "Fecund Ferncliffes" I have heard them called, for Abigail is the youngest of twelve brothers and sisters and has something like thirty-five nephews and nieces. Apparently even such an abundant population hasn't been able to deplete the family fortune. The joke going around is that with this union, the House of Baskerville (which has died out but for Sir Henry) will soon have an abundance of heirs.

Much of the evening was spent with him extolling his fiancée's charms, but toward the end he asked me about my limp. I told him about the coach that came out of nowhere and almost ran me over. He expressed his sympathy and asked when it had occurred.

"April 28th," I remembered. "A ghastly night."

"Ah. Rain, with flashes of lightning," he said promptly. "An hour before sunset, London was as dark as midnight."

"Amazing!" I exclaimed. "How did you remember?"

"That was the day my engagement was formally announced. Notice in *The Times,* party at her father's home. I remember every detail of the day."

Then the conversation turned to how perilous life could be in London these days, and I told him about the attack on Lestrade at the theatre. "It was around the anniversary of Holmes's death. I suppose Lestrade was determined to cheer me up, for he bought a pair of tickets to hear Miss Lotte Collins sing. It certainly seemed to cheer old Lestrade—he quite enjoyed the show! I think his inviting me was just an excuse to go himself. After the performance we were walking down a dark street not far from the theatre (with Lestrade whistling *Ta ra ra boom de yea,* if I recall rightly), when some fellow stepped out of the shadows and fired a pistol at Lestrade's head. Missed him, of course."

"Good Lord! What fellow?"

"No idea, couldn't see his face."

"Perhaps he was upset by Lestrade's voice," Sir Henry joked.

I laughed, because on the rare occasion that I have heard Lestrade sing, I've considered shooting him myself. Making light of the attack, I said how lucky I was to have been run down by that coach so that I was still armed with my cane. "I struck the fellow's hand with it and took out after Lestrade, who chased him down an alley. We never caught him, though."

"I'm glad no one was hurt," Sir Henry said after we stopped chuckling and the invisible Warrington had refilled our glasses and relit my cigar. "And if Lotte Collins is that good, perhaps I'll take Abigail to see her."

"Oh, I think not," I said, sobering. "Too risqué for young ladies, if you know what I mean." To change the subject I said, "Here, this is what I drove the fellow off with," and showed him my cane. "Holmes gave me this. Heavy enough for a cudgel. And see, inside it has a little compass. And twist this and out comes . . ." and I showed him the Italian stiletto. "And here in the center, turn this silver cylinder and look! A little flask for brandy! It was one of Holmes's favorite things," I added, letting Sir Henry examine it. "He always loved gadgets."

"What a noble mind he had," Sir Henry said sadly. "What a fine, if peculiar, character."

I found myself in danger of being overwhelmed by emotion. "I could desire nothing more in the world than to sit in this odd, overstuffed chair where Holmes once sat," I told Sir Henry with perfect sincerity, "and talk with you about your future with Abigail and my past with Sherlock."

"Well supplied with cigars and brandy," my host added, lifting his glass to touch mine.

"To past and future," I said and I quite meant it, feeling happy for Sir Henry and nostalgic for myself all at the same time.

As I left, old Warrington caught my eye for a moment, then glanced quickly downward. I blamed myself for talking so openly before a servant, even an invisible one, but he was most discreet as he showed me out of the club. As the heavy front door swung silently open, I gasped with surprise. The shadowy figure of a woman quickly turned away and fled down the stairs. Old Warrington was so startled by her sudden appearance that for a moment I thought he would fall down. I even put out a hand to steady him, but he jerked himself upright and very properly wished me a good evening.

"*Steady, Watson,*" a strangely familiar voice whispered in my head. "*What's this?*"

Several days later, Sir Henry generously invited my wife and me to dine with him in the Ferncliffe city residence to meet his fiancée and prospective father-in-law. Abigail Ferncliffe is indeed a beautiful young woman, and whether or not her family line is as fertile as it is reputed to be, her charms are every bit as alluring as Sir Henry indicated. Her father, the old Baronet, was cordial and hearty, a country man who enjoys horses and good port. It would have been an entertaining evening, for life in the country has not dulled the Ferncliffe wits, but Sir Henry spoiled everything. He seemed happy to welcome my wife and myself, but shortly after our arrival he stepped out of the room for a moment, and when he returned he seemed a different man.

I can hear Holmes now. *"What do you mean a different man, Watson? Surely you mean he was the same man, but something was different about him. What was it? Can you think?"* I think that when Baskerville returned to the room he seemed disturbed. He was not attentive to Abigail, who was plainly hurt when she whispered something in his ear and he answered her curtly, staring into space.

"How long was he gone from the room?" Yes, of course, that's it, what could have happened when he left the room that changed him so? But I don't know. He wasn't gone long enough to have done anything, barely long enough to have combed his hair. Or received a short message. At any rate, the evening ended on a sour note when Sir Henry abruptly proclaimed that he had to be up early in the morning and would we all excuse him.

And then in the middle of the night, that banging on my front door. It was Sir Henry, distraught, begging me to ask no questions, just bring my medical bag and follow him. He led me to a poor but respectable section of the city, up three flights of clean but rickety stairs to a tiny room almost bare except for a lady's dresser and armoire, where a woman lay injured on the bed. "Sir Henry, what's happened?" I demanded, but he was silent as I examined her.

I could not tell if her face was bruised, for she turned away from me, concealing her profile with her hand. Nevertheless, I could see that she possessed great beauty by the pleasing curve of her neck and the lustre and softness of her hair, which I was forced to touch as I examined a superficial gash on the back of her head. Her skin was of a golden hue with an underlying blush. As I bent over her, almost awed by her beauty, she slipped off a silken robe and lay face down on the bed, sweeping aside her raven tresses so that I could see her well-formed back and shoulders. I gasped. I did not need Holmes to explain what the marks on her body told me.

As a doctor I am not unfamiliar with the scars that some forms of depravity leave upon their devotees, yet never have I seen such marks on a woman's body as I saw that night. The man who had whipped her took savage pleasure in her pain. A web of welts criss-crossed her shoulders and back with perfect symmetry. Her slender thighs were red and bruised. I saw instantly that this was not the first cruel beating she had endured, for her back and sides were covered with a light latticework of scars, faint and white with age. As I leaned closer to see the extent of her injuries by the pulsing illumination of the smoking lamp, I saw with a shudder of revulsion that her tormentor had inflicted deep scars on her buttocks in the shape of the letter *B*. Cattle in America are branded in just this way to signify ownership, and I had no doubt that the perpetrator of these horrors had done this unspeakable act to lay claim to his slave.

While the Henry Baskerville that I'd known had always seemed the most sympathetic of men, I reflected now that I scarcely knew him. I glanced at him involuntarily and saw a short, dark-eyed man, sturdily built, even verging on corpulence. He had thick black eyebrows and a strong, pugnacious face. He seemed stricken with alarm and concern, yet at that moment the affection that I felt for him withered like a green shoot struck by an arctic wind. He had been raised in Canada, I remembered, far from England's public schools. How had he become infected with so vicious a form of corruption?

Barely able to look at him, I muttered that she should be taken to the hospital. It was the woman who emphatically said "No!" in a voice that was deep and musical, the sound of the vowel somehow exotic. Her face was still turned away from me, whether from shame or modesty I couldn't tell, but she issued a series of sharp cries and moans as I tended to her wounds. I left her with a draught of laudanum in case her pain worsened.

"For God's sake, Baskerville, what have you done?" I demanded of him when we were on the street again.

"Nothing, I swear!" he replied. "I merely found her here like this."

It was all I could do not to grab him by the collar and shake him. "Merely found her? You mean to tell me you just went out for a walk, wandered up here and found her by accident?"

"She sent a note saying she had something urgent to tell me, but—" He broke off, shaking his head. "Be my friend, ask no questions," he pleaded.

I advised him that if she were to show any signs of fever, he was to call on me so that she might be taken to Charing Cross Hospital. It was with the greatest misgivings that I returned home, just as a lifeless streak of light on the horizon heralded a grey dawn breaking over London.

I was exhausted, but my apprehension was so great that I returned to the little room well before noon. The woman was gone. Her landlady told me that she had been taken away by a gentleman early this morning, leaning heavily on the man's arm. "A fine gentleman 'e was, too," she told me, happy to elaborate when I offered her a guinea. "An' I figger 'e might be the one who pays 'er rent, y'know?" In that way I discovered that the woman's rent had been paid each month with a cheque mailed from a solicitor's office.

I have returned home to sit in growing apprehension throughout the afternoon. I find myself perusing my old notes on the Baskerville case and the lengthy correspondence I sent to Holmes while he was investigating the rumours of the mythical hound of that poor family. I read and reread my notes, especially Holmes's comments at the very end of the affair, committing his words to my memory. Rarely have I felt such a sense of misgiving.

May 24, 1893

Well, it all seems quite obvious now, if even more ominous, but I was too upset at the time to think clearly. I tried to contact

Baskerville all yesterday, sent runners to the club, went there twice myself. At last I found him in. A servant brought him downstairs to meet me in the smoke-flavoured air of the club's receiving room.

"The woman you treated for me is gone. Is she with you?" he demanded accusingly as soon as we were alone.

"No, she's not. Sir Henry, I must talk with you." A strange look passed over his face. Alarm? Relief? I couldn't be sure. "Is there some place where we could speak privately?"

"The India Room," he replied and led me up the stairs and down the hall.

The darkness of the late afternoon was broken by shimmering fingers of sunlight streaking across the window at the end of the corridor. Silent servants moved about us hurrying on errands for other, unseen members of the club hidden within the quiet rooms about us. When the door opened into The India Room, a familiar figure turned toward me from the mantle, his grey eyes peering behind his gold-rimmed glasses. "James Mortimer!" I exclaimed, clasping his hand in genuine pleasure.

"I just arrived from Dartmoor," Sir Henry's old friend and doctor explained. He squinted at me through his thick spectacles. "But you seem, like my friend Sir Henry, very troubled." He was a tall, stooped man, very thin with a light complexion and a pronounced nose. As he stood beside the shorter and wider Henry Baskerville, the contrast could not have been greater. Dr. Mortimer had been the first to welcome Sir Henry to England, and had forsaken his own obligations to accompany him on a long voyage to restore the baronet's health after the affair with the hound. I had no doubt of Mortimer's honour and decency. How much, I wondered, did he really know about his friend?

"There is bad business afoot," I said solemnly.

He nodded in agreement. "Would you like anything?"

"A whiskey."

"I went to meet Dr. Mortimer at Victoria Station," Baskerville explained. "I've told him everything. But when we looked in on that woman, she was gone. We've searched, but no one has seen her. We returned here less than an hour ago."

A whiskey, neat, was thrust into my hand. "Let's sit down," I said. "I have something important to ask you."

We were all whispering and moving quickly like conspirators. Mortimer was standing before the fireplace. Sir Henry crossed the room and sat down on the corner of the sofa and I turned to follow him. Before I could reach it, Dr. Mortimer flung himself down in the red leather chair and gave a ghastly cry. Struggling as though a powerful unseen force were pressing him back, he pulled himself up with great effort, then gave a gasp and fell face down on the floor. He was dead before my fingers could reach his pulse. "Great Scott," I exclaimed as I turned him over and saw a deep gash in his back beneath his left shoulder blade. "It looks like he's been stabbed!"

"Good God!" Sir Henry leaped to his feet, his eyes wide, his lower lip trembling. "How could that happen? He was just—"

I cautiously probed the seam between the cushions of the chair, jerking back my hand as I felt cold metal. A knife blade was tightly wedged in the stuffing of the red leather chair. "Sharp as a razor!" I explained when I had taken my bleeding finger from my mouth. "It would have killed anyone who sat in it. Don't move, Sir Henry. Don't touch anything!" The ever-present servants clustered by the door and I sent someone for the police, giving orders that no one should be allowed to leave the building.

The police arrived quickly and I was glad to see my old friend Inspector Lestrade in charge. His first act was to secure the building and see to the removal of the body and the chair, with its lethal blade still in place. Then he climbed the stairs to the crowded room. "Who was here at the time of the crime?" he asked.

"The deceased, myself, and Sir Henry Baskerville," I told him.

"And who had access to the room?"

"All the servants," Sir Henry put in. "Dr. Mortimer and I had just arrived."

"I thought you said that you came from Victoria Station an hour before," I objected.

"Barely that," he replied.

"Dr. Watson, come with me," Lestrade said formally.

An empty room was found for us, and we sat beside a bare fireplace while I told him everything that had transpired. Lestrade listened closely, wrapping his coat about his shoulders, for a chill filled the room that made us both shiver. I gave him the facts just as I have noted them here, just as I would have done with Holmes.

"Very well," was all he said when I was done. He went on to question Sir Henry and the servants, and it was several hours before he called us all together again at the scene of the crime.

"There is more than one crime here," the Inspector announced. "A woman has been beaten and abducted, a man murdered. I have sent men to investigate, and I have learned that for the past two years the woman whom you treated last night, Dr. Watson—her name was Mrs. Agrafe, by the way—was supported by a monthly cheque. Those cheques originated in the chambers of Lester Stanley, Esquire. Who is your solicitor, Henry Baskerville?"

"Lester Stanley," Sir Henry admitted.

"Yes, I thought so," Lestrade said. "Watson, what's the matter with you?" he added with some irritation.

"Agrafe!" I exclaimed. "That's 'staple' in French! Of course! I should have recognized her!"

"What are you rattling on about?" the Inspector demanded.

"The original crime, Lestrade!" I controlled myself and lowered my voice so that the servants and the policemen standing nearby couldn't hear. "Stapleton's wife, remember? I treated her when she was beaten by her husband just before he died fleeing justice. That woman in the room last night was Beryl Stapleton!"

"Are you sure? You said you never saw her face."

"But I saw . . . other things." I turned to Sir Henry. "It *was* Beryl Stapleton, was it not?" But Sir Henry only set his jaw and scowled. "I'm sure it was her! She had scars that corresponded to wounds Mrs. Stapleton suffered in the original incident."

"Why didn't you tell me this before?" demanded Lestrade.

"I only just realized it."

"Is there anything else you've neglected to tell me?"

"Well, yes, actually, but only for decency's sake," I crossed the room to whisper in his ear. "The lady had the letter *B* incised on her—ah. Well. On a private part of her body."

Lestrade's eyebrows shot up. "Thank you, Dr. Watson, you have just handed me the final element in this disturbing puzzle." He turned to Sir Henry. "Henry Baskerville, you are about to make a very advantageous marriage. Great fortune and many heirs seem inevitably yours." When Sir Henry nodded in reluctant agreement, Lestrade went on. "What will you do to protect that marriage?"

"Protect it?" The baronet was confused. "Anything! Anything at all!"

"Yes, I believe that," the Inspector nodded. "Just as I believe that your paramour became jealous. What caused you to beat her so savagely? Did she threaten to reveal your relationship with her?"

"Paramour?" Sir Henry echoed in what seemed like innocent astonishment.

"Don't try to deny it. This is a very intricate case, made more difficult because the original murder of your uncle, Sir Charles Baskerville, was solved by Sherlock Holmes. Mr. Holmes incriminated your cousin and pursued him to a terrible death in the quicksand of Grimpen Mire. The motives for the goings-on last night and today seem a separate puzzle. It's impossible to understand—unless one is clever enough to throw out Holmes's solution to that first case and start over. Do that, and the truth emerges as plain as the nose on your face."

Lestrade had a buoyant, cocky attitude and was, I felt, enjoying himself a little too much. I was becoming annoyed with his blatant disregard for Holmes's memory. "Really, Lestrade!" I protested.

"Admit for a change that Holmes could be wrong," he fired back. "Look at the matter with fresh eyes, Dr. Watson. Holmes had the wrong Baskerville! It was Sir Henry here, along with his accomplice, Dr. Mortimer, who conspired to kill Sir Charles in order to inherit the family fortune. He let his poor cousin take the blame and be hunted to death by Holmes and the rest of us."

"That's outrageous!" Sir Henry exclaimed.

"I must agree!" I declared.

The Inspector was undeterred. "Sir Henry stole the affections of his cousin's wife, Beryl, and brutalized her in a most despicable way when she threatened his chances with his fiancée's family. And finally, he's done away with her. Probably with James Mortimer's help," he added as an afterthought. "Why did you kill Dr. Mortimer? Was he threatening to blackmail you?"

"This is preposterous! I've done nothing!" Sir Henry protested.

"Wait, Inspector," I objected. "Sir Henry had no way of knowing that Mortimer would sit in that chair. There are chairs all over this room. In fact, that is *my* favourite chair and I might well have sat in it myself if Mortimer hadn't beaten me to it!"

Lestrade barely hesitated. "And don't think it hasn't occurred to me that you, Dr. Watson, were the intended victim. Although you don't realize it, you have come too close to the truth. Whatever Dr. Mortimer's fate, you would never have left this room alive, for you saw the evil that Baskerville has done to his lover, and it would be only a matter of time before you understood the situation almost as well as I." Unable to restrain a smug smile of satisfaction, he turned again to Sir Henry. "Baskerville, I am accusing you of the murders of your uncle, Sir Charles Baskerville, and of your accomplice, Dr. Mortimer. Furthermore, I suspect you are responsible for the assault, abduction and possible murder of Beryl Stapleton. I doubt we'll find that poor lady alive. What do you have to say for yourself?"

Sir Henry's face turned ashen and he sat abruptly on the

sofa as though his legs had buckled beneath him. "No," he croaked. "No, *No!*"

Lestrade turned to me and said with infuriating pleasure, "Sherlock Holmes had it all wrong."

"You can't let him get away with that, Watson."

"Wait just a moment!" I said, fighting to keep control of myself. "There's something you're not taking into account."

"What's that?" Lestrade growled.

"Character!" I blurted, not sure where I was going to go with this. "I knew James Mortimer, and he was a good man. And I know Sir Henry Baskerville. I was a guest in Baskerville Hall for several weeks. I watched him as he fell in love with Beryl Stapleton, saw his reaction when he learned she was married to his cousin. I saw him face death, and I know the nature of the man. It is, if occasionally too eager, a good and noble nature. I apologize for my earlier doubts, Sir Henry, but on reflection I know you could never abuse a lady or plot to kill a friend. Furthermore," I hurried on before Lestrade could interrupt, "I know the lady. Even though she was married to a man with a criminal mind, she managed to remain loyal to him while trying to thwart his malicious intentions. She is not the sort of woman who becomes someone's lover for money." I turned back to Baskerville. "Is it true that you were supporting Mrs. Stapleton?" But I saw by the rise of colour in his cheeks that it was. Lestrade snorted.

"There must be a perfectly logical explanation for this."

Unsure of where this would all lead, I pressed on. "Well, of course. It's perfectly logical that Sir Henry gave Beryl Stapleton money and, I dare say, perfectly innocent as well. After the death of her husband, the lady had no means of support. Sir Henry was grateful to her, for she had risked her life and suffered great harm from her secret attempts to save his life. I suspect that he was concerned that she should not have further hardship in what had already been a life marked with suffering. Knowing him as I do, I'm sure that you will find that the cheques began shortly after the death of her husband, about the same time that Sir Henry and his friend Dr. Mortimer began their trip around the world in an attempt to restore the baronet's health. I'm also confident that you will find that Sir Henry seldom, if ever, visited her, even though he has been in England for more than a year." Sir Henry glanced up toward me with a look of gratitude.

"All your talk about sterling character won't wash away the facts," Lestrade said. He halted abruptly as a constable threw open the door and stood back to allow into the room two of his companions. Between them they supported the bedraggled figure of a barely conscious woman. This time I saw her face and instantly recognized her.

"Beg your pardon, sir, but we just now found her tied up and gagged down in the club's cellar."

We leapt to our feet as one man. The constable carried Beryl Stapleton to the sofa, and Lestrade followed him, barking orders at his men while I snatched up a decanter and poured her a glass of brandy.

"A man has been murdered, Mrs. Stapleton," Lestrade told her as the constable set her down, "but at least we have managed to save you. Tell us who abused you so cruelly and abducted you."

Warrington, his silent servant role shaken by the sight of this woman in distress, took the glass from me and held it to her lips. "Here, madam, drink this."

She revived slowly, taking small sips and glancing apprehensively around the room. Sir Henry stood beside her, looking deeply into her dark eyes with a look of concern. "It was Henry Baskerville," she said at last in a small voice I could hardly hear. She buried her face in her hands and sobbed.

"There, there, madam, take courage," Lestrade said. "It is all over. You have only confirmed what I suspected from the start." He seemed pleased as he turned to Sir Henry. "Sir Henry Baskerville, I arrest you for the murders of Sir Charles and Dr. Mortimer, and for the abuse of this poor woman."

"Watson! Don't just sit there!"

"Wait, Lestrade, there is more to this than meets the eye," I protested. "May I ask a question?"

"What is it?" Lestrade asked with some impatience.

I turned to Beryl. She still reclined on the sofa, clutching the blanket that had been fetched to cover her shapely bare legs. "Just tell me, Mrs. Stapleton, why you came to this club on the evening of May 17th, the same evening that I visited Sir Henry?"

She seemed apprehensive. "It was not I."

"But it was! You must have wanted to tell Sir Henry something, but you were frightened off. I saw you at the door, but the instant that it was opened, you hurried away. What did you want to tell him, and what frightened you away?"

"I was not frightened! I was not there!" she cried, hiding her face behind shaking hands.

I stared back at her, dumbfounded. It had been no one else, I was certain.

"Take him away!" Lestrade barked at his constables and they stepped forward to take Sir Henry by the arms.

"Tell the worst, Watson, don't flinch!" The voice in my head propelled me to the center of the room.

"Wait, Lestrade! Your refusal to be logical forces me to admit that you are right about one thing," I said. "Sherlock Holmes *was* wrong—but not about Sir Henry Baskerville! Holmes was an excellent judge of character, and not for a moment did he suspect him. You can be sure that if Sir Henry were a fortune hunter, Holmes would have been onto him in a moment! No, Holmes proved beyond a doubt that it was Stapleton who murdered old Sir Charles, then tried to murder his heir, Sir Henry. But think of this. One month ago, Sir Henry announced his engagement to Abigail Ferncliffe. That very day, I was nearly run down by a coach and four. Not long afterward, someone took a shot at you. Some evil presence has been following both of us."

"Coincidence," Lestrade said.

"Holmes would say that there is no such thing as coincidence! Think of it! Almost everyone who knew of Sherlock Holmes's solution to the mystery of the myth of the Hound of the Baskervilles is under attack."

"Everyone but his lordship," Lestrade rasped. "And good reason for that, if he was the one doing the attacking!"

"But just think for a moment! Why should anyone want to murder you, Dr. Mortimer, and myself? Who would beat and threaten Mrs. Stapleton, forcing her to lie, as she is doing now? What do we four have in common?"

"Sir Henry is a murderer and philanderer," Lestrade explained to me as though I were an idiot. "Of course he'd want to kill Mrs. Stapleton. And if he were betrayed, he'd do Mortimer as well."

"That's fine as far as it goes," I agreed, "but why attempt to kill you? And if he were going to murder Mrs. Stapleton, why call upon me to save her? No. The only common link among the four of us is this: we all knew Stapleton before Holmes branded him a killer, when he was pretending to be a harmless bug collector!"

"Oh, well done, Watson!"

"But Stapleton died in Grimpen Mire," Lestrade protested.

I shook my head. "Mrs. Stapleton, you told Holmes that your husband had fled into that desolate swamp, yet we found hardly a trace of him. Impressed by that vast, trackless wilderness, Holmes deduced that Stapleton must have drowned. But no corpse was ever found."

"You believe that Stapleton's still alive!" Lestrade gasped. "Do you honestly think that Holmes could have missed something like that?"

"He didn't," I said with certainty, frowning as Warrington refilled Mrs. Stapleton's glass. "If Holmes had a fault, it was his genius for concealing uncertainties, rarely telling even me what he had in his mind until the facts seemed irrefutable. I know that he investigated the details of that case long after it was over, which was unusual for him. One of the things he discovered was that Stapleton had a man-servant named Anthony who assisted him in his crime and later escaped to the Continent."

"You have it now! Run with it, old boy!"

"But what if Beryl misdirected us that night, even as she is doing now?" I turned to glare at her and she dropped her eyes, a deep blush colouring her face. "Suppose it was old Anthony who died in the quicksand, and Stapleton who fled to Paris?"

"Hmm," growled Lestrade, impressed in spite of himself.

"Imagine if Stapleton were still alive and plotting to inherit the Baskerville title and fortune," I added. "Wouldn't he be compelled to murder Sir Henry before he could marry and beget an heir? And who could stop him?"

"Those of us who could recognize him on sight if he claimed to be the heir after Henry's death!" Lestrade agreed grimly. "I see what you've done. A simple example of 'Eliminate the impossible—' "

" 'And whatever remains, however improbable, is the solution,' " I finished for him, echoing the man we both respected so much. "Stapleton never went near Grimpen Mire that night. He was much too intelligent to flee to a place from which there was no escape. While Sherlock and I searched for him, he made his way to the Continent, probably disguised as old Anthony. Having eluded the greatest detective in the world, he was free to resume a life incognito in Europe. When he heard that Holmes was killed, he must have gloated over the demise of his adversary, then began to scheme again how he would inherit the estate of Baskerville."

"Yes," Lestrade added, "and he would have to hurry when he learned that Baskerville was marrying one of the Fecund Ferncliffes. Sorry, Sir Henry, but you must know how some people talk." He was embarrassed and reached for a tall glass on a silver tray offered by a silent servant.

"Don't drink that!" I said. "I'm deadly serious. I wouldn't trust anything served to us in this place."

Lestrade squinted critically at the violently foaming head of ale that stood before him. "Poison?"

"I shouldn't be surprised," I replied, trying to remember if I had sipped from the snifter that had appeared in my hand. "Who brought these drinks? Lestrade, see that no one leaves the room. I should think that—"

"Beryl!" cried Sir Henry. The deep blush had become livid, suffusing her fine features. The glass fell from her hand and she fell back, shuddering.

"She's dead," I told them a moment later. "Mute testimony to the potency of the poison in all our drinks. That can only mean—" With shocking quickness, a man brandished a pistol and leaped for the door. "Get down, Henry! Look out, Lestrade!" I had my own pistol in my pocket, but before I could pull it out a constable appeared from the other side of the door and wrestled down the old servant.

"Warrington?" Sir Henry exclaimed, aghast.

"If I'm not mistaken," I said, bending down, "it is Stapleton in a wig and makeup." A few tugs on his hair proved me right. I refrained from touching the envelope with traces of white powder found in his pocket.

Lestrade pulled Stapleton to his feet and pushed him into the arms of the constable. "Take him away!"

May 26, 1893

With Sir Henry safely back in the arms of his fiancée, this afternoon I sat with Lestrade in my study. "How did you know?" he asked.

"Start at the beginning, Watson."

"The poor woman's wounds," I replied. "I assumed at the time that Sir Henry was responsible and called upon me because he'd injured her. But when I'd had time to reflect on it, I realized that such depravity is the result of what is, for lack of a better way of putting it, an English schoolboy's vice. I have seen such injuries in men who as boys were caned for infractions at school (and who are not?) and then acquire a taste for it. It is shocking, but after a time some are not satisfied with a simple birching and cultivate a proclivity for the lash."

"Good God," Lestrade said, and took a gulp of tea. "That's the sort of thing only a doctor would know."

"But Sir Henry was raised in Canada," I went on. "Like Americans, in Canada they brand cattle and horses, but it is a mark of ownership because they can't afford fences, as I understand it. It's not deliberate cruelty. And while that didn't eliminate Sir Henry, it made it seem less likely that he would be such an enthusiast. So I cast about for another explanation and remembered that Beryl Stapleton had been beaten by her husband in just such a way. When I realized that the woman *was* Beryl, the rest became clear."

"In the beginning," Lestrade inquired, "even though she'd been beaten, Beryl misled Holmes by telling him that her husband had run to Grimpen Mire?"

I nodded.

"And although he beat her again, she didn't warn you or Sir Henry that the murdering fiend was back. She had the gall to come in here and lie to our faces, trying to blame poor Sir Harry!" He shook his head, baffled.

"Be kind to her memory, Lestrade. She recognized Warrington as her husband and was frightened by him. And, I suspect, loved him. Yet as soon as she learned that Stapleton had returned to London, she came to the club to warn Sir Henry. If someone other than Warrington had seen me to the front door that night, and if they hadn't recognized each other, she might have succeeded and poor Mortimer might still be alive. Stapleton must have traced her to her room and threatened her into silence."

"He abused her and he murdered her, yet she never said a word against him. I'll never understand women!" He was outraged, his lip curling in an angry sneer. Knowing his spouse, who was called by everyone, including the Inspector himself, "Mrs. Lestrade," I knew he was telling the truth.

Few men, certainly not Lestrade nor the average reader of *The Strand* could comprehend why I privately suspected that Beryl Stapleton was bound by more than just love. I was sure that, as some are addicted to drugs, she was doomed by what amounted to a sexual addiction to her husband, painful and humiliating as it must have been.

I came to a decision. "Lestrade, I must implore you to see that not one word of Holmes's involvement in this case ever comes before the public. I don't care how you manage it."

Lestrade agreed. "I'll not mention old Sir Charles and the earlier case. I'll see that Stapleton is charged only for his wife's and Dr. Mortimer's murders. He'll be hanged, if there's any justice. The name of Sherlock Holmes will never be uttered at the trial."

"Excellent. Try not to mention me, either."

"What is the matter with you, Watson?" he asked. "It was you who solved this difficult case. You've sent a master criminal to his just reward. Why not take credit for it?"

"I'd rather not."

"Oh, maybe just a small footnote, Watson," and I recognized the voice of my own vanity.

"When the Hound of the Baskervilles was killed and Sir Charles's murder solved, Holmes called it one of the greatest cases of his career," I explained. "I shall publish it as such someday, in memory of him. Just because he didn't live long enough to work out this—this *postscript,* I'll not have it made public that he erred."

"Suit yourself." Lestrade shrugged. "I respect your loyalty."

"But the truth is so perfect. The lie will be incomplete, unsatisfying," the voice pleaded.

"Be quiet!" I said firmly. "This is the end of it."

Lestrade frowned, hurt, thinking that I was talking to him.

Desperate Business

In the preceding section, Murder seldom raised its sanguine head, but the following quartet of adventures is rife with terrorism and wholesale slaughter. One tale was clearly suppressed for reasons of supreme tact and delicacy, whereas the French and Irish cases indicate reservations on the part of Holmes and Watson both. Perhaps most curious of all is "The Adventure of the Dying Ship," which ought to have been published in The Strand, *save for intervention from a completely unanticipated jurisdiction.*

*R*eaders *of* The Resurrected Holmes *(St. Martin's Press, 1996) will recall the incredible botch a certain "Beatnik" author made of the story of the French assassin Huret, which Watson first mentioned in "The Adventure of Wisteria Lodge." My scholarly colleague J. Adrian Fillmore concluded that the case was too well known in the newspapers of the era for Watson to bother writing up himself, but the manuscript we found in the lower compartment of his tin dispatch-box proves there was another reason why the story did not appear in print: one that concerns an important character in the following tale, Ida Minerva Tarbell (1857–1944). Ida Tarbell was one of America's leading muckraking journalists. In 1904, she wrote* The History of the Standard Oil Company, *which led to the exposure of malpractice and the prosecution of that firm.*

The Adventure of the Boulevard Assassin

BY KATHLEEN BRADY

O n the third morning of October the disaster Holmes had prophesied occurred. A bomb exploded in a Paris police station with such force and brutality that part of the body of one of the unfortunate victims was found dangling from a gas fixture in the shattered room.

Until then, most Parisians thought the danger had passed. The anarchists who terrorized the city in the late spring had been silent for months. Raw fear had faded to a general wariness that year of

77

1894. Most inhabitants of that marvelous capital had lived so long with feelings of dread that they could no longer identify their own anxiety. It was as if they had a chronic ache that seemed to fade because they simply learned to accommodate it.

Holmes and I came to be in Paris on that fateful day because a few weeks before, over breakfast in London, he made a decision. I was buttering the toast that the excellent Mrs. Hudson served on her little silver rack and Holmes was sitting with his right leg at an angle to the table reading the weather reports in *The Times*. He let the newspaper fall to the floor and turned his full attention to his rashers.

"The calm is about to end," he said. "The anarchists will come out of their holes with the approach of winter, Watson. They could not handle explosives safely during the hot months of summer because even the slightest rise in temperature can provoke a sudden detonation that will explode the operator into a score of pieces." He poured himself a second cup of tea. "We shall assist the Paris police whether they want it or not. On second thought, I shall set things in motion so that the Palais de Justice shall actually invite our help."

And so it came to be. Holmes's diplomatic contacts were such that he quickly received an official invitation. French officials were fairly frantic with eagerness to have Holmes come help them.

The task, to be fair, was impossible. Not even the esteemed Sherlock Holmes could tear out anarchism by its root. It had no root, no organized plan. It was an idea, a belief, a cause. There was no central conspiracy, only individual anarchists who believed in absolute freedom of the individual. They opposed every restraint, and believed as their social philosopher Proudhon did that "property is theft."

Building by building, anarchists tried to claim private property for the common ownership of all by blowing it to bits. In the process they murdered, as if by accident, people in the streets. First they dynamited a department store, then a bank, and finally one of their number assassinated the president of France. Over the steamy summer, the violent acts ceased as the wretched malcontents stewed in the torrid heat and made their plans.

Holmes and I settled into a hotel near the Palais de Justice on that fatal morning. We finished our croissants and café au lait and were longing for Mrs. Hudson's bacon and tea when we received an American journalist who came to interview Holmes for a new magazine. Normally, Holmes would not have considered granting an interview but this person represented a new type that Holmes thought he should become familiar with. She was an American spinster living in Paris on her own and supporting herself, God knew how, as a free-lance writer.

Her name was Ida Tarbell and she was from Titusville, Pennsylvania, the capital of America's oil industry. Holmes assaulted her with questions that she answered, hoping, I suppose, that eventually he would get around to answering hers.

She was intelligent, and not outwardly a blue-stocking. In fact, she tried to ask her questions in an intelligent manner in that flat, uninflected way Americans have of speaking. Holmes was not at all surprised to learn that Miss Tarbell had studied biology and chemistry and had a sound grasp of scientific methods of investigation. She was about thirty-five years of age, uncommonly tall and uncommonly thin, with dark hair and a complexion browned by riding in the open air atop Parisian omnibuses. She tried to ingratiate Holmes for the sake of her story, and she had a nice open smile. I wondered why she had never married. In short, I liked her. Having been the butt of some of Holmes's inquiries myself, I had some sympathy for her. When she insisted that The Great Detective figure her out for himself, Holmes did the usual trick of deducing where in Paris she lived—Rue Sommerard on the Left Bank—and the type of person she sat next to on the omnibus that morning.

"Yes, but what can you tell about *me,* Mr. Holmes?" she inquired.

I knew she had made a blunder that would rebound on her. "You have few funds, madame. Probably your editors are not paying what they owe you. Obviously, they like your work because interviewing me is a coveted assignment. Normally, that would go only to a reliable, and possibly gifted, journalist. I see you are low on money because your serviceable black dress is fading at the seams. The cut of your clothes shows that you are a woman of taste and would surely go to a dressmaker if you could. You have tried to make this dress seem less worn by colouring its frayed seams with ink."

"Holmes!" I cried, astonished that even he could behave in such an ungentlemanly manner. I was embarrassed to be privy to such rudeness and to her humiliation, but Miss Tarbell, to her credit, smiled a tight, rueful little smile and confirmed that his deductions were correct. She took notes of his deduction for her readers and regained her composure as she carefully incised every shaming word he had said in her notebook. As Holmes's official biographer, I know enough about writing to know she knew she was getting a terrific story, even if it was all at her own expense.

Perhaps the authorities rapped, but I cannot be sure. I know the three of us jumped as the door to the suite flew open and a policeman burst in. The concierge trailed just behind to act as interpreter. Holmes and Miss Tarbell spoke fluent French, but even I could interpret what the policeman said. "There has been another explosion. This time in the police station at the Boulevard des Italiens. You are wanted, Mr. Holmes. Please follow me."

I do not remember if we spoke during our ride there, although it went very quickly because we travelled in a carriage identified as that of the police. Never had I witnessed such devastation as we found at the scene. In Afghanistan there was much torn flesh and I myself was wounded, but I had never seen a building so destroyed, with an impossible section of its skeleton structure revealed where the stony muscle of the wall had been blown off.

We mounted a narrow, spiral staircase, made of ironwork. In the hallway on the second floor between two large windows, the body of a young clerk sat on a bench. He had no head. Where it had rested, his neck was a bloody, frothing pulp. We entered what had been until half an hour before the Inspector's office. That official was found still living in the corner, but there was nothing I could do to save him. Flesh had been ripped from his skull and his eyes were blasted from his head. Later, when his pockets were turned out, splinters from the metal casing of the bomb would be found embedded in the coins.

I surmised that the tiny islands of flesh in the pools of blood on the floor were his. The intestine that dripped blood from a gas bracket seemed to have come from the charred black body in the corner. What was left of the man's uniform indicated he had been a sergeant. Across from him was yet another corpse. His torso was a red crater and his trousers were grey like those of someone from the world of commerce.

To my amazement, I noted Miss Tarbell was with us still. Her face was drained white and if she had eaten anything that morning, she would have given it up in the carnage around us. However, she looked no worse than Holmes, who bolted from the ravaged room. I knew him too well to think he was being sick. I was stunned, and indeed too winded, to move as quickly as he, but I saw where he went and followed him to the sidewalk.

Holmes abandoned the body of one policeman as useless to his inquiry and stretched out to a second man in time to hear the dying man murmur "Darmaux." That word was his last. I was kneeling on the pavement, feeling his pulse, and when I turned my head from the dead man I saw that the hem of Miss Tarbell's faded black skirt was darkened now with blood. It was a dark day, stone-coloured with approaching rain. Were I to paint one of those nonsense modern paintings they turn out nowadays, I would do it in leaden, smoky tones with splashes of crimson, for it seems to me everything that day was hopeless grey except for taunting splashes of red.

Miss Tarbell saw she was standing in a puddle of that dead man's blood and jumped back. "Those poor men. God help their families," she said and covered her mouth as if to cut off further emotionalism.

By now the frantic policemen had stopped scurrying and stood in small groups. The chain of command in the station had been permanently broken, and surviving officers did not seem to know how to proceed. Anger is more comfortable than grief, so two officers argued over which station would take over jurisdiction of the scene. "Who saw what happened?" Holmes demanded of anyone who could respond. *"Qui a vu ce qui est arrivé?"*

"I saw them coming in when I was going out," a young policeman told Holmes miserably. He was whole and healthy, unharmed except by the horror of what he had seen. "Luc—his body is upstairs—was leading in a policeman and a clerk who was holding a large canister out in front of him. The man was carrying it like a waiter bearing a large fowl, and they put me in mind of a holiday dinner." The witness wiped his eyes.

"I was down the street when I heard the terrible sound. It was like the cracking of an iron bell—as if it were the day of judgement."

"What is Darmaux?" Holmes asked.

"A city in Lorraine," he replied, as if he were answering a headmaster's geography drill.

I would not have thought it possible, but Miss Tarbell was taking notes with her pen and pad. She said, "The Compagnie de Darmaux is a big industrial firm with interests in iron ore, Mr. Holmes. Its miners have been out on strike for some time. I have been following it in the papers."

"Where is its office?" Holmes demanded. A well-dressed man, whom we later learned was Monsieur Henri Troutout, who had been sent to the scene from someone in the Palais de Justice, gave Holmes an address a few blocks away on the Avenue de l'Opéra.

Troutout was a slight man with dark hair under a top hat. He wore the formal cutaway of the French civil servant of top rank. He could not have been more than forty, and when he spoke the corners of his mouth turned up slightly to reveal his teeth.

There was little time for conversation, however. Holmes, Miss Tarbell, Troutout and myself raced there, surely looking like what we were in truth—emissaries from the carnage of hell. But news of the disaster rippled out in waves to every part of the quarter. It was the calm person and not the agitated one who was out of place.

When we reached the building that houses the offices of the Compagnie de Darmaux, Troutout flashed his credentials and demanded to see the man in charge. One of the attendants led us to the president of the company. We mounted the marble staircase carpeted in deep, thick red. At the board room doors Holmes, wide-eyed and disheveled, banged his fist on one of the carved oaken panels and pushed his way in. The five directors, who had been safe and oblivious to everything but their deliberations, jumped in fear and outrage. The eldest of them, thin, frail and fast, cried "Anarchists!" in a strangled voice and dove below the table. The two youngest hurled themselves at Holmes, who was obviously our leader, but his knowledge of martial arts stood him in good stead. From the floor, the brave but hasty pair looked up at the rest of us and decided Troutout, Miss Tarbell and I posed no physical threat. The taller of Holmes's assailants, whose face was either marred or distinguished by a deep frown line permanently between his brows, was winded, but the younger, rounder one seemed not quite ready to give up the fight. Both brushed the lines of jackets back in place as Troutout introduced himself and Holmes.

Holmes's taller antagonist, whose name was Martin Kaspi, said in almost unaccented English, "My dear Mr. Holmes, I do beg your pardon. You can imagine—" But Holmes cut off his apologies with a nod of his head and began the story of the morning's events. "We are here because you may have been the target of an anarchist's bomb," The Great Detective said. "A dying man's last word was 'Darmaux,' which may have referred to your firm and the area you mine."

The directors resumed their seats, seeing that it was to their advantage to cooperate. Miss Tarbell took a place at the table, but the fourth director, who introduced himself as Georges Jacquot, seemed to question whether she should be allowed to stay. He was slight in build with a face under so much contained tension that one longed for him to release it in a nervous twitch. Miss Tarbell, who had no trouble expressing herself to any of the Parisians we encountered on that terrible day, pretended not to understand his French. Troutout and I saw no reason to intervene. The American stayed.

"Gentlemen," Holmes began, "did any of you observe any-thing unusual today?"

"We have been conducting business as usual!" said Charles Coman, the elderly director, who had been the first to take refuge under the floor.

"He wants to know if we noticed anything out of the ordinary anywhere this morning," snapped the plumper of Holmes's two attackers, a man named Edouard Knodler, who apparently had decided to release his aggression verbally, but not at Holmes.

The managing director, a plump man with a domed forehead and only a wide fringe of dark hair, looked at his colleagues as if deciding whether to speak. His name was Gilbert Daziell and he said, "I arrived early, before anyone else. The board room door was closed, and I saw a large round object covered in newspaper on the floor in front of it. It worried me. I sent for Picot, the concierge. There was quite a delay, but he finally appeared. Picot cut the string around it with his pocket-knife. The newspaper wrappings fell away and revealed a cast-iron canister. Picot picked it up and said it felt like it weighed five kilos. We neither of us wanted to open it, so Picot carefully held it upright and carried it away. The cast-iron canister seemed to be enough protection."

I had a vision of the corpse I'd seen with the grey trousers, and I might have asked what the porter was wearing, but Holmes ended our encounter by prevailing upon the directors to continue their important work. To his credit, the manager, Daziell, ended the meeting, instructed his secretary, a somber young man with a full moustache and pince-nez, to lead us to Picot the concierge's post. Daziell accompanied us.

His saturnine secretary had hair parted in the middle as if to form a curtain for the tragic mask that was his face. He had the manner of one who knew he would always be in a supporting position, and the weight of the responsibilities his superiors carried was something he himself had to bear. Holmes asked his name, and he said "Basil Pontell," as if surprised that anyone would want to know.

Pontell led us to the concierge's post, where, to our surprise, we found Picot sitting, alive and not at all a victim of the bomb. Picot was that same man we saw at the door when we arrived. Neither too slim nor too tall, he had the calm demeanour of a professional greeter who knows and facilitates all. He was about thirty, and so fair that although he was a city dweller, his face was blotched from the sun. He seemed about to ask us what we were about, but then our distracted attitude began to make sense to him.

"Where is Ernst?" the concierge demanded. "Do you know?"

"Perhaps you should tell us who Ernst is," said Holmes, not unkindly.

"Ernst went to the police station in the Boulevard des Italiens," Picot said in a strangled voice, seeming to age as he sat before us. "I found a package upstairs that was suspicious, so I called a gendarme. The policeman wouldn't touch it, so Ernst, one of our clerks, said he would take it to the station if the policeman showed him the way."

Certainly things looked grim for Ernst. Troutout, the representative from the Palais de Justice, told Picot that he would arrange for the concierge to view the body of one of the victims, who might well be the helpful clerk Ernst.

"Before you do so," the managing director said to Picot, "please place one of our offices at the disposal of Monsieur Sherlock Holmes."

The stricken concierge led us to an office on the ground floor that was probably used for maintenance staff, but the desk and chairs were all that we required. Miss Tarbell displayed no inclination to leave us, and Holmes was too preoccupied with the case to find the force to banish her, although normally he would not scruple to evict any unnecessary person at such a time.

"There may be no logical connection in this crime," Holmes observed as he seated himself behind his desk. "Even if this firm was chosen because of the strike, the anarchist may have had no personal connection to Darmaux. That's what makes these anarchists so damnably hard to find. Each must have a feeling of almost godlike power, but he does not accomplish a great deal beyond making martyrs of his dead victims. Holmes shook his head with rare anticipation of defeat. "We must now turn our attention to how the bomb came to be at the board room door."

Picot, still much shaken at the certain death of his friend Ernst, sat on the chair beside Holmes's desk. The concierge explained the late night schedule of the cleaning staff: "They are always out of the building well before midnight. During the night, one watchman guards the door. He stands inside the rear entrance, which is locked, as is the front door. The guard is expected to do nothing more than use a police call box if he sees anyone suspicious."

"When does he go off duty?" Holmes asked.

"At eight A.M., when those who work in the building arrive."

Picot told us that many people had access to the board-room: the directors, their secretaries, and a porter who brought an easel and various supplies that were sometimes wanted for meetings. "Monsieur Daziell summoned me personally just before eleven. Less than three hours ago," the concierge noted, forlornly checking his watch.

"Monsieur Daziell," said Holmes, "thought you were slow to arrive."

"I went as soon as I knew he wanted me."

"Who brought you word?"

"Basil Pontell, the president's secretary. The director must have told him to get me."

"Did Pontell return with you to the board room?"

"No. He said he had to go out on an urgent message for the president. In fact, Pontell asked me to accompany him because he thought he might need my assistance, and I was on the point of doing it, but then one of the porters came down from upstairs. Pontell got flustered and said he was so preoccupied he almost forgot to give me the director's message. He told me to go with the porter and then rushed out. It was most unlike him."

"How did Ernst get involved?" Holmes inquired.

"Ernst was coming out of the cloak room as I was bringing the package to my room. He thought the matter could be serious, so he went for the policeman. He was sure nothing would happen so long as the metal casing wasn't opened, and so when the policeman refused to pick it up, Ernst offered to carry the canister to the station. I sent word to his supervisor to explain Ernst's absence, and that was it. I hope, I still hope, that he will come back."

"What made Ernst think he understood bombs?"

"I don't know. But his observation about the cast iron made sense, we thought." According to Picot, Ernst was in his middle twenties and lived with his parents in Neuilly, where he was born.

After the concierge left, Miss Tarbell said, "You do plan to interview everyone in the building, don't you, Mr. Holmes? There seems to be no other place to start."

I knew the look that crossed Holmes's face when Lestrade volunteered his opinions, but unlike the London inspector, Miss Tarbell had not jumped to a conclusion, but only suggested a sound way to proceed. "Madame, I must keep my thoughts to myself," my friend said, with less rancour than I might have expected.

She seemed to realize that Holmes was about to ask her to leave. Her steady brown eyes rested on him as she made her decision. "I know you have work to do. Would you agree to finish our interview another time?"

Holmes was pleased by her proper sense of the mood of things. "Of course, madame. You may depend upon it."

She picked up her bag, wished us good day with a pleasant little smile, and walked to the door, closing it carefully after her. Holmes stared at the door as if lost in thought and then said, "Watson, follow her, but do try not to let her know it."

This last remark was of course gratuitous. Holmes knew he could trust me with my mission, but he was under some strain.

The guard at the front door told me he had not seen any women leave, and I was sure she had not gone out by the service entrance. I made a quick check of all the rooms on the first floor and learned that she'd had a brief chat with one of the porters. Then I started up the staircase. Jacquot, the director under so much contained tension, stopped me on the landing as he was coming down. He was clearly irritated. *"La femme américaine m'parlé en français!"* was the only sentence I understood. She had spoken to him in French, so he knew she had understood him earlier when he tried to make her leave the board room, but what she had just been saying to him I could not tell. He gave up in disgust and stamped his feet down the stairs. Somehow, she had offended him afresh, that much was clear.

Luckily, I caught sight of the hem of her skirt between the marble pillars of the second floor bannister as she walked on the floor above me. She seemed to be headed back down the hall towards the directors' room. The thick carpeting muffled my footsteps, but I must say that I was lucky that she did not think to turn around. She looked into an open door and greeted Basil Pontell, the managing director's melancholy assistant. His desk was in a large antechamber to Daziell's office, as I learned when I peeked in at them. Her back was towards me and Pontell's eyes were focused on her face so that he did not notice me. The work of the day had been suspended, so Pontell seemed to have little to do and sat with the tips of his fingers pressed together as if he clutched a ball of air.

As I moved out of eyesight and a few feet from the open door, I heard Pontell tell her that they could speak English.

"I believe I left my umbrella in the board room, Mr. Pontell," Miss Tarbell told him, and I tried to remember if I had seen her carrying one.

He led her back to the board room, which fortunately did not require them to pass the alcove where I was concealing myself behind an urn. It required a good deal of luck not to be discovered, but I had it that afternoon. I hardly had a chance to wonder if I could move closer to them when they reappeared in the hall.

"I must have left it elsewhere. It has been a distracting day," she said sadly. All the blood and carnage she had witnessed must have weighed in on her, because the flinty Miss Tarbell slumped into a straight-backed hallway chair. She seemed to study the bloodstain on her foot before looking up at him again. "As it happens, I know a great deal about bombs, Monsieur Pontell," she said. "This one was made with gunpowder."

"I doubt that, madame. Will there be nothing else?"

"Why do you doubt that it was made with gunpowder?"

"It was too powerful."

"But it was carried about the streets without exploding. Trust me, monsieur, it was made with carbon and sulfur, the ingredients of gunpowder."

"Gunpowder also contains potassium nitrate," he said with some impatience.

"I am sure that is not so," the woman insisted. "Carbon and sulfur are all that is required for gunpowder. I studied chemistry in America, which means I know."

"Madame, I studied chemistry at the Sorbonne. I can assure you, potassium nitrate is a component of gunpowder. There is no doubt."

Miss Tarbell stood up. "I don't believe it," she said, determined to have the last word. She took leave of him with a brisk and haughty air. Pontell must have been irritated: his exhale was like the snort of an animal and he walked stiff-legged back to his office.

I imagined Miss Tarbell's long strides down the corridor and the hem of her skirt dusting the stair carpet as she raced to Holmes's makeshift office. From the top of the stairs when I was coming down, I heard her rattling the glass panel of its door with her quick insistent raps. Her ladylike demeanour had been quite cast aside.

By the time I reached them, I was out of breath. I did not bother to knock, nor did they pay any attention when I came in. "Pontell knows about the makings of a bomb, Mr. Holmes," she announced. "I tricked him into admitting it."

"Have you been conducting inquiries, madame?"

"I talked to a few people. They had little to say, except for the secretary. I don't doubt you would have found it out yourself, but Pontell was less guarded with me. He was determined to put me in my place, and he did so with his knowledge of chemistry. This is important news, Mr. Holmes."

"Yes, Miss Tarbell, it is. But I cannot have you here when I interview him. I have to try to trick him into revealing himself to me, if such a thing is possible now that you've interfered and put him on his guard. I dare say he knows he made a mistake."

The journalist thought better of replying as she still wanted Holmes to finish her interview. "Must I leave the building?"

"No," he said as a concession to her help. "Just make sure he does not see you." With that she disappeared, we knew not where.

When he answered Holmes's summons, Pontell was calmer than Picot had been, but a good deal more sad. "I believe I saw the murderer, Mr. Holmes," he said.

"How is that?"

"I came in a little before eight so that I could go over the preparations for the morning's meeting. Just as I was going up the back stairs, a man who was too bundled up for this time of year came down."

"Why did you not ask who he was?"

"Frankly, I assumed he had business here. Our directors sometimes employ men who—let's say they do not always use gentlemen to carry out their commissions. I did not tell you about him in front of the directors for this very reason. Since this suspicious man was leaving, rather than coming into the building, I thought it was best to let him go and ask no questions."

"What did you do after Monsieur Daziell asked you to call the concierge?" Holmes asked him.

"Don't you care about this man?"

"What more can you tell me?"

"Nothing, but I think he should be found."

"I will leave that to the police. Tell me what you did after Monsieur Daziell asked you to get Picot."

"Why, I fetched him, of course."

"Both the director and the concierge report there was a delay."

"Perhaps the time seemed to drag because they were worried."

"But Picot could not have been worried. He knew nothing about the suspicious package until the porter appeared from upstairs and you finally gave him the message. Until then, you had been trying to get him out of the building."

"That is not my recollection. Obviously, Picot is under a strain."

"And you are not?"

"Of course, but Picot had more contact with the bomb." He sighed. "And he saw Ernst carry off the bomb, poor man."

"Who saw you arrive this morning?"

"The night watchman. As I came in a little before eight, I went to the back entrance."

"Were you carrying anything?"

Pontell smiled. "I brought nothing this morning. My hands were empty." He spread his fingers wide before him. "Not even a briefcase."

A party of police now arrived to interview people in the building, so Holmes told Pontell to return to his desk, advising him that no one was being allowed to leave.

The police took statements from everyone who had been in the building from the hour the doors opened until the minute the suspicious package was removed from the premises. By three in the afternoon, Holmes had a report of their findings. The night watchman had been interviewed at his home and confirmed that he had seen Pontell arrive. Ernst had been confirmed as a victim of the explosion. That morning, Ernst had entered the building with one of his colleagues at fifteen minutes after eight, according to those who had seen him. He spoke of his fiancée, whom he planned to marry at Christmas time. He was described by his colleagues as a frugal young man of no political beliefs.

"Hardly the description of an anarchist," said Holmes when he finished reading the report the police provided, "and they are too passionate to attempt to disguise themselves."

A clerk brought in some cakes and tea, and Miss Tarbell, who had rejoined us, set aside her notebook and pen to pour it. Holmes continued speaking, addressing his remarks to me, but of course he was aware that the American journalist was at our side.

Holmes could go without food or drink when he was working on a case, but as a concession to me and Miss Tarbell he partook of our little tea. Past experience of my friend taught me to eat at my own slow pace if food was to do me any good, but Miss Tarbell apparently felt compelled to gulp her tea and swallow her cake as if she would never be allowed another morsel. When the tray was cleared, she laid her hand on her stomach as if in dazed amazement.

Holmes resumed his synopsis of the police report. "Pontell has long-standing ties to the firm. His father, who only recently died, was a physician who attended Darmaux's workers in the northeast. Pontell applied here for a position last May and was quickly hired." Holmes closed the folder with an air of satisfaction. "He said nothing of his studies of chemistry. Let us go see this gentleman again."

The secretary was reviewing some reports when Holmes appeared, leading in a group that included Miss Tarbell, myself and a policeman. Holmes demanded to see his key ring. Pontell looked at the policeman in mute, useless appeal and then handed it over. It held five keys, which Pontell identified as belonging to the front door of his lodgings, his own room, and his employer's inner and outer offices. When he came to the fifth and smallest key, he paused. "Ah, that is to my parents' home. I carry it for sentimental reasons."

Holmes summoned Picot, but he was absent, having gone directly home from the morgue; however, an assistant to the concierge verified that the key looked like it might fit one of the porters' rooms. With that, Holmes led us on a pilgrimage to every door on the floor. We might have proceeded to every keyhole in the building, but the lock of a utility closet gave way to Pontell's fifth key. Inside the closet, instead of cleaning supplies, we found chemicals and wire that were easily identified as the makings of a bomb.

"Monsieur Pontell, you are discovered!" Holmes cried. "Officer, arrest this man." The assassin's resistance was instinctive and pointless.

He admitted nothing as he was led away, but his speeches, of course, came later, and we learned that Pontell nursed a grievance against the company that had used his father ill and left his family destitute. He railed against a society that victimized its weakest citizens . . . but as a murderer, these were things Pontell had done himself, and he met his end on the guillotine under his true name, Huret.

After Sherlock Holmes and I returned to London, neither of us gave much thought to the American journalist Ida Tarbell, until one day when Sam McClure, her editor, visited Baker Street to call on us. McClure, who was as rambunctious as any of the street-wise lads in the Baker Street Irregulars, came to us charged with his vision of his new magazine, which would be filled with reports of the wonders being unleashed in the world—X-rays, anti-toxins to diphtheria, and newly discovered portraits of Napoleon. Of course, Holmes had already heard of these things. Then McClure gave Holmes a look at the galleys of Miss Tarbell's story. It was filled with Holmes's brilliance. She glossed over his rudeness in the remarks he had made about herself. For that matter, she minimized her own part in the solution to the affair. I am sure Holmes would have unmasked Pontell/Huret, but the criminal was trapped before he could escape because Miss Tarbell's action was so quick.

Holmes set Miss Tarbell's work aside. "I have but one Boswell," he told the American. "That is Watson."

"But Miss Tarbell has written an excellent account," McClure protested. "You will be one of the most famous men in America, even if you live all your days in London."

"Nonetheless," Holmes said, "Watson has a drawer of manuscripts, and he, and he alone, will be writing more. I urge you to publish one of his stories rather than Miss Tarbell's. If you do, I'm sure he'll sell them to you exclusively in America."

"But what shall I tell Miss Tarbell?"

"Tell her I am loyal to my friends. She won't be angry at you if you pay what you owe her. Not just for this one. The other stories, too. You still owe her for them, do you not?" McClure shifted in his seat uncomfortably. "And why not give Miss Tarbell a job in America? Paris is no place for a woman alone."

So it was that my stories, published in *McClure's,* introduced Sherlock Holmes to America and made him almost a cult. Holmes's purpose in having Ida Tarbell's story of the Boulevard Assassin dropped was to help me, of course, and make my budding literary career more lucrative. Whether or not she ever knew it, Holmes tried to make it up to her by serving as her collection agent with McClure, who did indeed give her a job. She became one of the most famous journalists in America, writing a riveting biography of President Abraham Lincoln by interviewing everyone she could find who knew him as a boy. Then she turned her skills against John D. Rockefeller.

I ran into Miss Tarbell years later in New York. I walked into her office one afternoon at *McClure's,* where she was reading the proof of one of her articles. Her hair had strands of grey in it by then, but she was as thin as ever and clearly in command. She was peering at some galleys through little eyeglasses held at the end of a chain pinned to her blouse, and was telling her assistant what changes should be made to her copy. Although I interrupted her, she looked at me with a sweet warm smile, until she realized who I was. Her eyes narrowed.

"Dr. Watson, after all these years!" she exclaimed. "You are responsible for a great change in my life. Since the day I met you and Mr. Holmes, I have never allowed myself to use black ink on the worn spots on my dress." Nor did she have to wear worn and faded clothes after Holmes got her a good job, but I felt it prudent not to point that out.

"You know, Dr. Watson," she said, as if correcting a schoolboy. "Holmes should have let *my* story run."

In one of his memoirs, Watson mentions his notes of the "account of the Addleton tragedy and the singular contents of the ancient British barrow," which he admits would fulfill the requirements of a narrative. However, he declined to furnish it in favour of "The Adventure of the Golden Pince-Nez." In light of the grim implications of the ensuing chronicle, it is fair to say that Watson chose not to publish it for reasons more cogent than some supposed paucity of sensational elements, which it certainly contains in abundance.

The Case of the
Ancient British Barrow

BY TERRY McGARRY

The winter of early 1894 eased, for a brief spate of days, into a melancholy overture of the warmer weather to come. It was during this saturated lull that I found myself in a four-wheeler bearing east down Oxford Street towards Bloomsbury. The driver had been told to hurry, and the clatter of wheels over cobblestones sent corresponding jolts through the seats and the spine. I hoped to have all my teeth in my head when we arrived at our destination.

"Richard Addleton," said Sherlock Holmes, regarding with a frown the hastily scrawled note he held. It jounced in his hand, unreadable. "Low man on the totem pole, as it were, in the anthropology division of the British Museum."

"What does he say he wants?"

"He is faced with a dilemma of great weight, which he hopes I may help him solve, and he fears to walk the streets, or would never have presumed to summon me. I feel something very dark and very old looming over us, Watson, though for the life of me I can't tell you why." He lapsed into silence, his grey eyes focused inward rather than on the drear grey day outside.

The carriage slowed to pass with some care a group of workmen. A damp clay smell rose from the pit they had dug, ancient London exhaling into the modern. The scent of deep earth hung heavily on the wet air. Below the wheels of the growler, I reflected, was all the history of our great teeming city, laid down layer by layer, the new over the old.

I had no idea, then, to what astonishing and disturbing degree Holmes's dire presentiments and my own musings would twine together. I set it down here in hopes of easing my own mind on the matters that would so soon confront us—that will haunt me, I fear, forever. Whether or not so soiled a tale can be published remains to be seen.

We arrived at the Addleton house, a sedate old home tucked in among boarding-houses just off Russell Square, to find a young constable outside the premises speaking with a distrait elderly manservant, and a sergeant just venturing inside, his night-stick in his hand.

"Murders, sir," the young constable reported after Holmes had introduced himself. "Or so this fellow says—"

"Dead, both dead!" The manservant wrung his hands. "I come in as I do every morning at ten—I live with my family, you see, on Goodge Street—and there they was! And their brother gone for over a week with nary a word. What'll I do now? Who'll give me my orders like?"

"This is the home of Mr. Richard Addleton, is it not?" Holmes prompted. His soothing tone, wielded so effectively to calm witnesses into providing a clearer account, worked its magic. The manservant turned to him.

"Mr. Richard indeed, sir, who works round the corner there,

and his brother William the government clerk. Both dead. They'd had an awful row. But who could have done such a thing?"

"And this other brother you mentioned?" Holmes asked.

The servant's eyes went wide. "Oh, sir, it was never him. Raised them like his own sons, he did, him being so much older and all; they'd lived all their lives here in this house, parents died when the two youngest were schoolboys. Went up north on some business or other, Mr. James did—to Manchester, I think he said. They started in fighting right away. Mr. James was always the peacemaker, and it was terrible with him gone, just terrible. The housekeeper took her holiday early just to be away from it. And now this!"

Holmes thanked him, and with the constable's permission we followed his sergeant's path up the stone steps. The interior had the stale mustiness of an antiques shop, less from a housekeeper's absence than from the presence of many antiquated furnishings and tapestries, and mounds of carpet leaving not a floorboard bare.

"They're in here," the sergeant said, recognizing Holmes and gesturing to the dining room. "I've checked the upstairs; there's no one else about."

The brothers, dark men of small stature and middle years, were huddled together on a Regency settee, bodies twisted in the paroxysms of death. Their breakfast sat untouched on the table, a fragile crystal vase upright in the center. One chair was pushed back, far enough to ruck up the heavy Afghan rug behind it, and the other had toppled and lay on its back. Across another rug, an expensive Oriental in the center of the floor, a dark stain had spread. The eye naturally took it to be blood, at first, but there were no visible wounds on either man, and a closer inspection showed the liquid to be black coffee, spilled from an upset pot on the dining table. Holmes sniffed at the pot, then at each empty coffee cup in turn. Abruptly he turned away and cast his eye over the rest of the cluttered room.

"Something, Mr. Holmes?" the sergeant inquired.

"Hydrocyanic—also known as prussic—acid," Holmes said.

He lingered at what seemed an unremarkable lithograph hung over the mantel, then struck out to investigate the other rooms on the floor, calling behind him, "Administered in the coffee. It is a favoured method, as the smell of almonds in such a beverage would not inspire suspicion."

The sergeant moved to the window to call something down to his constable. From the doorway, Holmes caught my eye, and I followed him out to a small yard in the back.

I did not bother to inquire after his train of thought as the police-sergeant had. He was deep into the puzzle—perhaps unable, as yet, to articulate precisely how the elements were connecting in his mind—and there would be no diverting or distracting him until he had found what he sought.

With a pipe-cleaning tool drawn from an inner coat pocket, he made short work of unlocking the basement's outer door.

"Be ready," he admonished me as the door swung open.

Perhaps he believed the murderer was in subterranean hiding. I was prepared to be rushed the moment the light spilled in and announced our presence. Neither of us, however, expected to come upon what we did: a gleaming, well-appointed, unoccupied private museum.

Row upon row of glass cases shone softly in the light of a single gas-jet. Each was of professional quality, not the makeshift work one would expect of an amateur collector. Within the nearest lay crumbling notebooks, their anonymous covers closed. The farther vitrines displayed potsherds, beads, stone tools, and human bones. Most unsettling, however, were the nearest and longest cases, tightly sealed against the air. Their contents seemed at first to be three sprawling mud or clay lumps, but something in their shape suggested a human aspect, despite the extreme decay they had undergone. The substance of which they consisted did not appear ever to have been flesh—more like tree bark steeped too long in foul water—and there were no bones or cartilage. Yet I was certain these monstrous artifacts had once been human.

It was an extraordinary exhibit, a private collection of some magnitude, though whether from one archaeological excavation or several, I could not tell.

"There are no tags or legends of any kind," I said to Holmes in consternation. "Do you suppose this Richard Addleton stole these items from his work place?"

Holmes shook his head in a distracted way; he had perused the volumes in a low shelf, found them unilluminating, and begun to check the back and sides. "Hah!" he said at last. From under the clawfooted shelf he came up with a sheet of foolscap, balled up and cast aside, as if in anger, to roll out of view and be forgotten.

"A letter from the British Museum to Richard Addleton," he announced. "It concerns a property near Trowbridge, and says that all funding has been withdrawn, no reason given."

Holmes smoothed the paper, folded it in quarters, and slid it into an inner pocket. We slipped out of the strange private exhibit and back into the world of the present with a sense of surfacing. "I'm afraid we have a train to catch," Holmes said to the sergeant.

"But I've just sent for the inspector!" the man replied, vexed. "He'll want to talk to you!"

"I will of course be available to the inspector as soon as I return," Holmes said, whistling for a hansom.

The train to which Holmes referred was the next one bound for Wiltshire. As soon as we were settled in seats of relative privacy, I exclaimed, "What extraordinary events! I am well aware that you know, or suspect, far more than you are letting on, Holmes, but I cannot restrain myself from asking: Who killed the Addleton brothers, and how on earth do you expect to find some unnamed property near Trowbridge?"

Holmes waved a hand perfunctorily. "There was a map of Wiltshire over the mantelpiece," he said. "For a locality so irrelevant to the personal history of lifelong Londoners to occupy so central a position in the household imbued it with import beyond the decorative. The letter merely confirmed it. Our destination was pinpointed on the map, although I have only the slightest inkling of what we may find there."

"And the letter itself?" I asked. "Perhaps they quarrelled over the withholding of funds for some pet project."

Holmes shook his head. "I estimate from the accumulation of dust that this sheet had been under the shelf for some months, and the quarrels, according to the house servant, began only after the missing brother took his leave. You are right on two counts, however: there was a pet project, as clearly evidenced by the basement display—and it was that project, or something germane to it, that caused them to fall out." He allowed himself a nearly inaudible sigh. "Pity that the rift was so wide, and the project so controversial, as to cause one brother to kill another and then take his own life."

Horrified, I said, "Surely it must have been the older brother, James, no matter what a loyal servant might have said."

"Alas, the evidence is all there, and whichever inspector turns up will have little trouble seeing it. The housekeeper was on holiday and the brothers were left to fend for themselves. The resulting meal was atrocious: eggs full of shell fragments, burnt rashers, toast the consistency of charcoal. A nervous, frightened man, with little kitchen experience and half out of his wits with fear of the deed he was about to do, would cook such a meal—knowing it would never be consumed, merely going through the motions to allay suspicion, and far more concerned with the coffee the housekeeper's absence had allowed him to poison."

"Out of his wits, indeed, to drink of it himself," I said.

"I am sure he intended it. And afterwards he tipped the mugs and drained the pot onto the floor, lest anyone else partake of his fatal brew. A man, therefore, who wished no one ill—whose crime was an act of deepest desperation. Something dire must have hung over his head, to push him to poison his own brother, quarrels notwithstanding. This was not a crime of rage, Watson, but of despair."

"Perhaps he meant the poison for himself, and committed suicide when he realized that his brother had accidentally shared it."

"Why, then, add the prussic acid to the pot and not simply his own mug? No, it was no scene from *Hamlet*. His brother drank first, and when he stood up, knocking the chair back, our murderer ran to catch him before he fell, and staggered with him to the settee, where they died in each other's arms."

"William, then, was the murderer," I said slowly. "Unless Richard summoned us in hopes we would be first upon the scene."

"Richard hoped we would aid him in unravelling their dilemma," said Holmes. "He had no knowledge that his brother William had come up with his own, extreme solution."

The tragedy of it, and the mental picture of their last moments, weighed on my heart for the rest of our journey.

The property in question turned out to be an estate some miles south of Trowbridge, near a small village where we succeeded in hiring a horse and buggy. We were denied access at the main gate by a surly attendant who refused to tell us the owner's name, and when we drove around the perimeter we found ourselves followed and were soon accosted by a gang of groundskeepers who warned us vehemently away.

There was nothing for it but to take lodgings in town. I had no doubt that Holmes would not be dissuaded, and we quickly made plans to return later that night, our circumnavigation of the property having had the advantage of revealing what appeared, from a distance, to be an excavation site. The connection to our strange private collection and the British Museum letter seemed indubitable. We had also noted the location of a concealed point of entry through a long hedge not far from the site.

We spent the remainder of the daylight making discreet inquiries in the village. I feared such activities would give away our clandestine plans, but the locals had a horror of the place, and when Holmes and I reconvened for a light supper we regaled each other with the tales we had collected. Legends of shadowy apparitions on the estate, witchcraft and druidism, dark demons on the loose who would suck the marrow from the bones of anyone foolish enough to venture on the grounds after dark. That such stories existed was no surprise in the vicinity of a site of archaeological interest—located on an estate of mysterious ownership, to which access was denied to all but a few taciturn sentries. Any suspicious nocturnal activities would be likely to warp into tales of ghostly intrigue.

The landlord of the pub in which we secured rooms told us that the groundskeepers lived on the estate, but never ventured out after dark, which would certainly, we thought, facilitate our later entry. More than that he would not say, claiming it was bad luck to discuss the matter; but his wife confided, somewhat later, that there was known to be an ancient tomb on the site, an evil, haunted place from which terrible cries had once issued, now silenced, only the ghosts remaining. She suspected that we planned to return, and although she begged us to change our minds, she offered the use of a lantern should we persist in our mad course.

We set off on foot after full dark, the lantern unlit. When we had cleared the village, Holmes produced his small pocket lantern to light our way unobtrusively down the long curve of the road, through the hedge at last, and across the springy vegetation of a bog which showed no signs of ever having been cut for fuel. The legends of the unnamed estate had cost the locals many a cold night, it seemed.

A new-cut entrance to the mound was shored up by timbers. The work had been abandoned some months ago, judging from the weathering of the wood, which corresponded to Holmes's estimate of the age of the Museum letter. The interior confronting us was a dark, endless throat. I was not prone to conjuring imaginary demons, but in my memory still resided the inexplicably human-looking shapes in their sealed vitrines, and I rather wished I had brought my pistol.

Holmes lit the lantern, and we entered a long stone passageway with a downward incline. There was an unmistakable scuttling sound from somewhere deep within the tomb. Holmes suddenly halted, but not in response to the sound: rather, he had spied something incongruous about a thinner section of stone wall.

"It's been moved several times, once recently," said he, examining the arc of smoothed earthen floor. "Come—let's find out what's behind it."

With Holmes's prodigious strength, the two of us managed to slide the rock in its carven path. Within was a side passageway. The lumber that maintained the structural integrity of the passage was decades older than that at the entryway, afflicted with rot and sagging at many points. I cautioned against an infirm ceiling, but Holmes forged onward, undeterred by physical danger.

We were stopped at last by what appeared to have been a cave-in. "They were trying to continue digging," Holmes said. "See here, and there, where tunnels were started and abandoned. The bog was too soft to hold open, but they continued to try, it seems—and there, where the soil tumbled down—a more recent hand was at work there, and there . . ." He did not finish, but instead knelt down and set himself to continuing the half-finished, small-scale excavation.

An hour later, something that had once been human emerged from the damp peat. Then another. And a third.

They were the size and shape of men—larger precursors of what we had seen in the Addleton exhibit. But only the one-time flesh remained; the bones were entirely gone.

"I cannot countenance it," I said. "How in the world were the bones removed?"

"In fact, Watson, it is quite simple," Holmes said, "though chemically extraordinary. These bodies were preserved from oxygenation by the medium of the bog. Fleshly elements were replaced by the earthen elements iron and sulfur, while the bones dissolved in the acidic water. Quite the opposite of the conventional process of decay. It is as I suspected when I saw the contents of those vitrines. These bodies will jellify rapidly now that they have been exposed to the air. But some chemical solution might be found to retard such decay, and I suspect that the Addletons, or their colleagues, used such a solution on the creatures we saw in the exhibit."

"Which must have come from here," I supplied.

"I have no doubt of it."

"How long, then, have these bodies been buried?"

"That, Watson, is the question. This tunnel is not Neolithic, though the barrow itself most certainly is. This tunnel was dug sometime in the last quarter-century. So who, then, are these men?" He paused, eyes narrowed, and then pounced on a metallic glint I had not noticed—a small tin box recently shoved into the peat.

"Open the box, Watson," Holmes whispered, "and make as much noise about it as you can." As I followed his directions, the rusty hinges emitting a gratifying shriek, Holmes melted into the shadows of the main passageway.

Before I could study the documents, there came a cry and a scuffle from deep within the barrow. I stuffed the papers into my vest, snatched up the lantern, and ran down into the heart of the tomb.

Holmes was holding a white-haired man in an iron grip. The man was gibbering in unintelligible gasps, but at last he managed to say, "Let me go, please. I can not run now that your friend has blocked the way."

Holmes complied, and we stood there for a moment staring at each other, the only sound our laboured breathing.

At length Holmes said, "James Addleton, I presume?"

The man nodded. The resemblance to the two poor souls in Bloomsbury was unmistakable.

Holmes questioned him, but the man would say nothing, certain we were Government men sent to assassinate him. Only when Holmes convinced him of our identities did he relax somewhat. "My little brother Richard," he said, "has a great respect for your work."

"The papers in the box," Holmes began again—no doubt he had heard me riffling through them and deduced the contents. "They pertain to this excavation?"

"Scandal!" Addleton burst out. A tic picked up a wild rhythm in his cheek. "Scandal that could rock the very foundations of government. A great man ruined. My heart breaks to think of it!" The man was filthy from what must have been a week here underground. What he lived on I will never know; but he had clearly confronted some demons of his own, and they were getting the better of him.

"Perhaps you might start from the beginning," said Holmes, and we sat down among the scattered bones and artifacts and listened to James Addleton's terrible but disjointed tale.

"I'm a geologic surveyor and contractor, you see," he said. "Such careers run in the family, a love of the past, a respect for preserving detail. My brother William spent his life cataloguing the minutiae of political events: keeping the minutes, writing the reports and memoranda. Richard shared his love of details, but turned his talents to scientific and scholarly pursuits, though he never could advance past junior curator—too much backstabbing in the division. How ironic, how sad, that our careers should intersect upon such a terrible point! And that we cannot agree on how next to proceed. Oh, if I'd only known how it all would come together, the terrible revenge exacted upon my family . . ."

He took hold of himself with some effort. Holmes and I exchanged a glance; this was not the time to break the news of his brothers' tragic deaths.

"I didn't know, you see, that there was anyone *here*. No one knew who owned the place. All you could get out of the villagers were stories to frighten children, or so I thought—or so they were then, before I—oh, God forgive me. In 1864, I was ordered to open this mound up, for an archaeological excavation, they said. It was a Government commission, they didn't want to use a local man, I didn't know why and didn't ask, I needed the work. And then, a month later, they had me back to cave the entrance in again. I couldn't figure it, but I did what I was told. I did my job quickly, efficiently, and I left. I never heard the screams . . ."

"There were men down here, then? An excavation crew not notified to leave in time?"

"No." The elder Addleton shook his head miserably. For a moment his eyes went wild, and he clawed at his cheek as if to yank the persistent facial spasm out; then his terror subsided, and he cast

Holmes a piteous stare as he said, "They were slaves, black-skinned men from Africa, kept here on Gladstone's estate for years, working for him, tilling his land, maybe cutting his bog, I don't know. But someone in the Government found out about it, and was going to expose his terrible hypocrisy, and so he had to cover it up. Gladstone! Gladstone, who did so much to end such tyranny—" He began to wail and tear at his hair, and it took all of Holmes's persuasive soothing to calm him back into something resembling a coherent narrative. "The order came down to open this mound up—and then cave it in again, *with the men inside.* I didn't put them in! I didn't know, I heard nothing, I did what I was told!"

"Who found those papers?" Holmes asked quietly.

"William," said Addleton, wiping tears from his eyes with a soil-blacked cuff. "A stickler for details, for order. He was cleaning out old files in the Government records, and he found those letters, memoranda. The thought of what it would do to Gladstone—an old man, his sight failing, what use in bringing him down now? Then we realized what it meant to Richard's work. I had told him about the barrow, you see, and he'd gotten funding for an excavation, it was a coup for him, an unplumbed Wiltshire barrow when the archaeologists thought they'd all been discovered long since. He let ambition cloud his judgement, for he was bitter about his career, and he lied to the Museum about the location of the barrow. He didn't tell them that he'd never established who owned the grounds. Just came in here with his men and started digging. He preserved and catalogued everything he found, but then Gladstone must have found out. The Museum revoked its funding. Richard was furious. He moved his exhibits to our cellar, secretly, put them under lock and key and told the Museum they'd been disposed of as requested. But William couldn't bear the thought of any evidence that might hurt Gladstone. No matter what terrible things he had done—had ordered—he was still a good man, Gladstone, and William is nothing if not loyal. He wanted the exhibit and the papers destroyed. Richard was horrified. 'Suppress it, yes; destroy it, never!' he cried. 'History is far too precious a thing.' We could not agree on what to

do, any of us—and I feared that William would do something terrible, so I took the papers away, I brought them here, I put them in
with the grave of the men whose death they ordered. Ever since
William found them, ever since I realized what I did . . . I can't sleep
for hearing the screams, they never stop . . ."

He covered his ears and curled around himself, rocking back
and forth, weeping softly.

I was reeling from his tale, but Holmes seemed more focused
on the man than on the information. "They tried to tunnel out," he
said. "They died in a cave-in because they hadn't the means of
shoring the sides up adequately. The cave-in killed them, Addleton,
not you. You did not know those men were here."

His words were mesmeric, utterly convincing, perhaps because he was wholly convinced of their truth. Addleton looked up
slowly. "But the screams," he said. "Don't you hear them? Can't you
see the shadows lurking? Fifty men, dead. Fifty poor imprisoned
men, dead in their final prison under the ground, so that Gladstone
might save his reputation . . ."

"Then Gladstone was the killer," Holmes said. "You were
merely an unwitting tool. Unwitting, Addleton." He rose slowly
and held out his hand. "Come," he said. "We'll take you back to
London."

Addleton followed, docile now, his madness subsiding somewhat under Holmes's calming influence. What would become of
him, I didn't like to think, as we climbed slowly up the sloping passageway and breathed again the clear night-time air. The news of his
brothers' deaths would surely send him into the chasm of insanity
whose edge he already skirted.

But it was not to be. As we came closer to the entrance we saw
other lights bobbing outside. We had been followed after all.

Addleton deserted us with a cry, certain these were the Government men he feared, and fled back into the passageway—
whether into the side tunnel or the tomb we could not tell, for this
time his fears were justified. The men awaiting us were not the
groundskeepers; they did not identify themselves. They escorted us

back to the village, silently, unswayed by Holmes's attempts to ca-jole information from them, stern and unyielding in their task. One of them stayed with us through the late-night carriage ride back to Trowbridge and saw us onto the last train for London. Over-whelmed by all that we had discovered, still I found myself relieved that we had paid for our rooms in advance, for we never saw the publican or his wife again.

"We must go back at once," I said as the train pulled out of the station. There were no other passengers at this hour. "We cannot leave Addleton like that."

"For the moment I'm afraid we have no choice. The property is too well guarded, ghost stories notwithstanding, and until we find out who employed those men we can exert no pressure upon them. Addleton has hid well for many days now. We can only hope they got no glimpse of him before he ran. Now, show me the papers."

I pulled them out of my vest with some reluctance. Gladstone ruined . . . It seemed too much to bear, and yet surely the facts must come to light. We could not suppress such a thing.

"It's all here," I said, when we had traded the papers back and forth to read them all with care. Ship manifests, schedules, deeds and titles and work orders signed by Gladstone. In 1852, a slave ship had been diverted on its route to Cuba and delivered fifty captive men onto English soil, where they stayed for over a decade, working Gladstone's land in secret—and were then ordered buried alive when it seemed the secret would get out. "It will be Gladstone's downfall. I must admit that I share Addleton's discomfiture at bring-ing ignominy down on a man at the end of a lauded tenure."

"Gladstone has brought himself down," Holmes said, still peer-ing closely at the papers, as if further hypocrisy and death and mad-ness might be woven into their very fibres. Then he looked up at me, and a slow, terrible smile spread across his sallow face. "But not because of this. The claim of failing eyesight is an excuse for him to step down, after his latest defeat in the House of Lords—an ad-mirable effort on behalf of the downtrodden, as was ever his wont.

He has never abandoned his principles, Watson. What we have here is scandal indeed, but of a far more insidious nature."

"I cannot imagine what you mean," I said, weariness edging into irritability. I wanted no more ghastly revelations this night.

"These papers are forgeries," said Sherlock Holmes. "The hand of Burkum Stacy, if I read it correctly, with later additions by Pearce and Kirkland, both dead now. Whatever horrors were done on that estate, Gladstone had no part of them. They were a heinous construct to discredit an honourable man. It would have been too easy, I suppose, to forge documents showing his ownership of a slave-trading ship; he could have disproved such a fiction easily, and none of it would have outraged the public, which is well aware that English ships were engaged in transporting slaves to Cuba, and thence to Virginia, until the American civil conflict put an end to the market. As a nation, we could be proud of having abolished such enslavement on our own land, and later in our colonies, while still profiting from its continuance elsewhere."

I began to see what he meant, a larger vision of the forces at work. "But for a man like Gladstone to employ such workers on his own land at home . . ."

"It would be more than the public would stand for. Oh, fools, to make such an accusation a reality! Never seeing that what they had done was so much worse than what he would have stood accused of. I will get to the bottom of this, Watson, mark my words. The careers and reputations of Richard and William Addleton were so soiled, so jeopardized, by this that they died tragically, and all to preserve both their precious History and the reputation of an innocent prime minister on the eve of his retirement. Poor, mad James Addleton was the shovel that buried fifty men, but I will find the hands that wielded that shovel and see prison manacles around their wrists."

I felt a deep unease at this proclamation, and it only deepened after our return to Baker Street. The forged papers were put safely away and not a word said to the inquiring inspector, as the Addleton tragedy was solved in every matter but motive, and that, Holmes believed, was well outside Scotland Yard's bailiwick. Then Holmes went off in search of the retired forger Burkum Stacy, and sent me to the Diogenes Club to have a preliminary word with his brother Mycroft, who should know more than any man alive about such an insidious plot—or at the very least be able to find out.

The elder Holmes merely shook his head. "You must stop him, Watson," he said. "You have some influence with him, a friendship, that I lack. Tell him that this is one case that must be left buried where he found it, no matter what tragedies it may have engendered. What's done is done, and no more harm can come of it. You must convince him, as his friend, for the best result he will achieve is frustration and the worst I prefer not to contemplate."

It was as dire a warning as I ever hope to hear from those lips. I returned to Baker Street immediately, turning over in my mind the various means I might use to put Holmes off this case, only to find him in a hellish rage, our lodgings a shambles, and Mrs. Hudson terrified and in tears.

"They just bullied their way in!" she cried. "Threw me out of my own house and then turned it all topsy-turvy! I've never been so frightened in my life!"

I looked at Holmes, pacing in helpless anger through the loose papers and debris. His obsessively indexed commonplace books, his scrapbooks and collected biographies and agony columns, seemed undamaged but lay strewn about, their pages fluttering in the breeze of his long stride.

"The forged documents are gone," he said, as I knew he would. "Taken by force, and with further vandalism that can only be meant as punitive. Do they think this will daunt me?"

I calmed Mrs. Hudson as best I could and persuaded her to return downstairs and fix a cup of tea, hoping the panacea of a routine task would soothe her, and keep her away long enough for me to convey Mycroft Holmes's warning.

I had hoped that Holmes would heed his brother's unimpeachably expert advice in this matter. To my dismay, the caveat, which I had felt strongly worded, had no effect but to tighten his jaw and sharpen the resolve in his eyes.

"What of the forger, then?" I asked wearily, thinking that his hopes of a resolution might have been fanned from that quarter.

"Gone," he said, and knelt to begin the task of reassembling his books and papers. "Packed up and left for the Continent early this morning. If I had started my investigation last night, I might have caught him. But it is no matter now. I will not be so tardy again."

"The other forgers, you mentioned, are both dead?" I said, as a reminder, one more small attempt to dissuade him.

"Syphilis and hanging, respectively." He shrugged, his back to me. "I've set the Irregulars to watching the Addleton house," he said. "We'll find out who comes and goes, we'll track them down, unravel the web of connections."

"It goes very high, Holmes," I said quietly. "Higher than you or I can aspire, I fear."

He made no answer, and I left him to his organizing and his thoughts, taking a cup of tea with Mrs. Hudson and assuring her that she could sleep the night safely before going to my own bed in hopes that I had not told her a lie.

It seemed only moments later that I was pulled up through layers of nightmare to find myself buried not in smothering peat but in my own woollen blankets. A street arab was shaking me awake, saying urgently, "Mr. Holmes sent me to fetch you—the Addleton place is burning!"

It was indeed in flames, and its basement exhibit with it. I disembarked from my cab and walked slowly over to stand next to Holmes. His face was unreadable, the conflagration starkly illuminating its harsh angularity. Dawn was a nacreous glow over the house, dimmed by the grasping flames and the firefighters they silhouetted.

"The water will put an end to what evidence the fire doesn't destroy," said Holmes in a flat voice. He turned to me at last. "Have you seen the morning edition? It's just out."

I shook my head, not bothering to remind him that I was not

a nocturnal creature such as he, nor to ask him what efforts had kept him out roaming through the dark hours.

He handed me the folded newspaper and pointed to the article.

The barrow in Wiltshire had been destroyed. The item referred only obliquely to reports of a deafening explosion on an unnamed estate south of Trowbridge, and to presumed connections with an unidentified lunatic found wandering. The man was questioned, then given over to the care of a noted asylum.

"He'll spend the rest of his life in there," said Holmes.

"Perhaps." I held out some hope that we might contrive for his release upon the grounds that he was grief-stricken over his brothers' deaths, but said nothing, preferring to withhold encouragement now that the last blow had been dealt. James Addleton had no home to return to now, in any event.

"The bodies would have disintegrated upon being exhumed," he added. *"Corpora delicti* forever unmet. Perhaps that was the intent all along. A master stroke, if so." There was no tone of admiration in his voice.

"There is much buried under the decades, Watson, much we do not know, perhaps much tragedy still to come to light. We enslave each other to this day, the brotherhood of mankind enslaving itself. Do I exploit you, as friend, as chronicler? Do you exploit me as your subject? All-powerful Great Britain enslaves her neighbors, and her colonies, and even her own people under the yoke of poverty and the factory—what Gladstone spent a lifetime attempting to rectify. These are cold ironies, Watson. They chill me to the bone." He fell silent then, and looked past me into the greying shadows.

I did not think I could be any further amazed, after all that had transpired, but once again, as so often, I was proven wrong. Mycroft Holmes, who so rarely deviated from his customary path, walked slowly towards us, bundled heavily against the rising wind.

"It is no failure, Sherlock," he said, coming to stand by us. "It is an old and a dead thing, and better left so."

At last expression flickered to life in Holmes's face. "Better left so? Better for the Addletons? Tell me, Mycroft, how many times have I safeguarded our national security, how many secrets have I kept on behalf of a Government capable of such abhorrent acts? Fifty men criminally enslaved, then caused to die hideously in a foul bog. Mass murder, and England responsible."

"You do not know who was responsible."

"Don't I? D— is gone these thirteen years, his secrets lost to the grave. But he was in power then, and well threatened by Gladstone, whom he loathed. His part in this is clear as the day now dawning. And his fondest admirer despised Gladstone, despises him still. Together they contrived this, and obscured it beyond even my powers to reveal."

"I will not contradict you," Mycroft said mildly. "But why this, Holmes? You know what happened in South Africa, what was done to our people and to theirs. Can you be sure that even Watson has told you all of what he saw in India? You know precisely what our Empire is and what she is capable of. Why does this one instance gall so? You are not so naive as to think its like has never been seen before."

"Not on home soil," Holmes growled. *"Not on one of my cases."*

Mycroft smiled, having proved some personal point. For a moment he let his brother's words hang in the smoky air, drifting like the bits of charred debris. Then he said, "The murders were done thirty-odd years ago, Sherlock. It's over. Let it be buried, and be glad you were not buried with it."

"Oh, it is buried," Holmes replied bitterly. "Buried forever and most literally, with priceless historic artifacts, with two misguided brothers who should not have had to die for such a thing. Buried legally by an overwhelming absence of evidence. And buried in a madman's mind, where anyone who can see it will give it no credence."

"An apt summation," Mycroft said, offering no solace, for there was none to be had.

"All that remains to be answered is the question of why they never used this weapon of hypocrisy they created." Holmes turned to his brother and waited.

Mycroft's agile brain seemed to be weighing what he knew and what he was willing to divulge. In the end, all he said was, "They concluded that it would misfire."

"Too dangerous a weapon, and so they put it in the ground, where it could never discharge? Then allowed local legends to wreathe its tomb in mist? They underestimated the thoroughness of their own bureaucracy, that fosters clerks like William Addleton. It discharged after all. Into innocent faces."

There was no more to be said, no more to be done. We moved away from the smouldering remains of the Addleton home. The water that extinguished the flames was now running into the sewers with a noisy gurgle. The winter wind had come in with the dawn.

I fear that I am as a man in a tunnel deep underground, speaking to himself of dire matters long past. I suspect I will find that I cannot publish this under the current Government; for this one tale, at least, my publisher's ethics will no doubt flee to parts unknown, as the forger fled to Europe. The very lack of evidence bemoaned herein could cast aspersions on all the other chronicles, cause them all to be read as fabrications with no basis in fact. I would not so damage my friend's well-earned reputation.

In the end, perhaps, I will lock this away, like a diary buried under a mattress. Perhaps my heirs will exhume it, when its contents will do less harm. For now, it exists only to ease my own burden, for I could not leave the story untold. It shames me as an Englishman, as it shames Holmes, and as it must shame all England. I only hope that, having committed the events to these pages, I can bury the memory of them deep in my own mind, and dwell on them no longer.

When the Titanic *went down on its maiden voyage, one of its casualties was Jacques Futrelle (1875–1912), author of the short mystery classic "The Problem of Cell 13," as well as other entertaining mysteries involving Professor Augustus S.F.X. Van Dusen, Ph.D., LL.D., F.R.S., M.D., etc., better known as The Thinking Machine. Futrelle plays an important role in "The Adventure of the Dying Ship."*

The Adventure of the Dying Ship

BY EDWARD D. HOCH

I write of this late in life, because I feel some record must be left of the astounding events of April 1912. I am aware that prior attempts to record my adventures personally have suffered when compared to those of my old and good friend Watson, but following my retirement from active practice as a consulting detective late in 1904 I saw very little of him. There were occasional weekend visits when he was in the area of my little Sussex home overlooking the Channel, but for the most part we had retired to our separate lives. It was not until 1914, at the outbreak of the Great War, that we would come together for a final adventure.

But that was more than two years away when I decided, quite irrationally, to accept an invitation from the president of the White Star Line to be a guest on the maiden voyage of R.M.S. *Titanic* across the Atlantic to New York. He was a man for whom I had performed a slight service some years back, not even worthy of mention in Watson's notes, and he hardly owed me compensation on such a grand scale. There were several reasons why I agreed to it but perhaps the truth was that I had simply grown bored with retirement. Still in my mid-fifties and enjoying good health, I had quickly learned that even at the height of the season the physical demands of bee keeping were slight indeed. The winter months were spent in correspondence with fellow enthusiasts and a review and classification of my past cases. What few needs I had were seen to by an elderly housekeeper.

My initial reaction upon receiving the invitation was to ignore it. I had never been much of a world traveller, except for my years in Tibet and the Middle East, but the offer to revisit America intrigued me for two reasons. It would enable me to visit places like the Great Alkali Plain of Utah and the coal mining region of Pennsylvania, which had figured in some of my investigations. And I could meet with one or two American bee keepers with whom I'd struck up a correspondence. I agreed to the invitation on one condition—that I travel under an assumed name. For the voyage I became simply Mr. Smith, a name I shared with five other passengers and the ship's captain.

Early April had been a time of chilly temperatures and high winds. I was more than a little apprehensive as I departed from London on the first-class boat-train to Southampton, arriving there at 11:30 A.M. on Wednesday the 10th. Happily, my seat companion on the boat-train proved to be a young American writer and journalist named Jacques Futrelle. He was a stocky man with a round, boyish face and dark hair that dipped down over his forehead on the right side. He wore pince-nez glasses and flowing bow tie, with white gloves that seemed formal for the occasion. Because of his name I took him to be French at first, but he quickly corrected my misapprehension. "I am a Georgian, sir, by way of Boston," he told me, "which might explain my strange accent."

"But surely your name—"

"My family is of French Huguenot stock. And you are—?"

"Smith," I told him.

"Ah!" He indicated the attractive woman seated across the aisle from us. "This is my wife, May. She is also a writer."

"A journalist like your husband?" I asked.

She gave me a winning smile. "We both write fiction. My first story appeared in *The Saturday Evening Post* some years back." She added, "The maiden voyage of the *Titanic* might provide an article for your old employer, Jacques."

He laughed. "I'm certain *The Boston American* will have any number of Hearst writers covering the voyage. They hardly need me, though I do owe them a debt of gratitude for publishing my early short stories while I worked there."

"Might I be familiar with your books?" I asked. Retirement to Sussex had left me with a mixed blessing, time to read the sort of popular fiction which I'd always ignored in the past.

It was May Futrelle who answered for him. "His novel *The Diamond Master* was published three years ago. I think that is the best of his romances, though many people prefer his detective stories."

The words stirred my memory. "Of course! Futrelle! You are the author of 'The Problem of Cell 13.' I have read that gem of a story more than once."

Futrelle smiled slightly. "Thank you. It has proven to be quite popular. My newspaper published it over six days and offered prizes for the correct solution."

"Your detective is known as The Thinking Machine."

The smile widened a bit. "Professor Augustus S.F.X. Van Dusen. I have published nearly fifty stories about the character in the past seven years, and have another seven with me that I wrote on our journey. None has equalled the popularity of the first, however."

Fifty stories! That was more than Watson had published about our exploits up to that time, but Futrelle was correct in saying the first of them had been the most popular. "Have you two ever collaborated?" I asked. May Futrelle laughed. "We swore that we never would, but we did try it once, in a way. I wrote a story that seemed to be a fantasy, and Jacques wrote his own story in which The Thinking Machine provided a logical solution to mine."

The talk shifted from his writing to their travels and I found him a most pleasant conversationalist. The time on the boat-train passed quickly and before long we were at the docks in Southampton. We parted then, promising to see each other on the voyage.

I stood on the dock for a moment, staring up at the great ship before me. Then I boarded the *Titanic* and was escorted to my cabin. It was suite B–57 on the starboard side of Bridge Deck B, reached by the impressive Grand Staircase or by a small elevator. Once in the cabin I found a comfortable bed with a brass and enamel head- and foot board. There was a wardrobe room next to the bed and a luxurious sitting area opposite it. An electric space heater provided warmth if needed. The suite's two windows were framed in gleaming brass. In the bath and WC there was a marble-topped sink. For just a moment I wished that my old friend Watson was there to see it.

I had been on board barely a half-hour when the ship cast off, exactly at noon. As the tugs maneuvered it away from the dock and moved downstream into the River Test, I left my stateroom on the bridge deck and went out to the railing, lighting a cigarette as I watched our progress past banks lined with well-wishers. Then we stopped, narrowly avoiding a collision with another ship. It was almost an hour before we were under way again, and the next twenty-four hours were frustrating ones. We steamed downstream to the English Channel and then across to Cherbourg where 274 additional passengers boarded by tender. Then it was a night crossing to Queenstown, Ireland, where we anchored about two miles offshore while more passengers were brought out by tender.

When at last the anchor was raised for the final time Captain Smith posted a notice that there were some 2,227 passengers and crew aboard, the exact number uncertain. This was about two-thirds the maximum capacity of 3,360 passengers and crew.

As I watched us pull out at 1:30 P.M. on Thursday, April 11, I suddenly realized that an attractive red-haired young woman had joined me on deck.

"Is this your first trip across?" she asked.

"Across the Atlantic, yes," I said to discourage any discussion of my past.

"I'm Margo Collier. It's my first, too."

Women seldom have been an attraction to me, but there were exceptions. Looking into the deep, intelligent eyes of Margo Collier I knew she could have been one of them had I not been old enough to have sired her. "A pleasure to meet you," I replied. "I am Mr. Smith."

She blinked, or winked, at me. "Mr. John Smith, no doubt. Are you in first class?"

"I am. And you are an American, judging by the sound of your accent."

"I thought you could tell from my red hair."

I smiled. "Do all Americans have red hair?"

"The ones that are in trouble seem to. Sometimes I think it's my red hair that gets me in trouble."

"What sort of trouble could one so young have gotten into?"

Her expression changed and in an instant she was coldly serious. "There's a man on board who's been following me, Mr. Holmes."

The sound of my own name startled me. "You know me, Miss Collier?"

"You were pointed out by one of the ship's officers. He was telling me about the famous people on board—John Jacob Astor, Benjamin Guggenheim, Sherlock Holmes, and many others."

I laughed. "My life's work has hardly been comparable to theirs. But pray tell me of this man who follows you. We are, after all, on shipboard. Perhaps he only strolls the deck as you do yourself."

She shook her head. "He was following me before I boarded the ship at Cherbourg."

I pondered this news. "Are you certain? One does not suddenly board the maiden voyage of the *Titanic* because he is shadowing a woman who has done so. If what you say is true, he must have known of your plans well in advance."

She grew suddenly nervous. "I can say no more now. Could you meet me in the first-class lounge on A deck? I'll try to be in the writing room tomorrow morning at eleven."

I bowed slightly. "I'll expect to see you then, Miss Collier."

There was a chill in the air on Friday morning, though the weather was calm and clear. Captain Smith reported that the *Titanic* had covered 386 miles since leaving Queenstown harbour. I ate an early breakfast in the first-class dining saloon and after a stroll around the deck spent some time in the ship's gymnasium on the boat deck. The idea of using a rowing machine on this great ocean liner appealed to me, though I'm certain Watson would have groused about it, reminding me of my age. Finally, shortly before eleven, I went down one flight of stairs to the writing room.

Margo Collier was seated alone at one of the tables, sipping a cup of tea. The reading and writing room adjoined the first-class lounge. It was a spacious, inviting area with groups of upholstered chairs and tables placed at comfortable intervals. I smiled as I seated myself opposite her. "Good morning, Miss Collier. Did you have a good night's sleep?"

"As well as could be expected," she murmured, her voice barely carrying across the table. "The man who's been following me is in the lounge right now, standing by that leaded glass window."

I turned casually in my chair and realized that Jacques Futrelle and his wife were seated with an older man in a black suit. Seeing them gave me an excuse to walk into the lounge and get a better look at the man she'd indicated. I paused at their table with a few words of greeting, noting that the man with them was studying the tea leaves in one of the cups.

"Mr. Smith!" May Futrelle greeted me. "You must meet Franklin Baynes, the British spiritualist."

The man eyed me solemnly as he stood up to shake my hand. "Smith? What is your line of work?"

"I am retired from a research position. This voyage is strictly for pleasure. But I see you are at work, sir, attempting to divine the world in a teacup."

"The Futrelles asked for a demonstration."

"I will leave you to it," I said, continuing on my way into the wood-paneled lounge. The man Margo Collier had indicated now stood a few paces from the window. He was almost bald, with a growth of greying beard along his chin, and his left hand was clutched around the knob of a thick walking stick. As I approached he turned on me with blazing eyes.

"Has she sent you to confront me, sir?"

"Miss Collier says you have been following her since Cherbourg. You are frightening the poor woman half to death. Would you care to identify yourself?"

The bearded man drew himself up until he was almost my height. "I am Pierre Glacet. Cherbourg is my home. I am like yourself."

"And why do you follow her?" I asked, not quite understanding his remark.

"Because she runs away from me. Margo Collier is my wife."

I cannot pretend that the news did not astound me. I had noticed the faint indentation on her ring finger, but I assumed it was only the sign of a broken engagement in one so young. Likewise, the manner in which she approached me had seemed quite sincere.

"I find that difficult to believe," I told Glacet.

"Ask her! We have been married for more than a year, though we are living apart at the moment."

"Under what circumstances?"

"That is a personal matter, sir."

"How were you able to obtain a booking on the voyage at the last minute in order to follow her?"

"The ship is not fully booked at these prices."

"Forgive me, sir, if I have done you an injustice." I retreated back to the writing room where Margo Collier was waiting.

"Did you confront him, Mr. Holmes?" she asked immediately.

"I did. The man claims to be your legal husband. Is that true?"

"We are separated. He has no business following me about!"

"I am sorry, Mrs. Glacet. I am, or was, a consulting detective. I have never been a marriage counselor."

"Mr. Holmes—"

"Pardon me, madam. I can no longer help you." I turned and walked away.

For the rest of that day and the next I managed to avoid both Margo Collier and Pierre Glacet. The *Titanic* covered 519 miles on its second day, though it received several warnings of heavy pack ice from other ships. Captain Smith assured us via his posted notices that ice warnings were not uncommon for April crossings.

On Saturday evening I dined with the Futrelles and the spiritualist, Franklin Baynes, in the first-class dining saloon. He was an interesting gentleman, well steeped in occult lore. Futrelle seemed especially taken with him and I could only assume that the author was researching a possible idea for one of his detective stories. It developed that the spiritualist was travelling to America for a series of lectures and demonstrations.

"You are a showman, then," I proposed, as much to bait him as anything else.

"No, no!" he insisted. "Spiritualism is as much a science as Madame Curie's radiology."

May Futrelle spoke. "Mr. Baynes has invited us to his cabin after dinner for a demonstration of some of his devices. Perhaps you could join us, Mr. Smith."

"By all means do so!" Baynes urged.

I agreed with some reluctance and following dessert we took the elevator up three floors to his stateroom on the promenade deck. It was even larger than my cabin, and I wondered if this too might be a reward from the White Star president. The spiritualist went directly to his steamer trunk and opened it. He removed a crystal ball some six inches in diameter, mounted on a wooden base with an electrical cord attached. Quickly unplugging the cabin's electric space heater by the bed, he plugged his device in its place. The crystal ball sprang to life with a bright intense light.

"Look in here, Mr. Smith, but not too long or you will be blinded."

"What am I supposed to see?" I inquired.

"Perhaps those who have gone before you into the great beyond."

I glanced at the brightly glowing filament for an instant and then looked away, its image burnt into my retina. "I see nothing of the past," I told him, "though something of the future might be had in lights like this."

Franklin Baynes unplugged the crystal ball and brought out an oversized deck of cards. I began to suspect he was more magician than spiritualist. "You are not a believer in the hereafter, Mr. Smith, in that other world where our ancestors await us, where it is always spring and the fairies and elves flit across the meadow?"

I smiled slightly. "I have my own vision of the hereafter, Mr. Baynes. It is not the same as yours."

May Futrelle seemed to sense that the visit to his cabin had been a mistake. "We really should be going, Jacques," she told her husband.

The spiritualist shook their hands. "Thank you for dinner. It was most delightful. And you, Mr. Smith. I trust we can discuss our differing views before the ship docks in New York."

"Perhaps," I agreed.

I left the cabin in the company of the Futrelles and walked a few steps to the elevator. "Obviously the man is something of a charlatan," May said, "but Jacques thinks he might get a story idea out of this."

"It's always possible," I agreed.

The elevator arrived and I opened the folding gate for them. He peered at me and asked, "If it's not too personal a question, Mr. Smith, are you a detective?"

"Why do you ask?"

"Our steward told us you were the famous Mr. Sherlock Holmes."

I laughed as I stepped into the elevator with them and closed the gate. "My secret seems to be a secret no longer. You're the second person who's confronted me about my identity."

"We won't tell anyone," May promised, "though Mr. Baynes has heard it, too. Certainly it's an honour to meet you. Jacques was inspired to write his stories after reading Dr. Watson's accounts of your cases."

"Watson glamourizes me, I fear."

"How is the old fellow?" Futrelle asked.

"Fine. He comes to see me on occasion, though it's been some time now since I've had the pleasure of his company." I got off one flight down on the bridge deck. "I'll see you tomorrow," I told them.

Futrelle grinned. "Good night, Mr. Smith."

Sunday, April 14—the longest day of my life—began with divine services held in the first-class dining saloon. I had overslept and when I went for breakfast at 10:30 I found the services in progress. That was how I happened upon Margo Collier again. She spotted me at once, standing in the back of the room, and pushed through the late arrivals to join me. "Hello, Mr. Holmes."

"Hello, Mrs. Glacet."

"Please don't call me that. If you would grant me time I could explain the entire matter to you."

Something in her desperate tone made me regret the harshness of my earlier dismissal. "Very well," I said. "Join me at dinner tonight in the first-class saloon. I will be in the outer reception room at eight o'clock."

"I will be there," she promised, brightening at once.

During the day I continued to hear reports of ice sightings from the other passengers. In the twenty-four hours since noon Saturday we had covered another 546 miles, and the map showed us approaching the Grand Banks off Newfoundland. The temperature had remained in the forties much of the afternoon, but after 5:30 as darkness descended it plunged quite quickly to 33 degrees. Captain Smith altered the ship's course slightly to the south and west, possibly as a precaution to avoid icebergs. Lookouts in the crow's nest would remain on duty all night watching for ice. Looking up at them from the top deck, I decided it must be the loneliest of shipboard tasks, even though there were two men up there.

Exactly at eight o'clock, Margo Collier met me in the reception room on the saloon deck. "My cabin is in second class," she confided. "I feared they might put another woman in with me to occupy the other bunk, but happily I'm alone."

"That is more pleasant," I agreed as we were shown to our table.

"Did you know that the passengers' maids and valets eat in a separate dining room on Shelter Deck C? I saw it yesterday as I was touring the ship. They just have long communal tables, of course."

"Nothing about this ship would surprise me," I admitted. "It must be the grandest thing afloat." At the far end of the dining saloon an orchestra had begun to play.

The menu was a delight, as it had been each night of the voyage thus far. Margo Collier ordered the roast duckling with apple sauce. After some debate between the lamb and the filet mignon, I chose the latter with boiled new potatoes and creamed carrots, preceded by oysters and cream of barley soup.

"Now let us get down to business," I told the young woman. "Tell me about your marriage to Pierre Glacet."

She sighed and began her story. "As you can see, there is a great difference in our ages. I met him on a weekend holiday in Cherbourg last year, and he persuaded me to work for him."

"Work? What sort of work?"

"He is a consulting detective like yourself, Mr. Holmes."

At last I understood the meaning of the man's words, "I am like yourself." He too knew my identity, as most everyone on the ship seemed to. "Being in his employ hardly necessitated marriage, did it?" I asked.

"He specializes in cases involving family matters. Often his investigations involve checking into hotels to keep certain parties under surveillance. He needed me to pose as his wife, and since he was a moral man he felt we should be truly married if we were to share a hotel room."

"You agreed to this?" I asked with some astonishment.

"Not at first. The idea of being married to a man more than twice my age, who had a greying beard and walked with a cane, was more than I could imagine. I agreed to it only when he assured me it would be a marriage in name only, for business purposes. The pay he offered was quite good, and I agreed to try it for one year."

"What happened next?"

"We went through a brief civil ceremony, which he assured me could be easily annulled. I quickly found out, Mr. Holmes, that I had made a foolish mistake. The first time we shared a hotel room while shadowing someone he was a perfect gentleman, sleeping on the sofa while I took the only bed. After that things began to change. He mentioned the troubles with his leg and how uncomfortable hotel room sofas were. I allowed him to share the bed but nothing more. Gradually he began taking liberties and when I objected he reminded me that we were legally man and wife. After a few months of that I left him."

"And he has been following you ever since?"

"No. Even though I remained in Cherbourg through the winter months he made no effort to bother me. It was when I decided to go to America and purchased my ticket on the *Titanic* that I saw him again. He wanted me to stay in Cherbourg."

Over a dessert of Waldorf pudding I tried to learn more about the French detective's cases. "Were they all divorces?"

"No, no. Some involved confidence men trying to swindle wealthy widows. I remember a pair of them, Cozel and Sanbey, who operated as a team. We followed them to Paris once and I kept Mr. Cozel occupied in a café while Pierre searched his room." She smiled at the memory. "We had some good times together."

"Then why did you seek my protection?"

"He wanted more than I was willing to give," she said with a sigh. "When I saw him on the ship I feared I would end up having to fight him off."

"I will speak with him again before we dock in New York," I promised. "Perhaps I can persuade him to leave you alone."

We parted around eleven as the orchestra was playing *The Tales of Hoffmann,* and I decided to go up to the boat deck for a stroll. The temperature was just below freezing, with a mist that cut visibility sharply. I thought of the poor seamen in the crow's nest and shivered for them. Then I retreated inside to the first-class smoking room on A Deck. I could hear the orchestra still playing. May had already retired for the evening, but Futrelle was sitting alone enjoying a nightcap. I joined him and ordered one myself. We were having a lively conversation about detective stories when there was a faint grinding jar to the ship.

"Iceberg!" someone shouted. Several of us ran outside to look. We were in time to see a giant berg, almost as high as the boat deck, vanishing into the mist astern.

"That was a close call," Futrelle said. "I think we actually scraped it going past!"

We went back inside to finish our drinks. After about ten minutes I observed that the level of liquid in my glass was beginning to tilt a bit toward the bow of the ship. Before that fact could register in my mind, Margo Collier came running in. "What is it?" I asked, seeing her ashen face.

"I've been seeking you everywhere, Mr. Holmes. My husband has fallen down the elevator shaft! He's dead."

It was true. One of the first-class stewards had noticed the open gate on the top deck. Looking into the shaft, he'd been able to make out a body on top of the elevator car four floors below. Futrelle and I reached the scene just as the broken body of Pierre Glacet was being removed.

I stared hard at the body as it lay in the corridor, then said, "Let me through here, please."

A ship's officer blocked the way. "Sorry, sir. You're too near the shaft."

"I want to examine it."

"Nothing to see in there, sir. Just the elevator cables."

He was correct, of course. The top of the car had nothing on it. "Can you raise it up so I can see to the bottom of the shaft?" I asked.

Futrelle smiled at my request. "Are you searching for a murder weapon, Mr. Holmes?"

I did not answer, but merely stared at the bottom of the shaft as it came into view beneath the rising elevator car. It was empty, as I suspected it would be. Some first-class passengers came in to use the elevator, but the officer directed them to the main staircase or the aft elevator. "Why is the ship listing?" one of the gentlemen asked.

"We're looking into it," the officer said. For the first time I was aware that we were tilting forward, and I remembered the liquid in my glass. From far off came the sudden sound of a lively ragtime tune being played by the orchestra.

Franklin Baynes, the spiritualist, was coming down the stairs from the boat deck. "What's going on?" he asked. "The crew is uncovering the lifeboats."

Captain Smith himself appeared on the stairs in time to hear the question. "It's just a precaution," he told them. "The ship is taking on water."

"From that iceberg?" Futrelle asked.

"Yes. Please gather your families and follow directions to your lifeboat stations."

Margo Collier seemed dazed. "This ship is unsinkable! There are waterproof compartments. I read all the literature."

"Please follow instructions," the Captain said, a bit more sharply. "Leave that body where it is."

"I must get to May," Futrelle said. I hurried after him. There would be time for the rest later.

Within minutes we were on the deck with May. She was clinging to her husband, unwilling to let go. "Aren't there enough lifeboats for everyone?" she asked. The answer was already plain. The *Titanic* was sinking and there was room enough for only half the passengers in the lifeboats. It was 12:25 A.M. when the order came for women and children to abandon ship. We had scraped against the iceberg only forty-five minutes earlier.

"Jacques!" May Futrelle screamed, and he pushed her to safety in the nearest lifeboat.

"Now what?" he asked me, as the half-full lifeboat was being lowered to the dark churning waters. "Do we go back for our murderer?"

"So you spotted it too?" I asked, already leading the way.

"The missing cane. I only saw Glacet once but he walked with the aid of a stout walking stick."

"Exactly," I agreed. "And I'm told he used it regularly. It wasn't on top of the elevator car and it hadn't slipped down to the bottom of the shaft. That meant he didn't step into that empty shaft accidentally. He had help." We were on the Grand Staircase now, and I spotted our quarry. "Didn't he, Mr. Baynes?"

He turned at the sound of his name, and drew a revolver from under his coat. "Damn you, Holmes! You'll go down with the ship."

"We all will, Baynes. The women and children are leaving. The rest of us will stay. Glacet recognized you as a confidence man he'd once pursued, a man named Sanbey—a simple anagram for Baynes. Somehow you got him into your cabin tonight to stare at your electric crystal ball. When the bright light had temporarily blinded him, you helped him to the elevator, then sent the car down and pushed him after it. Only you forgot his walking stick. That probably went over the side when you discovered it."

The great ship listed suddenly, throwing us against the staircase railing. "I'm getting out of here, Holmes! I'll find room in a lifeboat if I have to don women's clothes!" He raised the revolver and fired.

And in that instant, before I could move, Futrelle jumped between us. He took the bullet meant for me and collided with Baynes, sending them both over the railing of the Grand Staircase.

Somehow I made my way into the night air. It was just after one o'clock and the orchestra had moved to the boat deck to continue playing. The remaining passengers were beginning to panic. Suddenly someone grabbed me and shoved me toward a lifeboat. "Only twelve aboard starboard number one, sir. Plenty of room for you."

"I'll stay," I said, but it was not to be. I was pushed bodily into the boat as it was being lowered.

It was from there, an hour later, that I saw the last of the great *Titanic* vanish beneath the waves, carrying a victim, a murderer, and a mystery writer with it. Two hours after that a ship called the *Carpathia* plucked us from the water, amidst floating ice and debris. Margo Collier was among the survivors, but I never saw her again.

A final note by Dr. Watson: It was not until 1918, at the close of the Great War, that my old friend Holmes entrusted this account to my care. By that time, my literary agent, Arthur Conan Doyle, had embraced spiritualism. He refused to handle a story in which a spiritualist was revealed to be a sham and a murderer. This most dramatic of adventures has remained unpublished.

Imagine Sherlock Holmes consulted by a client so appalling that the detective would never want word to get out that he'd actually helped him. Now imagine who that client might possibly be. If the answer hasn't immediately occurred to you, then read "The Revenge of the Fenian Brotherhood," a riveting adventure that took place approximately eighteen months before the dire events recounted in Watson's famous tale, "The Final Problem."

The Revenge of the Fenian Brotherhood

BY CAROLE BUGGÉ

We have received many unusual visitors in our rooms on the second floor of 221 Baker Street, but I cannot remember any appearance more unexpected than that of the personage who appeared at our door on a cold, wet November night in 1889. I was, in fact, left speechless for some time—though Holmes, displaying his usual *sang-froid,* calmly motioned our visitor towards the sofa.

"You realize, of course, my distaste in coming to you for assistance in this matter," said our caller, settling his thin, bony frame into the depths of the sofa.

"Naturally," Holmes replied, digging his long fingers into the Persian slipper which served as his tobacco tin.

I stood staring as foolishly as a schoolboy, until Holmes laid a hand gently on my shoulder.

"Please sit down, Watson; you are making me nervous."

I sat slowly in my usual chair in front of the crackling fire, never taking my eyes off our guest. I don't know what I thought he would do, but although I had never laid eyes on him before I was certain that this was a man you did not turn your back on.

Holmes was more sanguine, however, and deliberately turned his back to procure a match from the mantelpiece. At this our visitor chuckled.

"Always the showman, eh, Holmes?" he said in a low voice, hissing his *s*'s, his grey eyes as hooded as a viper's. He turned his steely gaze on me, and it was then I first made eye contact with the late Professor James Moriarty.

"No more than yourself," Holmes replied, lighting his pipe and turning to face the Professor.

"Now it is you who are making me nervous, Holmes—sit down, please," I said, my eyes still trained on Moriarty; some instinct deep within me would not let me take my gaze off him. I had always thought of him as the personification of evil, and yet now what struck me about his face was how deeply pain was etched into every line, every crevice—as though someone had taken a sharp knife and carved out a mask of suffering. His eyes were dead, though, as cold and lifeless as the lidless eyes of a fish.

Holmes sat in the winged armchair opposite mine. "Now, then, Professor, what can I do for you?"

Moriarty gave off a long, slow exhalation of breath, which made a low hissing sound like air escaping from a tyre. There was a long pause as he rose and walked to the window, pulling aside the curtains to look out on the street below. I tensed in my chair, ready to spring, my mind racing—it occurred to me that he might be giving a signal of some kind. I glanced at Holmes, who appeared utterly unconcerned; he sat smoking peacefully, his eyes half closed, fingers folded in repose on his lap.

Finally Moriarty spoke.

"What a pitiful sight mankind is," he said, still gazing out onto the street, "hurrying back and forth like so many ants, and all to what purpose? To work and spawn and die, with no more mindfulness than a doomed salmon swimming upstream towards his death."

"You certainly did not come here to philosophize with me," said Holmes. "May I ask——"

"You are unaware, perhaps, that I have a brother?" Moriarty interrupted, swivelling to face us, and again I was struck by the pain which had hardened into the lines of his face.

"I had heard something of it," Holmes replied, "from my own brother."

"Ah, yes, Mycroft," Moriarty said, his thin lips curling into something resembling a smile.

"I believe he lives in Ireland, does he not?"

Again Moriarty sighed, but when he spoke his voice was a sneer. "If anyone could be said to actually 'live' in Ireland. He is, in fact, a Catholic priest."

If Holmes felt any surprise at this revelation he betrayed none of it. Moriarty, however, snickered. "Yes, it is ironic, isn't it? A brother who is a man of the cloth—when I have devoted myself to quite another kind of priesthood."

"He is in trouble, your brother?"

Moriarty nodded, his large head swivelling precariously on its long, thin neck; it was as though the head of a bull had been set upon the body of a giraffe.

"We had a—falling out, shall we say—and have not spoken for some years, and yet, when I came by the information that I am about to tell you I had no choice but to intervene."

"No choice——?"

Moriarty smiled, and though I would not say it was a warm smile, some of the hard lines on his face softened. "It may surprise you to know that even I have areas in my life which are—sacred, so to speak."

"Not at all," Holmes replied. "I would have assumed as much."

"I am afraid that it is so unoriginal as to be a cliché, but I made a promise to my dying mother that no matter what came, I would look after my younger brother, Sean. And I have kept that promise—until now, that is."

"I see; pray continue."

Moriarty walked back to sit upon the couch again; his gait swayed like that of a large flightless bird.

"You have perhaps heard of the Fenian Brotherhood?"

"I have heard of them, yes—they are essentially a terrorist organization bent on the eradication of British rule in Ireland. Is your brother mixed up with them?"

"On the contrary; he is their sworn enemy. I have reason to believe they have kidnapped him."

"I see." Holmes's face was as stoic as ever, but he could not conceal the gleam of interest in his grey eyes, which burned dark as coals in the dull November light.

"So you see your involvement in this case would be for the good of England as well. If you don't believe me, ask your brother Mycroft; he is privy to every bit of international intelligence, is he not?"

Holmes just smiled in reply. "Why do you come to me for assistance when you have a network of your own upon which to draw?"

Moriarty's face hardened again, and his dark eyes clouded over. "Because my brother must know nothing of my involvement in his rescue. He knows my agents, and he knows the way I operate. He has taken great pains to disassociate himself from me—"

"And yet you protect him," I blurted out.

"As I said, Dr. Watson, every man has some things that are sacred."

"Say no more," Holmes said graciously; "I see your predicament. Do you know whether Scotland Yard has been informed of this matter yet?"

Moriarty let out what could have been taken for a laugh—a short, brutal exhalation of air. "If they have, they have not learned it from me."

"Why don't you tell me what you know?"

"There isn't much to tell. My brother was invited to preach at a notoriously pro-Fenian church here in London, and his subject matter did not sit well with certain factions in the congregation . . . The next day he went out in the morning and did not return."

"I see. Naturally you suspect elements of that organization."

"Let's just say there's a strong certainty, Holmes." Moriarty's eyes narrowed and darkened. "It's well for them that I am not handling this myself . . . I would make them pay in ways you cannot imagine," he said in a cold, flat voice.

I shuddered at not so much his words as the way he said them.

Holmes rose from his chair. "I will begin working on it immediately."

Moriarty rose stiffly and walked to the door in his peculiar, swaying gait. When he reached the door he paused.

"You realize, of course, that this changes nothing between us?"

Holmes smiled. "Of course."

Their eyes met briefly and they exchanged a look extraordinary in its contradictions—it was full of understanding without friendship, admiration without affection; the sort of look two opposing generals might give one another on the eve of battle. Without another word Moriarty turned and was gone. I listened as his footsteps descended the stairs, and only when I heard the front door latch behind him did I turn to Holmes.

"I didn't know he had a brother."

Holmes shrugged. "Neither did I."

"But you said—"

"My dear Watson, with a man like Moriarty it is better not to admit ignorance on any matter if you can avoid it."

"But how did you know he lived in Ireland?"

"That was a lucky guess; Moriarty is an Irish name."

"But what if this whole thing is a trap?"

"I think we can rule that out easily enough," he replied, opening the door to the sitting room. To my surprise, our landlady, Mrs. Hudson, was standing in the hallway outside. She wore an apron and there was flour on her hands.

"Yes, Mrs. Hudson?" said Holmes with a smile.

"I just thought I'd come up and see . . . if everything was all right—that is . . ." she said, flustered.

"Quite all right, thank you," Holmes replied, scribbling something on a piece of paper. "Would you see that Master Tuthill of the Baker Street Irregulars gets this?" he said, handing the note to Mrs. Hudson.

"Yes, sir," she answered, tucking it into the pocket of her apron. "Mr. Holmes, may I ask you something? That fellow who was just here . . . he—what I mean is, was he—?"

"Yes, Mrs. Hudson, he was. And now don't let us detain you any longer; please return to your baking."

"What—? Oh, yes," she said, looking at her flour-covered hands. "Yes, of course . . ."

"Good-bye, Mrs. Hudson, and thank you," Holmes said firmly.

"You're welcome, Mr. Holmes; quite welcome, I'm sure." She looked as if she wanted to say something else, but Holmes escorted her gently to the door and closed it behind her.

"The less she knows about this the better for her," he said, heading for his bedroom.

"He's telling the truth, you think, then?"

"We shall find out soon enough. It's time for a visit to Brother Mycroft."

The Diogenes Club was in Pall Mall, across from Mycroft's rooms, and a short distance from his office. His routine rarely varied; he could be found in his office until precisely four forty-five, at which time he made his way to his club, then at exactly seven-forty trundled off to his lodgings. It is ironic that the physical universe inhabited by this extraordinary creature was as limited as his mental world was expansive. Holmes had once confided to me that Mycroft was not only his intellectual superior, but that "one might even say that Mycroft *is* the Government." Holmes was not a man given to exaggeration, and so my respect for his brother Mycroft was considerable.

We entered the august edifice which housed the club, a heavy grey stone building typical of the mid-Victorian period, and headed straight for the Visitors' Lounge, the only room in the cavernous structure in which conversation was allowed. Mycroft Holmes was seated in an armchair, and I thought he had grown a tad heftier since our last encounter. His grey eyes were as keen as his brother's, however, and his massive skull was evidence of the same magnificent brain power. I sat—or rather sank—down upon a low overstuffed armchair.

"You are dealing with an offshoot of the Fenians called the Triangle," he said, without any conversational preamble. "They call themselves The Invincibles, or Clann na Gael. Some of their darker deeds include the murder of Lord Frederick Cavendish, shortly after he was appointed Chief Secretary for Ireland, in 1882; they are also suspected of crimes in the United States. They are ruthless and will stop at nothing to achieve their goal of Irish independence."

He paused and lit the pipe which sat on the arm of his chair, and thin reeds of smoke curled around his broad head.

"The Government has already received a ransom note in the matter of Moriarty's brother, offering to exchange him for Fenian prisoners. An exchange is of course out of the question. The men we hold are directly implicated in the dynamite campaign of 1883, in which a number of bombs were set off all over England, some of which killed innocent people.

"One more thing," said Mycroft; "we have reason to believe that a bomb will be planted in a major edifice somewhere in London within the next few days. I needn't tell you that the consequences could be catastrophic." He handed Holmes a piece of paper. "These password phrases may or may not work; however, it is the most current information we have."

"I see," said Holmes. He studied the paper, his lean face tight, his grey eyes gleaming like coals in the dim light of the Diogenes Club.

Mycroft walked us to the door, and as we turned to leave, he laid a hand on his brother's shoulder.

"Be careful, Sherlock."

I was struck more by the uncharacteristic gesture than by his words, but Holmes just nodded.

Outside, we stood for a moment watching a dimly glimmering twilight settle over London. Holmes stood upon the stairs, his sharp profile silhouetted against the waning light in the western sky. I wondered what thoughts were racing through that quicksilver brain when suddenly he shook off his mood, sprang into the street, and hailed a cab. The cab ride back to Baker Street was spent in silence; Holmes sat in the corner wrapped in thought, and I knew better than to disturb him at times like this.

When we arrived at Baker Street, Holmes went straight to his bedroom without a word. I sat down on the couch and filled my pipe. I didn't like this, any of it, but I was so accustomed to deferring to Holmes in most matters that I didn't know if I should say anything. My concern turned to astonishment a few minutes later when Holmes emerged from the bedroom dressed in a black suit and clerical collar.

"What do you think, Watson?"

"Good heavens, Holmes!"

"I admit it's a bit of a stretch, but it's necessary under the circumstances."

"But—"

"Oh, I know; my soul could go straight to hell."

"I didn't mean that, but don't you think it's a bit—"

"Sacrilegious? I suppose it is, but I'm sure I've committed worse sins. And now if you'll excuse me, I shall be off," he said, throwing his black ulster on over his priestly garb. "Tell Mrs. Hudson I shall be back in time for dinner and that I look forward to the fine fruit tart she is preparing for us."

I didn't even bother to ask Holmes how he knew it was a fruit tart. I closed the door after him and wandered around the sitting room for a while, trying to make sense of the strange events of the morning. Finally I lay down upon the couch and attempted to immerse myself in some medical texts which I had recently purchased. My mind was having none of it, however, and soon I drifted off into uneasy dreams in which masked gunmen tried to pull me off the couch where I lay. I clung to my pillow, though, until I heard Mrs. Hudson's voice coming from one of the gunmen.

"Dr. Watson, wake up! There's a message for you."

I sat up abruptly and took the slip of paper which she held in her hand. I opened it and read: "Meet me at Paddy O'Reilly's— Holmes. P.S. Bring your revolver."

"Thank you, Mrs. Hudson." I rose from the couch, groggy from the sleep which still clung to me. I thrust the note into my pocket and, with trembling hands, took my service revolver from the desk drawer and loaded it.

"I'm going out, Mrs. Hudson," I said, smoothing my hair and buttoning my cuffs. My wife had just given me a beautiful new pair of gold cufflinks with my initials engraved on them, and I was very taken with them.

"Wouldn't you like some tea before you leave?" she said, picking up the sofa pillows which I had flung about the room in my dream-tossed slumber.

"No, thank you—I haven't any time."

As I closed the door behind me, she was fussing about the room muttering something about "regular hours" and "all this dashing about."

The weather had cleared, and a brisk wind had picked up from the river. I pulled my coat about me as I stood waiting for a cab to arrive; and soon I was seated in a hansom rumbling east along the cobblestones.

London's East End is sometimes referred to as "the other London." This catch-all description includes the opium dens and whore-houses in neighborhoods such as Whitehall and Spitalfields; it also describes the colourful but less ominous environs in which respectable working-class English people and foreigners made their homes. The men and women who cleaned the houses and chimneys of the richer folk, who shod their horses and shined their shoes, who baked their pastries and sewed their clothes—these hard-working people to a large extent lived in the eastern sector of the city. Holmes and I often journeyed into these places—as a source of information, the pubs and tea rooms of the East End were invaluable. The Irish pubs of Spitalfields were no exception. In London in 1891 an Irishman was regarded as closer to a foreigner than an Englishman. They retaliated by taking their business en masse to the East End.

An Irish pub is not like an English pub. It is noisier, more boisterous and more vital. There is usually music, there is often dancing, and there is always drinking—not polite social drinking, but serious, determined drinking, the consumption of alcohol serving as a revolt against the insults of the world. I am half Irish myself, and as a child I saw what motivated that kind of drinking, and also what it could do to a man.

Paddy O'Reilly's was the kind of place you could go to forget the insults of the world—to drown them in a glass of stout if that was your choice, or to lose them in a reel played hard and fast on a concertina and a tin whistle. The sound of the music reached me even before I put my hand upon the handle of the heavy oaken door. It was a tune I recognized—"Mary's Wedding," a Scottish melody—and it was being played at breakneck speed on a fiddle and concertina, with a tin whistle supplying a kind of obbligato or counterpoint. I stood in the doorway for a moment, pushed back by the harsh smell of tobacco, sawdust and beer. The concertina player was middle-aged, with the heavy-lidded eyes of a Scotsman, and he sat pumping his instrument with a grim determination. Four or five dancers stomped out something close to the Highland fling, and a few other people watched them, clapping and laughing with a bleary-eyed euphoria.

I made my way across the sawdust-strewn floor, heading for a lone figure sitting hunched over at a table at the back of the room. I was very nearly drawn into the dance by a raucous young woman, who attempted to link her arm around mine. Her red hair was wild; her eyes were wilder, and I extracted myself from her clutches, mumbling a polite excuse, and made my way to the back of the room.

When I reached the solitary man, who was seated at a dimly lit table in the corner, I sat down. When I looked at his face I thought I had made a mistake; surely the ruddy complexion and full cheeks did not belong to my friend Holmes. I began to rise, but I felt a strong hand upon my shoulder pull me back down.

"Sit still, Watson! Do you want to call attention to us?"

It was unmistakably Holmes's voice, and I could not prevent the look of astonishment which crossed my face.

"Holmes!" I whispered, "it *is* you, then!"

"Of course it is. Now keep still and try not to look suspicious."

Holmes ordered two glasses of stout from the surly waiter, whose cigarette perched upon his lower lip, defying the laws of gravity and physics.

"Try to look inconspicuous," Holmes muttered as the man set two foaming mugs in front of us.

"By the way, what happened to your last disguise?" I said, taking a sip of the heavy, sweet dark liquid in my glass.

"It was very useful for a time." He smiled. "I'm afraid I violated the sanctity of the confessional, but as you know, Watson, I am not religious."

"You mean—you posed as a priest to hear confessions?"

"The Fenians are Catholics to a man, and a Catholic may do any number of heinous deeds, but if he is a good Catholic he will always confess it to his priest."

"Holmes—!" I was raised Church of England myself, but still I admit I was shocked.

"Yes, Watson; no doubt I am a sinner, and if there is a hell, I shall end up there." He dismissed the thought with a wave of his hand. "No matter; I now know the identity of at least one of the conspirators. You see that man there?" he said, indicating a large, heavy-shouldered man who stood watching the dancers as they spun and bobbed to the music. With his thick unruly hair and massive torso, he resembled a large brown bear.

"Yes?"

"He is a good Catholic; he is also a kidnapper, and very probably a murderer."

Just then, as if he had sensed we were talking about him, the man turned towards us, and I saw his lips part to reveal a mouth of large, yellowed teeth. His face was heavy and thick-featured, a crudely sensual face, and I shuddered at the sight of so many teeth set between those thick lips. His eyes moved about the room but did not settle upon us, and when he turned back to watch the dancers I exhaled heavily; I had been holding my breath.

"So you—you followed him here?" I whispered to Holmes.

"Yes, and it was no easy feat, let me tell you. A priest attracts more attention on the street than an ordinary man, and several times I had to dart behind buildings to make certain he didn't see me. But when he went in here I had some time to apply the makeup which you see I now wear."

I shook my head; there seemed to be no end to my friend's ingenuity.

"So what do we do next?" I asked, but just then Holmes's hand gripped my arm.

"Shhh—it is time!" he said in a low voice.

Our massive friend was now bending over a tableful of men, a serious expression on his florid face. The others at the table were a grim-looking lot, and a tall, sallow man who appeared to be the leader was speaking, his head lowered; all the others listened to him intently.

"Time for what?" I whispered to Holmes.

"The thing we have come here to see. Avert your gaze; don't let them see you looking at them!" Holmes murmured as one of the men at the table let his eyes roam idly around the room. It was too late, however; our eyes met and he nodded to me. His face would have been handsome except for his deeply pockmarked skin; his eyes were large and lustrous, and the high cheekbones bespoke an aristocratic heritage. My skin chilled as he bent over and said something to the thin sallow leader, who nodded and looked over at us.

"You have your revolver?" Holmes whispered.

"Right here in my pocket." I closed my fingers over the handle of the gun; the cool smooth metal was reassuring in my hand.

The pockmarked man straightened up and walked towards us, and my fingers tightened around the revolver. However, when he reached us he smiled.

"Are you finding it unusually warm in here?" he said in a cultivated, educated voice with just a trace of an Irish accent.

"The weather can be unpredictable this time of year," Holmes replied smoothly.

The man nodded, then turned and walked back to his table; once again he leaned over for a consultation with his leader. I held my breath; this was evidently the password which Mycroft had referred to, but he had said he was not certain if it would work. To my surprise, the man motioned to us, whereupon Holmes rose and walked over to the other table. I followed him, and I could feel the men's eyes on us but I tried to look unconcerned. I am not the actor Holmes is, though, and I am afraid I did not manage to look any more nonchalant than I felt. In truth, my heart was racing and my palms were oozing sweat. I have been under fire in wartime and managed to remain rather cool, but there was something in the stares of these men which sent tingling threads of fear up my spine.

The thin sallow man regarded us through half-closed eyes; he reminded me of a long yellow cat.

"I understand you are interested in the current climate," he said.

"My brother usually knows when it's going to rain," Holmes replied calmly.

The sallow man nodded, and motioned to his pockmarked lieutenant, who indicated that we should follow him. He led us across the sawdust-strewn floor, behind the musicians and other patrons, and through a narrow door on the other side of the bar. We followed him down a set of steep steps to a dimly lit basement room. A few chairs were scattered about the room, and a podium stood underneath a flag of Ireland, which had been tacked up on one wall.

"Wait here," he said, and with that, he left us and went back upstairs. Holmes and I stood listening to the sounds coming from upstairs. Someone was singing in a faltering tenor:

> "Oh Danny Boy, the pipes, the pipes are calling
> From glen to glen and down the mountainside . . ."

I wondered what we were waiting for, and was about to ask Holmes what was going on, but just then I heard the sound of footsteps upon the stairs. Our pockmarked friend reappeared, followed by the large, thick-lipped fellow we had seen earlier, as well as the sallow man whom I took to be the leader. The rest of the men in his entourage were close behind, as well as a few others whom I supposed had been scattered among the pub patrons. I estimated that there were perhaps two dozen people in the room, including ourselves.

To my surprise, the wild-haired redhead was also among them, the only woman in the group. Holmes and I took our seats among the other patrons, and as we did, the young woman caught my eye and smiled. Though I averted my gaze, she came and sat next to us, brushing my leg with her long skirt as she did so.

"And what might your name be?" she said in a voice somewhat the worse for whiskey.

"Uh . . . Raoul," I said uncertainly.

"Oh, are you French, then?"

I looked at Holmes, but he sat staring straight ahead.

"On my mother's side."

"Oh, the French are very romantic, aren't they?" she replied, snuggling up closer to me.

"I—I don't know," I said miserably.

"Oh, but you should know . . . I could teach you, you know."

Just then our pockmarked friend banged a gavel upon the podium at the front of the room.

"All right, it's time we began," he said, and the room quieted down. "Let's all listen to what Brother Kerry has to say."

The wan-faced leader took the podium. He stood for a moment gazing at his audience and then he spoke.

"Our fight has just begun. As most of you know, we are ready to strike a blow which will leave our English oppressors reeling. I will let Brother O'Malley tell you about it."

With that, he stepped away from the podium and allowed the pockmarked man to take his place.

"This is the grandest plan we have ever conceived," Brother O'Malley began, but just then the intoxicated young woman grasped my hand in hers. I pulled away, but her grip was tight, and as I pulled away, the cufflink on my right sleeve came off and fell to the floor. She bent down and picked it up, and then her eyes fell upon the engraved initials: "JHW."

"You said your name was Raoul," she said in a loud voice. Brother O'Malley stopped in mid-sentence and looked at us.

"Is there a problem?" he said in a stern voice.

To my horror, the young woman stood up, swaying uncertainly.

"Yes, Annie; what is it?" Brother O'Malley said impatiently.

"We have a spy among us," she said, pointing at me. At that moment my blood froze and ran cold in my veins; I felt as if the floor had suddenly been removed out from under me.

"Oh?" replied O'Malley in a wary voice. "What makes you think that?"

By now everyone was looking at us. I looked at Holmes; he sat utterly still, his face impassive, barely breathing.

"This cufflink!" Annie declared, holding it up for all to see.

"What about it?" said Brother Kerry, a gleam of suspicion in his eyes.

"Well, he told me his name was Raoul, but his cufflinks have the initials JHW! I say he's a spy!"

There was a murmur of voices in the room. I slipped my hand into my pocket and gripped the revolver.

"Hmmm," said Brother O'Malley, and he walked slowly towards us. I cursed myself for having worn these cufflinks, and for having the misfortune to attract the attention of the inebriated young woman.

It was too late, however; I think Holmes also knew the gig was up, because he stood up when O'Malley reached us.

"How did you manage to procure our password?" said O'Malley.

Holmes shrugged and did not reply. O'Malley nodded to the large bearlike fellow, who was looming nearby. To my horror, the huge fellow took two steps towards Holmes and suddenly rammed his massive fist into my friend's stomach. Holmes groaned and fell to the floor. I drew my gun, but with a quickness I would not have given him credit for, the giant flicked his hand out with lightning speed and delivered a crushing blow to my wrist, sending the gun flying. Cradling my wrist in my other hand, I dropped to the floor.

"We don't take too kindly to spies, you know," said Brother O'Malley in a flat voice. He bent over Holmes, who lay gasping for breath.

"Who sent you?"

Holmes shook his head. O'Malley shrugged and turned to me. "Perhaps you will tell me—or it will not go well for your friend here." He motioned to the bearlike man again, and before I could stop him he kicked Holmes in the ribs. Holmes moaned and lost consciousness.

Just then Annie interposed herself between O'Malley and us. "Stop it—stop it, I say!" she screamed, clawing at him wildly.

O'Malley nodded to his goon, whereupon the man lifted her off her feet and carried her from the room.

"I always said women should not be allowed to be a part of this," muttered Brother Kerry, walking over to us.

"What shall we do with them?" said O'Malley.

"Oh, I think we can put them with our other friend for the time being—at least until we finish our meeting," he replied, looking down at Holmes. "He's no good to us right now, anyway."

O'Malley nodded to several of the men, whereupon I found myself being half carried and half dragged from the room. Several of the men followed behind, carrying Holmes. A blindfold was placed over my eyes, and abruptly locked into darkness, I experienced the sensations which I imagined a blind man must feel. My world consisted now only of my other four senses, and I was suddenly very aware of the sounds and smells around me. The smooth voice of O'Malley faded into the background and was replaced by the heavy steps of my captors, whose laboured breathing indicated that they were unused to such strenuous exercise.

I was carried along for some ten minutes, and then I heard the high-pitched cry of seagulls and smelled the thick brackish aroma of the Thames; we were near the river. A door was opened and we entered a room; then another door, and then we stopped. I was shoved rudely into a chair, and I felt my hands and feet being tied. Then the blindfold was removed, and when my vision cleared I saw that I was in a long, low-ceilinged room, the walls and floor entirely made out of crude wooden planks; the kind of room you would see in a warehouse by the docks. Buoys and rusted anchors hung from the walls; coils of rotted rope sat in corners gathering dust; the warehouse had evidently been abandoned for some time. The room smelled of mildew and salt water.

The massive fellow, whom his comrades addressed as Connors, was engaged in tying Holmes to a chair. O'Malley stood, arms folded, gazing out of a small window at the other end of the room, the pale light highlighting the craters on his face. It was then I noticed there was a third figure in the room: along the far wall, in the shadows, I could barely make out the form of a man upon the floor, sitting slumped up against the wall. I strained my eyes to see better, but just then O'Malley turned and spoke.

"You stay and stand guard outside, Connors; we'll deal with them later," he said; "I have to get back to the meeting. Well, gentlemen," he continued, addressing himself to me, "I trust you will introduce yourselves to each other; I shall return as soon as I can."

With that he turned smoothly and left the room, followed by the other two men who had helped carry us here. Connors looked around the room, grunted, and then left. When he had gone I heard a bolt slide into place from the outside. Shortly afterwards I smelled cheap shag tobacco, and surmised that Connors was passing the time by having a smoke. I turned my attention to Holmes, who had begun to stir. My wrist throbbed but I was far more concerned about his injuries than mine.

"Holmes, are you all right?" I whispered, not wanting Connors to hear our conversation. A moment passed, and then he replied in a weak voice.

"I'm all right, Watson—I was just stunned, that's all."

I didn't tell him that I suspected he had a broken rib or two. Instead I strained to make out the man in the corner.

"Holmes, there's someone else in here with us!"

"Really?"

"Yes, over there in the corner!"

He twisted around to see, a move which caused him to wince in pain.

"Who is it, do you think?"

"I don't know; he looks as though he's been drugged, though."

"Yes, I expect you're right. Holmes—do you suppose it's—could it be—?"

"That would be the most logical conclusion, certainly."

Just then the man stirred and moaned softly.

"Hello—I say—hello there!" I whispered as loudly as I could.

He stirred again, and lifted his head. To my surprise, he chuckled softly.

"Well, well . . . Sherlock Holmes and Dr. Watson, fancy meeting you here. I thought my brother might send you to rescue me."

"So you are—"

"Father Sean Moriarty, at your service," he said in a voice which had the same sibilant softness as his brother's but without the restrained violence underneath. "I am correct in surmising that you are here at the behest of my brother?"

"Your brother and I are enemies," Holmes said evasively; "we are here on behalf of the British Government."

"Very well, have it your way," Sean Moriarty said with a sigh. "I know he does not wish me to know of his involvement."

"What is important is not why we are here, but how we are going to get out of here," Holmes replied. "Are you able-bodied?"

"You were correct in surmising that I have been drugged, but the effect is now largely worn off; I thought it best to pretend I was still unconscious when our friends were here earlier."

"Good," said Holmes, and I mused that craftiness seemed to be one trait which remained consistent in both brothers.

"If they are going to kill us, they will not do so for at least one hour," Sean Moriarty continued.

"Why is that?" I said, my tongue going dry at his words.

"Because high tide is an hour away, and that is by far the best time to dispose of bodies; the outgoing tide would sweep them out toward sea."

"Admirably reasoned," said Holmes, and I felt a pang of jealousy at the approval in his voice.

"There's more at stake than just us, too," our fellow prisoner continued. "I overheard them plotting something else, something big involving a bomb."

There was a silence between us. I had already tried to work free of my bonds, but had only succeeded in giving myself rope burns; we were very securely and professionally bound.

We were evidently near one of London's busier docks, because I could hear the cries of costermongers outside, advertising their wares.

"Pickled eels—fresh, oy!"

"Get your cress, fresh watercress—penny a bunch!"

Holmes was listening too, and even in the dim light I could see the muscles of his face working. Suddenly he pursed his lips and emitted a low, soft whistle. He paused and listened for a reply, and to my surprise it came almost at once, the same exact whistle! Holmes whistled again, this time repeating the same tone in short, staccato bursts. Again the answer came, and again Holmes replied. I was wondering where this was all leading when I saw a face appear at the window. It was a weathered, wizened face, with broken veins on the cheeks and a nose red from drink, but never in my life was I so glad to see a face!

Holmes nodded to the man, who nodded and then disappeared from view. A moment later there was the sound of glass being cut, and I saw that the sound was being made by a thin blade inserted between the pane and the window frame. The three of us in the room held our breath as the glass was cleanly and skillfully separated from its base. Moments later another face appeared, followed by a body. This time I recognized the face: it was Master Tuthill of the Baker Street Irregulars. The boy wriggled his thin form through the window, dropping noiselessly to the floor; then he crept over and began untying us one by one. He had just started to untie me when the door flung open and Connors's enormous bulk filled up the door frame.

"What's going on here?" he said. Before he could make a move, Holmes sprang at him, knocking him backwards through the door. His strength was enormous, though, and he tossed Holmes off him as easily as if he were a rag. Holmes staggered and then went at him again, landing several blows to the big man's torso. Connors grunted and struck out, but Holmes was lighter and quicker than his opponent, and easily avoided his blows.

"Hurry, Tuthill!" I cried as the boy struggled with my bonds. "I'm goin' as fast as I can!"

Holmes was aiming his punches to Connors's face now, and the huge fellow was beginning to slow down when suddenly Holmes tripped over a coil of rotting rope. Connors took advantage of this and swung with all his might, landing a blow to Holmes's ribs, whereupon my friend doubled over and slumped to the floor.

Free now from my restraints, I threw myself at Connors with a roar, but didn't even get near him; a blow to my head from one huge fist made me dizzy and I crumpled to the ground. My head spinning, I looked up through a haze of pain and saw Sean Moriarty rush at Connors. I closed my eyes, not wanting to see the results, but when I opened them moments later I saw Connors stretched out on the floor. Moriarty was standing over him, breathing heavily, rubbing his knuckles. I staggered unsteadily to my feet.

"Good Lord! What did you do to him?" I gasped.

"I did a bit of boxing before I was called to the priesthood," he replied modestly, and I stared at him in wonder. Though possessed of the same wiry frame as his brother, I would not have thought he could floor the big man like that. Tuthill stood looking at Moriarty with an expression of adoration.

I turned my attention to Holmes, who lay upon the floor looking very wan; I feared his injuries were causing internal bleeding.

"Dr. Watson," Moriarty asked, "how are you at knots?"

"I'm excellent, sir," Tuthill piped up; "I've worked on shipboard."

Moriarty regarded the lad. "Good," he said, pointing to Connors; "see that you tie him up well."

"Yes, *sir!*" said the boy, and grabbing one of the ropes formerly used on us, he set to work.

"We must get out of here before he comes to and tells the others," Moriarty said sharply, and then he bent over Holmes.

"Can you move?"

Holmes nodded, and we helped him to his feet. Gripping his side, his face deathly pale, he spoke in a raspy whisper.

"What can you tell me—about what they—are planning?" he said, pausing between words to catch his breath. I felt strongly that moving him was not a good idea, and yet we could not leave him here.

"I remember they said something about 'the third time's the charm . . .' "

"What else did they say? Can you remember anything else?"

"It's difficult; I was drugged at the time . . ." Moriarty paused, and then his face lit up. "Wait a minute—yes, they said, something about 'the bird will have flown for the last time!' "

"Excellent!" cried Holmes, and then he winced and paused for breath. "Quickly, we must hurry!"

"Where are we going?" I said, following him out of the warehouse.

"To St. Paul's Cathedral!"

I immediately grasped Holmes's reasoning. Twice destroyed by fire, a bombing of St. Paul's would indeed be "a third time." The "bird" was a veiled reference to Christopher Wren, the architect who designed the current building.

"May I come along, Mr. Holmes?" said Tuthill.

"No, Tuthill, it could be very dangerous," Holmes replied; "but you have rendered us a great service today which I won't forget." The boy's beaming face showed the impact Holmes's praise had on him, and again I felt myself foolishly wishing those words had been spoken to me.

The night was dark and overcast but as the three of us scrambled up the bank of mud which led away from the river I could see the sweat gleaming on Holmes's forehead. When we reached Cannon Street we flagged down a cab.

"There's an extra guinea for you if you hurry!" Holmes cried to the driver, and soon we were rattling along the cobblestones at a brisk canter. The driver earned his money, for we arrived there within minutes.

St. Paul's Cathedral's reputation as one of the greatest cathedrals in Europe is well deserved. Its dome dominates the skyline of the City like a mountain rising majestically out of foothills. Christopher Wren's design displays a harmony and balance which is both calming and exhilarating, and as we dashed through the marbled entryway I couldn't help feeling overwhelmed by its grandeur.

Suddenly Holmes gripped my arm. "There—there he is!"

I followed his gaze and saw the thin form of O'Malley dart behind a column.

"He's seen us," said Moriarty.

"Go around the back way, Watson; Moriarty and I will separate and cover the entrances."

I nodded and crept around the row of silent marble columns, my eyes straining to catch a sight of our quarry. The smooth floor and resonance of the walls made it difficult to move quietly, but I tiptoed as softly as I could. I stopped and listened. There was no sound except my own breathing, and I listened vainly for the echo of other footsteps.

Suddenly my eye caught a movement behind one of the columns. I froze and stopped breathing for what seemed like an eternity, then crept slowly forward.

"Well, Dr. Watson, I must congratulate you. I don't know how you escaped, but now you will die a glorious death for the cause of Ireland."

I spun around to see O'Malley holding a gun pointed at my chest. Under his arm he carried an ominous-looking package wrapped in brown paper.

"Don't do it, O'Malley; think of the loss."

"Oh, but we're all thinking about loss all the time," he replied, his dark eyes narrow. "The loss of our homeland—the Ireland that once was but is no more thanks to the British Government."

"But this won't solve anything," I said desperately; "you'll only be killing innocent people."

O'Malley shrugged. "Do you know how many people died in

the potato famine because of the greed and indifference of British landlords? An eye for an eye. It's in the Bible, you know."

"And a tooth for a tooth."

O'Malley turned around to face Holmes, who stood there looking as pale as a ghost. As he did I threw myself at him, knocking him to the ground. I grabbed for the gun, and we fought for possession of it. Then suddenly a shot rang out. O'Malley's eyes stared wildly into mine, then his body went limp.

"Watson, are you all right?" Holmes cried, sinking to the ground beside us.

"Quite all right, thank you," I said, secretly pleased at the desperation in his voice. He was not a man given to emotional outburst, and it warmed me to the core to hear the concern he felt for my safety.

"Thank God," he said, and then gingerly picked up the package from where it had fallen on the floor. We opened it, and found that the timing device had not yet been set to go off. "I think we'd best take this to Scotland Yard," he said as Sean Moriarty joined us. The commotion caused by the gunshot had already attracted several policemen, and I convinced Holmes to give them custody of the bomb and go back with me to Baker Street.

Only once we were safely back in our sitting room did I get a close look at Father Sean Moriarty. He had the same high domed forehead, the same thin lips as his brother, but without the cruelty about his mouth. His black eyes were softer, and as he sipped the tea which Mrs. Hudson insisted on serving us, he shook his head, reminding me of the strange reptilian head-swivelling which was peculiar to James Moriarty.

"My brother must have felt a bitter humiliation when he came to you for help." At Sean's insistence, Holmes and I both had finally stopped denying the involvement of James Moriarty.

I wanted to ask him how he and his brother had ended up at such different ends of the moral spectrum, but I contented myself with a question for Holmes, who lay on the couch at my insistence; after much protest, he had allowed me to bandage his ribs and administer some morphine.

"How did you know that they would take us to Sean if we were made prisoners?"

Holmes stared at me for a moment and then let out a laugh, which caused him to wince and hold his side.

"Good Lord, Watson—you actually thought I *planned* to have us captured?"

"Well, didn't you?" said Moriarty.

"Good heavens, no; I was just there to infiltrate their meeting. Everything that happened afterwards was a complete surprise to me."

"But how did you know Tuthill was outside the window?" I asked.

"I didn't, but you may remember I sent him a note earlier, suggesting that he keep an eye on our movements. He occasionally works as a costermonger's assistant, and as you can see, he did a good job of tracking us." Holmes smiled. "Well, Watson, I'd rather you didn't write this one up—I was employed by Professor Moriarty, nearly failed to prevent the destruction of St. Paul's, and was rescued by a priest and a little boy. Not a very successful case, I think."

"The public might enjoy knowing you are human after all, Holmes."

He turned his face towards the pale light of dawn creeping through the curtains. "I think not, Watson; if they knew I was human, why on earth would they want to read about me?"

My Blushes, Watson!

". . . You have heard me speak of Professor Moriarty?"

"The famous scientific criminal, as famous among crooks as—"

"My blushes, Watson," Holmes murmured, in a deprecating voice.

"I was about to say 'as he is unknown to the public.'"

"A touch—a distinct touch!" cried Holmes. "You are developing a certain unexpected vein of pawky humour, Watson, against which I must learn to guard myself."

The above well-known excerpt from The Valley of Fear proves that Sherlock Holmes was fully capable of laughing at himself. Yet he did have his petty vanities, such as his irritation at Watson's penning of "The Yellow Face" (for details, see "Too Many Stains" in my 1996 anthology, The Resurrected Holmes) or his presumable embarrassment over the three tales in this section.

In "The Adventure of the Mazarin Stone," *Watson is told by Billy, Sherlock Holmes's page, that the day before, his master disguised himself as an old woman carrying a baggy parasol. In the following case, Sherlock employs a similar ruse, but considering the outcome, it is probable that this was the last time Holmes chose to go around in "drag"* . . .

The Affair of the Counterfeit Countess

BY CRAIG SHAW GARDNER

You are Dr. Watson, I presume?"

I looked up from my perusal of that day's *Times,* a bit startled by this intrusion. Before me stood a tall woman of mature years, dressed in the current layered style so favoured by women of breeding. She was a striking woman in more ways than one, her face arrestingly angular. The bits of colour she had applied to her cheeks and lips accented the paleness of her complexion and made her seem a bit severe. She was still a handsome woman in her way. But what was she doing in our drawing room in Baker Street? Why hadn't Mrs. Hudson announced her?

"I am the Baroness Von Stuppell," she ventured when I did not reply. From the directness of her gaze and the strictness of her bearing, she was a woman used to getting her way.

"Pardon me for my rudeness," I said, quickly rising from my chair. "Does Mr. Holmes know of this appointment?"

She nodded curtly. "Oh, I am quite sure Mr. Holmes is currently aware of my every move."

So the baroness and the detective were previously acquainted. Still, I wondered why Holmes had not apprised me of this appointment. I felt the slightest concern; what if something had happened to my friend?

"Well, perhaps there is something I can do for you until Mr. Holmes returns." I waved at a chair placed across from mine. "If you would care to take a seat?"

She sat with the practiced grace of a gentlewoman, and pulled a fan designed in the Oriental style from the large and ornately appliquéd bag she had brought with her. She took a moment to fan herself, no doubt fatigued by the lingering summer heat. She paused and observed me from behind her fan. "Doctor, I trust that I might confide in you, for you are certainly a man of the world." She turned her eyes down to the floor. "That is, if I do not presume too much."

"Forgive me, Baroness," I sputtered. There was something about her total propriety that took me aback. I wished for an instant that Holmes were here. Still, my powers of observation would have to serve. I struggled to find the proper words. "Baroness, there seems something about your manner. You seem to wish to keep a distance, as if you might have something to hide."

"Something to hide? Why, Doctor, whatever could you mean by that?" Despite the surprised tone of her voice, she did not remove her fan from before her face.

"Perhaps it is your nerves," I added quickly, "or perhaps—" I realized then that there was something else that I recognized about my visitor, something I had yet to put my finger upon. "—something we might yet determine. If we are to help you, you must confide in us completely. If you indeed know Mr. Holmes, you know there is no other way."

The baroness's laugh was most unladylike. "Watson, you are wise to my game!"

Holmes's voice shifted to his regular register. I should not have been surprised by the detective's deception. After all, he had played these tricks before. Still, I had to admit to a certain annoyance. "Holmes," I began. "Why must you always—"

The detective answered before I could even complete my thought. "As a doctor, you are trained to be observant. If my disguise might fool you, even for these few brief moments, I might then be able to pass out into the world."

"Pass out into the world? Then you mean—"

Holmes pulled off the bonnet and the wig beneath. "Yes, we must once again visit a certain embassy."

"Wearing a disguise?" I shot back, my annoyance still all too plain. "Pardon me, Holmes, but do you believe this is the best—"

"After what occurred yesterday morning?" He cut me off with a single motion of his lace-covered hand. "Watson, it is the only way."

At that, I thought back on recent incidents. My annoyance evaporated at once, for I had to agree.

It was only the day before that we were introduced to the troubles of a small Balkan country. Holmes asked me to accompany him to an appointment involving a case "of some interest," as he phrased it. Though I pressed him on the topic, he would say no more.

Holmes and I were less than a block away from the tiny foreign embassy in a very fashionable section of London when we heard the explosion.

"A bomb, no doubt," my friend remarked to me, not even breaking his stride. "In a carriage in front of the embassy. I had been expecting as much."

It was all very well for Sherlock Holmes to expound upon his theories, but I was a doctor and felt it was my duty to rush ahead to aid the wounded. I ran about the corner to see a great blackened spot before the iron gate that guarded the embassy. I called out my profession, in case there were any in need of me.

A tall, well-appointed man in a well-pressed uniform stepped from the middle of the devastation. A large hole stood in a brick wall by his side, the iron-work to either side twisted hideously by the force of the explosion.

The man smiled pleasantly at my approach despite the fact that he obviously had been shaken by the explosion.

"Most generous of you, Doctor. However—" He paused, and bowed to another who came up by my side. I glanced that way and discovered that Holmes had only been seconds behind me. The fellow in the uniform was a gentleman of such breeding that he immediately put us both at our ease. He nodded to me, to acknowledge that his answer now included both Holmes and myself. "The damage has been done to property, rather than to people, in large part due to your letter."

"You are Colonel Gelthelm?" Holmes enquired.

"The same," the colonel agreed. He smiled at the detective. "Most fortunately, no one was hurt. We are most grateful for your warning."

So Holmes had already alerted the embassy. Apparently the explosion had only been a surprise to me. I looked at my old friend. He spoke before I could even frame a rebuke.

"Watson, the evidence was everywhere. Most obvious, of course, were certain developments in the foreign columns in the news."

I nodded. Even I knew of the great upheavals all these small Balkan republics had been experiencing of late.

"And of course," Holmes continued, "a quick glance at the shipping news told me of the arrival of a boat from this embassy's home country. And it would be remiss of me not to have noticed that announced lecture series to be delivered by Professor Van Zummann."

"Van Zummann?" Here was a name that even I was familiar with. "You mean the anarchist?"

That he was lecturing should have come as no surprise. Living in such a metropolitan district as London, one might be exposed to every view imaginable. All very well when people were willing to conduct themselves in a civilized fashion. However, things seemed to happen about Van Zummann that were anything but civilized.

Holmes nodded. "Despite his radical views, Van Zummann has committed no crime."

I could not believe that Holmes was discussing this fellow so calmly. "No crime for which he has been convicted!"

Holmes nodded. "Most astute, Watson, for I know from my dealings with Scotland Yard that Van Zummann's name has arisen on more than one occasion concerning unsolved crimes—and murders." He nodded to the blackened gate before us. "There is an assassin at large, Watson—a man, I believe, who considers himself a master of disguise, for the description of the guilty party varies slightly in every case, even though there are certain common qualities of stature and bearing." The detective's tone was dismissive, for both he and I knew the true master of disguise here. "And Van Zummann has often been found, a day or two before the event, in the vicinity of these heinous crimes."

"Pardon," Colonel Gelthelm interrupted. "But a gentleman of your acquaintance has been here before you, and might hold something useful." He pointed to the embassy steps, still unharmed beyond the blasted gate. "I took the liberty of calling the police."

"A wise precaution," Holmes agreed. Both he and I turned towards the steps to see a familiar figure scowling in our direction as he approached.

"Inspector Lestrade!" I called. He winced at the mention of his name, as though, at the moment, he found no joy in being a policeman. Still, he nodded at both of us in turn.

"Mr. Holmes. Dr. Watson. I have passed a most unrewarding few moments within these walls."

"Then you were here before the explosion, Lestrade?" I asked.

My question only caused his grimace to deepen. "A lot of good it did." I had rarely seen the inspector so out of sorts.

"There was little you could do," Holmes replied. "The carriage would have appeared quite suddenly."

"It was an apple cart, actually, with no horses attached," the uniformed gentleman amended most politely. "One moment, there appeared to be a great crowd about the thing, half a dozen people or more. The next, the crowd was gone, and the cart was pushed against the gate."

Holmes nodded as if this was precisely what he had expected to hear. "It is the manner of such things. If I recall, there was a similar occurrence in Belgrade only three months ago."

"So you know of Belgrade?" the colonel asked with obvious admiration. "Because they were unprepared, the devastation to that embassy was far worse."

Holmes glanced back at the street, his face disturbed by the slightest of frowns. "I do not expect this to be their only attempt. And the next will be far more subtle." He turned back to the uniformed man. "I will need to speak with everyone within the embassy."

For once, the other lost his smile. "I am afraid that is quite impossible."

"I assure you," Holmes replied calmly, "I am the soul of discretion."

"Your reputation precedes you in this matter," the other agreed. "Unfortunately, even that will mean nothing to the Grand Duke."

"I can certainly vouch for that," Lestrade interrupted. "The difficulty, that is. He simply refused to see me!"

Colonel Gelthelm nodded his head brusquely at Lestrade's statement. "The duke has taken over our little embassy in order to put some distance between himself and the troubles we are having at home. Perhaps in reaction to that, he guards his time jealously."

"Even if the Duke's life is in danger?" I asked incredulously.

"Alas, the duke is a difficult man. He deals very brusquely with affairs of state. Nothing is allowed to interfere with his social calendar."

"Perhaps," my friend replied, "we might find a way around that difficulty."

Holmes's voice pulled me from my reverie. "You recall how we left the embassy, Watson. I have been in touch with the uniformed man with whom we spoke, Colonel Gelthelm. He will provide us certain assistance."

Once again, Holmes's plans were far beyond me. "Assistance? Assistance with what?"

"The embassy is hosting a tea this very afternoon, and the baroness will put in an appearance."

"You mean you intend to go into this strange place, alone and in disguise?" Even though I knew Holmes made a habit of this sort of thing, I thought it particularly unwise in this instance, for more than one reason. "There is no telling where Von Zummann may strike!"

"Exactly, Watson. I will not make a move without you."

"You wish *me* to come along?" Apparently, I was to be continually astonished.

Holmes rose then, smiling as he straightened his skirt. "It is not at all out of the question for the baroness to bring her personal physician!"

So it was that, later that afternoon, I found myself once again at the embassy gate, this time in the company of the Baroness Von Stuppell.

I had decided, for the ruse to succeed, I would indeed have to think of Holmes as the baroness. As Holmes reminded me, our primary purpose was to prevent Von Zummann from causing any more mischief. Anything else would be unthinkable.

The baroness stumbled a bit as she descended from the carriage. She gave me the slightest of coquettish smiles. "I could have had a bit more practice with the shoes." I felt my cheeks redden slightly at Holmes's—rather, the Baroness's—difficulty. Perhaps it would be better if I looked straight ahead.

Colonel Gelthelm was waiting for us at the gate. "Ah. The tea has just begun. Punctuality is much prized in my country." The colonel, ever the gentleman, did not comment on Holmes's appearance.

He waved us forward with a white-gloved hand. "Come. There is a side entrance reserved for special guests."

The baroness curtsied ever-so-slightly and followed the colonel along the walk to a second iron gate. I took up the rear, following her small, quick, yet measured steps, her bustle swaying ever-so-slightly before me. Even I, who knew him so well, found all traces of Holmes absent from the actions of this noblewoman.

Taking a ring of keys from his belt, the colonel unlocked the second gate. He led us through a doorway beyond, into the interior of the embassy, filled with rich drapes and even finer carpets. From the quiet opulence of the halls, there was certainly no hint of the unrest in their home country.

But even the rich carpets could not hush the commotion rapidly approaching behind us.

"Out of my way!" a voice shouted hoarsely. "State business!"

The colonel turned to look at the disturbance. "Please, Count Orlock. These are our guests."

"Guests?" the voice called back derisively. "All step aside for the decision makers of the realm!"

At that, the baroness and I turned about as well. We were being approached by three men in dark suits, two of whom were quite tall and muscular. The third individual was much shorter and smaller boned than the others. He was also the one doing the shouting.

"I warn you! Out of the way or heads will roll!" With that, the diminutive count walked straight into the baroness, no doubt proposing to brush the intruder aside. The count bounced off the baroness's ample chest. The baroness did not move. Count Orlock picked himself off the floor as if he had meant to fall there all along. He quickly walked around the lady, shouting for the others to follow. The two larger men glared at the baroness as they passed as well.

The colonel coughed apologetically. "You will have to forgive Count Orlock. He becomes frustrated with the way the grand duke conducts his affairs."

The baroness spread her fan so she might look over it to the military man. "I have heard rumours of this, that he surrounds himself with women?"

Colonel Gelthelm nodded ruefully. "Our duke has gotten on in years, and claims he will spend what little time remains to him in those pursuits he truly enjoys."

I might have found this more astonishing if there were not so many things here already beyond belief. Still I felt compelled to ask, "How does any business get done?"

The colonel's expression became even more pained. "The duke will entertain certain matters of importance, so long as they are presented to him by members of the fairer sex."

"So my information was correct," Holmes replied softly. For an instant, his tone reflected the detective and not the baroness.

The colonel sighed in agreement. "It is a game—but then, can't the same be said of all politics? But come, I must announce you to the duke."

He led us further down the hall to a double doorway guarded by a pair of men in grey uniforms similar to the colonel's. They snapped to attention as we approached, then, at a single word from their colonel, they smartly reached forward and swung the two doors open wide.

A grand salon lay beyond, filled with fifty or more finely dressed people. What struck me first about the crowd before us was that it was primarily composed of females; at a cursory glance, women seemed to outnumber men by five or six to one.

"The duke is in his glory." The colonel spoke to both of us in a low tone. "If you would follow me?"

We boldly followed our guide into the room filled with women. And such women, ranging from their early twenties to perhaps four times that age; yet all shared such a richness of dress and refinement that even a world-traveled physician such as myself felt close to overwhelmed. The baroness, in her superbly tailored but sensible tweeds, seemed decidedly underdressed in such a company. Still, she glanced neither right nor left as she followed the colonel to our goal, paying no mind to the hushed conversations of the many women we passed, all of whom turned to regard the newcomer as we strode near.

"If you might forgive us, my Duke!" the colonel called out as we approached a tight-knit group before us, with half a dozen women surrounding a white-haired man.

The man looked distractedly away from where one lovely young lass stroked his brow.

"Eh?" he muttered. "How dare you disturb my conversation?"

"I do not mean to disturb you in the least," the colonel interjected smoothly. "Rather, I wish to bring added interest to your afternoon's socializing." He motioned to the woman at my side. "May I present the Baroness Von Stuppell?"

"You certainly may." The duke freed himself from the crowd of women and approached the baroness, his face lit by the brightest of smiles. "It is an honour. You are a distant relative, I hear? It is a problem with royalty. We are all related somehow!"

With that, he glanced at me, his voice shifting quickly from pleasure to disdain. "And who is this?"

"Only my personal physician," the baroness replied. A lace-covered hand rose to her brow. "Doctor, my salts!"

The baroness swayed back and forth, nearly overcome by her surroundings. I fished in my medical bag and found a small bottle that would look appropriate to the purpose. I handed it to the baroness, who allowed one delicate sniff before returning it to me.

"I am afraid I am quite overwhelmed to be in this place," the baroness cried, fluttering her fan in our host's direction. "I have so looked forward to being in your presence."

I feared the baroness might be overreacting, but the duke appeared quite charmed.

"We should give our new arrival a seat!" He shooed away a nearby matron. "Baroness, if you would please?"

She very definitely curtsied this time. "So kind."

"You are the sort of woman to whom I could act in no other way!" the duke declared.

"I have heard, my good Duke, many tales of your refinement." She giggled ever-so-slightly as she took her seat. "I must confess, however, that I did not expect to find someone so intelligent. Or so vital."

The duke puffed out his chest and stroked his medals. "We do not have enough contact with the London gentility. Surely, if more women like you exist beyond these walls, my embassy becomes more like a prison."

"More like a retreat, I would say, a beautiful place where one might find refinement"—the baroness looked at the duke with a certain directness—"if one only knew where to look."

Colonel Gelthelm drew me aside.

"The duke, my dear Doctor, is totally smitten. Finally, a cool, continental noblewoman of mature years who can challenge him."

I was struck speechless. Didn't the colonel know the baroness's secret? What if Holmes had not told him of the deception?

"I can see the wisdom now in the detective's plan," the colonel continued in a confidential tone. "Perhaps the duke will heed our warning if it should come from such a source."

What could I do but nod?

I heard a delicate cough near my shoulder. I glanced over to see a much calmer Count Orlock. He nodded pleasantly to both myself and the colonel, perhaps wishing to make up for past improprieties.

"The duke will have a new conquest before the night is done," he said in a voice just above a whisper.

Perhaps, I thought, the baroness was being a bit too successful. I looked back to where she was still engaged in conversation with the duke. She made a small excuse and took a step away. The duke laughed heartily and took a step to close the gap.

"Surely," the baroness said demurely, "I am taking up far too much of your time."

But the duke only laughed again. "My time? It is our time now! The only way you shall be free of me is if you disappear from the face of the Earth!"

"You flatter me far too greatly." The baroness waved her fan. "I am just a poor child of the Continent, adrift in London society."

"No matter!" the duke rejoined. "With me you shall be very rich!"

The baroness looked away. "A breath of air would be nice. You will excuse me while I take a look at the stars?"

But the duke would give no ground. "The only stars I need," he purred, "are in your eyes."

The baroness's fan fluttered faster than ever before. "Doctor! My salts!"

Even her suitor took a step away at that. "A glass of water for the dear baroness!" the duke called.

I thought a little distance might be in order here as well. I purposefully stepped between the duke and the object of his affection. "Water will do her no good if you do not give her air."

The duke and his entourage dutifully took a few more steps away.

"Thank you, Watson," the baroness whispered close by my ear. "I'm afraid the duke's attentions can be a bit suffocating. Still, I think we should remain. The assassin might strike at any time!"

A glass of water was thrust into my hand. I glanced up, a bit taken aback by the heavy-set serving women, so different from the delicate nobility all around us. The serving staff had no doubt been recruited from the peasant class back home.

The baroness raised her fan so that she might sip her water in private.

"Ah," she said at last as she relinquished her glass to one of the servers. "I am better already." She lowered her fan. "Duke, there is much I would love to ask you about your country."

The duke smiled at that, stepping close once more. "Surely then, you will stay and join us for dinner."

But one of the surrounding women spoke up. "You monopolize our new arrival, you naughty duke! Come, Baroness, we will get you some air. Let us go and freshen up!"

My worst fears were realized. We had fallen victim to the habits of women everywhere. The baroness could do nothing but obey! I watched helplessly as the baroness and half a dozen other women moved towards that place where no man might go.

Count Orlock had once again placed his short stature before me. He seemed to want to make small talk about the baroness's habits. I could not truly concentrate on the conversation. Excepting a certain woman in green, Holmes had never seemed to have much use for the fairer sex. How would he fare among the company of women?

The count went on and on. I could do little but nod. Once I had evaded his questions concerning my companion, the small man wanted to talk about nothing but politics!

"I have so little opportunity to explore the English mind. Compared to my home country—pfahh!"

I am afraid that the conversation was getting on my nerves. I snapped a response: "Perhaps you might have more opportunity to explore things if you presented yourself a little less—forcefully."

The count seemed unfazed by my anger. He simply shook his head and replied, "One must make one's own opportunities, my dear Doctor."

But the women had returned. And they were laughing, the baroness along with all the rest! A certain young woman at the edge of the group turned to me with great excitement.

"Oh, Doctor!" the young woman related in the most breathless of tones. "Your baroness is a marvel! She is a fountain of information—what she has told us of skirt length and fabrics and the changes in number of petticoats. She knows every variation of dress over the past fifty years! I had no idea that fashion was so fickle!"

I smiled at the news. Holmes would of course lead with his strengths. My worry had been needless once again. Throughout our association, the detective would never cease to surprise me.

I turned back to the baroness, and saw her waving for me with her fan.

"I have gained some useful information as well, Watson," the baroness confided when I reached her side. "Unless I am very much mistaken, the assassin will not be among the women. Or at least these particular women."

I longed to ask the detective how or why he had discovered this, but the duke approached again, ending all attempts at conversation.

"I have taken the liberty to have my kitchen prepare some of my country's specialties." He waved about the room, and I saw that the heavy-set serving women had returned, this time bearing great silver trays piled with foodstuffs.

The duke leaned close to the baroness. "The Breaded Codfish Soaked in Beer is a particular delight!"

The baroness fanned herself. "Indeed?"

The duke discerned her meaning. "Ah." He leapt forward to snatch something from a passing tray. "Perhaps you would care for something lighter? These pastries are filled with our native berries."

The count was once again before us. "But Duke! Surely you wish to sample the Fannsnufel!" One of the large serving women was at his side, her tray piled high with some large, puffy white concoction.

"Ah, Count!" The duke swallowed the berry trifle and nodded to the bloated white things. "Fannsnufel is my passion! Well— one of my passions." For once, both duke and count were all smiles. Only the baroness was frowning.

The count waved away the questing fingers of the duke's entourage from the silver tray. "We should always let the duke sample first. As he said, it is his passion. And I understand that this plate was made specially."

The duke acted as if he barely even heard the small man, his gaze fixed resolutely on the tall woman in tweed. "These are indeed the pride of my native land. Perhaps we should give some to our honoured guest."

The count stared at the duke as if the elder man had spoken the unthinkable. "What if they are sour? You know yourself that if the heavy cream, brown sugar and wartroot are not mixed precisely, disaster may result."

But the duke did not take his eyes from the baroness. "Perhaps, then, we might sample them together. I will feed one to you, and then, perhaps—"

The baroness raised her fan. "As eager as I am to sample the delights of your kitchen, I feel that I must pass, and I suggest that you pass as well."

"So you suggest I save my appetite for other things?" On a commoner, the look upon the duke's face might have been taken for a leer.

"No," the baroness replied. "The count appears as if he is much neglected. I suggest that the first taste of Fannsnufel should be his."

"A capital suggestion from a generous lady!" the duke agreed.

But the count looked pale. "I have no appetite for pastries."

The baroness stared at him. "Especially none prepared with your sister's recipe?"

The count gasped. "What do you know of my sister?"

"Only that before she left, she hired and supervised the kitchen and serving staffs. She had always felt the position beneath her. Not to mention that she conveniently left just before you arrived." The baroness smiled slightly in my direction. "It is amazing what you might learn in a private conversation with the women of the court."

"Ah, that countess," the duke murmured. "A beautiful woman, but so private. She did not wish to have too much known about her family, I believe. The very existence of Count Orlock here came as a complete surprise!"

"What are you insinuating?" the count demanded, his voice breaking with the emotion.

Colonel Gelthelm stepped to my side.

"Is there some difficulty here?"

"Ah!" the baroness cried. "A wonderful source of information! I pray, Colonel, you may allow me to ask you a few questions of a delicate nature?"

"If the duke does not object, I am your man."

"You will have to stand in line behind me, Colonel!" the duke rejoined. "But by all means, answer the delightful lady's questions!"

The baroness nodded graciously. "I understand that, besides the count, the embassy staff is very—close knit?"

The colonel cleared his throat. "Ah yes, well, you see, I am a married man. But I have heard that certain of my officers are somewhat—familiar with certain ladies of the court."

"They are all strangers together in a strange land," the baroness agreed. "It is to be expected. Yet the count seems to be as standoffish as—say, his sister?"

The count seemed genuinely uncomfortable. "I find my pleasures elsewhere."

"In Fannsnufel, perhaps?" The baroness snatched one of the large and gooey pastries from the tray. "Come, take a bite."

The count turned his head away.

"Perhaps knowledge of your family has taken away your appetite," the baroness coaxed. "You see, I know of your stepfather, a certain Professor Van Zummann."

"Van Zummann?" Colonel Gelthelm cried in alarm.

"Perhaps when bombs do not work, Count," the Baroness continued, "you find subtler means of death, like poisoning the Fannsnufel. Or should I say—Countess?"

"Enough!" The count pulled a knife from deep within his coat. His—or was it her?—voice seemed to rise with every word. "Poison is too good for this lecherous duke. I will kill him myself!"

The colonel took a step forward, hoping no doubt to intercede. He paused as he saw that three of the serving women had drawn knives as well.

The baroness reeled away. "Doctor, my salts!"

Everyone turned to look at me as I fumbled for my medical bag. I wished I had had the foresight to bring my revolver from Baker Street. What did Holmes want me to do?

"If you wish to get to the duke, you will have to get by me first." I looked up to see that the baroness stood once more, but now, in her hand, she held my revolver!

"It is amazing what one can carry in one's bag," she remarked casually. "But I assure you, Countess, I know how to use this, and, should you approach the duke, I will not hesitate to fire!"

"You are a woman of action!" the unmasked countess exclaimed. "Oh, how I have longed for a life such as yours. I was forced into this by my backwards nation! Look at this pitiful duke, so typical of the ruling class! Only someone as versed in politics as myself should be allowed to rule this land!"

But the baroness would not be moved. Colonel Gelthelm quickly shouted orders, and the uniformed sentries entered the room, their own guns at the ready.

"You see," the baroness explained as the miscreants were led away, "the countess, no doubt working under her stepfather's orders, set up the means to poison the duke. But since she was in charge of kitchen staff, she would immediately fall under suspicion if such a thing were to happen. That is why she had to disappear, and the so-called Count Orlock took her place."

"A countess masquerading as a count!" the grand duke marvelled. "Who could imagine such a thing!"

The baroness dropped her gun into her bag and once again took up her fan. "Oh, I assure you, my dear Duke, I can imagine that and more."

If anything, this all appeared to make the duke more excited. "But Baroness, you reveal a new part of your personality. You are indeed a woman of action! It makes me desire you all the more!"

The baroness bowed her head. "Alas, my Duke. I am afraid my destiny lies elsewhere. I must go."

She turned and strode gracefully but briskly from the ballroom. I nearly had to run to follow.

"You cannot desert me like this!" The duke's voice followed us from the room. "My life shall never be the same! If you exist, I shall find you!"

"Then," Holmes spoke softly to me, "the baroness must cease to exist."

Indeed, not a week later, we received a sealed letter at 221B Baker Street from that same embassy, a letter from the grand duke, a missing-person case. The duke was beside himself. Price was no object.

Holmes, regretfully, had to tell the duke he was otherwise involved. It was one case, in fact, that Holmes said might elude him forever. And a case that, while I write of it as I do all the rest, might best stay sealed for an equal time.

Irene Adler got the best of Sherlock Holmes in "A Scandal in Bohemia," and twenty years later, her daughter did the same (according to "The Second Generation," a radio dramatization by Anthony Boucher and Denis Green, available from Simon & Schuster Audioworks). In the suppressed, oddly timely manuscript below, however, the woman actually seeks Holmes's aid, and this time, at least, she means to play it straight with him. Or does she?

The *Woman*

BY ALINE MYETTE-VOLSKY

Our visitor that winter evening was a lady, and a lovely one, most modishly turned out. I noticed Holmes's keen eye narrow as he bent over her ringless hand, a hand surely meant for the display of expensive rings, or so most observers would have thought. In fact I myself had noticed the obvious lack. Perhaps my close association with my friend was beginning to lend a sharper edge to my own powers of observation, or perhaps the fact that the lady's hand was gloveless as well as ringless had pointed it out to me.

I awaited his first words with some curiosity.

"Mrs. Norton" (so he had recognized her). With a nod he indicated a comfortable chair near the hearth where the firelight and the mantel lamp would conspire to light her facial expressions. To my shame I felt only amusement as I saw her balk his purpose by shifting her chair slightly as she seated herself. Now her features were somewhat shadowed and more difficult to read. In the face of

177

this small setback Holmes showed no discomfiture. I should have been surprised if he had.

"Mrs. Norton," he repeated, "I am pleased to renew your acquaintance, although the signs of urgency which mark your arrival at my door give me cause for a certain amount of concern on your behalf."

Her head came up at that. "Signs of urgency, Mr. Holmes? I am unaware of displaying any such signs."

"When a lady has left home in such a distressed frame of mind that she has forgotten to wear gloves, and her journey has been so precipitous that her veil blows in and out with the swiftness of her breathing, I take these to be signs of anxiety."

She nodded slowly. "Of course you are right, Mr. Holmes. I had almost forgotten the observant study you habitually make of your visitors. And yet it is for that very reason that I am here, to take advantage, if I may, of those powers for which you are so justly famous."

"Thank you for your faith, and I assure you that my so-called powers will be put to work for you as willingly as they were used against you during our last meeting."

He referred, of course, to the scandal in Bohemia when the king of that country, about to be married, had called upon Holmes to retrieve certain compromising letters and photographs of the glamorous opera star Irene Adler, as she then was. The great detective consultant had developed a respect and admiration for *"the woman,"* as he thereafter referred to her, which to my knowledge he conceded to no other of her sex.

Irene Norton sighed and lifted her veil, revealing the beautiful face and great glowing eyes which had helped to make her the toast of Milan and the jewel of La Scala. "I have long been the designer of my own destiny," she told us, "or so I have thought myself. To a woman as independent as I, the reminder that there are influences which can work me personal harm or financial damage comes as an unwelcome surprise. And although I have racked my brain—and believe me, Mr. Holmes and Dr. Watson, I have!—I have been completely unable to discover the source or sources of these attacks on me or the reasons behind them."

Holmes's long chemically stained fingers, witnesses to his years of scientific experimentation, tapped the arms of his chair. "When you mention attacks, madam, surely you do not mean attacks against your person?"

"Oh, but I do mean that. On a number of recent occasions I have been deliberately shoved by passing strangers; yesterday I was even pushed into an open doorway by a gang of street arabs—not hurt, mind you, but nasty language was used and my garments pulled about quite roughly." She took a deep breath. "Now I am not unfamiliar with harassment, sir. If you will recollect my experience with the king of Bohemia—"

"But in that case you held something which was dangerous to him and which you refused to relinquish. So there was a reason."

"So there was a reason. Yes. But in this case I pose no danger to—to anyone, so why am I being harassed in this increasingly alarming fashion? Who is my enemy? And what does he—or she—want of me?"

Holmes got up and moved over to the window which over-looked Baker Street, where he stood holding aside two inches of the drapery so that he could look out into the lamplit darkness. "No one in sight," he remarked. "For the moment, at least, you seem to have shaken off your annoyers. I am, however, not convinced that the minor rudenesses you've been subjected to are actually anything more than coincidences. Your street arabs, for instance . . ."

" 'Minor rudenesses,' Mr. Holmes? Such as the burglary of my suite in the best hotel in London? The theft of my jewels by my new lady's maid after three days in my employ?"

Holmes moved his length away from the window to stand beside the fire, his look suddenly more attentive. "No, I must admit that where there occurs a sudden series of uncommon events, either all good or all bad, the probabilities are that they are being directed by a purpose rather than by chance. Please describe to me more precisely the occurrences which have brought you to me in such haste this evening."

"You wish me to describe each incident in detail?"

"As minutely as possible, if you please."

She frowned in thought for a moment and Holmes took his keen gaze away from her face, as if to allow her a sense of mental privacy while she cogitated. It occurred to me that he was not always so thoughtful.

After a moment Irene Norton spoke again, her voice reflective. "To begin with, I would guess that this—campaign against me—"

Holmes pounced. "Campaign?"

"Yes, that is how I am forced to see it: a campaign of persecution. The petty annoyances such as the theft of my newspaper from before my door in the mornings and the scorching of a Worth gown I had given to my maid to be pressed (that incident was what led me to hire a new maid). As I've mentioned, she stole every piece of jewelry I owned, left my boxes bare of a single personal treasure—oh, but she was a merciless little thief!"

Her remarkable eyes flashed and Holmes darted an amused glance at me. "As far as thieves are concerned, madam, mercy toward the victim is not their strong suit. They do not leave consoling souvenirs behind them."

"I'm aware of that, sir, but in this case I had a confidential conversation with this girl and found her so sympathetic in manner that I confided to her my deep regard for one or two special jewels, gifts from a very highly placed Personage: a diamond sea horse, my set of emeralds . . . And to think she stole those from me as well—oh, I suppose I've been a trusting fool and I'm ashamed to have you gentlemen see me in that light."

"Madam," Holmes said quite gently for him, "feel no shame. Your faith in humanity is far from unbecoming. Now do you have more of these hostile acts to relate to us?"

"Yes. On another occasion I was riding in a hansom cab on my way to an appointment in Threadneedle Street, and a man jumped onto the cab's running board. He swung himself into the carriage and ordered me to avert my face so I couldn't see his. I simply sat there, terrified, and did as I was told."

"Not surprising. A ruffianly type, was he?"

"No, that was the odd thing: he was well dressed and his voice was—I can only describe it as gentlemanly." She shook her head slightly. "When I think back on it I find myself puzzled. That voice—"

"Had you heard it before?"

"I can't say that exactly, but the tones themselves were somehow familiar, not dangerous— Oh, I know I'm not being helpful, but—"

She broke off. Holmes was strolling the hearthrug back and forth, his head bent. "I assure you that you *are* being helpful, Mrs. Norton. What exactly did he say, this unwelcome fellow passenger of yours?"

"That is the strangest part of all. He said, 'Just continue to do what you're doing and your life as you know it is over.' "

" 'And your life . . . is over' In other words he threatened your life?"

She hesitated. "It sounded more like a warning than an actual threat."

"But he didn't indicate what it is that you've been doing that is so displeasing to—someone?"

"No."

"Well, it is clear enough to me that the plan against you aims at subtlety, but the mind which evolved it is not devious enough to achieve it. For example," said Holmes, hands flat upon his thighs as he leaned forward, "I submit that the person or persons who developed this plot are not criminals but people of British background, education and interest and that they firmly believe they are serving their country."

"Against *me?*" Even in the dimness one could sense her sudden pallor. "But that would be dreadful! What on earth would lead them to suppose such a thing?"

"They have their reasons. Some strong conviction is moving them, of that you may be certain, since they are hiring various substitutes to terrorize you and being careful to keep their own identity a secret—at least so far. I expect that to change. Perhaps one of these hirelings can be bribed to name a name if only we can lay our hands on him long enough to make him an offer."

"You mean a bribe." Her foot tapped the carpet in involuntary protest. Holmes asked abruptly, "Do you have any idea at all what all this could be about? Have you any reason to think you have enemies here in London? Any reason whatsoever?"

She shook her head, her eyes on her own fingers as they smoothed her velvet bonnet ribbons.

Holmes regarded her thoughtfully, the firelight flickering on his gaunt features. Then he spoke. "If you will permit me to put it slangily, this campaign, as you term it, does not hang together. You tell me of a burglary *and* a threat *and* physical harassment—no. It offers too many different features, and the picture which they present is like an eccentric portrait, the mouth of which has been painted by Gainsborough, the eyes by Holbein, the nose and chin by Reynolds. You may imagine what the resultant picture would be: utter confusion. But where is the connection, one would ask. There must be, there has to be a connection which will tie these features together."

He turned to me abruptly. "Do you follow my reasoning here, Watson?"

I have seldom been able to follow his reasoning at the start of a case and he knew it, but he always had hopes. "Not clearly, my dear fellow. I must admit that any connection between the episodes Mrs. Norton has just described eludes me."

"Exactly so. It has all been deliberately designed to elude us, Watson, because that very important connection will uncover the mystery of this entire unpleasant persecution."

"I hope so," Mrs. Norton sighed. The clock struck nine and she rose to leave, pulling down her veil and settling her wool-and-velvet outer garments about her. "I've taken up too much of your evening . . ."

Holmes saw her downstairs and walked her to the nearest hackstand, where he put her into a cab.

When he returned to our rooms he said only, "The woman has agreed, but only reluctantly, to offer a generous reward, a bribe, actually, for the name of her enemy." He shook his head again. "It's a step in the right direction, but she isn't being candid with us, Watson. She is holding something back, and whatever it is might very well jeopardize my defense. However, I am determined to triumph in her behalf in spite of her."

That was all he would say. He then made a beeline for his pipe and his pouch of what I considered inhumanly strong tobacco. Seated in his favorite armchair he sank into such a brown study that I knew myself to be invisible to him for the remainder of the evening, and I retired quietly to my own quarters.

Holmes was certain where he wanted to begin his investigation. On the following morning, he and I visited the lobby of the Hotel ————, which Mrs. Norton was making her temporary London home. She had been vague about her future plans as well as the whereabouts of her seldom mentioned husband, Mr. Godfrey Norton. Privately I wondered what had happened to that marriage but personal gossip rarely interested Holmes and he had not pursued it.

I was therefore the more puzzled when he moved directly to a table near the front desk that held the latest newspapers for the convenience of the hotel's guests. He picked one up and turned his attention to, of all things, the society pages.

"My dear fellow," I protested, "may we not at least sit down to read?"

Absently and without setting aside his paper, Holmes moved to a nearby banquette which could seat the two of us, and we sat there side by side, he reading, I silent. He was completely unconscious of his surroundings, or so he seemed. He continued to absorb every frivolous word of the engagement notices, entertainment descriptions and birth announcements, and I continued to wonder why.

At last he nodded to himself, folded the paper and looked about him with interest, although there was little of interest to be seen, to my way of thinking. A tall man stood a few feet away leaning against the desk, smoking and conversing with the clerk; a cleaning woman knelt in a far corner working at removing a fresh stain from the carpet; a young couple on a neighboring banquette spoke together in low tones, and various other guests or visitors moved about in different directions. All seemed very ordinary.

It was not to remain so.

Holmes rising, I rose also and accompanied him as he walked over to the desk, waved the clerk to one side, and to my embarrassment addressed himself to the tall man without a moment's hesitation. "I am Sherlock Holmes and this is my friend, Dr. Watson, who is, like you, a veteran of the sunnier climes of India."

The stranger looked uncertain. His gaze moved from one to the other of us. "Do I know you gentlemen?"

"No," Holmes said baldly, "but I believe we know you. Late of Her Majesty's Service, I should say at a guess: perhaps too fond of gambling but far from lucky, which has been an unfortunate combination for you. It probably got you cashiered and brought you to your present level of threatening women for money."

"Sir!" He was tall enough to stand eye to eye with Holmes, which he did, and his look was not cordial. "It is too early in the day for public drunkenness but I can attribute your behaviour to nothing else—"

"How much were you paid to abandon your standards as a gentleman, ex-Captain, or is it ex-Major?"

The man paled and seemed to lose an inch or two of stature. "I don't understand—you must take me for someone—I deny—"

Holmes cut him off. "Your denials will serve no purpose.

What I propose instead is more practical, a gift of money, a generous gift, for the identity of your employer."

The man stood silent, his tongue moistening his lips.

"Well?" Holmes, sharp-voiced.

"I cannot oblige you with any names, sir," the ex-officer said stiffly.

"You refuse?"

"I repeat, I cannot oblige. The simple fact is that I myself do not know the identity of my employer. The instructions regarding my—er—meeting with the lady were slipped under my door along with a sum of money, and the source is as much a mystery to me as it is to you. So I can be of no help whatsoever in the matter of naming names."

Holmes's expression did not alter. He merely reached into his pocket and withdrew a small tip. The other man's eyes did not meet ours as the coins slid into his own pocket.

Holmes was shaking his head as we left the hotel.

We next made the rounds of a few jewelry stores in the vicinity of the Hotel ——— and in the third one Holmes's questions brought results. Yes, the proprietor did occasionally buy valuable pieces from private parties. No, never from doubtful sources, only from persons whose obvious quality justified their claim to ownership. He was certain that Mr. Holmes would understand how careful one must be of one's business reputation. Yes, he had in his cases just such pieces as the gentleman described: the diamond sea horse, the emeralds. Magnificent, were they not? Worthy of Her Majesty herself, although naturally she would never wear such inappropriate pieces with her mourning. But alas, no, the lady who had sold them to him had remained incognita. Yes indeed, her quality had been unmistakable, but he had no idea of her identity and no description to furnish. One must understand that with the heavy veils the ladies wore nowadays . . .

"Failure again, Holmes," I commiserated with him as we regained the sidewalk.

"Quite the reverse, my friend. We are beginning to make rapid progress: in fact we are two-thirds of the way to the answer we seek."

I looked my surprise. "Oh, come now, Holmes! The single fact which you've ascertained is that a lady presented Mrs. Norton's jewels for sale. It could even have been Mrs. Norton herself. Has that occurred to you?"

"It has even occurred to me that it could have been a man dressed as a woman. Remember, Watson, 'with the heavy veils the ladies wear nowadays . . .' "

The winter wind drove against us as we walked, and I thrust my hands deep into my pockets. Holmes, however, seemed serenely unaware of the cold. He had lost himself in his puzzle, and although I usually respected his moments of distraction I was now curious enough to break rather rudely into his thoughts.

"What on earth led you to believe the man in the hotel was Mrs. Norton's fellow-passenger in the hack?"

"Eh? Oh, as it turned out that was fairly easy. By sitting near the desk, I could note the speech patterns of anyone addressing the clerk. Those patterns were important to listen for: You'll recall that Mrs. Norton had not felt threatened by the man in the hack simply because his speech had been similar to that of her friends, her peers, so that she was unconsciously almost comfortable with him. That in turn indicated that the man presumably had been well educated and seen better days. Another expected factor: Our man in the hotel seemed almost to be stationed there in the lobby. Did you notice how casually he leaned against the desk? What better place to watch the comings and goings of the woman? There had to be someone assigned to do that. I suspect he's probably paid a crown or two a day to keep a watch on her."

"Assigned? By whom?"

"Well, yes, 'whom' is our problem, Watson, isn't it? But not for long. As I told you, we're closing in."

"But did you have no other clue that he was the man who had

jumped aboard the cab when you confronted him so—so brusquely?"

"You mean so rudely, Watson. Say what you mean precisely. Yes, naturally, I did have other clues: He was obviously a man who had lost his place in society, else he would never have been seen conversing so familiarly with a hotel employee. That in itself was highly indicative. And of course you must have noticed that the garments he wore, although once expensive, now have the seedy look of the over-worn and over-brushed, sure signs of a man's comedown in the world.

"So: Here we have an officer, ostracized by his own class, too young to be retired and athletic enough by the look of him to have swung himself aboard a moving carriage; and down on his luck besides, which in the army always means gambling; but one whose pride persists in trying to keep up appearances. Not exactly unusual, I'm afraid."

"Well, that all sounds plausible, I must admit, Holmes, but my curiosity is up over something you said last evening, something to the effect that your client was not being candid, as you put it, and her defense being in jeopardy."

Without answering, Holmes suddenly swung about so abruptly that I was startled, for with my coat collar pulled up about my ears I myself had noticed no sounds behind us. But he had.

"Aha!"

Following us was a small shabby group of small shabby boys. Woollen mufflers were secured about their necks and hung down to their broken-down boots, and running noses were the order of the day. They had stopped in their tracks at Holmes's "Aha!" and now they stood their ground, impudent and unafraid, or so I had to deduce from the fact that they made no attempt to sheer off.

"You've been following us for several hundred paces," my friend accused the tallest of the group. "Why? What do you mean by it? What do you imps of Satan hope to gain from trailing us, hmm?"

"Wot do anybody 'ope to gain from toffs like you? Not no hinvitation to tea, we don't. Wot we wants is to sell you sumfin. Got money on you, gents? Paper money? We seen you give 'im back there in the 'otel some o' your brass, but we don't take nuffin' wot rattles. So 'ows abaht it, gents? Make it worth yor wile, we will."

"I've been waiting for this," Holmes told me out of the corner of his mouth. "Now we're in business." And to the young bargainer, "I'm no banker and you'll get no pound notes from me, boy. But here …" He reached into a pocket and withdrew a few crowns. "Very well, then, if you're about to begin, begin. What is it you have to sell? We already know all about your jostling-about of a certain lady a few days ago, so don't think to sell us that; but on the other hand if you can tell us who put you up to it—" He jingled the coins in his hand and there was some muttering among the boys, but after a moment or two the leader stepped forward, almost tripping over his own muffler as he did so. I shall not attempt to reproduce more of his hideous Cockney sounds on paper, however.

"We was walking along that big crooked road in the park when along comes this great carriage, shiny and mostly bright black it was, with a gold picture on the side of it of one of them 'orrible animals sorta like a tiger with horns but not ezzactly. There was a lady inside and she called to us. Wasn't nobody else around, not no bobbies nor nothin', but we wasn't scared so we went closer to 'er. She leans out and tells us about the hotel lady and how to know her when we sees her, and how to pester her and follow her and bother her good when we gets the chance, scare her but not to hurt her, we wasn't. And then the lady in the carriage hands over paper money with her fingers held all stiff like she didn't want to touch us with her gloves on, even. She said for us not to tell nobody and looked at us bloody hard down her nose but like I said, we don't get scared easy. Expeshully not by no woman. Now ain't that good enough for yor bloody crowns, mister?"

"Almost good enough, Oliver Twist," Holmes told him. "Only

one more thing: Did the man who drove this 'bright black' carriage wear a uniform? That is to say, special clothes?"

"I well remember he did that, mister. All black and yellow like the carriage, it was."

"So," Holmes murmured aside to me. "And since everyone recognizes the Fitzbarry colors as well as the crest on her carriage it would seem she's decided to come out in the open at last. Perhaps now she'll dispense with the unpleasant pranks."

"Lady Fitzbarry? Isn't she the one they say is so close to the Queen?"

He cut me off. "No names, please, my friend. Not now, not ever. We are stepping close to the edge of perilously high places here, and we'd best watch our footing."

Turning back to the boys, Holmes began doling out crowns to each of them, which the leader promptly confiscated despite a momentary buzz of protest from the ranks. Another moment and they had all disappeared at top speed.

Holmes frowned after them absently. "It's time for us to begin pulling her chestnuts out of the fire—if we still can. At least now we know the 'whom' involved."

"But first," I said, "tell me this: will she be in danger? I mean Mrs. Norton, of course."

"I hope not, I intend not, but didn't I tell you she was not being candid? And mark my words, it could cost her dearly."

"Not her life, Holmes! Don't tell me that—"

"Oh, no, not her life, but her musical career as well as her entrée into Society, not only here but everywhere on the Continent. Remember the soldier's prediction? 'Life as you know it will be over.' He was speaking the truth. Actually, for a woman like her it would be as much murder as if they had slit her throat. A kind of bloodless assassination."

"Do you believe she's fully aware of the trouble she's in?"

"No, because like all beautiful women she is overconfident, and in this case the admiration of a very highly placed Personage would serve to keep her safe, or so she thinks. She is wrong, of course."

"Holmes, I'm freezing . . ."

Inside the welcome warmth of a small nearby coffeehouse we loosened our coats, placed our hats on the shelf under our chairs, and over the coffee's steam and the smoke from Holmes's cigarette I prodded him to continue his character description of the woman who was his client of the moment.

"I was talking about how unaware she is of the depth of the trouble which threatens her," Holmes replied. "She is hiding behind her previous successes and she will go on hiding behind them until I can pry her loose from her delusions. You see, Watson, in order to understand Irene you must realize that her beauty is the currency of her life: It's what she has always used to buy everything she has ever wanted and it has never failed her. And now she's using it (and this time unwisely) to enjoy the favours of a very highly placed Personage. Why not? Her personal history tells her that she never fails, so she employs her wit, charm and beauty (and for this particular conquest a talent for playing cards and an eye for horses as well)— all irresistible to him. Small wonder his people are worried, eh, Watson? He has already been cited more than once in the divorce courts. Why does he persist in persisting, as it were, only with married women? His mother is quite naturally furious. His wife turns her eyes away like Patience on a Pedestal while *l'affaire* Norton is endlessly discussed in the society pages of newspapers such as the one I examined this very morning. It told the world that he and she are seen everywhere together: at the Cowes Regatta, weekending at Sandringham or Blenheim, the races at Ascot— Truthfully I cannot blame his mother for her attitude towards the woman."

"But you did agree to accept her as your client, therefore you have no alternative."

"And wouldn't take it if I had. The woman has rare spirit.

Right or wrong, she deserves support because of her courage and the fact that she is so far out-numbered in this battle; she faces such overwhelming forces. Well, you and I know what and who they are, Watson, and we know she cannot win. But yes, I believe I can still extricate her from her trouble without a public disgrace, although she cannot maintain this 'friendship' . . . she's over-matched and must be brought to admit it. For once she'll have to bow to a stronger power."

From one of his coat's great square pockets he withdrew his notebook with pencil attached. "A discreet ad in the personal column of the papers should bring about a meeting with his mother's loyal emissary, don't you agree?" He was writing busily, holding the notepad at an angle which allowed me to read it as he scribbled:

> Tall dark gentleman who enjoys a walk in the park around ten A.M. and is in sympathy with the dealings of patriotic Lady with military men, nimble-fingered maids and urchins-for-hire seeks meeting with above-mentioned patriotic Lady. Object: to relieve her and Others of problem arising from unsuitable Friendship. Perfect satisfaction and discretion guaranteed if face-to-face meeting can be arranged. No written response necessary.

He pocketed his pencil and glanced over at me. "I hope this will bring results."

"I'd almost wager on it," I assured him.

I t went much as I had foreseen," he told me a few days later, rubbing his lean hands together and looking somewhat smug. "Veni, vidi, vici, as Caesar would have put it. Not that the encounter was comparable to the Gallic wars, perhaps, because to tell you the truth the lady was—well, in all respects a lady. The threats were real enough but our discussion was courteous and we found ourselves in accord at the finish."

He went on to relate how the black and yellow carriage approached him as he walked in the park. He knew it instantly and also Lady Fitzbarry, who descended from it to join him on the walkway. The carriage moved slowly along the drive behind them as they talked, she first:

"They—that is, the Family—are all of one mind. This affair must cease at once. The Empire must not be witness to yet another fall from grace. The lady in this case could even be dangerous to the Succession."

"In what sense, madam?" Holmes inquired. ("Although I knew the answer quite well, Watson.")

"In the sense, Mr. Holmes, that she seems to hold the key to all his preferences, and his infatuation with her has become so obvious that he is now publicly ignoring the responsibilities of his station. As for her, she has been given increasingly pointed warnings and has chosen to ignore them."

"Is it possible that she does not connect her own actions with your 'warnings'?"

Lady Fitzbarry slanted a scornful glance at him. "Apparently we have a higher respect for her acuity than you do. *She knows!* And still she's made no retreat from her position nor seems inclined to do so. Frankly, sir, we cannot allow it to continue."

"I think I understand, madam. What do you suggest that I advise my client?"

"You may tell her that the Family sees no recourse but to use its influence here and abroad. Believe me when I say that her way will not be easy. The great opera stages of Europe will never welcome her again. The Society which she values so highly will now be closed to her. She's gone too far in her belief in her own power, and this arrogance cannot be tolerated. She is about to feel the effects of true Power. We are all reluctant to use harsh measures and we regret the necessity, but—"

"Are you so certain of the necessity, Lady Fitzbarry? Why must the Power you mention stoop to crushing one individual? I can think of alternatives to be considered."

"Can you? What would you propose?"

"It seems to me," Holmes said slowly, "that if the lady in question were to take her personal attractions elsewhere, to another scene, another place, in fact to another country . . . ?"

She stared directly at the path before her. "And all contact between the parties would cease permanently?"

"Permanently, but with the assurance that my client would remain safe from any damage whatsoever to her career or to her reputation now or in the future."

"That might be acceptable," she said, and then, "Very well, then."

"And—?"

"There is no 'and.' If she abides by these demands (and make no mistake, sir, they are demands, not requests), her life can continue on its present course—except in England. Here she will be henceforth persona non grata. The end. Finis. She has brought it upon herself."

"With his help, madam . . ."

Her eyes met his and she bent her head slightly and signalled to the carriage with the same motion. A moment later Lady Fitzbarry was gone.

. . . So you may see how well I had gauged the situation, Watson! The best I could have hoped for was that there be no spiteful desire on their part for vengeance, no need to ruin her future."

"But still—" I said doubtfully. "How did Mrs. Norton take it?" I asked, thinking of the proud high-held head and the independent spirit of the woman.

He rubbed his chin. "She was shaken, but she took it surprisingly well," he told me seriously. "And yet, I shouldn't say 'surprisingly.' When a champion shows quality it should surprise no one, and she is—you may judge for yourself, Watson, for if I'm not mistaken she's on her way up our stairs at this very moment, or my faith in her punctuality is ill placed."

He was turning the doorknob as her knock sounded. "Dependable as ever, I see, Mrs. Norton," he greeted her. "Won't you come in and be seated?"

But she remained standing in the doorway, straight and tall. "No, Mr. Holmes. I requested these few minutes with you only to offer a few more words of appreciation for your efforts. I fear that the last time I saw you my—my—humiliation was so complete that I failed to do justice to them. To your efforts, I mean. Your results were not what I had hoped for, but after a few weeks or months have passed I'm certain that my pride will have recovered sufficiently for me to fully appreciate them. Even now, while my self-confidence is so badly mauled, my more rational side can and does thank you most sincerely. With the handicap you had working against you (and yes, I do mean my own lack of frankness), as well as the Power aligned against you, you managed to salvage a great deal of my life to go on with. In your own way you are—incomparable."

"Madam, I thank you and I return the compliment with full confidence that wherever you go, your life will continue to be a pleasant and successful one."

She smiled. "So, then, the time has come to bid one another good-bye, Incomparable Sherlock Holmes." She extended her hand, which he shook, and nodded to me, then the door to 221B Baker Street closed behind her.

A few hours later I was struck with the irreverent thought that today must be Ladies' Day at this same 221B Baker Street, for when the next knock sounded on our door, it was opened to frame the figure of an angry Lady Fitzbarry. A more icily furious woman I had never encountered in all my life. I am not anxious to repeat the experience, even though I was not the one on whom she poured what some have referred to as "vials of wrath."

She swept into the room before Holmes could invite her to enter, and her accusing index finger pointed so directly at his heart that he took an involuntary step backwards.

"You!" The finger still threatened. "Was *this* your advice to your client? Do you own no conscience whatsoever? What sort of a man are you, to bear me such spite, such deep-held malice simply because I won the honours in the bargain we struck in the park?"

Holmes raised a hand, his face pale with his own resentment at this attack. "I assure you——" he began, but she broke in hotly.

"Oh, yes, assure me, assure me! My God, man, much good may that do me now! All I know is that only days ago my husband had no thoughts of this woman, none at all, and now, at this very moment, they are aboard the Dover-to-Calais——"

"Who?" Holmes interrupted, but I knew by his look that he had guessed.

"Who but that—*creature*—that singer or whatever she calls herself. As if you didn't know who! 'Off together for a lengthy tour of the Continent,' his note said, and may the boat go to the bottom of the Channel with the both of them!" She was flushed and trembling with temper.

"Madam," Holmes said expressionlessly, "I know nothing of any of this. I had nothing to do with it. Their—plans—might well have been made some time ago."

She glared at him. "Impossible."

"Why so?"

"Because Lord Fitzbarry knew with whom she was connected, and what loyal Englishman would have interfered under those circumstances? No, he would have never—but since your meddling fingers have stirred the waters, all that has changed and now—he's gone! Your fault! Your fault!"

"My 'meddling fingers,' " he said coldly, "have merely served your own purposes, madam, as you outlined them to me. If the outcome is different from what we both expected it is none of my doing and I refuse to accept the blame. Therefore, Lady Fitzbarry, although I deeply regret the distress this has caused you—"

"Does it not occur, even to one such as you, how ignoble a deed it is to sunder a marriage for such a spiteful personal reason?"

Holmes had heard enough. Without another word, he walked to the door and opened it significantly.

For a long moment she stood there, indecisive, and then she threw him one last hateful look and departed.

He closed the door and leaned against it with his back to me. His shoulders were shaking and I stood watching him, shocked to see him display his emotions so openly. Another man might very well have felt and shown signs of stress after such a scene, but I had thought my friend more in control of his own nerves.

But when, after a moment, he turned towards me, I saw his face alight with the deepest amusement he had ever revealed to me. I was startled, and naturally Holmes, being Holmes, caught my expression. He clapped me on the shoulder, chuckling aloud.

"Watson," he said, "was there ever to your knowledge another so wilful, so charming and so deceitful as Irene Adler Norton? I tell you, wherever she goes the woman can upset the world around her. And mine also, my friend. Mine also. At least temporarily," he added, still chuckling.

And throwing himself into his armchair he pulled out his pipe and leaned back. "But you realize, Watson, that this is the second time that this same female has played me one of her sly tricks. I find myself embarrassed. 'Fool me once and shame on you. Fool me twice and shame on me!' Therefore spare my blushes, old friend, and keep this particular story to yourself, will you?"

I saw his point. I said I would and I have.

In my 1996 St. Martin's collection, The Resurrected Holmes, *my colleague J. Adrian Fillmore explained that Dr. R., the Philadelphia collector who bought the tin dispatch-box, hired many authors to ghost-write Watson's notes into full narratives. Many writers tried, but few succeeded in submerging their own distinctive literary styles in favour of Watson's. Dr. R.'s ledgers reveal that though the bulk of the next tale was penned by Inspector Lestrade himself, the frame and certain characters and situations were embellished by Arthur Stanley Jefferson (1890–1965), a young English comic who, stranded in 1912 in Philadelphia, made the acquaintance of Dr. R., who recognized Jefferson's genius and many years later asked him to write up "The Little Problem of the Grosvenor Square Furniture Van." Aficionados will recognize in it the germ of an idea that later won an Oscar for Jefferson (a/k/a Stan Laurel) and his partner Oliver Norvell Hardy. Mmm-mmm-MMM!*

The Little Problem of the Grosvenor Square Furniture Van

BY *"PATRICK LOBRUTTO"*
(ASCRIBED TO ARTHUR STANLEY JEFFERSON)

In the thick London night, a lemon-tinted, coal-fouled fog swirled. Although everything beyond ten feet became wavering and indistinct, sound seemed magnified, heavy. Voices, hoofbeat and footfall, the sodden sound of wooden wheels thudding on wet cobblestone came out of the night from all directions.

Two men stepped into the flickering gaslight on a corner by Cavendish Square. The blockier of the two stopped, moaned softly, held a hand to the side of his face for a brief moment, then walked on, his pace quick and determined. His companion hurried to catch up.

They walked through the night, turning west at Wigmore Street. Never uttering a sound, they strode on. At the foot of Baker Street, they turned north, increasing their pace. At Crawford, they stopped and stood in front of the corner shop bearing the sign CURTIS & CO. CHEMISTS. The lean, grey-eyed gentleman with the deerstalker cap waited quietly while the other went into the shop. He returned after only a few moments, holding a small, square package in one hand.

"I have what I came for, Holmes." His voice was thick with pain. "We must press on."

"Yes, Watson. We can go home now."

Walking back south on Baker Street, they entered 221, walked up the seventeen steps and entered B, Holmes's apartment.

Inside, with the door closed behind them, their coats still on, they paused and looked at each other. Watson nodded. "I'll be only a moment. I hope the laudanum will ease this pain; we must decide what we are to do." He pulled a sheaf of papers from a pocket inside his coat. "Once you have *observed* these, you will understand my urgency, and why I have ventured out into the streets with this damned toothache when I would much rather be soothed by the tender ministrations of my new wife." His ill temper was evident and sharp.

Holmes nodded and removed his coat. "Of course, Watson, of course," he said soothingly. He took the proffered papers. Printed in block letters across the top of the first page were the words:

Mr. Holmes and the Grosvenor Furniture Van or
The True Facts As I Seen Them with My Own Two Eyes
BY Inspector G. Lestrade

Holmes sighed heavily and stared up at the ceiling. "What a revolting development this is," he said, and began to read . . .

It was a bright and sunny afternoon when I come to Baker Street to speak to Mr. Sherlock Holmes of 221B, an amateur detective who has occasionally been of some assistance in a few official police matters, and Doctor John Watson, a writer of magazine stories. These two gentlemen—especially Holmes—have accumulated a great deal of the public's admiration in recent times at the expense of our efficient and hard-working Metropolitan Police. By means of this testimony, I hope to address the balance . . .

Holmes stopped and said, "Who could have foreseen, nearly a year ago, that the little sallow, rat-faced fellow would be such a snitcher. I think we shall both be in need of whiskey, Watson, and much of it, before this is done."

"It's *elementary,* my dear fellow," said Watson in a sharp tone, wincing with discomfort. "He is, no doubt, having his revenge for the times you went out of your way to show him up."

"Might I remind you, old friend," Holmes replied, "that it was you who wrote about it."

For the briefest of moments, the two men held each other's gaze.

Making a visible effort to rein his billowing temper, Watson said, "Nothing to be done for that now. I'll do the honours. Read on, won't you."

Holmes said, "Yes, yes, of course," and did so . . .

. . . When I arrived, on that day, Mr. Holmes and Doctor Watson both were engaged in an attempt to bring a piano into their apartments on the second floor. I would have thought that Mr. Holmes's way with a fiddle would have been enough to fill any house but now it seems that he must have the tinkle of a piano for Baker Street. Perhaps Mr. Holmes thought to accompany himself whilst he played the violin. I do pity the neighbours.

Holmes put down the papers and looked over to Watson, who stood by the bow window rubbing his sore cheek. "I say, old man, what *do* you suppose Lestrade meant by that remark about my violin playing and pitying the neighbours?"

It seemed, for a few moments, that Watson hadn't heard the question. Slowly, he turned towards the seated detective. He stared at him for a long moment, and said, finally, "Just read on, won't you?"

"Yes, of course."

Me, I been seeing to the duties of an officer of the law twenty years nearly, learned it the hard way—through the records division—and I say it's the old hound what's best, when all is said and done. I concentrate on the job and the evidence before me and hunt down criminals. I shall leave fancy theories to amateurs.

Now you take this case here at hand. The search for the mysterious, and missing, S. Terry, the Poet Laureate of the West End, had led me into many strange and dangerous situations with little result. I knew I needed to talk to someone with very specialized and unsavoury information. I took myself, therefore, to Number 221B and attempted to see if some of that useless information in Holmes's skull might be of some use to the good people of London.

The instant I observed the proceedings, I saw that I would have a difficult time in pursuing my original purpose. Old Mrs. Hudson, no fool she, was in a state, indeed. The poor old dear couldn't stop wringing her hands, telling all who'd listen, as well as them that wouldn't, how worried she was that somewhat would befall the house, what was left her by her good dead man, that was her sole support in her old age. You see, Mr. Holmes had hired a driver and a helper to bring the piano in question up the stairs. The two he hires are rather . . . underbalanced . . . and somewhat high-strung. Perhaps they could have done the job, if they hadn't been driven off . . . but I get ahead of my tale.

The helper is a dour, little bald-headed jockey of a Scot, name of Finlay—couldn't have weighed more than seven stone or stood higher than fifteen hands. Moustachioed like some Baghdad *pasha,* he hardly stood still a second, bobbing about in a birdy way. Had the oddest way of cockin' one eyebrow, too—like it was pulled up by a string—and growling low when his ire was ruffled.

The driver's a hale, *stout* Irishman, Cannady, he calls himself, and he's twice as tall and twice as meaty as his assistant. He's no happy bloke, either, and don't have much more hair than that damned Lowlander. Always clenching up his face like a great wrinkled fist and scowling. Dumb as pisswater, he was, and slow moving, lumbering. Strong as an English ploughhorse, however, I'll say that for him.

They drove up in a van with the words *Grosvenor Square Furniture* written across one side, and *We Haul Ash* on the other. No sooner do they step out than I attempt to ask Holmes a few questions, since I had no intention of getting involved with this piano foolishness. Holmes wouldn't deign to answer—walked away without a word like I hadn't spoken.

Suddenly, I felt an eye boring into the back of me skull. It was this little Finlay fellow. I turned to him like a gentleman, raised my hat, and introduces myself as an officer of the Queen. He juts his neck forward and glowers at me first with the one eye, and then the other. "Officer, ye say," he growls, then turns away and quick looks back like I was trying to sneak up behind him. He turns, takes a step away and to my utter amazement, swings back yet again! Muttering something incomprehensible and Gaelic—and insulting, I have no doubt—he finally walks right past me. Well. I had never seen the like.

Finlay and Cannady drag the piano to the edge of the wagon, then Cannady jumps down and Finlay pushes one side of the instrument off the wagon onto Cannady, then jumps down, slides it over and tries to lift his end. Unfortunately, Finlay can barely hold it aloft at all. Trembling like a new bride, he sinks to the ground caterwauling, "WhaehaeyedoonyeHiberniansavage?OHHH!" waving his arms and legs frantically. The Irishman sighs and has to set his end down and go over and push the piano off his partner. Who gives him not a word of thanks. Instead, he leaps to his feet and barking, "Back, ye scrofulous Saxon scum!" Finlay clears a path as the sweating Cannady pushes the business up to the door.

All the while, Holmes has been busy . . . in his own way. With Watson in his wake, he's been walking around whistling tunelessly, peering into, over, around and under everything with a magnifying glass. Since he's bored, obviously, with nothing to do, I make another attempt to engage him in a discussion of my case. "It is your duty, sir, to aid the police in whatever manner possible. Now, here are the facts . . ."

Ignoring me completely, Holmes announces in a loud voice, "I have investigated all of the available evidence and I have deduced the single most efficacious method of bringing the object up the stairs. Based upon that deduction, I have formulated a plan of action." A hush settles upon Baker Street as the silly blighter continues. "The piano must be pushed up the stairs a stair at a time."

As if that were a great revelation. And there's seventeen stairs (Holmes ain't the only one to have a sharp sense of the world about himself). Throwing my hands up in the air, I have to walk away.

The crowd by now has grown raucous—so raucous, in fact, that it even penetrates the glaze around Holmes. Once the piano, surrounded by Finlay, Cannady and Watson—and myself, of course; by now I have decided there is more entertainment than information to be got at Baker Street—is in the foyer of Number 221, Holmes closes the door, though the rumbling of voices outside can still be heard.

Well, up Cannady goes, pushing the piano, whilst Finlay bleats encouragement at him in that horrible Scots bray.

Poor Mrs. Hudson is making little high noises in the back of her throat, knowing that the weight and banging is doing damage to the steps. It doesn't help when Watson suddenly turns to her,

smiles and gives his tie what I'm sure he believes is a reassuring little wiggle from the bottom.

Nearing the top step, Cannady puts on a last burst of fantastic strength and the piano turns straight up and crashes to the floor
of the landing, cracking several of the wooden slats. Mrs. Hudson
screams in anguish.

"EXcuse me, Holmes!" yells Watson. "Stand aside, Watson!"
orders Holmes.

Finlay decides to act the peacemaker and push the two gentlemen apart. Holmes shoves him back; the Scot collides with Watson, who pushes him towards Holmes. Before you can say "Robert
Peel," Finlay's grimacing something fearful and latching his scrawny
hands around Holmes's throat, shaking for all he's worth. Doctor
Watson gets him by one of his legs trying to pull him away, but pulls
instead on Finlay's pants, the only place he can get a grip.

Leaning against the wall, arms crossed in front of my chest, I
can only shake my head. I am a trained professional and I can see
that there is an exceptional situation developing here. I'm thinking,
too, that a *professional* policeman'd be trained in taking his man
along, but your civilian thinks he can do without training. Which
explains why the doctor's got Finlay by the pants leg, pulling the
man's breeches half down. Which is just what the little blighter is
screeching—except when it comes from his gizzard it sounds more
like "YERPUILLINM'TROOZERSDOON!OHHH!"

Cannady, up top of the steps, bellows loyally, "I'm a'comin,
Finn!" and barrels down the stairs with a full head of steam. Holmes
sees the Irish juggernaut and shouts to Watson, "Look out, old
man!" They drop the squirming Finlay and dive to either side. Cannady, unable to stop, trips over his helper and sails through the
door—the *closed* door—with a resounding *CRASH*. Leaving a
neat hole the width of his shoulders in the wood, he tumbles like
a boulder into the crowd pressed thick right up against the door. His
size and the force of his flight is such that perhaps twenty all told
are laying about moaning and rolling around in the filth of the

street. Those that are left standing take to their heels yelling for the police.

As I walk up behind Holmes and Watson peeking through the hole, the great deducer, Holmes, says in very cool tones, "Deucedly difficult getting good help these days. Don't you agree?"

Finlay sees this as an opportunity to attack from behind. Unfortunately, his pants are still around his ankles, so he trips and falls flat on his face. Holmes at this point has had quite enough—and I must say that I concur. He turns to Watson and says, "Heave-ho, eh?" Watson smiles and opens the door. "Quite so."

I step aside as the two take Finlay by his arms and legs, swing him several times and heave him—pants still around his ankles— into the crowd around Cannady. The hollow *ratatat* of night-sticks beating the sidewalk can now be heard in the distance. Whistles screech, sounding closer, as the brave protectors of London's citizenry answer the call for help.

Holmes and Watson take all this in, look at each other, smile and nod emphatically.

The police arrive as Cannady is helping Finlay pull up his pants. Finlay, is caterwauling at the top of his lungs and bouncing quite energetically, so Cannady is having a hard time of it.

Not surprisingly, the police jump onto Cannady, and Finlay, who rushes to his partner's defense yelling a battle cry of "Sodamtin'NormansOHHH!" at the rather surprised officers. A wave of police break over the wildly struggling Cannady and Finlay and they drag the two off into a wagon and away.

Back in Number 221, we go up to the first floor and attempt to help Mrs. Hudson. Holmes sits cross-legged (he has brought up the piano stool with him) trying to soothe the ruffled feathers of his landlady, who is swatting at the floor with a broom and mumbling angrily. When Holmes says, "Well, at least the piano has gotten up the stairs," Mrs. Hudson gives him a most fearsome glare and sweeps even more furiously. Thus, she doesn't watch where she's going, bumps into Holmes's knees and falls sitting right on his lap like some dance-hall tart. No sooner does she hit than she pops straight up with a loud *Whoop!* I will swear in a court of law that she flies a clear six feet through the air, hitting Watson and the door to Holmes's rooms with such force that the door flies open and she tumbles, arse over teakettle over Doctor Watson, right through a table littered with the most amazing collection of papers, pipes, tobacco pouches, knives, revolver cartridges and chemical apparatus, knocking the whole mess over and onto the floor.

Holmes comes running to help the old woman but stops as he takes a good look. Her hair is a frightful mess and her clothes are all rumpled and filthy and she is lying atop the stunned Doctor Watson. Even the "great detective" of Baker Street senses he must approach with caution. She glares at him for a moment, but Holmes realizes he must try to pull her up. He almost gets the old dear to her feet, but his sweaty hand can't hold the grip, and both fly over backward—him into a hinged, full-length dressing mirror which swings about striking him a hard whack on the head—breaking the mirror—and her into the mess of chemicals, tobacco, gunpowder and Watson, still on the floor.

Mrs. Hudson has been driven, by all these shenanigans, quite literally beyond the use of coherent speech. Her visage resembles that of an animal attempting to pass an egg that is too large. Even though I have several weapons on my person, I do not think it wise to approach too closely. I am content to watch while standing just outside the room.

Mrs. Hudson frantically searches for a suitable method of demonstrating her feelings and grabs a washbowl full of water. She flings it at Holmes who ducks, and the cold water hits the rising Watson full in the face. Holmes laughs uproriously; in a quite ungentlemanly way, I might add. "Oh ho, old man!" he shouts. "I wish you could see yourself! Ho ho!"

Watson, too, seems now quite discombobulated. He walks up to Mr. Holmes and kicks him, firmly, in the right ankle. Holmes hops about for a few moments then, game as a cock, leaps back, and kicks Watson in the backside as hard as he can. Balling up their fists—or their feet, I should say—Holmes and Watson begin shin-kicking in real earnest now. And something it was to see. My money would be on an Army veteran like the doctor, except that Holmes is spinning around yelling suspiciously French words at the top of his lungs and putting through some very fancy Froggy kicks at the doctor's poor legs. I'd like to say that this does nothing but prove what I always say on the subject of people always falling to their natural station in life, but I'm too polite to say so either then or now. So I won't.

Watson is clearly getting the worst of this, I'm sorry to report, and begins casting about for some way to get some of his own back. Suddenly, he runs over to the candlestand, grabs a candle, and wallops Holmes on the head with the thick candle. He is rewarded by the most satisfying *bop!* I have ever heard in all my years on the force. Holmes, recoiling from the blow to his head, falls against the piano. It holds him . . . for a moment, then rolls to the edge of the stairs and over.

Everyone, including myself, screams as the piano sails down the stairs and through the closed door. The unmoveable force meets the irresistible object as both door and piano are smashed into a million smithereens . . .

All is silence. We all realize that nothing will ever be quite the same . . .

Then Mrs. Hudson lets go a bloodcurdling cry that has everybody jump straight up in the air. She runs downstairs, yelling incoherently. A tremendous racket of banging pots and pans and breaking glass and Mrs. Hudson's angry yelling comes up the broken stairs. We all rush to investigate, but Holmes and Watson contrive so strenuously to be first that they succeed only in tripping and undermining each other and come rolling down the stairs in an angry heap, breaking the bannister into splinters on the way.

The noise has gotten even louder and Mrs. Hudson is shouting things that t'would leave a sailor gaping in awe and respect. As Holmes and Watson stop just before the door to the stairs leading down to the kitchen, all noise stops and there's a dead, ominous silence.

The two men look at one another and then at the yawning doorway. They back up several steps, fearfully. Unwilling to be anything more than an innocent bystander, I am behind them in the hall. Watson hits Holmes in the shoulder and motions towards the door; the brave Holmes shakes his head No vigorously. Watson pushes Holmes. Holmes takes a sliding step towards the door while trying hard to lean away from it at the same time. He's about to start down the stairs when an egg flies out and Mrs. Hudson, bellowing, charges right out after it.

Eggs start flying, and the two men run and fall all over themselves to get out of the way. I press myself against the wall as she comes rushing past, holding a big pot filled with eggs. Chasing them out of the house, scattering the crowd, they disappear down Baker Street. The last I seen is Watson and Holmes, knees and arms pumping, running for their very lives—curiously, their bowler hats are still on—Mrs. Hudson, the avenging Valkyrie, merely a step behind the detective and the scribbler.

I do not know how them two got themselves home or how far they travelled, or who cleaned up the colossus of a mess that was made in Mrs. Hudson's house, for I strained myself nearly into herniation with laughing.

I joyful took my leave then and came straight to pen and paper. I sat myself down to narrate this account in a fresh green memory. It all happened just as you see it set down here. This, I believe, will once and for all paint the true picture of the famous Mr. Holmes for the world entire to see. My duty as I sees it.

As a postscript, I must mention that Finlay and Cannady were released the next morning . . . but there is still the little problem of the Grosvenor Square Furniture van, which disappeared and has not yet been recovered.

* * *

Holmes turned the last page, stood and ripped the papers to tiny little shreds, kicking the pieces across the floor.

"That was a copy," Watson said tersely. "Lestrade has the original. He wants . . . one thousand pounds. He will suppress this . . . tale, and he will keep his mouth shut." Watson walked over to pour himself another whiskey, his third. Drinking it down in two gulps, he added, "Forever, God willing. I recommend, for both our sakes, that we pay him. If this were to become public knowledge, we would be the laughing-stock of all London—at the very least—and you would see precious few cases in the future."

Holmes stood speechless, quivering, for long moments, then shouted, "He's mad I tell you, mad! We must . . . How he . . . Why I . . ." Sherlock Holmes stopped, shoulders slumped and said resignedly, "Pay him and have done." He took long strides to his bedroom, stopped with his hand on the door, and before going in said, "What *did* happen to the van? I wonder . . .

"But do see Lestrade immediately. You are quite correct—if this story were ever to be published, I should have to retire to Essex and raise peas!" The door slammed behind him.

Watson was silent a moment, then growled with a sudden pain in his tooth, and said derisively, "Raise peas. . . . Why, the very *idea!*"

À la Recherche du Temps Perdu

Seldom will Sherlock Holmes speak of bygone times, and Watson, except for his war wounds, is even more close-lipped about his past. It is quite a coup, therefore, to offer two glimpses into certain painful childhood memories of each of our heroes. This section also contains another early case of Sherlock's, as well as a fascinating diplomatic exploit that happened during that melancholy period when the world believed Holmes to be dead.

The supernatural never obtrudes into the ordered world of 221 Baker Street, but sometimes, as in The Hound of the Baskervilles, *it comes mighty close. "A Ballad of the White Plague," whose title refers to the chilling folk song, "The Mistletoe Bough," circles even closer. Here is a powerful memoir of Holmes's childhood that tells a bit more about the detective's family, a subject he hardly ever mentioned to his friend Watson.*

A Ballad of the White Plague

BY P. C. HODGELL

Denn die Todten reiten schnell,' " Holmes quoted in a sudden, mocking voice. " 'The dead travel fast.' My dear Watson, we are not dead yet, but that may soon be remedied if you overturn us in a ditch."

I was almost startled enough to do exactly that, so long had it been since last he had deigned to speak to me—as if our current plight were entirely my fault!

Lightning flared to the north, broken forks seen through a black canopy of oak leaves, and a moment later thunder rolled down on us like a run-away cart full of rocks. The pony's hooves clattered nervously on the rough stones of the old Roman road. Our rented trap bounced and swayed. With nightfall, a cold wind had pushed aside the heat of the August day, and now we stood a good chance of being half drowned, if not pelted with hail or struck by lightning.

"My dear Holmes," I said, mimicking his tone to cover my

own quite natural nervousness. "You must admit that our situation approaches the gothic, if not the ludicrous. Lost in the wilds of Surrey! What time is it?"

"The dead of night," he replied in a hollow voice. "The third watch. The witching hour."

"In other words," I said crossly, "about midnight. At this rate, we will never make Bagshot in time to catch the last express to London."

"It was your idea to drag me off for a drive in the country."

"And yours that we return through this wretched wilderness . . . Oh really, this is too much!"

" 'The children of the night!' Holmes quoted again, listening to the distant howl. " 'What music they make!' "

The howl ended in a most unromantic yelp, some exasperated farmer probably having clouted the hound. We were, after all, only five or six miles from civilization, cutting across the woodland that surrounded Surrey Hill. Sandhurst lay to our southwest, Ascot to our north, and Bagshot to our east. If we followed the Roman road far enough, we would rejoin the world, but not in time to return our rented trap and catch the last train home or, it seemed, to escape a drenching. On top of that, Holmes was in a strange, wrangling mood that made me long to shake him.

"You may jeer at my romantic tastes and complain that I reduce your cases to mere sensationalism," I snapped, "but you yourself have just quoted from Bürger's "Lenore" and *Dracula*. Now, admit: sensational or not, Bram Stoker knows how to tell a tale."

Holmes snorted. "A tale of arrant nonsense. The living dead . . . ha! Some people will devour any story if it is sufficiently fantastic, as your readers have repeatedly proved. Sometimes I wonder how gullible you yourself are. Next, you will claim that, once upon a time, we really did confront a vampire in Sussex."

"I never thought so, any more than you did. That was real life, not fiction."

"I am glad that you acknowledge the difference," said Holmes tartly.

"Nonetheless," I said, pursuing my own thought, "there are sometimes curious coincidences between the two. For example, take names: Carfax Abbey, where Stoker's undead monster lay hidden in his coffin by day, and Lady Frances Carfax, whom we plucked living from the tomb only a month ago."

When Holmes made no reply, I shot him a look askance. The brim of his hat was pulled down over his eyes and his chin had sunk into the collar of his grey travelling-cloak, leaving only the predatory hook of his nose. He was ignoring me again.

I knew that the Carfax case still bothered my friend. At first, I thought that that was because he had so nearly failed to deduce Lady Frances's whereabouts in time to prevent the villainous Holy Peters and his female accomplice from burying her alive. As it was, we had barely removed her from the coffin in time to prevent her asphyxiation from the chloroform with which she had been drugged.

The Carfax case took place in July of this year [1902].

Soon after, I moved to my own rooms on Queen Anne Street and for a fortnight did not see my friend. When we met again, I was disturbed by his haggard appearance. He had not been sleeping well, he said, and muttered something about a recurrent dream. In it, his fear apparently was not that the lady would fail to escape her premature grave but, oddly, that she would.

For the intensely rational Holmes to admit to any dream was rare. Far worse was his tacit admission that one was actually robbing him of his sleep. True, I had known him to stay awake for days on end when working on a case, but this case was over, successfully solved, if at the last minute.

It had crossed my mind that Lady Frances might have stirred a latent taphophobia in Holmes. By 1900, the fear of premature interment had grown to epidemic proportions. Recently, an elderly female patient had presented me with a first edition of Tebb and Vollum's *Premature Burial and How It May Be Prevented*. If she died while in my care, so great was her fear of waking in the grave that she strictly charged me to cut her throat before allowing her to be buried. Glancing through the book's bibliography, I counted no less than 120 works in five languages on the subject, in addition to 135 articles, forty-one university theses, and seventeen pamphlets published by the London Association for the Prevention of Premature Burial. By God, that gave *me* nightmares, before I ever heard of Lady Frances Carfax.

But Holmes had never shown any such weakness, nor did it seem likely with his cool, almost clinical approach to any case. In short, I was at a loss to know why the Carfax affair still haunted my friend, and I was worried. Hence my ill-fated attempt to divert him with a country drive.

"Turn here," said Holmes suddenly.

I could see no crossroads, but to the right there was a dark break in the trees. At a tug of the reins, the pony swung down off the causeway, the trap lurching after him. We would end in the ditch after all, I thought, but then the wheels crunched on unseen gravel. We were following a hidden drive through a tree-lined tunnel of darkness. High grass swished around the pony's legs. Branches scraped the trap's sides. The first fat drops of rain began to tap imperiously against the overarching leaves.

"Holmes, I don't think that this is the road to Bagshot."

"No. It is, however, the road to shelter, if you don't mind a ghost or two."

I was about to demand what he meant when we emerged from the trees. Ahead, indistinct against the dark flank of Surrey Hill, sprawled an enormous building. Then a lightning flash revealed my mistake: The house itself was fairly small, a country manor in the Georgian fashion. Surrounding it, however, like a series of broken eggshells set one inside another, were the ruins of at least three far older structures. Then the darkness fell again like a thunderclap, and again the house seemed huge and misshapen, devoid of light or life, yet watching, waiting.

The wind swooped and rain came spattering down, mixed with a handful of stinging hail. As I secured the pony in the lee of the house, Holmes disappeared inside. Following, I hesitated in an entryway as black as the bowels of the earth, stinking of wet wood and rot.

"Holmes? Holmes! Where are you?"

His voice came hollowly from within: "Welcome to Morthill Manor."

As I groped toward him, the storm breathing loudly down the hall at my back, his words reached me in snatches:

"The name or some variation of it . . . said to date back to Neolithic times, designating the huge barrow mound which itself is the hill. Druids . . . circle of standing stones within the oak grove on its summit . . . 60 A.D., human sacrifice there to ensure Boadicea victory in her revolt against the Romans . . . Following her defeat, Roman soldiers slaughtered the priests, overthrew the stones, and cut down the sacred oaks to build a country villa . . . said to have sealed Celtic infants alive under the floor as foundation sacrifices . . . Watson, you spoke?"

"No," I snapped. I had run my thigh hard against a table and sworn, as much at Holmes and his ill-timed games as at the pain to my old war injury, already aching with the change of weather.

My left hand lost contact with the wall. I stood in the doorway of a long dining room, its dimensions briefly defined by a flash of lightning outside tall, broken windows. Holmes was moving about at the room's far end, apparently in search of something, still lecturing like some infernal cicerone:

"Many structures have risen on this site since then, each built with the bones . . . I mean, the stones of its predecessor, each with its foundation sunk deep into the same thirsty darkness. In the Middle Ages, a convent rose on the villa ruins, but was abandoned because of 'straunge noises under-ground.' Later, it was learned that the abbess had ordered thirteen young novices to be walled up alive for 'consorting with the dead of the mound.' During Elizabeth's reign, the house was rebuilt, but again abandoned after tainted water from a new well shaft killed nine children. In 1645, Roundheads burned it to the ground under the impression that the wife and children of a Royalist supporter were hiding inside. Unfortunately, they were. Ah."

A candle flared. The light flickered across Holmes's sharp-boned face, and then across that of the young woman behind him. I could not suppress a cry, even as I realized what I was seeing. Holmes turned and looked at the portrait over the fireplace. I believe that its sudden, spectral appearance startled him, too, though the only sign was a quiver, instantly controlled, in the hand which held the candle.

"The current structure dates from 1725," he said. "Its last owner, to my mind, was its worst. There, if you please, is the portrait of a true vampire."

The light called her forth from the shadows, ghostly in her pallor, yet strangely, avidly alive. The pose and style were reminiscent of da Vinci's *Mona Lisa*. Her hair, the shade of anaemic strawberry, was pulled back from her white brow to tumble luxuriously down below her waist. Her eyes were a pale, almost luminous green. White teeth—the incisors, not the canines—showed between unexpectedly full, red lips. She was smiling. I thought, despite myself, that she looked hungry, and Walter Pater's description of that famous painting came unbidden to my mind:

> She is older than the rocks among which she sits; like the vampire, she has been dead many times, and learned the secrets of the grave.

No. This would *not* do.

"Really, Holmes. Next you'll claim to have known this lady."

"Of course I did," he snapped, turning. "Her name was Blanche Vernet. She was my cousin."

Then a strange expression flickered across his face. He was staring at something above my head. Hastily, I crossed the threshold and turned to look up. Over the doorway, chained to the lintel, hung a giant, skeletal branch of mistletoe. It moved slightly in the unaccustomed draft rushing in from the hall, its leafless fingers scraping on stone.

" 'The mistletoe hung in the castle hall.' " Holmes quoted the old ballad in an odd tone, as if surprised to remember it. " 'The holly branch shone on the old oak wall . . .' "

His voice faltered. For a moment, he looked . . . "haunted" is the only word—but that moment quickly passed.

"You have heard me mention my maternal great-grandfather, the French painter Carle Vernet," he resumed briskly. "Besides his son Horace, also an artist, he had another son, Charles, who became a doctor."

"Your great-uncle," I said, working this out.

"Yes. For a doctor, he seems to have been singularly unfortunate: His first wife, a Frenchwoman, did not survive Blanche's birth. His second wife, the daughter of a minor Wallachian diplomat, died some twelve years later under similar circumstances, leaving behind twin infant girls, Alice and Alyse. That was in 1853, I believe, after the family had moved to London . . . Watson, am I boring you?"

"What?" I jerked my attention back to him, away from a second face that stared grimly from the end wall opposite Blanche out of the heavy gold of a mock Byzantine icon. "Holmes, who is *that?*"

"Irisa," he said curtly, noting the direction of my gaze. "The second wife's sister and the twins' aunt. She descended suddenly from some aerie in the Carpathians and stayed to tend house after her brother-in-law removed his family here in the summer of '62."

Severe, black clothing, an ornate Greek cross on her breast, black brows drawn together over inimical black eyes . . . she was like the shadow cast by Blanche's hectic light, watching her niece down the length of the dining room with the unfathomable stare of a death's-head.

Sodden branches lashed the windows. Atop Surrey Hill, the Druids' desecrated grove seemed to pull lightning down from the sky.

Flash. CRACK.

I blinked in the after-glare, seeing not the room but its image burned into my mind, stark black and white. Instead of portraits, the family themselves stood silent and watchful against the walls: black-browed Irisa, pale Blanche, and two little girls in white, side by side in a corner, regarding us solemnly . . . but then my sight cleared and again they were only paint on canvas with dust-blurred eyes. Of the two girls, however, there was no sign.

I cleared my throat. "Dr. Vernet painted these?"

"He did," said Holmes. "Art in the blood will out, one way or another. His last portrait was that which you see over the mantel, but his true masterpiece was its original: his eldest daughter, Blanche."

" 'The baron beheld with a father's pride,/ His beautiful child, young Lovell's bride.' " I quoted the ballad's next verses sarcastically, still half convinced that Holmes was pulling my leg, not wanting to prove myself as gullible as he thought or as I had just been given reason to fear.

"Oh, yes," he said, ignoring my tone. "He doted on Blanche, for whom nothing was good enough. My own father, Siger, on business in London, wrote home that Blanche's coming-out ball was the hit of the season and she the nonpareil, upstaging even that other 'Pocket Venus,' the notorious Florence Paget. Oh, my lovely cousin had many admirers, but, as women will, she fixed her wild heart on the least suitable and seduced him."

This was blunt, even for Holmes, surprising bluntness from me in return. "Who?"

He ignored my question.

"In the midst of her triumph, she contracted a cough which proved to be consumption. At that time, Dr. Vernet sold his London practice, bought Morthill, and moved his family here in a desperate attempt to find a cure."

In this, Dr. Vernet had my sympathy. The only "cure" for tuberculosis is fresh air and sunlight, but most victims die anyway, usually from inanition, sometimes from drowning as bodily fluids flood into their destroyed lungs—a far cry from the romantic image of the disease in Dumas's *Lady of the Camellias* or *La Bohème*. In the mid-nineteenth century, the disease which we now call the White Plague killed millions, if not tens of millions, with no end in sight even today.

"I fear," I said, "that Dr. Vernet's effort was gallant, but doomed."

"Call it rather his obsession, matched only by his daughter's ferocious will to live. Tiny as Blanche was—hardly taller than a child—she proved remarkably tenacious of life. Summer passed, and then fall. In the last, bleak days of the year, a black-edged envelope finally arrived—sent by Blanche to announce her father's death."

"Of consumption?"

"Yes. Remember, this was before Villemin proved tuberculosis to be contagious, although it had already been noted that while the disease dawdled with some victims like a fond lover, it galloped off pell-mell with others. This had been Dr. Vernet's fate. Moreover, Blanche informed us that she had inherited all her father's assets, including a large debt owed by my father, Siger Holmes, to hers. She asked—no, demanded—that Father immediately attend her here at Morthill to discuss terms. And so, perforce, he came, bringing me with him."

Holmes looked up again at the leafless branch chained and creaking over the lintel.

"Forty years ago one Christmas Eve, when I was a boy of eight and that bough was fresh . . ."

Viscum album, the boy Sherlock thought, regarding the spiky greenery over the door. The traditional kissing bough. How seasonal.

He tried to keep his thoughts on this subject—*parasitical, sa-*

cred to the Druids . . . —but unease gnawed at him, as it had all that long, dark day on the increasingly silent drive to his cousin's house.

Looking back, it seemed that none of their household had been easy since Father's return from London the previous spring. That was when the letters started to arrive. At first, awkwardly joking about some "damned importunate suitor" in a civil case, Father had carried them away to read in private.

Finally, in a stony voice, Mother said, "Burn them."

From then on, self-consciously, Father did—unopened, in full sight of the family—until they slowed and stopped at summer's end. Intrigued, Sherlock slipped back into the breakfast room to rescue the last one from the grate. All that remained was a piece of red paper, ripped on one side and charred on the other, overlaid with a filigree of light ash.

Then, that morning, another envelope addressed in that same impetuous hand, edged in black, lay beside Father's plate.

"Open it," Mother said, and he did.

As he read, Siger Holmes's face blanched. "My God. So much money. This will ruin us." He looked at Mother, turning paler still. "I must go."

Mother was silent for a moment and then suddenly said, "Take Mycroft with you."

Mycroft looked grim at this. At fifteen, seven years his brother's senior, he took their mother's side in whatever-it-was that had upset her since the previous spring. Father glanced at him and then quickly away.

"No. I will take Sherlock. A child may soften her."

Now here they stood—Sherlock and his father—in their cousin's cold, disordered dining room beside a long table laden with dirty dishes. Their pony and rig were tied at the outer door; no one had come to take charge of them, the servants having all fled.

"A plague house declares itself," that grim woman in black (Aunt Irisa?) said as she let them in. Then she saw Sherlock, and drew her breath in sharply. "You fool, to bring a child here! Do you know what happens to children in this house?"

The boy wondered about his two little cousins, Alice and Alyse. As he entered the dining room, Sherlock thought he saw the white hem of a child's dress flick out by the far door. *Girls are timid,* he reminded himself, clutching for the warmth of superiority. Cold as the room was, Mycroft would laugh at him if he shivered: *What are emotions to the superior mind? What is physical weakness?*

Father hid his emotions poorly. He was pacing now, shooting glances at the door.

Quick footsteps out in the hall, a flurry of white—Blanche stood there, breathless, under the bough, corsaged with holly and crowned with mistletoe. Once she had been as tiny and perfect as a porcelain doll. Now her unbound hair, thinned by illness, floated up about her in the draft from the hall and her eyes glistened. When she looked at Father, the tip of her pale tongue slid as if with a life of its own across the bruised ripeness of her lips. Then she saw the boy, and the smile froze on her face like ice mantling over a corpse.

"What a dear little chap, Siger!" she cried with feigned delight. "My cousin Sherlock, is it not?"

She embraced him as if she would gladly have broken him in two. There was strength there yet, though he felt the rack of her bones beneath the white shroud of her gown and smelled the sweet rot of her flesh mingling obscenely with attar of roses. Then she began to cough and pushed him away. Flecks of her blood speckled his face.

"How shall we . . . entertain you?" she cried, collapsing into a chair, struggling to catch her breath. "I know . . . a treasure hunt! There is a paper . . . a promise in writing to repay my dear dead father . . . oh, such a great amount of money! Find it, and perhaps you may keep it." She clasped her hands against her wasted breast, gazing at his father. "Look for it . . . under a broken heart."

The boy left the room by the far door, forcing himself not to run. A stair led upwards to the second floor. He climbed.

The window at the far end of the upper hallway was small and round, silvery with twilight. It seemed a great distance away, and yet Morthill was not large. After all, it only had two central corridors, one on each floor, with rooms opening off to either side. It should be easy to find his cousin's bedroom. Women liked to keep their secrets hidden close. He hesitated a moment, uncertain, and then turned to the first door on the left, which stood half open.

His boots crunched on broken glass as he stepped inside. The door closed behind him. He edged forward in utter darkness, his feet now rustling as if through fallen leaves. He ran into something, hard. A table edge. More glass fell and broke. Now he could see the vague outline of a window. Advancing on it, he pulled down the black velvet which muffled its long, narrow frame.

Twilight glimmered into the ruins of Dr. Vernet's laboratory. Here was the squat hulk of an alchemist's athenor; there, rows of shattered retorts like jagged, crystal teeth; everywhere, the pages of books ripped out and strewn in drifts about the floor. Chemical formulae, astrological symbols, and Celtic runes tangled in black charcoal across the white-washed walls.

Bon sang ne peut mentir, read one notation. *Le sang c'est la vie,* proclaimed another—and a third, simpler and more raggedly written: *Sangsue.* Leech. Bloodsucker.

Scrawled over it all, in letters almost too large to read, was a single, repeated word: *NON, NON, NON . . .*

There were secrets here, but they belonged to the doctor, not the daughter. He must look elsewhere.

The boy dragged the door open again, grating over shards of glass. Beyond, however, lay not the hall but another, smaller room. He must have lost his bearings in the dark, he thought. Thin light showed him two iron cots, bolted together side by side. One was draped with leather straps. The floor beneath it was dark, and greasy, and there was a smell.

The boy paused, thinking that he heard the distant voices of children, singing. Alice and Alyse must have come upstairs before him. This was a cold, lonely place. He would find his little cousins and ask for their help.

But each door only led to another room, never to the hall.

As night fell, the boy wandered on, deeper and deeper into the house. How cold it was and how silent, except for a chill winter's rain stealthily tapping on the windows. Where were his cousins? Where was he? Maybe he was no longer even in the same house which he had entered—oh, such a long time ago, it seemed. What if tonight all the Morthill manors down through the ages had come back, stone, and oak, and human bone?

("Do you know what happens to children in this house?")

What if, even now, black-robed monks were walling the little novices up alive? In the dark, gagged and bound, they beat their heads against the newly set stones: *Ta-thump, ta-thump* . . . and from within the mound came the slow, heavy answer: *THUMP. THUMP. THUMP.*

What if, even now, Roman soldiers were bending the limbs of a child to fit into an oak-lined cavity under the floor? "The earth is still hungry," the centurion in charge would say—in Latin, of course—and they would come tramping through the house, looking for another child to bury alive . . .

Then, to the boy's relief, he heard the singing again, closer now, almost clear enough to understand the words. They were playing hide-and-seek with him. He hurried on through door after door, room after room, following the thread of song, until at last he entered a chamber which reeked of roses.

At the foot of an unmade bed was an oblong chest, the size of a child's coffin. Was this what his little cousins had wanted him to find? He listened for them, but only heard the rain, tapping on the window panes. The box was oak, black with age, bound with iron. He traced the crude carving on its lid—a spray of mistletoe, split by a finger-wide crack. Then, gingerly, he opened it.

Within lay a welter of Blanche's under-garments.

At first the boy thought that the bosom of the negligeé uppermost was soaked with blood, but then he saw that the red was the backing of a lace paper valentine, ripped down the middle. He had found Blanche's broken heart, whose other half his father had burned almost but not quite to ashes.

The boy looked on, detached, as his hands shredded the paper. *("What are emotions to the superior mind?")* Crimson fragments fell into the chest like a sprinkling of blood.

Then he knelt to burrow beneath the shattered "heart," through layers of not-very-clean linen. The smell made his head swim. Breathing through his mouth, he clambered inside the chest so as to be done searching as quickly as possible. Camisoles, chemises, drawers, petticoats, no, no, no . . . yes! Here was a legal document: his father's promissory note, tucked into the bodice of a peignoir.

Then the chest's heavy lid crashed down on his head.

Darkness. Pain. Confusion. Fear.

The reek of sweat and perfume clotted his lungs. He . . . couldn't . . . breathe. Her arms were wrapped around his neck, tightening as he struggled . . .

Don't struggle. Listen. The children are singing:

> *"The mistletoe hung in the castle hall,*
> *The holly branch shone on the old oak wall,*
> *The baron's retainers were blithe and gay,*
> *Keeping the Christmas holiday . . ."*

Mistletoe. He was inside the mistletoe chest, tangled up in his cousin's clothing. There was a crack in the chest's lid. He was not going to suffocate.

Be calm, he told himself, still more than half dazed. *Breathe deeply. Never mind the woman smell. Mycroft says women will kill you if you are weak . . . if you feel . . .*

Then, when his heart finally stopped hammering and he caught his breath, he tried to lift the lid. At first it resisted and he thought (*. . . be calm . . .*) that someone was sitting on it, but it was only stuck. At last he was out of the chest, of the room, down the stair, into the hall . . .

Blanche sat on the dining room hearth, beneath her portrait. Father bent over her. She had looped her long, pale hair around his neck and he was staring down at her like a rabbit at a snake. The boy's eyes were dazzled—by the firelight, he groggily supposed—but it seemed to him that a darkness loomed over them both, as if the house itself stood there, watching, waiting. Then Blanche drew his father down. They kissed. And the darkness smiled with Irisa's thin, cruel lips.

The boy heard a strange sound, then realized that he himself had made it.

Father broke away from Blanche, as glad of the interruption as of a rescue. He fussed over his son, brushing fragments of red paper out of the boy's hair, staring when his fingers came away stained with blood. The chest lid had struck hard. The boy looked blankly down at his own hand, at the stiff legal paper which he still clutched.

He heard singing. No, he was singing:

> *"The baron beheld with a father's pride,*
> *His beautiful child, young Lovell's bride,*
> *While she, with her bright eyes, seemed to be*
> *The star of that goodly company,*
> *Oh, the mistletoe bough!"*

Blanche stood rigid, glaring like a Gorgon at father and son. "Siger, why did you bring this brat? Was it to remind me how false you are, what other bed you have shared?"

Darkness moved. For a moment, the boy stared directly into Irisa's black eyes, inches from his own, and then she retreated, taking the promissory note with her.

"Go," Irisa murmured to Blanche in her heavily accented English. "Take this. Lure him to your narrow bed. The song guides you."

Blanche looked blankly at the paper which her aunt had thrust into her hands. Her full lips framed the song's next line. Then she caught her breath in a gasp of laughter and began raggedly to sing:

> *"I'm weary of dancing now, she cried:*
> *Here tarry a moment, I'll hide, I'll hide,*
> *And Lovell, be sure thou'rt the first to trace*
> *The clue to my secret lurking place."*

"The clue, 'Lovell,' the clue!" Blanche cried, waving the note in Father's face as he stood as if turned to stone. "Find me and—perhaps, perhaps—you may keep it!" Then she thrust the paper into her bosom and ran from the room, her aunt following like her a shadow. And again the boy sang, as if possessed:

> *"Away she ran and her friends began*
> *Each tower to search and each nook to scan,*
> *And young Lovell cried, oh where dost thou hide?*
> *I'm lonesome without thee, my own dear bride,*
> *Oh, the mistletoe bough!"*

But the boy was singing to himself. Siger Holmes had left the room. Trailing after him, Sherlock found his father standing irresolute at the foot of the stair, listening to the voices above—the aunt's low and intense, her niece's shrill with rising anger.

"Leave me alone!" Blanche suddenly cried out loud. "Why do you prattle of the dead? The dead are nothing! Only life matters. I am alive, and I will live, do you hear? *Arrêtez! N'y touchez pas . . . !*"

A hollow thud cut off her words.

Father ran up the stairs. The boy stumbled after him. Irisa stood in the upper hall before the closed bedroom door, stern as Fate, implacable as Nemesis.

"Leave," she said. "She is my business now and none of yours, nor should she ever have been. Leave, and the debt which you owe this house is buried forever."

"What have you done with her?"

"Can you not guess? Sing, boy!"

And the boy sang:

> *"They sought her that night, they sought her next day,*
> *They sought her in vain when a week passed away,*
> *In the highest, the lowest, the loneliest spot*
> *Young Lovell sought wildly, but found her not . . ."*

"Stop!" cried Father. "I can not . . . I will not understand! Why are you doing this?"

"In my homeland, we know how to deal with such heartless *stregoica* as she, who must feed their lust at whatever cost to others, who prey upon those whom they should first protect."

"You think her a *vampyre*, like Polidori's Lord Ruthven or Prest's Varney?" Father tried to laugh. The boy could see that he thought her mad, and that she frightened him. "Come, the pallor of her cheek and the blood upon her lips are the curses of her illness, nothing more. You are an educated woman. Surely you can not believe such wild tales!"

Irisa smiled, and her smile was a terrible thing.

"I believe in evil. I believe that no place on earth is immune, including your oh-so-civilized England. Do you think that only *nosferatu* prey upon the innocent? Shall I tell you why this woman still lives while her little sisters lie side by side in the grave? Because that hero of science, their father, stole the blood from his infant children's veins to transfuse into hers. There."

A black-gloved finger stabbed like a lance towards the laboratory's closed door across the hall.

"He took and took and so did she until there was nothing left to give. Too late did I understand those devils' marks scrawled across the wall, those iron beds of pain! Too late, his remorse, too late. Oh, my dear little nieces, my sweet Alice and Alyse . . ."

For a moment, grief cracked the dark mask of her face and

something darker still glared through, beyond reason, beyond mercy. Then by ruthless will alone she pulled herself back together.

"Leave," she said again to Father, with such awful, cold scorn. "You weak, foolish man. Once you willingly embraced her corruption and now she has breathed death into your mouth. I know. I saw. Leave. Soon enough, you will join her in the grave's narrow bed. Listen: already she calls to you."

And they heard. Inside the bedroom. Muffled. Raging. Thuds. Long, scraping sounds. Fists beating against the coffin lid. Nails scratching . . .

Father made a choking sound. Then he snatched up his son and fled. Behind them, Irisa laughed and laughed.

No one ever saw Blanche again.

> *"And years flew by, and their grief at last*
> *Was told as a sorrowful tale long past,*
> *And when Lovell appeared the children cried,*
> *See the old man weep for his fairy bride,*
> *Oh, the mistletoe bough!"*

The echo of Holmes's voice died in the room, swallowed by its dank decay. The storm was muttering off into the distance, leaving the melancholy drip of water outside the manor and in.

"Curiously enough," Holmes said, with a shaky return to his normal, dry manner, "that ballad is based upon a tragedy which befell a family in Rutland named Noel. We cannot seem to escape it or the Christmas theme—or can we? Gone she was, but my father did not weep. He died within four months, coughing blood. I nearly followed him. As I lay ill, I overheard that Irisa was also dead, of self-inflicted starvation. A refusal to consume, if you will. Nonetheless, some curses are . . . very persistent. Even now, in my dreams, I hear it: fists beating against the coffin lid, nails clawing . . ."

I stared at him, speechless, then blurted out the first question that came into my mind. "B–but what about the two little girls?"

Holmes drew a thin hand over his face. "How can I have forgotten? Of course, they were already dead. I saw their gravestones among the trees as we drove away."

This was too much for me. "And they, I suppose, are the 'ghost or two' which you promised me before we entered this foul place, not to mention a Wallachian madwoman, an evil scientist, and a vampire in the linen chest. Oh, well done, Holmes. Bravo! And you call *me* romantic!"

His attention sharpened and he threw up a hand for silence. I, well trained, instantly obeyed.

We listened. Water dripped, the wind soughed, the old house creaked . . . and then it came again, from above us somewhere on the second floor: a faint rasp, a muffled thump.

"Oh, really!" I exclaimed.

Snatching the candle from his hand, I limped hastily down the hall to the far door. There was the stair, with water cascading down the steps. The decayed remains of a carpet made them as slippery as moss in a river-bed as I climbed, clinging to the bannister.

I did not want to believe my friend's story. It frightened me the way he had groped after details, not as if making them up but as if drawing their memory out of a half-forgotten childhood nightmare like splinters from a long neglected wound. And such details! Was I really to believe that . . . ? No, I would not.

But I had to be sure.

Here was the upper hall as Holmes had described it, eerily long, lined with doors. I hesitated on the upper landing, suddenly unsure. After all, here I was, with a guttering candle, in the upper storey of an abandoned house miles from anywhere, on a dark and stormy night, hunting ghosts. For all I knew, we might instead be sharing Morthill with an escaped axe-murderer—which, at that moment, I would almost have preferred.

The first door to the left stood half open. From the darkness within came a furtive rustle, as if of shifting paper.

A hand closed like a vise on my arm. "Don't go in there," snapped Holmes.

I was startled, so quickly and quietly had he come up the stair on my heels, and I was annoyed to find myself whispering. "Why not?"

"Because the way in may not be the way out. And besides," he added, somewhat lamely, "the floor may be unsound."

"A fine time to think of that. Very well, then; if not this door, which?"

He would not answer me, but his eyes betrayed him, sliding involuntarily to the first door on the right. When he made no move to open it, I pushed past him and gripped the knob. It came off in my hand.

I glanced back at Holmes, suddenly as reluctant as he. Candlelight flickered across his face, shadows pooling in the hollows beneath cheekbones and eyes. He stood as if rooted before the door from which his father had fled.

There was no way forward but one.

I set my shoulder to the warped panels and pushed. The lock broke in a shower of rust and the door squealed open on clutching hinges. Mindful of the house's tricks, I reached blindly inside, fished out a high-backed chair, and wedged the door open with it. Holmes stared into the darkness, then entered as if drawn. I followed.

Candlelight flickered on mouldering clutter: a disordered bed whose canopy long since had fallen down across its foot, rags of once elegant clothing strewn about the floor, a pair of long, dingy gloves draped like flayed skin over the back of a chair. More confusion littered the dressing table—age-dull bottles, lotions, notions and trinkets tumbled together.

One of Carle Vernet's lithographs hung on the nearby wall, depicting an extravagantly dressed eighteenth-century belle seated at her dressing table, admiring herself in its large mirror.

"The picture is called *Vanity*," said Holmes, behind me, "not that Blanche probably understood why. She had a certain imitative cleverness—like a monkey—but no real imagination."

I looked again, and recoiled. The mirror's rounded shape was that of a naked skull, the twin images of the woman's head and her reflection its hollow eyes, the cosmetic bottles her teeth bared in a cryptic smile. This print, not the *Mona Lisa,* was the original of Blanche's portrait in the hall below.

"*Sangsue,*" her dying father had scrawled in horror over his meticulous notations. Bloodsucker. *Non, non, non* . . .

I turned to Holmes in triumph, just as he threw back the collapsed canopy. At the foot of the bed was a chest, no bigger than a child's coffin. A crude spray of mistletoe was carved into the age-blackened oak of its lid. At its farther end, caught in the crack, were several long strands of pale hair.

Holmes hesitated a moment. Then he gripped the lid and, with a sudden effort, attempted to lift it. It rose a quarter inch and stopped with a jar that dislodged his fingers. Belatedly, he looked at the key, still turned in the lock. For a long moment we stood there, he staring at the key, I at him. It had grown very quiet outside. Inside, all I heard was the distant, forlorn drip of water. A long, scraping sound made me start. It came from the window. Outside, the fingers of a dead oak again drew restlessly across the glass and tapped against the pane. Then Holmes sighed.

"No ghosts need apply," he murmured, turned, and walked past me out of the room.

I suppose I stood with my mouth open a good ten seconds, and then I swallowed. There was the chest; there, the key. Stealthy moonlight pooled about it on the floor, and a breath of air sighed through the broken window. The strands of pale hair stirred . . .

I ran down the treacherous stair after my friend, in danger of adding one more ghost to the house by slipping.

Below, the dining hall had filled with shifting moonlight and shadow. I paused in the hall doorway, searching the walls not for the painted smile of a "da Vinci" or an icon's baleful glare, but for those two white blurs in the corner, forever side by side. They were not there. Something outside the window caught my attention. There the two dead children stood, white frocks glimmering among the moon-silvered birch, watching, waiting . . . for what, or whom? Their pale, unblinking eyes gazed upwards, as though toward the window of a second-storey bedroom.

Cold water dripped on my head. I started and looked up. Above me hung the mistletoe, that filthy parasite, each bare twig glistening with a drop of condensation like so many sparkling poison berries.

When I looked out the window again, I cursed my gullibility. Not children but two small, white tombstones leaned toward each other in the family plot, almost touching.

We reached Bagshot in time to catch the last train. Holmes slept all the way to London.

We have never spoken of that evening again.

Was the whole adventure a practical joke—Holmes's attempt to cure me by surfeit of my foolish romanticism? I want to think so, but I can not shrug off the story. It haunts me. In my dreams, I wander through endless, dusty rooms, sometimes hearing distant song, sometimes distant laughter. Last night, all too close, there was a muffled voice crying and the sound of nails breaking against wood as hard as iron . . .

Let me out, let me out, let me out . . .

Thus, I have felt compelled on this Christmas Eve to make what sense I can of that strange night four months ago. Perhaps I have read more into my friend's words and especially into his silences than he ever intended. Perhaps he is waiting for me to publish this fantastic tale to have the last laugh. Perhaps, in the beginning, that was his only goal.

I believe, however, that he found himself telling a deeper story than he intended, digging up the buried horror that poisoned his sleep. What he can not endure is the inexplicable, the irrational. Mere ghosts will never bother him, for he does not believe in them. For him, the mystery is solved. That is enough.

In that, he is more the detective than I have proved the story-teller. Before that sullen, silent chest, my courage faltered, and the story's end remains untold.

[1902]

ADDENDUM

Story-tellers die, but do stories ever really end? If you are reading this, then perhaps I, too, am dead, and the guardianship of these hitherto unpublished accounts passes to you.

Whatever my other failings, I have found myself too much both the story-teller and the detective to destroy evidence. At the bottom of this old tin dispatch-box is the last stanza of "The Mistletoe Bough," wrapped around a key—two keys, as it were, to a single mystery. The dispatch-box itself sits upon an oblong chest made of age-blackened oak, bound with iron, with a crude mistletoe carved into its cracked lid. Without telling Holmes, I had carters convey it unopened from Morthill Manor to the vaults of Cox & Company.

Here, then, are the ballad and the key; there is the chest. As my dear friend once said of another case, "It can't hurt now." Do what you will.

At length an oak chest that had long laid hid
Was found in the castle, they raised the lid
When a skeleton form lay mouldering there
In the bridal wreath of that lady fair.
Oh sad was her fate, when in sportive jest
She hid from her lord in the old oak chest,
It closed with a spring and a dreadful doom
And the bride lay clasped in a living tomb,
Oh, the mistletoe bough!

[1929]

Considerable historical detail corroborates the truth of the following manuscript, a case that Watson alluded to in "The Adventure of the Sussex Vampire." In the words of its editor, Roberta Rogow: "The Duchess of Marlborough's jewels were indeed stolen in a daring 'snatch-and-grab' at Victoria Station en route to Sandringham. The jewels were never recovered. William Henry Vanderbilt's appearance is accurate, a conclusion I base on a photograph taken at the time of the Vanderbilt Will trials, a scandal about equal to the O. J. Simpson case. As for Alva Smith Vanderbilt, later Belmont, she really deserves a book to herself! Her determination, aggressiveness and sheer chutzpah got the Vanderbilts into Society."

The Adventure of Vanderbilt and the Yeggman

BY ROBERTA ROGOW

There are very few times I have ever seen my friend Sherlock Holmes refuse to help a prospective client. I was present at our lodgings in Baker Street when such an occasion arose. It led to a revelation so shocking in its implications that I have never set it down before. I only do so now in the interests of completing the record of the cases undertaken by my famous friend.

It was November of the year 1896. Holmes and I were preparing to leave London, in pursuit of one of the most elusive criminals we ever encountered, when the bell rang, and Mrs. Hudson announced that a "Mrs. Churchill" and a "Mrs. Jerome" wished to speak with the famous detective.

Before we could stop them, two women strode past our faithful landlady; a tall, slender lady, in a fashionable morning-suit of blue velvet entered, followed by a shorter, stouter woman in an equally striking dress of dull rust color. Both wore the huge hats common to that year, with veils that were supposed to conceal their features. The piercing eye of Sherlock Holmes penetrated the veils, and he bowed to the taller veiled woman.

"Good morning, Your Grace," he said.

The woman lifted her veils to reveal the delicate features made famous by the illustrated newspapers the year before, upon her marriage to His Grace, the Duke of Marlborough. The other woman shrugged and lifted her veil also.

"I told you, Consuelo, he can tell everything at a glance," she said, in an unmistakably American accent. I recognized Lady Randolph Churchill, known to London Society as Jenny. Like Her Grace the Duchess, Lady Randolph's face had been photographed and popularized in the Press.

Her Grace turned to Holmes. "Was I so obvious?" she asked, in clear but timid tones.

Holmes restrained a smirk, but his lips twitched as he said, "If you wish to be anonymous, Your Grace, you should not go about carrying a handkerchief with the Marlborough crest on it, like the one I see in your reticule."

"Of course." The duchess looked about her. "May I sit down?"

"We were about to leave . . ." Holmes said. I bustled forward with a small chair. The young duchess looked quite faint, whether with fatigue or fear I could not say.

"It is quite important," Lady Randolph said, with the air of one who is usually obeyed instantly. "Consuelo . . . that is, Her Grace's jewels have been stolen."

Holmes strolled to the fireplace where he took his familiar stance, leaning against the mantelpiece. "Indeed. A burglary . . . ?"

"No, not at all. It was when Marlborough and I were invited for the shooting at Sandringham last month. A man came out of the crowd at the railroad station, grabbed my jewel case as it was being loaded, and ran off. The police have not been able to find him and I thought . . ." Her voice trailed off, as she looked at Holmes. Even seated, she retained the noble posture of one trained from birth to a Position in Society.

Holmes frowned. "Not a burglary," he muttered to himself. "A vulgar snatch-and-grab. In this case, Your Grace, I must defer to the efforts of Scotland Yard. They are the experts in petty thievery, not I."

"Petty thievery!" Lady Randolph exclaimed. "Those jewels were worth several thousand pounds!"

Holmes's eyes never left the young duchess. "For you, Your Grace, that would be a mere bagatelle. The Vanderbilt fortune will surely make up the difference."

I suddenly remembered that the Duchess of Marlborough had been Miss Consuelo Vanderbilt, the daughter of the American multi-millionaire. The marriage had been the subject of lewd gossip and surmise in the clubs for months, both before and after the event.

Her Grace rose in one graceful motion. "Come, Jenny. I am sorry I troubled you, Mr. Holmes. Good day." She took a hesitant step towards the door. "Mr. Holmes," she said, a slight frown marring the porcelain perfection of her features, "you seem familiar to me. Have we ever met before?"

Holmes face was still as marble. "It is not likely," he said slowly. "If we did, Your Grace, it was long ago, and in another life."

The duchess shook her head, disguised herself once again, then swept out, leaving Lady Randolph to turn her disapproving gaze on my friend.

"Randolph thought the world of you, Mr. Holmes. He said you could do anything. He had his faults, but he was rarely wrong about people. I wouldn't have talked Consuelo into coming here if I didn't think you could help her."

Holmes flinched under that cool disdain. "Under other circumstances, Lady Randolph, I would be able to assist. In this case, I would recommend that the pawnbrokers and receivers of stolen goods be examined. If there had been a burglary, I would have been of more use, but in this case . . ." He shrugged.

With a toss of her head, Lady Randolph Churchill followed her young niece-in-law down to Baker Street. Holmes watched from the window as their carriage trotted away.

"Come, Watson," he said. "Our train awaits, and we are already late. Let us hope we are on time, or our bird will have flown, and we shall have to lay our traps all over again."

We were lucky enough to get a cab, and caught the train with seconds to spare. Once we were settled into our carriage, and I could breathe again without difficulty, I asked Holmes the question that had been nagging at me all during the interview.

"Holmes," I began, not liking to take my friend to task, "you were almost rude to Her Grace the Duchess this morning. Could you not have given her some sign of hope? I know we are not free to assist her at the moment, but . . ."

Holmes held up a hand. "I know, Watson. I was abominably brusque with her. She is not more than a child, barely out of her teens, and she is not to blame for the sins of her elders, but I have my own reasons for avoiding the Vanderbilt family, and their connections. I believe I once mentioned the case of Vanderbilt and the Yeggman?"

"I have seen the name on your files," I admitted.

"It was not one of my finer moments, Watson. However, the telling of it will while away the time until we get to Sussex, but I must request that you not reveal what I am about to tell you to anyone. It is a matter of personal honour."

I was much mystified by this, and readily swore not to do more than jot down notes for my files. Holmes drew out his pipe, filled it, lit it, and leaned back to make himself comfortable before he chose to speak.

I believe I have told you (Holmes said) that I spent my youth in restless pursuit of some employment that would suit my talents. I finished University, and was somewhat at loose ends when a chance meeting led me to a brief career as an actor. I played in Shakespeare, as Cassius in *Julius Caesar* and Mercutio in *Romeo and Juliet* but I modestly admit my greatest role was as Malvolio in *Twelfth Night.* It was in this character that I appeared in New York City in the season of '79–'80, and it was during that period that I encountered both Vanderbilt and the Yeggman.

I played under the *nom de théâtre of William Escott, and it was as "Mr. Escott" that I was addressed by the young woman playing Maria, Miss Margaret Magill, a petite Irish beauty, of great verve, and a talented comedienne. She was later to become a great favourite in the United States. This was her debut, and she had made a great hit. Her dressing-room was always crowded with flowers, and her "stage-door Johnnies" filled the Green Room after each performance.*

One would think that such a charming young woman would have no troubles, but I could not but notice that on a particular evening during our run, in the middle of January, she was in difficulties. During the performance of *Twelfth Night,* she missed cues and nearly forgot her lines. Since my effectiveness as Malvolio depended in large part on her liveliness as Maria, I felt constrained to ask what was wrong, in hopes that it might be corrected before the next performance. I therefore approached her in her dressing-room.

"Are you decent?" I asked (this being the accepted greeting in the Profession).

She had obviously been crying. Her eyes were red, and several crumpled linen squares (usually used for removal of stage-paint) littered her dressing-table. "I'm sorry for what happened during the letter scene," she apologized. "It's just that I got a note from my brother. He's been taken up and he's in the Tombs. Here's his note. They let him get word to me, so I can find him a lawyer, but I don't understand the American system of law . . ." She began to cry again. I took the note, written on coarse paper with a pencil that had obviously been sharpened with a knife:

Maggie, I'm in the Tombs, they say I cracked Vanderbilt's safe, but I swear on Ma's dear soul, I never did! Get a shyster, and get me out! I won't go down for something I didn't do.—Mike

"It seems your brother has gotten himself into a pickle," I said. "Why would he be accused of cracking Vanderbilt's safe? And which Vanderbilt? There are a number of them, as I recall: Mr. William Henry Vanderbilt and his sons, Mr. Cornelius Vanderbilt and Mr. William Kissam Vanderbilt. I have seen their names on the list of patrons using boxes at our performances."

Miss Magill controlled herself long enough to repair the damage wrought to her complexion. Then she turned to me and explained: "Mike came over long ago, when I was just a wee thing. He was the eldest of us, you see, and when Pa died, he was to go to America and make his fortune, and send for Ma and the rest of us."

"I presume he did not make his fortune," I said.

"Oh, but he did, at first. He sent money back home, enough to let Ma send me and my brothers to the school, to learn to read and write and speak genteelly. Once my brothers Patrick and Antony were out in the world, they could take care of Ma and me, and a good thing, too, for the money from Michael stopped coming, and no word did we have from him at all." In the press of her emotion, Miss Magill's brogue emerged from hiding.

"He seems to have surfaced again," I noted, tapping the letter.

"That he did! He saw Magill on the stage-bills and came around to see if it was one of his own, and it was me! Oh, Mr. Escott, there's nothing like knowing you have family nearby!" Her face was radiant. I prudently kept my own thoughts on family connections to myself.

"Evidently, your brother has made some unsavoury friends," I said, "or he would not refer to a lawyer as a 'shyster' nor would he refer to a prison sentence as 'going down.' That is thieves' cant. If you insist on seeing your brother, then I insist on accompanying you. The Tombs is the New York City jail, where prisoners are held before being arraigned before the magistrate. As I understand the American system, according to their Constitution every prisoner has a right to see a lawyer. Of course, this may be more honour'd in the breach than in the observance, but I will be glad to assist you in any way I can."

"Oh, Mr. Escott . . . William!" She leapt from her chair and threw her arms around me. "I know it's very late, but will you come with me now, and see Mike? I have to know he's all right! You hear awful things about American jails."

I permitted the embrace (she was an extraordinarily pretty young woman, and I was quite young), but evaded the kiss she was about to plant on my cheek. We bundled up against the cold of January in New York City, where the wind sweeps over the island of Manhattan with a fury known only on the Steppes of Russia, and made our way from the Theatre District of Broadway downtown to the Tombs, a massive brick pile that dated from before the notorious Tweed Ring's depredations on the New York City treasury.

The Tombs was not only the City Jail but the Police Headquarters as well. We were forced to run a veritable gauntlet of uniformed warders and guardians of Public Safety before we were allowed into a barren cell, brick-walled and lit only with one flaring gas jet, containing two wooden chairs and nothing else.

A massively built policeman shoved Mike Magill into the room, and announced, "Yer got fifteen minutes!"

The accused burglar was not more than forty years old, small and wiry, with Miss Magill's quirky eyebrows that she used to such effect as Maria. On her brother, they appeared to be pasted on. There was enough of a family resemblance that I put aside the unworthy thought that he had imposed upon the successful young actress for his own ends. No, this was indeed a family reunion, and I had to make my presence known with a cough before the brother and sister would acknowledge that a third party was there.

"Mr. Magill," I asked, "why should the police light on you as the one who, as you put it, cracked Vanderbilt's safe?"

He looked at the floor. "I was in the house," he admitted. "On business," he added. "I'm a trained locksmith." He turned to Miss Magill. "When I come over, there was a man aboard who saw that I was clever with me hands, always making little toys and such for the children down in steerage with us. So, when we landed, he said he'd take me on as a 'prentice, like. Only, it was a terrible temptation, seeing all that money going into those safes, locked up with my keys."

"And you fell," I said.

"I did. I was able to take a little here and there, not much, just to send to Ma and the rest of you."

Miss Magill looked horrified. "You mean Pat and Tony and I all went to school on stolen money!"

Mike protested, "Them what I took it from never missed it! Most of 'em probably never even knew it was gone!"

"Then how did you, um, 'go down'?" I asked.

"How did you know?" He turned to me in surprise.

"You stopped sending funds to your family. They did not hear from you. I can only assume that you were caught and sent to prison."

He nodded and shook his head. "The only time I ever took anything but cash. It was a ring. I was going to give it to a certain girl I was seeing, but she took and hocked it. The coppers came and found me, but as I was a first offender, all I got was seven years, and that got cut down to five for good behaviour. I was able to set up my shop again thanks to Mr. Vanderbilt. He's not at all like his Old Man, the Commodore, is Mr. William Henry Vanderbilt. He came up to Sing Sing and read us a lesson on mending our ways, and offered to stake those who'd take the Pledge and swear never to break the law again."

"And you took advantage of this generous offer," I concluded. "Mr. Vanderbilt seems to be quite the philanthropist."

Mike Magill grinned, and the resemblance to his sister was accentuated. It was with just such a grin that she hatched the plot that led to Malvolio's downfall. "Oh, the old Commodore was a character, I'll give you that. But Mr. William Henry's a gentleman."

"Yer time's up!" the uniformed Cerberus at the door announced.

"One moment, please?" Miss Magill turned her piquant little face to the door.

"I don't understand. Which Vanderbilt safe are you supposed to have robbed?" I asked.

"Mr. William Henry's, which I was supposed to be putting in. See, Mr. Vanderbilt had me put in locks on the offices at the New York Central Railroad, and then he sent me over to his new house on Fifth Avenue to do the same. And I looked over the old safe, and made a few suggestions to Mrs. Vanderbilt, who was watching my work. I mean my boss's sister-in-law, Mrs. Alva, Mr. W. K.'s wife," he explained. "And then I was taken into the conservatory, which is a room where they keep all kinds of plants, right in the house! Fancy that!" He shook his head at the vagaries of the rich.

"And you put in the locks?" I prompted him, ever conscious of the policeman at the door.

"That I did, with a big bruiser in a red velvet coat looking on all the while, to see I didn't pinch one of the flower-pots, no doubt. And I went to the kitchen to have a bite of luncheon, and suddenly there was a screeching and Mrs. Alva come a-running and yelled that I'd been at the study safe!"

"Which you had just examined," I said, to get the sequence of events straight.

"But I left it as I found it," Magill stated. "When the copper came in from Fifth Avenue, the whole room had been turned upside down, and money and papers were all over the place. And the big bruiser, what they call a footman, looked inside my tool-kit and says he's found a packet of money in my tool-kit. But I swear to you, Maggie, and you . . ."

"Mr. Escott," Miss Magill introduced me.

"I never touched that safe! I was downstairs in the conservatory, attending to the outside locks. I wouldn't treat a fine piece of machinery like that! Twisting the handle, breaking the hinges . . . sloppy, that is."

"But the money in your tool-kit was in a neat packet?"

"So it was," Magill said. "And I will swear up and down, I never put it there!"

There was a disturbance at the door. The guard was shoved aside, and four more men entered the cell, filling it to its capacity. I found myself being shoved into a corner, while a burly policeman in the uniform of a sergeant announced, "Mr. Vanderbilt is here to see yer, Magill!"

Mr. William Henry Vanderbilt was a stout man of middle years whose face was adorned with a pair of streaming side-whiskers, which by then were already out of fashion. He was dressed in evening clothes that were well made but not particularly flashy. One would never suspect by looking at him that he had nearly doubled his original patrimony, and was probably the wealthiest man in America at that date. He regarded Mike Magill with the look of one who had expected better things.

"Why did you do it, Magill? I thought you had turned from crime and become an honest man."

Magill began to snivel. "I swear on me mother's grave . . ."

"Ma's still alive," Miss Magill put in. Vanderbilt turned to look at her.

"My sister," the yeggman introduced her. "She's on the stage. And this is . . ."

"Mr. Escott," I said, with a bow. "I came to see no harm comes to Miss Magill. Mr. Vanderbilt, if I may put in a word for Magill, I think he is telling the truth. Miss Magill is a fine actress, but I do not think her skill is hereditary."

Vanderbilt nodded. "You may be right, young man. That's why I brought Hargreave along. He looks into things for me."

A man in a greatcoat and battered bowler hat nodded briefly to me. "What else d'ye think, younker?" he asked.

"It strikes me as odd that a man should rob the house with so many people about. Besides yourself, Mr. Vanderbilt, and your brother's wife, Mrs. Alva Vanderbilt, who else was present?"

The millionaire considered for a moment. "My own wife was out paying calls. Alva came to see me about some matters pertaining to the new house she's building near mine on Fifth Avenue. I mentioned that the locksmith was in the house, and she asked to see his work, thinking, I suppose, that she might have him do the locks on the new house. It would be a step up for you, Magill. I truly thought that you had taken the Bible-classes to heart, and were reformed."

"But I am!" Magill wailed.

Vanderbilt sighed. "Hargreave, look into it," he ordered. Then he turned to the fourth man, a wispy-looking individual in a shabby overcoat. "I will pay his bail. I'll give you one more chance, Magill!"

"Oh, thank you, Mr. Vanderbilt, sir!" Magill called out, as the millionaire stalked out of the cell.

The lawyer sneezed heartily, as well he might, for the cell was totally unheated. "You'll have to spend the night in jail, Magill, but I've got the writs all signed. Mr. Vanderbilt thinks you didn't do it, and that should be good enough, but it looks very black for you, very black indeed."

"Time's up!" the guard announced. Magill and Maggie kissed tenderly, and he was led away. Hargreave and I were left alone to size each other up, as the sporting men have it.

"Well, Escott," he said at last. "So you think Magill didn't do it. Would you like to tell me why? Just because his sister says so?"

"No," I said slowly. "Because the scene is so improbable. To commit a robbery in a house where the family is still in residence requires great daring, and a certain *panache*, which is certainly lacking in our yeggman. In fact, when I spoke with him, he seemed most upset at the treatment dealt out to the safe. Whoever broke into it apparently did damage, which infuriated Magill."

"Not bad, for a Limey," Hargreave said. "Educated at their University, too. A real toff. Well, I'm no toff, younker. I've been around the block a few times, and I tell you it smells fishy to me, too. A yeggman like Magill doesn't pull off a quick job like this. It's not his style. Crooks get into habits, see; that's how they get nabbed in the end."

"Excuse me," I said, "but . . . you are not with the police, are you?"

Hargreave smiled. "Private inquiry agent," he said. "Not Pinkerton . . . at least, not yet! But Pinkerton's too big. I take on one case at a time, just me. Mr. Vanderbilt back there is one of my best customers. I work quietly, and I get the goods. Watch, and learn, younker."

"Thank you," I said. "I have been of assistance in several small problems in England, and I should like to observe a professional consulting detective at work. May I join you?"

Hargreave laughed heartily. "You've got brass, kid. Okay, you meet me at Mr. Vanderbilt's house tomorrow morning, nine sharp, and we'll take a look at the scene of the crime, so to speak."

With a touch of his hat to Miss Magill, he left. Miss Magill and I were very late getting back to our boarding-house, incurring the wrath of the landlady for "carrying on after hours!"

Nevertheless, I was up early the next morning and made my way north on Fifth Avenue to the brownstone mansion inhabited by Mr. William Henry Vanderbilt and his large family. The previous day's sleet had changed to ice, and the city was covered with a glittering sheet that sparkled like crystal, lending a magical air to the drabbest of tenements, and causing the streets to become treacherous as skating-ponds. Just beyond Mr. Vanderbilt's house I could see a construction site, with workmen swarming about like ants erecting a new hill. This, presumably, was the much-talked-about palace being constructed at the whim of Mrs. William Kissam Vanderbilt, the imperious Alva, who had accused Mike Magill of theft.

Hargreave was waiting for me. He boldly went up to the front door, instead of walking around to the servants' entrance in the areaway behind the house. He and I were let in by a maid, who passed us on to an imposing footman in antiquated livery. The footman, in turn, showed us into Mr. William Henry Vanderbilt's study, the scene of the crime, as Hargreave had put it.

If a room takes on the character of the man who lives in it, then this study proved once again that Mr. William Henry Vanderbilt was the most modest of millionaires. The walls were panelled, not with expensive mahogany or elaborate tracery, but with honest oak. The few paintings were of bucolic landscapes, not particularly impressive, but pleasing to the eye. The furnishings were solid, armchairs and a sofa, upholstered in sombre but serviceable style, and a massive carved desk, where Vanderbilt presumably did his business.

Mr. Vanderbilt, dressed in morning coat and silk vest, was overseeing the repair of his safe, with the assistance of a young lady in fashionable attire. She looked the two of us over and apparently dismissed us as not worthy of her attention. Mr. Vanderbilt, however, stood up and nodded to us.

Hargreave stepped forward. "We're here, Mr. Vanderbilt, like you asked," he said. "You asked us to clear up a few points."

"There is nothing to clear up," the woman snapped, before Mr. Vanderbilt could utter a word. "The locksmith was there. The money was found in his tool-kit. He is a convicted criminal. Surely, that is enough?" She smiled sweetly, her voice suddenly turning to honey, and her accent assuming the liquid slur of the Southerner.

"I don't like to think I was mistaken in Magill," Vanderbilt said. "Alva, are you sure you saw the money in his tool-kit?"

I looked closer at Mrs. Alva. On inspection, she did not appear to be particularly daunting; she had a round face made remarkable only by her penetrating eyes, which seemed to mesmerize anyone who gazed into them too long. For the rest, she was a well-formed woman verging on thirty, with dark hair, dressed in the height of the most elaborate fashions of that year of extravagance.

"May I inspect the safe?" I asked, stepping forward. The safe was little more than a square box set into the fabric of the wall, closed with an old-fashioned key, rather than one of the newer combination locks. The handle had been wrenched away bodily, and the door to the safe sagged on its hinges. I nodded to Hargreave, as if to tell him to note this fact.

"What was usually kept in this safe?" I asked.

"Household money. Private papers," Mr. Vanderbilt said.

"Private . . . ?"

"Some letters, which dealt with family matters. My Will. Leases on family property."

Hargreave nodded. "And how much money was taken?"

"We're not sure," Alva put in. "Mr. Vanderbilt usually keeps ten thousand in the safe, for household expenses. There was money all over the floor." She made a sweeping gesture.

"I see. Where was Magill when all this was going on?"

Alva turned her expressive dark eyes on us. "Why . . . here, of course!"

"I meant to say, ma'am, where was he supposed to be?"

Vanderbilt spoke up. "I told him to do the conservatory locks first. A burglar might get in through the garden, you see."

"The conservatory it is, then," Hargreave said.

"Charles, show these men the conservatory," Alva ordered.

The huge footman marched us through the house, from the study to the conservatory, both on the ground floor. Once inside the glass-roofed extension to the mansion, I felt as if I were hacking my way through an exotic jungle, even in the middle of January. The cold air was whistling through a broken pane of glass, and the conservatory attendant was moving his precious charges away from the draught as if they had been children, while a glazier was fitting a new pane into the door.

"Why was the glass broken?" I asked.

"According to Mrs. Vanderbilt—that's Mrs. William Kissam Vanderbilt, Alva, who we just met—the yeggman must have got in this way."

"But that's absurd," I said. "Magill was already in the house. Besides . . ." I stooped down and checked the flagged floor of the conservatory. "If he had broken the glass from the outside, there would be shards of it here, whereas"—I opened the door and stepped outside, stooped, and found what I thought I would find— "the glass was broken from the inside. Here is the proof." I held up a shard of glass. I also noted some red-brown stains on the snow outside the window.

"I believe our thief may have scratched himself on this glass," I said.

"So, who are we looking for, younker? You want to tell the Old Man?"

"I should think we are looking for someone fairly large, with very strong hands," I said. "Which Mike Magill is emphatically not."

"Right you are," Hargreave said. "And why should he bother to tear the safe apart when he had the keys? That's his M.O., kid; put in the safe, then visit it when the family's away and lift a few bills, neat and clean. All that mess . . . papers all over the place? That's not like Magill. Not like any yeggman I know, either. They like to leave things real tidy. Takes the marks longer to figure that something's missing, you see!"

"But . . . if Magill didn't do it, who did?" I wondered, as Charles showed us back to the Vanderbilt study.

Hargreave smiled and tapped the side of his nose. Alva Vanderbilt was still in the study, sorting through Mr. Vanderbilt's papers.

"What a dreadful mess that criminal made," she said, as she examined each of the documents. "Why look, Mr. Vanderbilt, here's your Will! How ever do you suppose it got across the room like that?" She fanned the papers out, as if to put them in order, then laid the papers together in front of her father-in-law, who took them up and placed them into one of the drawers in his desk. She looked up and saw Hargreave and myself.

"Well?" she asked snappishly. I was forcibly reminded of a Pekingese dog disputing the ownership of a bone.

"Magill is innocent," Hargreave pronounced. "I'll go his bail myself. He couldn't have done it, ma'am; his hands are too small."

"Then who . . ." Mr. Vanderbilt asked in confusion.

I noticed the footman, who had been hovering nearby. "Mr. Hargreave," I said, in a conversational tone, "have you noticed the size of this footman's hands?"

"Good-size feller, too," Hargreave remarked. "Been in the ring? Let me see them hands." He seized the footman's wrists, before the servant could move. "Looky here, Mr. Escott. You were right; the thief did cut himself on the glass. Why'd you do it, Charley?"

The footman seemed to sag, then wrenched himself away and landed a perfect uppercut on Hargreave's jaw that laid the big man out on the floor. I launched myself after him, conscious of my bravado, for the footman was at least two inches taller than I, and correspondingly broad in the shoulders and arms. He shook me off like a terrier shakes off a rat, and made for the door at the end of the passage leading to the kitchen.

I followed, yelling as I went, "Call the police!"

Charles and I ploughed through the kitchen and out to the area, a paved yard below the street level. Like the street, the courtyard was covered with a thin sheet of ice. Charles crashed through the kitchen door, took one step, and landed ungracefully on his rump. I tripped over him, and thus I was accorded the honours when the police arrived to take the wretched man away. To add to his chagrin, the officers hauled him out the front door, onto Fifth Avenue, before a gawking crowd.

To my astonishment, Alva appeared, overseeing the removal of her footman. She fixed him with that basilisk stare of hers, as if daring him to speak out. "Don't you worry, Charles," Alva said. "Vanderbilts take care of their own. I will see that you have a good lawyer."

Charles stared helplessly at her as he was being led away. Hargreave followed, to give his deposition, and Mr. Vanderbilt retreated to his study, leaving me at the back of the hall. Before I could make my presence known, a tiny child, barely three years old came in, with her nurse. The child's eyes were red, but whether the tears were from the cold or another reason I could not say.

Her mother, Alva, spared a glance for the child. "How was your party, Consuelo? Did you have a good time?"

"I wanted to skate, Mama, but the Astor children would not skate with me. They said that Vanderbilts are not the thing."

Alva straightened up. I could have sworn I saw the light of battle in her eyes. "Not the thing!" she muttered to herself. "Vanderbilt money's not good enough for the Astors? We'll see about that!" Then she patted the child on the shoulder. "Never you mind, dear. Nurse, take Miss Consuelo up and see she is kept warm. Consuelo, you listen to me. When you are a duchess, they will come begging to play with you!"

"Am I to be a duchess, Mama?"

"Or a princess. Trust your mama, you shall be."

The child thought gravely, then said, "But I may not wish to be a duchess."

Alva stiffened. "I'll tell you what you wish, child. Get upstairs."

Consuelo noticed me for the first time. She gravely curtsied, then scampered up the stairs, followed by her nurse.

Mrs. Alva turned and saw me, lurking, as it were, in the shadow of the grand staircase. She smiled, and turned those remarkable eyes in my direction. "Why, Mr. Escott . . . it is Escott, isn't it? I thought I recognized you. You were in that amusing play . . ."

"I am delighted to know that my performance was so memorable." I began to edge towards the door.

Alva's smile became almost fierce. "Actors lead such difficult lives, I hear. Audiences are so fickle. Why, someone who was enormously popular one day can be cast aside the next. All it takes is a word or two in the right ears . . ."

I suddenly realized what she was driving at. She could destroy, not me, but the entire company, with a whispering campaign that would turn our success to a miserable failure. If I voiced my suspicions about her inciting Charles to his robbery, or implicating Magill, she would see to it that everyone connected with me suffered. I understood that much well enough, Watson. That woman was positively demonic! She would let nothing and nobody stop her from attaining her ends, no matter how petty they may be.

I reached the front door. Without another word, I bolted! I practically slid down Fifth Avenue until I caught up with Hargreave, who was watching Charles being stowed into the Black Maria, to be hauled off to the Tombs in place of Mike Magill.

"Had enough of Alva, younker?" Hargreave chuckled, as we began the walk downtown.

"Then you agree that it was she who spurred Charles on?"

"Had to be," Hargreave said. "But he'll never rat on her. He'll do his time and there'll be a nice job waiting for him somewhere. Unless he's sent out West. I'm still not sure what he was after, though."

"The Will," I said suddenly.

"Eh?" Hargreave looked sharply at me.

"Was there not some difficulty about the terms of the old Commodore's Will?"

Hargreave chuckled. "You bet there was, younker. A whale of a scandal. Lawsuits and everything. After all that, no Vanderbilt will ever dare question a Will again!"

"So that if Mr. William Henry Vanderbilt were to die tomorrow . . ."

"Whatever they find in his safe will stick!" Hargreave shook his head at the audacity of it. "And Mrs. Alva wanted to see how much she would get—"

"And possibly take steps to correct any 'error,' " I concluded. "But we have no proof of any of this, Mr. Hargreave, and the Vanderbilts are not about to let two private inquiry agents—"

"One agent, one actor," Hargreave reminded me.

"I stand corrected," I said. "This will never be made public."

We walked along for a few more minutes. Then I said, "I am intrigued that you actually make your living investigating crimes that have baffled the police. As far as I know, there is no such creature in England."

"Well, kid, if you want to give it a whirl, I say, go to it," said Hargreave genially. "Only not in my town! New York is mine!"

"At the moment, sir, you can have it," I said. "May I tell Miss Magill that her brother will soon be a free man?"

"I think she knows," Hargreave said. I realized that we had already reached the theatre, where I saw Miss Magill throw her arms around her brother, who was stepping out of a horse-car. I was pleased, but not satisfied, for Justice had not truly been served.

Our train pulled into the station, and Holmes began to wrap himself into his famous tweed greatcoat and deerstalker cap.

I followed him through the station to where our local transportation, a farmer's dray, stood waiting. "But, Holmes . . ." I said, puffing a little. "I don't understand the secrecy. Surely, you could have spoken out when Mr. William Vanderbilt died, and his Will was read."

"That was in 1885," Holmes said. "As you may recall, we were extremely busy that year. By the time I knew anything about it, Mr. Vanderbilt's Will had been read and probated. According to its terms, his fortune was divided more or less evenly between Mr. Cornelius and Mr. William Kissam Vanderbilt, with Mr. George Washington Vanderbilt and the various Vanderbilt daughters getting substantial, but not extravagant bequests. Mrs. William Kissam—Alva—became a leader in what passes for Society in America, and did make her daughter a duchess . . . as you have seen. I was quite surprised that Her Grace recalled my face. I have changed somewhat since then."

"But . . ." I still protested. "You could have come forward with your suspicions."

"To what end?" Holmes asked wearily. "After the scandalous

trials of the Commodore's Will, none of the surviving Vanderbilts would question another Will. Without proof, there was nothing I could do. The case of Vanderbilt and the Yeggman was closed. It was one of my earliest successes, and one of my greatest failures. I still am chagrined when I think how I cravenly ran from that woman. It is the only time I ever ran from anything, and I can only excuse myself by recalling how many others she managed to ride over in pursuit of her goals. She bullied her way into that Society that rejected her, and married her daughter into the highest circles of our aristocracy."

"Yes . . . the Duchess of Marlborough," I said.

"You are right, Watson. I was abominably rude to her. I shall write to her and apologize, explaining that the pressure of a case vital to the Empire prevented me from assisting her. I cannot possibly explain that her whole marriage might have been based on a fraud."

"Might have been?" I echoed.

"Watson, don't you see? Mr. William Henry Vanderbilt could have altered his Will any time between the robbery in 1880 and his death in 1885. It is possible that Alva Vanderbilt merely influenced her father-in-law, rather than actually inserting a clause into that infamous Will, but without proof, I can say nothing. Nevertheless, when Miss Consuelo Vanderbilt married the Duke of Marlborough last year, it was with the understanding that a large part of her fortune would revert directly to him. His title, bought with her money. A dreadful bargain, Watson; I do not think the Duchess of Marlborough is a happy woman. I shall not add to her unhappiness by accusing her mother of theft and possible forgery. No, Watson, I must insist that you keep this case confidential. Now, let us be off!"

AFTERMATH:

It was indeed rumoured that William Henry Vanderbilt's will was tampered with by Alva, or at least that she influenced him to divide his enormous estate between his two eldest sons. A third son, George Washington Vanderbilt, was given a substantial bequest, but nothing like the fifty million or so that Cornelius and Willie K. Vanderbilt inherited. Consuelo Vanderbilt's marriage to the Duke of Marlborough was stage-managed by her mother, although both parties were attached to other people. (They separated in 1909, and were finally divorced in 1920.) As soon as her daughter's engagement was announced, Alva divorced her husband and proceeded to marry one of his best friends, Oliver Perry Belmont. As Mrs. Belmont, she spearheaded the drive for woman's suffrage and the Nineteenth Amendment.

As stated earlier, Sherlock Holmes was presumed dead, smashed at the foot of Reichenbach Falls along with his arch-enemy Professor Moriarty, from 1891 until 1894, when he finally revealed himself to Dr. Watson. When his friend asked Holmes what he'd been doing during this undercover period, the detective spoke of time spent in Tibet, Persia, Mecca and Khartoum, and some months spent in research at a laboratory in the south of France. But he neglected to mention the diplomatic mission undertaken for his brother Mycroft that led to this supremely unromantic sleuth's . . . marriage?!!

The Secret Marriage of Sherlock Holmes

BY SHARIANN LEWITT

The mission was an imposition, but I could not say no to Mycroft. Usually his inquiries were of an intriguing as well as important nature, and provided an opportunity to serve the Queen in a unique capacity.

Still, I did not desire to go to Arabia in 1893. Work on the laboratory was progressing nicely in France, and my mind was on research for my own edification. There was much promise in some recent work in Germany that I wished to pursue, and I had spent some time and a good portion of funds to obtain the equipment and supplies I would need.

It was with great regret that I boarded the ship at Marseilles and watched green France recede from the rail. In my pocket I carried the sealed leather envelope that Mycroft had given me to deliver in Mecca to a representative of the Ottoman Turks, along with several other missives that were destined for officials stationed throughout Arabia.

There was little employment for my talents in this mission. Mycroft could not send a courier from the Foreign Office, as the contact was not a public one, but he had no need of my skills and abilities.

"Nonsense," he replied when I told him that any one of a dozen Orientalists could fulfill the task better than I. "None of them have the nerve for it. And you do have the language and knowledge of the culture to enable you to penetrate the forbidden city of Mecca as Burton did. No one else exists who is better suited."

So now I was sailing away from the work I found so fascinating in France in order to deliver the mail in fancy dress. When I could tolerate looking at the shore no longer, I retired to my cabin to read yet again the exploits of Sir Richard Burton, the great Orientalist, in Mecca some forty years earlier.

But I was not to travel the usual Pilgrimage route. The delivery in Mecca was but the last of several interviews and letters to be given to Arabs and Egyptians as well as Turks in various parts of Arabia. Not only was this to be a dull task, but an uncomfortable one as well. The itinerary that Mycroft had prepared would require me to cross the Empty Quarter if I were to make the timetable so subtly included in the list of addresses where I was to call.

Mycroft knew perfectly well that the Empty Quarter is the most inhospitable and barren desert in the world. There are no wells and what few sources of water there are are poisoned. Even among the Arabs there are few who can survive there, let alone track across the moving dunes and guide a traveller to the other side. Only one or two of the fiercest Bedouin tribes would undertake the journey. It sounded quite unpleasant in the comfort of Mycroft's club; in the full furnace heat of Jedda I wished for a moment that I had argued more fiercely against taking the mission.

The aridity of the peninsula was worse than the heat. Simply disembarking from our ship was a nightmare. My suit was soaked through with sweat and my mouth was dry before I even picked up my bags to walk down to solid land. The stench hit before I stepped into Arabia proper, the unwashed throng of beggars and porters and navvies all crowded on the narrow accessway, each of them yelling for work or alms. There were also water sellers festooned with grimy bottles half-full of water, which they were hawking for prices that would buy two pints of ale at any pub in London. And yet I was so thirsty that I contemplated the price and mentally sifted through my change to see if I had the sum at hand.

Before I could purchase the water, my bags were snatched out of my hands by a wiry young man with dark skin and a scowl. "Give those back," I ordered, but he did not stop until he had reached the street. Or the poor excuse for one, since it was not decently paved.

He dropped my things on the hard-packed dirt and started yelling and waving his arms to every vehicle that moved. Finally a small cart drew up. "You are going to Riyadh, sir?" the porter asked as he handed my cases over to the driver. "This is my cousin Salah, he will take you to Riyadh. Only two pounds, is very cheap."

"No, sir, it is very expensive," I replied in Arabic. "I will not pay more than one and a half."

The porter grinned broadly and his white teeth blazed in his leathered face. Then he touched his heart, his lips and his forehead with the fingers of his right hand and held it open to me. "Why did you not tell me you were a believer, sir?" he asked in his own language, his tone conveying just a hint of petulance. "I would not charge you as I do an infidel. Salah will take you for half that price, unless you wish to go to the Pilgrim's area. Then he will take you for nothing, and our honour to welcome you to the holy places."

It was quite evident how Sir Richard Burton had managed to enter the city closed to all but Muslims. Though, indeed, he knew more of the customs and religion of Islam than any man in Britain before undertaking the Pilgrimage himself. This was going to be even less interesting than I had first thought.

"Thank you, I am going to Riyadh first," I said. "So your offer will be fine. Good day." I gave him tuppence and climbed into the cart, which smelled of camel milk and old wool. I steeled myself for the long journey to the capital, which turned out to be only a full day's ride. We approached just at sunset, as the muezzins chanted the call to prayer from all the minarets in the town. To see those dizzying white towers against the darkening sky and hear the call echoed and repeated all around reminded me that this was truly an alien place. The stars were clear and bright, outlining the graceful towers in the falling darkness. It was very beautiful in a foreign way, but also brought home to me how much I would prefer at that moment to be sitting in a clean sitting room in a comfortable wingback chair.

The air chilled rapidly but there was no comforting moisture in the coming night. Indeed, my throat was dry and rasping and I would have happily paid for another sip of water had there been any left in the canteen. My guide, Salah, stopped the cart, took out his prayer rug and began to pray. He looked askance at me, as if expecting me to join him, but I wandered far enough to give him privacy in his devotions.

Darkness falls rapidly this near the equator. The long gentle twilight full of pinks and ambers is a stranger to this place of harsh contrasts, of endless desert and fervent faith. When Salah had finished at his prayers, we both climbed back into the cart and rode the last two miles to the outskirts of town in much less time than I had expected. With the darkness came cool air that seemed to breathe life into the one sorry roan gelding hitched to the cart, and he picked up his ears and started to move with something that approached vigour. No longer beaten down by the anvil of the sun, he showed himself to be a fine animal, alert and ready to go home.

"It is too late," Salah protested when we found the gates of the city closed for the night. Riyadh is the center of a very strict sect of

Islam, and its gates are shut after evening prayers. "We shall have to find the camp where my brother-in-law lives. They are close to here, I have gone with them often. We are not entirely soft city folk, no, we are proud of our Bedouin family. Now two of my nephews are with the band as well, learning the ways of the desert so they do not grow up to be spoiled, lazy, irreligious city boys. When my sons are thirteen I will send them to their uncle in the desert to train them."

As there was no choice in the matter, I was quite content to let Salah drive until he found a ragged outcropping of tents along a ridge. I had noticed the irregularity of shape in the shadows, but would not have immediately recognized this as a Bedouin encampment. The fires were all well hidden by the deep sand pits, around which men sat on fine carpets and smoked a water pipe.

Salah approached one of the elders, a gentleman with skin as dark and lined as the waterskin that lay empty under the driver's seat. Under his keffiyah his hair was no doubt as white as his long desert robe, and his nose was a monument to both the size and sharpness of the organ. Indeed, it looked more like a beak than anything human.

The old man rose with grace that belied his years and welcomed us among the Murrah tribe of the Bedouin. "We are happy to fulfill the obligation of hospitality that is the law of the desert, and in so doing to give of charity as we are commanded as believers. For did not the Prophet say that to remove the obstructions in the way of true belief is itself a form of charity? That to smile at someone is charity, to give greeting is charity. And so we are honoured to welcome you to our fire and conversation."

Salah bowed and introduced us. "This gentleman is a European who has need to travel. His name is Sherlock Holmes, and he serves his ruler, the Queen of England."

The old man jutted his chin with approval and pointed his nose to a place that had been made on the carpet next to him. "I am Bader ibn Abdullah of the Murrah Bedouin. We await the arrival of a young man of Riyadh who wishes our escort to cross the Empty Quarter."

Immediately my interest was aroused. "You cross the Empty Quarter? I had heard that even the Bedouin prefer to go around that place." For it is surely the most desolate spot on the earth, I added mentally, with perhaps the exception of the South Pole. There is no water there, nothing at all grows in the shifting dunes, and it is full of treacherous quicksand and springs where the water is tainted with toxic chemicals leached from the sands.

Ibn Abdullah smiled as if what I said had pleased him greatly. "This is so indeed, Mr. Sherlock. Of all the Bedouin, only the Murrah will make the crossing more than once. We know the ways of the Empty Quarter, and we can take anyone across it for a price."

The young man who was serving Salah coffee made a face. Then he offered me a thimble-sized glass edged with gold on an ornate brass tray. I sniffed at it slightly; the beverage was heavily laced with cardamum but from the way the men regarded me it was obvious that I was required to drink. Not to do so would be an insult to my hosts. I quaffed the whole in a single mouthful, and while the strangely spiced coffee was odd it was also decidedly appealing and refreshing.

"Delicious," I said quite honestly to my host, and added a smile to the young man serving. He smiled back brilliantly and immediately poured me another cup. This one I savoured slowly.

"When do you think you shall leave across the Quarter?" Salah asked.

Ibn Abdullah shrugged. "In a day and a night, maybe two nights, God willing. But we cannot wait much longer. In two weeks it will be too late to attempt to cross before the windstorms become too dangerous. Then we shall have to wait until the end of the windstorm season, which will not suit our customer in Riyadh." Then the old man's face broke into a deep smile. "But there will be good hunting along the way for the falcons, and I am sure that this fat, Western-taught Rasheedi will not be up to the hunt. I do not think he can handle birds at all."

A few deep laughs joined the old man's. I was curious and hoped he would speak more. Certainly I already knew that the traditional ruling family of Riyadh had been driven from the city and the Rasheedi were considered upstarts and pretenders by everyone in the region. But the two families had been feuding for a very long time and one of them ascendant over the other meant nothing, or so I understood.

"So one of the new royalty has hired you as guides?" I prompted just a bit more discussion of the matter. "Surely he has other matters more important to attend."

Ibn Abdullah smiled slowly, and this time there was a hint of slyness under the white teeth. "Ah, perhaps the rest of the family does," my host agreed with me. "But young Mahmud has just returned from studies at Oxford and also in Switzerland and thinks himself rather above us here. Tell me, sir, have you ever been to Switzerland? Is there some reason that he would learn to deny his people, his heritage, his duty to God there? Those who go to the West all carry the taint of irreligious thought and no longer think that the ways of the Murrah are good enough any longer. 'This is a new age,' they say. 'We should be settled and have automobiles.' Tell me, sir, what is your thought on automobiles?"

"That they would be quite absurd in the desert," I answered truthfully. "They are made for carefully paved roads. Here the sand would get into the engine and then it would break down."

The old man slapped his palm against his knee. "Just so! And when it has broken, you cannot eat it or drink from its stomach or its blood, you cannot use it to warm you. And it has no sense, it cannot smell water under the ground, it cannot tell which wells are tainted and which are sweet and pure. No, I do not think that a camel is of the past and that this automobile is the way we shall overcome the desert. Though I do not hate all things Western," he said expansively, trying to be more generous towards me. "Look." He pulled back the white sleeve of his beautifully laundered and pressed *thobe* to display a Swiss timepiece as fine as any I have ever seen on a gentleman's arm, and I lost no time in telling him so.

"Then I must give it to you," he said immediately, taking the watch from his wrist.

"No, not at all, sir," I protested. "It would be unseemly and un-gentlemanly for me to accept such a gift on so short an acquaintance."

"Not at all," the old man insisted, tossing the watch into my lap. "I would be honoured if you would wear it always and re-member our friendship. Besides, it is not so good to have it. Our young people must learn to read the shadows and the sun to know when it is time to pray, and not become the slaves of some foreign timepiece that could break. Only Allah's own clock can keep time precisely enough so that we will never miss the correct time for worship. Everything else is false."

Try as I might I could not refuse. Arabians, especially the Bedouin, judge themselves not by education and achievement as we do in England, but by piety, generosity and courage. It gave Ibn Abdullah great esteem among his people to be so conspicuous in his gift-giving. Even knowing that did not erase the last shadow of guilt, however. I should have realized that this was the proper time to have admired the watch on his wrist, to say how finely it suited him, instead of simply stating the obvious fact of its fine precision and manufacture. But the Bedouin are more sensitive to such things and while I was quite comfortable with the language and customs of the city-dwellers in places like Egypt and Syria, there were sub-tle differences with these desert dwellers that promised at least some diversion on the long journey ahead.

I thanked him deeply and then put the watch on my wrist. It has resided noplace else since, not only to honour Ibn Abdullah but to honour all those people of the Peninsula that I came to know and find quite admirable and respectable in a way that is not generally commonly assumed in England. There the Arabs are seen as inno-cent natives, all quite noble and primitive when they are not being sneaky and underhanded.

The moon rose high above the camp in a midnight blue sky. It was a thin crescent sliver shimmering among the stars, and in this clear dry air it was easy to distinguish hundreds of the lesser stars. They spilled across the sky so richly that it seemed that all heaven was ablaze with hundreds and hundreds of tiny lights. Indeed, there were even stars I could not recognize or name, and briefly wondered whether they all had names in English.

The boy who had poured my coffee showed me quickly to a sleeping place, a pile of elaborately woven rugs in the men's area of a tent. Two others were already asleep and snoring, one of them being my driver Salah.

"Please to let me show, if you need. I happy to serve, honour the Murrah," the boy said in heavily accented English. I was quite surprised that he attempted the language at all. I wondered idly if he were literate.

"Indeed, I can read the Koran and the Hadith and can write well enough, though my tutor said that my letters are harder to read than a camel track in the sand," he replied in elegant Arabic. There was no question at all that he had been well schooled. "Will you be travelling with us? I would like to improve my English and my French, too, if that is possible."

Indeed, the fact that this band was crossing the Empty Quarter and leaving immediately was an advantage. My errand in Riyadh should take no more than the morning, and it appeared that the group would not leave until the next day in any case. Besides, that would mean that no one could easily track where I was headed; Mycroft did impress me with the need for discretion in this task. There would be no record of my asking for guides, buying supplies, and making a fair show in town.

"If that is amenable to your leaders, I should find it very convenient," I replied. "But surely you can practice English and French with this Rasheedi. He was educated at Oxford, so I understand, and studied in Switzerland. I should think that he would be most accomplished in those languages."

The boy sneered. "I will not speak with him at all. He is the enemy of my family and some day I shall bury him in the desert and pray for his soul."

I raised an eyebrow. "You are of the House of Saud, then?" I asked, though I hardly needed the question. The Rasheed family had unseated the ibn Saud from their royal position in Riyadh, though if it weren't for the education he had received I could easily believe that this boy was Bedouin and felt that the Rasheeds had been responsible for some personal misfortune. However, he was far too well educated for a Bedouin, and too commanding in the company of his elders. The mark of Royal bearing was unmistakeable.

"I am Abdul Aziz ibn Saud," he said proudly.

Not simply a member of the Royal family then, but the deposed young prince himself. Mycroft had spoken highly of him and his father in years past, and praised the boy's keen intelligence and political bent of mind. "He will be a fine king one day, and if we do well by him he will be a good friend of England for life," I remembered Mycroft saying from the recess of a great leather wing-back, veiled in cigar smoke.

But the ibn Saud had been displaced by their old rivals the Rasheeds, and the boy had been driven into the desert with his sister Noura. The whereabouts of his parents and other family members were still unknown, and very likely they were dead.

"Your Highness," I said, rising and nodding sharply to him as I would to a European aristocrat of high rank. "I am honoured to make your acquaintance. My name is Sherlock Holmes and I am in Arabia on a mission from my Queen."

"Sherlock Holmes?" the boy asked quickly. "I have read about the way you have solved many difficult crimes. Always those were the best things in the English papers that I studied. It is I who am honoured to meet you."

He said the last in very creditable English.

That was when I decided that I would indeed accompany this band of Bedouin across the Empty Quarter. I wanted to know more about this Saudi princeling who seemed so much at home as a

Murrah youth. And I wanted to meet the Rasheed who would be traveling with us as well. The information might never become important, but at least it would provide some intellectual stimulation while on the way.

The next day I accomplished my business in Riyadh by noon. Salah had driven me to both of the houses where I was to call, and threw in the ride back to the Murrah Bedouin camp for free. "It is too late to get a good fare now, anyway, and I enjoyed meeting ibn Abdullah," the carter said with a pleasant smile. "And I will be home before the gates close for the sunset prayers."

I gave him a generous tip before I approached the aged Bedouin leader to ask for a place on the journey. Ibn Abdullah might have lived all his life in tents on the sands, but he was as fierce bargaining over fees as he was flying his hawks. Finally we agreed upon a price that was rather higher than I would have liked and well below the budget Mycroft had set. I would have my own small tent furnished with several rugs and blankets and take my meals with the Rasheed party, which would be served by the teenage boys in the band.

I requested that Abdul Aziz be assigned to me, to pack and set my tent, to care for the camel I would ride and to make sure I was properly mounted every night. The old man insisted that there was no Abdul Aziz among the boys and that he had never heard of the House of Saud. I shrugged and said there was a boy who wanted to practice some English and French with me, and that was the one, no matter which name I had "misunderstood." Ibn Abdullah nodded sagely and agreed that I would have such an assistant.

The Rasheed party did not arrive until the next day near sunset. They rode fine horses that ibn Abdullah insisted be sent back to Riyadh. "They will never survive the Empty Quarter," he said, but as he surveyed his guests it appeared that he thought they would not survive it either.

There were four men in the group. Ahmed al-Rasheed was precisely the kind of Arab noble one found with such ease in Western universities. He was handsome enough, and would have cut quite a figure had he not already begun to indulge in the excesses for which his people are known. He was perhaps twenty-five years old, but already his body was thickening and his face had heavy jowls. His skin was red and blotchy, attesting to far too much fondness for drink. He would find the long road ahead difficult indeed, then, since ibn Abdullah was not about to tolerate any alcohol in his camp.

Though I am not myself a Muslim, I must admit that I admired the Murrah leader. He allowed no deviation in his faith, not in himself and not among his people. He could not be a hypocrite of any form; indeed, his absolute honesty and unfailing devotion was among the most unswerving I have ever observed. I wondered why Ahmed al-Rasheed, who appeared so much the opposite of the old man, had chosen to travel with him.

Among al-Rasheed's traveling companions, two were servants and the third was a school friend of lesser rank among the Arab people but most likely as much wealth. He had the unlikely name of Khalid ibn Peterson, which presaged a story I was curious to hear. This Peterson probably had far more native ability than al-Rasheed, and less devotion to his vices—as is common among such friendships in England.

I watched idly, smoking my pipe, as the servants put up Rasheed's tent. It was a grand affair with at least three rooms, several brass chandeliers and tables and several chairs carved of fine wood and inlaid with mother-of-pearl. A second tent was provided for the friend, much smaller but equally opulent with oil lamps and worked brass fittings.

Abdul Aziz, the young prince in his role as my squire, squatted in the shadows a bit behind me as we watched this luxury constructed in the midst of Bedouin austerity. "He does not respect his betters from the desert," Abdul Aziz spat. "He tries to show he is superior and he only proves his own foolishness. And he thinks he will eliminate me on the way—he is a fool, indeed."

I took a deep pull on the pipe. "It is never a good idea to underestimate one's enemies," I pointed out neutrally. "Though I would be interested in knowing why you find his furnishings foolish."

"He is a fool because we will use every drop of all the water we can carry crossing the Empty Quarter," the boy replied firmly. "We must rely on the camels, and even many of them have died on this trail. Everything they carry, every bit of weight, must be balanced against how long the camel can go without water. And if they are asked to carry too much they will die of thirst like any other beast. If the camels die, we die."

"Hmm," I said, gazing at the tent that was now finished and ready for occupancy. The blend in my pipe was excellently satisfying, and Abdul Aziz's assessment of the Rasheed fit my own. The boy certainly had more talent than many Royals through Europe. Indeed, the Foreign Office could do worse than wish that some of the Hapsburgs were so astute.

Shadows moved around the sand and Abdul Aziz slipped away before Rasheed's servant approached me. He bowed and touched his heart and forehead as if to a believer. "Please, sir, my master would like you to honour his poor tent as a guest at dinner tonight. He has heard that you are the great Sherlock Holmes of England. And as he has spent much of his life in that fair land, he considers it his true home and you a countryman of his."

"I would be delighted to join your master at dinner," I replied. "Let me change into something more appropriate and I shall be with him directly."

The servant bowed again and scampered away. I ducked back into my tent with its serviceable hurricane lamp and took off the long white *thobe* I wore along with the native headdress. I was not attempting any deception by the guise, but the Arab robe is much cooler and more comfortable than woolen trousers and a starched collar. People who live in harsh climes know best about how to make them most tolerable, and it would be senseless to ignore their collective wisdom. However, I dressed in one of three suits I had brought along, with a fresh shirt-front and collar, to represent the England that Ahmed al-Rasheed knew. Then I crossed the small space between our tents and was ushered into what appeared to be a city palace from the inside. I was seated on a carved chair softened by silk pillows while my host came out and greeted me effusively. Then he took the ewer of rosewater while a servant held a bowl beneath my hands. Al-Rasheed himself poured scented water so that I might wash, and did so so graciously that I wondered if I had misjudged him and he would prove to be a delightful companion. Al-Rasheed offered the towel to dry my hands, and then went through the entire ritual for his friend Peterson as well.

"It is so fortunate that we have some civilized company here," he said. "Mr. Holmes, we are deeply honoured by your presence among us. Who in all the fair land of England has not read of your most brilliant service to the cause of justice? You are the last of King Arthur's knights among us, and your presence in my humble tent is a memory that I shall cherish all my life and into the next world as well. Especially since I heard *you* have in the next world . . ."

"Thank you, sir, though I fear you overstate the case. The papers have made far more of my inquiries than is appropriate. My putative death suits the mission I am on. And it is I who am honoured to meet you, a prince of the reigning House of Rasheed. And you as well, sir," I nodded in the direction of Peterson.

"This is Khalid ibn Peterson, a friend of mine from our earliest days in school," al-Rasheed said.

"Peterson?" I asked blandly. "That is not an Arab name."

"No indeed, sir," Peterson said. And as I looked at him closely in the light it was evident that his was a mixed heritage. He had the dark eyes of Arabia and the profile, but his skin was too light for this desert sun by half and what hair showed under his keffiyah was auburn, something between the deep near-black of the Arabs and what I would expect was his father's blonde. Unlike al-Rasheed, he wore his *thobe* as if it were the dress of a king, and from his movement and his face I could see clearly that he was slim and well muscled and had not fallen victim to the indulgences of food and drink and sloth.

"My father came to Arabia as a student of Sir Richard Burton and one of his party. His name was George Peterson and his father, my late grandfather, was Richard Peterson, Lord Phillipsbourne," Peterson said in unaccented English. "My father studied Arabic in Oxford, and also the True Faith, but it remained merely an intellectual exercise for him until he came to Arabia to further his knowledge of the region. As I understand it, my grandfather was quite proud of his talent for languages and foreign cultures and hoped that some day George would be appointed Ambassador to Egypt or the Ottomans.

"But my grandfather was not so pleased when his only son went off to Arabia with the great adventurer Sir Richard Burton. My father has always had a great passion for the truth, and for discovering things for himself. He left Burton's party to study with a great scholar of Islamic law in Jedda, and became so convinced by his teacher and what he had learned that he converted to the Faith of the Prophet in his second year here. He had to give up a great fortune in England, as his family quite disapproved and disinherited him.

"My father was so highly regarded by his teacher that he was brought to Mecca as a great jurist and introduced to the leading imams of that holy place. One of these leaders, the great poet Isa ibn Khalid, was so very impressed by the young Englishman that the poet arranged a match with his daughter. My mother was the greatest prize in Mecca, as famed for her piety and learning as for her beauty. Her father was one of the great imams of the Holy Places as well as a distinguished poet, and quite wealthy besides. Therefore, I grew up in a good Arab home with all the advantages of education and property. But what I hold most dear and for which

I have the greatest gratitude is that both my parents and my grand-parents were people of great wisdom and deep faith. After my three uncles died in battle, my grandfather adopted my father as his son, and now that my grandfather is so old, my father stands to inherit the whole."

"But George Peterson did inherit from the Petersons," I said, remembering the papers. "He was the only male heir of direct lineage, and a very old codicil in some ancestor's will insisted that the property belong only to a direct descendant. The courts upheld the decision even though much of the family was horrified."

Khalid smiled. "Yes. I am my father's second son. My brother will inherit what is here and will take his place as one of the great scholars of the Shari'a. And I will be sent in exile to hold our land and house in England. For that reason I was sent to school there, to learn the workings of English law as thoroughly as my brother learns the Islamic. He is my brother and I love him, and I honour his place in the family as my elder, but I do wish that our fortunes were reversed."

"While I wish I could live in England forever," al-Rasheed sighed. "But there are advantages to being here as well. Anyway, it should be time for dinner. Would you care for a drink, Mr. Holmes? I have some very acceptable brandy and a decent Scotch."

Both Peterson and I took water while al-Rasheed poured himself a generous whiskey. "I understand that my friend Khalid does not drink because he is Muslim and wishes to avoid the appearance of sin. Though he did like his beer in England. But you, Mr. Holmes, you are not Muslim. Why do you prefer water to good Scotch?"

"My body is not accustomed to this climate, Your Highness, and alcohol dehydrates one rapidly. Perhaps for one who is more used to desert conditions it is not a concern, but since the Empty Quarter is known to be the most arid place on Earth I think it best to refrain."

Al-Rasheed nodded and put his own glass aside. Servants arrived bearing platters of lamb and rice and vegetables, which they set on the largest brass table directly in front of me. Then they brought china and silver and large serving spoons, which is much a Western affectation here. The Bedouin eat with their hands from the central dish, so the ceremonial washing of hands is a sanitary procedure as well as a welcoming gesture. The food was excellent, and I was sorry that Watson was not there to sample it. He is fond of mutton and this was delicious.

As we ate, the conversation turned towards Mr. Peterson's coming marriage, which had been arranged by his parents. "Khalid seems to have gotten religion since we have returned," al-Rasheed sighed. "At school he was too serious by half, and took a first in Law. He never went out with us drinking and at the bawdy houses he always married the girl."

"It is easy enough and an old tradition," Peterson protested. "And I always divorced them before I left. Besides, none of the girls even know what I said since it was in Arabic. It made no difference to any of them."

"Yes, but it made a difference to you," al-Rasheed said with a grin that could very easily become a sneer.

"Excuse me, but how is it possible to marry anyone for a few hours?" I asked, both curious and hoping to divert what appeared to be a long-standing argument.

Peterson waved his hand as if brushing off a fly. "In order to marry, according to Muslim rite, a man need only say 'I marry thee' to a woman three times. The divorce is the same, he merely has to repeat 'I divorce thee' three times and it counts as a legal divorce. It is the common custom here for men who do not have true wives with them to enter a temporary marriage for a set period of time so they can enjoy the comforts of home."

These simple marriage customs seemed all too dangerous to me. While I myself found the idea simply foreign and strange, some men who have great weakness for the fair sex could find themselves married dozens of times. Watson, for example, would have married before he was out of public school, had the opportunity been so easy!

And yet it was such customs that kept these people primitive. If something as sacred as marriage can be entered with no more than the muttering of a few words, if Church and State both are not required to be present to sanction the union and all forms of ceremony are not established, then there is little public recognition for the most civilizing institution known. Indeed, marriage is known to civilize men, and the Arabs remain utterly wild with their constant raiding and incessant tribal wars.

"I always thought the English ladies much more intelligent," al-Rasheed broke in. "They only provide what a man needs most and make no commitment for more than an hour, while the temporary wives here are expected to cook and wash and take care of the household as well. And though they are usually paid a reasonable sum upon the divorce, it is not so much as the ladies at Doll's make in a single week."

"But the employees of this establishment, they must pay for their own room and board and clothes and expenses all the time," I pointed out. "While I suppose a temporary wife is supported in all these things."

Khalid nodded and he smiled. "Just so. They are often given valuable gifts as well, clothes and jewelry and carpets, that they keep along with the payment."

"Still, those unfortunates who have been forced to work in bawdy houses are rendered unmarriageable in the true sense, and when they grow older they are left to charity if they have not been prudent," I remarked, thinking of the poor unfortunates in charitable establishments throughout my native land.

Even al-Rasheed blinked with surprise. "Unmarriageable?" he asked. "Why would a temporary wife be any more unmarriageable than any other divorced woman? Sometimes a second or third wife who is older, a fine cook and a good housekeeper, can make a household run far more smoothly. What does it matter if she is no longer beautiful?"

I had also forgotten that Muslim men were permitted four wives as well. Watson is very fortunate that he has never come to Arabia, for to have four wives a man must support all of them and treat them equally well. Upon reflection, it is no wonder that most Arab men marry only one wife at a time.

Khalid Peterson shook his head. "You must forgive my friend," he said to me. "He is worried about marrying a young and fiery-tempered Bedouin girl who can't do anything but milk camels and shake carpets. Even Ahmed must serve his family as I have served mine, though it is to neither of our liking."

Al-Rasheed shot Peterson a hard look, and I began to wonder if the word "friend" did describe their relationship. Perhaps Peterson had been sent with al-Rasheed as his keeper at school, and had kept the role when they both returned. Certainly there was little warmth between them.

"We all must make sacrifices to serve our families," I said, remembering only too acutely that I was not as unfamiliar with the concept as they appeared to believe.

Then a servant arrived with dessert, a pastry far too sticky and sweet for anyone over the age of ten. With the change of course came a change of conversation that was quite welcome. I already knew that I was not looking forward to spending the next weeks crossing the harshest desert in the world with these men.

Five days out of Riyadh, al-Rasheed was already begging water. He had gone through his ration as though he did not believe that there was no oasis, no spring, no place at all to get water until we crossed the sand. I did not feel obliged to share with him; apparently neither did anyone else.

"That is good," Abdul Aziz said after he got my tent set and served me a portion of hard bread and dried dates. "Then he will die soon, and he won't be able to kill me."

"Why do you think he wants to kill you?" I asked.

"That is why he was sent with us," Abdul-Aziz answered with

the world-weariness of a youth. "I am the prince, the next in line to be king after my father. And I do not have any brothers. If he kills me, then he has defeated our line and we shall never be able to claim the throne in Riyadh again."

"I think if he had wanted to kill you he would have attempted it by now," I replied. "At least he would have begun looking for you, and he clearly shows no interest in anyone among the Murrah with some exception of the women. Though I think that he finds the veils disturbingly old-fashioned."

Abdul Aziz smiled grimly. "With men like him to watch, it only proves that a veil is the only hope for a woman who wishes to retain her privacy and self-respect. And not to become the prey of something like him."

Abdul Aziz would not mention the Rasheed name, and the boy tried to spit even at the pronoun, though of course he was too dry. We were all too dry, doling out our rations a drop at a time. The thought of spitting out precious moisture was abhorrent.

"But it would still be good if he died," the boy said again, as if to make up for his inability to complete the gesture of contempt.

Abdul Aziz sat in silence while I ate. One of the veiled women of the camp came up to the youth and handed him a plate with the same food that I had on mine. This happened every evening, and by now I could tell it was the same girl.

I was certain this was a girl or very young woman from the way she moved. It is interesting that when all other visual information is removed, one can still observe movement and pick out the finest detail that could indicate age or condition or even comfort under that concealing veil. I had concluded this must be Abdul Aziz's sister, Noura.

Usually she did not speak, but on this evening she did so. "Brother," she said very softly. "I would like you to come to my tent to stay the day and not remain with the other camel-tenders. I have heard some things that are disquieting, and would prefer your company. Perhaps we can discuss again the strategies of the Prophet when he fought the unbelievers at the Battle of Badr."

"Yes, yes, of course I'll be there," he agreed quickly. "You don't have to worry about coming up with conversation, I understand that the situation is not comfortable for you with the other women there. And all of them trying to find you a husband, too."

"I just feel uneasy with one of *them* among us," she said, with an involuntary turn of her head towards al-Rasheed's tent.

"I am sorry, I have neglected you," Abdul Aziz apologized quickly. "I wish you had told me sooner; of course you must not stay without a man in your tent to protect you."

The girl said something that I didn't catch and then appeared to float away, her great veil drifting over the sand.

Abdul Aziz looked at me and coloured. For a moment he had forgotten that they should not talk in front of me, that I could understand as well as any countryman of their tribe. And he could not mention her, not her name or her relationship to him, without dishonouring her and me both.

I was not concerned. The girl had said more than enough for me to be quite sure of who she was and in what relationship. And that she was uncommonly sensible and well educated for any woman in this world. The fact that she offered to discuss battle strategies with her brother was most forward. In fact, she reminded me of the young ladies who aspired to study at the great universities and would not permit the gentleness of their sex to blunt the acuity of their minds. I had never expected to find such a woman in Arabia—they were rare enough in England, after all.

Noura's voice and accent told all the rest of the story. She had addressed Abdul Aziz as brother intimately and had every right to do so. It was apparent that they had even been schooled by the same tutor.

I stretched mightily and made a great show of being ready to sleep, so that my young prince could hide from the shame of my knowing that he had a female relative with him among the Murrah. "Time to turn in, I think," I said crisply. "Thank you."

Abdul Aziz bowed graciously, took my now empty plate, and walked through the street of tents, though he did not follow the direction of the other camel-tenders to go off to their own place near their four-footed charges.

I was just as glad that he had left. I found myself hoping that Peterson would arrive with his special smoke this evening. Some nights he would appear at my tent just before we were to retire to enjoy a smoke, though Peterson did not use tobacco. He had his own special blend that he shared with me, the effects of it being somewhat familiar and very useful. We could not spare the water for the bubble pipe that was traditional, so one of my pipes was sacrificed to the cause, and could not have been put to better use.

It was almost impossible to sleep through the heat of the day. The heat more than the dryness stuck to the skin and pressed downward. Every breath was pain, every hope of shadow welcome. The hot air rasped into our lungs, leaching out any hope of coolness or moisture. And the heat was unrelenting, constant, unchanging until sundown when the temperature would plummet suddenly with the darkness.

This is when we travelled. In the morning camp was set, the boys assigned to the guests, as we were called, and the veiled women taking care of the rest, women who, under their veils, could seem almost invisible as they went about their chores around us. Had I not just heard the conversation with Abdul Aziz's sister, I would not have realized just how invisible they were in this world.

As usual, I invited Peterson in. We both reclined on the carpets as he prepared the pipe, not breaking our silence until we shared some long, thoughtful puffs and began to feel the ancient poppy relax our minds along with our bodies.

"They say that al-Rasheed will die," I started. "Because no one will give him any water. Certainly I hope you will not. You have already helped him out of too many scrapes altogether."

Khalid shrugged. "He has taken his servants' rations. Taken them completely, not shared any of what they have hoarded. That is not the way the Holy Koran tells us we should treat our servants and slaves, not even the unbelievers."

"You do not seem terribly upset," I noted.

Peterson smiled bitterly. "It affords me the opportunity to build my credit for Paradise," he replied. "And of the requirements of a believer, charity is the easiest."

I said nothing, though I knew that sharing water here could not be called easy at any time.

"Why do you tolerate him?" I inquired, though were it not for the relaxation of the pipe I certainly would not have asked such a personal question.

Peterson shrugged. "As long as I act as his caretaker, I can remain here. And perhaps I can do more charity by keeping him from some of the serious harm he could do others. Often I can distract him, or suggest something that is less evil than his original plan. This, I think, can be counted a charity."

"Yes," I agreed.

And then the drug took us both into the long periods of silence that were our habit. We smoked one more bowl together. By then it was the full blaze of near noon and I drifted with some help into a deep and dreamless sleep.

When I awoke I suddenly knew for certain what was going on and what al-Rasheed meant to do. I had known it earlier, but exhaustion, extreme discomfort, and distraction from the problem had slowed my normal processes. There were two royal personages in this caravan—a young prince and an unmarried princess. Rulers have used marriage as frequently as murder to gain or keep a throne.

Al-Rasheed was indeed up to no good, but I didn't know how I could tell Abdul Aziz. To mention that his sister even existed was to treat her with contempt. And yet, he was in as much danger as she. If al-Rasheed married Noura as he intended, the young prince would never be able to take the throne. That would be as bad as death for the youth, and far far worse for all of the people of Arabia. To say nothing of the Foreign Office and England.

I knew nothing of the dispatches I had been sent to deliver, but I could not ignore the fact that Europe had been stable for a long time. There was an undercurrent brewing, some shift in the wind as Mycroft put it. "Be assured," he had said, "that this is the quiet before the storm. We have been blessed with undeniable good fortune, but the Queen cannot live forever and the Prince is, well— he is the Prince. With Germany courting the Ottomans and the Hapsburgs trying to expand and consolidate an empire too large by half, to say nothing of the Russians, this blessing of peace we have now cannot last."

Arabia and its Holy Cities make it a crucial place for policy throughout the Middle East and North Africa. In Egypt, Syria and Transjordan, people are swayed by mullahs and kings of Mecca. Even to the Sultan of the Ottoman throne, the word of the Arabians carries weight. And while the Ottomans might be rotting of corruption and their empire splintering under their fingers, they are still a powerful force and not to be dismissed at all.

No, eliminating Abdul Aziz as an ally and contender in this area would hurt England and all of Europe. Al-Rasheed might *appear* a better ally on the surface, but he is cruel and selfish and without true nobility. He would make a dangerous ally and an untrustworthy friend, always ready to jump for his own advantage and sacrifice all the treaties signed and loyalties pledged.

No, it was not for Abdul Aziz and Noura alone that I was so concerned. Abdul Aziz is the prince that all wish Edward would be; al-Rasheed would be the self-serving monarch all civilized men despise. And he was ready to pounce on my young friend in a way that I could never explain. Not within the confines of Arab propriety, and not without grave consequences.

Abdul Aziz arrived as always, with a camel ready to be packed up with the tent and my belongings. My riding camel would not be saddled until he finished those tasks.

"Did you have a good rest?" I asked, as I did every evening.

"Yes, thank you, I slept very well," he said in English. We were practicing, as usual, and so it was difficult to express complex thoughts.

"Did you hear that al-Rasheed has taken his servants' water?"

The young Arab prince stepped back in sheer horror. "No. Oh no. That is, that is . . ." Even in Arabic he could find no word for how terrible an act that was. "That cannot be true," he finally said, though his face gave lie to the statement. He knew it was true.

"Yes, it is true," I said. "Khalid ibn Peterson told me so after we ate this morning. He is giving the servants some of his water, so perhaps they will not die. I was curious because I think that Peterson seems to be a good man, and yet he remains in the company of someone so untrustworthy."

"Untrustworthy," Abdul Aziz repeated. I gave him the word in Arabic and he shook his head and then spoke in that language. "No, he is much worse than untrustworthy. He is abomination, he is the portrait of the immoral man, the apostate, the man who is lower than the beasts."

Then we heard the screams just as I caught the first scent of smoke on the air. "Fire, fire!" The youths who tended the camels ran among the tents to rouse help. "Near the camels," someone yelled with a clear and authoritative voice.

This was al-Rasheed's move, creating a diversion that would cover his absence and any cry for help from the princess who was his target. As men rushed out of tents among the Murrah, I raced through the now-familiar route to where Abdul Aziz's sister had her tent. Abdul Aziz had left moments earlier; I saw him dash out half dressed and race to where the other grooms were already busy smothering the fire with sand. There was commotion enough to cover the coming of the Apocalypse.

As for the fire that al-Rasheed had set, I was certain that, given his cowardice, it would not be anything truly dangerous. Most likely he had lit a few oiled rags that he had brought for the purpose and placed them well down-wind of the beasts. Even Ahmed al-Rasheed knew that if the camels died, then we would all die.

I only hoped that I could run fast enough through the crowd to get to the young lady before al-Rasheed arrived. Though he had the start on me, to set the fire he had been further away. And being so close to the site of the fire, he must have had to make some token effort to fight it, along with all the men of the Murrah. Still, I ran as hard as I could. Al-Rasheed must be close behind. This was his diversion, and he had already worked out the timing. I needed to arrive at the tent before the chaos was over, though the heat pressed around my chest like dry fingers squeezing the air from my lungs. A deep, sharp burn pierced my side. I did not slacken my pace, for I knew what was at stake.

I could see someone's shadow in the tent. Though the gender was not clear, the stature was markedly small; it had to be Abdul Aziz's sister. I knocked on a tent-post to get her attention, without impugning her honour by asking for admittance.

"Miss, I must speak to you," I whispered urgently.

"Sir? I do not recognize your voice. You must speak to my brother," the young woman said firmly.

"I am Sherlock Holmes, a friend to your brother and I hope to yourself. You are in great danger."

I saw al-Rasheed approach from the vaguely defined street and make his way boldly to this tent with his two servants behind him.

"Quickly, Your Highness, come out here through the back," I instructed her.

Al-Rasheed disappeared from sight. I heard the main door of the tent being pulled open. "Come, come, Miss Noura." His voice carried through the thick goathair felt that made up the tent walls and partitions. "You know that you are contracted to me, and I have waited all this time. Now come out and do not force me to be impolite."

A sword cut through the heavy felt like it was butter. "Inside, quickly," Abdul Aziz's sister ordered me, sword in hand.

In any other circumstance I would hesitate. No woman could ever be alone in the company of a man who was not a relative. The word "haram" comes from the Arabic word for "forbidden." It was forbidden for a man to even mention the names of women not his immediate relations. Being found alone with a woman was punished by death for both. Noura and I both would die simply for being found here together. It would be the only option allowed, and it would be Abdul Aziz's place to kill us—or else he would lose all honour and respect and position.

But given al-Rasheed's protestations outside her tent, I had no other option. I took the sword from the princess's hand and strode forward to the *majlis,* the men's more public side to the tent where al-Rasheed waited.

"No," she whispered urgently. "Just marry me and wait here."

"I marry thee," I repeated to her three times in Arabic, and looked into her unveiled face without realizing what I had just done.

"That's it, you have forced my hand," al-Rasheed whined from beyond the black felt partition. "I would not have intruded on any lady, let alone my intended wife, had she appeared decently as commanded by her husband." He flipped open the entrance drape and took two steps into the women's quarters.

"You are not my husband," the princess said, snatching the veil over her. "He is."

Al-Rasheed looked at me for a moment before he sighed. "Well, if he is your husband you shall soon be a widow. And we know that it is an act of charity to marry a widow."

I raised the sword but al-Rasheed did not move. He appeared unarmed and at ease. Instead he clapped twice and his servants appeared through the opening, the very servants he would have killed through thirst. Each of them had a pistol in his belt.

"Kill him," al-Rasheed ordered them.

The servants regarded him for a long moment, then looked at me. Neither of them touched their weapons.

"Fire," al-Rasheed charged them more harshly this time. "Kill that man. I command you."

One of the servants dropped his hand to the pistol; the other frowned at him in disapproval and shook his head almost imperceptibly.

"I see we shall have to do it the old-fashioned way," al-Rasheed sighed, then drew the ceremonial sword he wore and waved it about in front of me.

"I take it you were not on the fencing team," I observed as I launched into my opening attack.

Al-Rasheed dropped the sword and turned to run.

Only he couldn't run very far. Peterson was standing blocking the entrance of the main part of the tent.

"Oh, Khalid, good. You must kill him and let me out of here. And serve as my witness, as you were here to do in any case," al-Rasheed panted. Certainly he was out of breath quickly for very little exertion.

"No, Ahmed," Peterson said. "I am here under orders of the Imam, who suspected you of treachery. You will wish that Mr. Holmes had been kind enough to dispatch you here. After the religious courts hear how you took your servants' water in the Empty Quarter and tried to marry a young and royal virgin against her will, I think that you will wish that you had been left on the sands in the hot sun. But I am not disposed to be charitable today. Not when we are only a few hours from the oasis. You could too easily get away."

"Why did you not shoot?" al-Rasheed asked his servants.

The man was impossible. "They did not shoot because you took their water. They felt no loyalty to you," I said rather brusquely.

"Oh, that was definitely the final straw," Peterson agreed. "But

I recruited them into the Imam's religious police. They are now deputies and will help me in making certain that you are turned over to the proper authorities."

"A royal virgin?" al-Rasheed continued to protest while the two servant-deputies tied his hands. "She claims that this man did not dishonour her and that he is her husband."

"If she claims that, then I think the matter is quite clear." A new voice entered the discussion. "He must be her husband. And I for one am very honoured to have Mr. Sherlock Holmes as my brother."

In the desert fashion, Abdul Aziz embraced me and kissed my cheek. "The fire was a little thing. He is too much of a coward to make a fire that was really dangerous. We shall celebrate this marriage when we arrive in the village. I will buy a whole sheep and everyone will feast."

The reality of what I had done suddenly hit me. "It is the only way to save her honour, really, under the circumstances," Peterson said. "You must be publicly seen to be Miss Saud's husband so there was nothing untoward about your being there to defend her in the end."

"Indeed," I said, switching languages back to Arabic. "If it is for the princess's good, then I can hardly refuse."

"Then it is all settled," Abdul Aziz said. "We leave within the hour.

As a matter of record, Abdul Aziz bought two sheep, not one, and everyone in the village as well as the Murrah band feasted our wedding. I did not, of course, visit the bride. And six days later, as the Murrah readied to march on towards their traditional grazing land, I divorced her most privately and with the greatest respect, for she was resourceful and intelligent and had uncommon good sense as well.

Abdul Aziz said as we took our leave, "Though you have divorced my sister you are always my brother, and hers as well. And I shall always be proud to tell the world that the great Sherlock Holmes is my close and dear relation."

He laughed as he got on the camel. The bells rang and he disappeared into the desert, and though I read of his exploits often in the papers I never saw him again.

And finally, here is a recollection so painful for Dr. Watson that his ratiocinative friend assumes the role of psychologist and prompts him to exorcise his demons by committing them to paper. And what demons! Had Holmes not prevailed upon him to set this dreadful history down, Watson surely never would have done so, and the only record we would have is Holmes's brief allusion to Vittoria early in "The Adventure of the Sussex Vampire." Warning: Events in this tale are uncharacteristically explicit for a Victorian writer.

The Case of Vittoria the Circus Belle

BY JAY SHECKLEY
N.B.: this case *not* for publication!—JHW

As Irene Adler shall always be *"the* woman" to Holmes, so Miss Madeline Snow shall ever to me remain *"the* girl." I am not (and surely not in Mr. Holmes's case) speaking of Romance, but of that identity gained simply by virtue of a radiant and unsurpassedly pure "She-ness." Such a creature can only be underestimated, and one could be on his guard against that danger if she were not so altogether disarming.

Holmes has asked me to write this, and I do so now in his chambers which used to be also mine, not out of any great desire to confess to the sins I've witnessed (and thereby mayhap contributed to?) but because I'm disturbed this evening, shaken to my core, and because my friend Sherlock Holmes has asked me to. I can not know if authoring a memoir will illumine any of the mysteries on my mind today, but yes, Holmes, I believe that the practice is otherwise helping.

Only yesterday the news came to me, with the day's twelfth visit from the postman. Good that it arrived within the final delivery, for I haven't been able since to concentrate sufficiently to read a letter. My dear wife Mary brought me the post herself, along with a cup of tea, and sat beside me on the striped horsehair divan. I took the envelope from her kind hand and turned it to see the black wax seal. Within, the black-bordered note was without ornament. I have it here:

> *My dear cousin John,*
> *Our Randall, Earl of Norris, has passed on from this Life.*
>
> > *The suddenness of events comes as a shock to all of us, but none is wholly surprised save his son. Let us say the Earl's heart had been troubling him more often than not.*
> >
> > *Your presence in a crisis I have always found steadying. Perhaps you would be good enough to drop by to-morrow to pay a condolence if not console his Widow Lady Jane, and I'd like you to see dear Randall the younger, whose stoicism very much resembles incomprehension.*
> >
> > *Do again convey my regards to your lovely Mary. In any event I do ever remain your grateful admirer,*
>
> > > > *Maddy*

I read, and at once the strength drained from me. As if the missive were soaking up my power, the document itself seemed to grow in weight until my right hand, which held it, fell to my knee.

Naturally, Mary took this to mean I was handing her the letter, which she slipped out from my hand and quickly read.

"Oh!" Mary said, among a number of other sympathetic noises. It is to my discredit I cannot recall most of what she said then. Noting my distraction, she asked, "Was Randall a dear comrade of yours?"

"No," I said quickly. "He was not."

Whatever she mistook my vehemence for, it aroused her feeling.

"Oh! Was he then a patient in your care? His heart—"

"His heart, if he had one, was no concern of mine." My harshness surprised us both. I took Mary's hand in mine, but found myself unable to speak further to her of the [here the word "man" is scratched out] subject.

Nor could I tell her of Madeline.

I think Mary drank the tea. I'm not sure of much. I remember pacing most of the night, muttering. Mary believed me feverish, but it wasn't that.

Would that it were!

When at last the sun leaked its first weak rays onto the grey city, inspiring a squadron of blackbirds to register complaints, I fell into a hard, dreamless sleep. When I finally awoke I no sooner recalled who I was then I became again quickly agitated, as if an accursed mood could be donned as simply as the previous day's hosiery, and with the same malodorous effect.

Food was of no interest. To please Mary, I ate as if taking medicine, or stowing goods in large quantity for a compulsory journey. When I departed the house without a word, Mary didn't drop a stitch.

I walked and walked as if trying to escape myself.

Twice I passed the house Randall kept in town, where he had lived with Lady Jane and young Randall and Madeline, Lady Jane's constant friend. I could see pairs of callers climbing the front stairs. I wasn't ready to join them. I kept walking.

All of London seemed ordered and reasonable as I stormed throughout it. I was moved by the array of dry goods laid out before the shops, and watched a man leisurely choosing a writing instrument from a bundle of fine white goose quills. Everywhere was the calm relation of the hansom drivers to their horses, hoofbeats and big wheels turning in time, the wheels like perfect cogs in The City's majestic clockworks. Even street urchins seemed at uncommon peace today. Dazzled at the ease about me, I turned Northwest, and by the time I found myself at Baker Street my feet ached from stamping on cobblestones. I passed one of those small dirty street arabs we called The Baker Street Irregulars. The child appeared to be waiting for someone.

As I mounted the seventeenth stair, Holmes opened the door, holding a large and evidently heavy earthen crock. I stumbled into his lair.

"Bullet severed the aorta," he said, conversationally.

"Holmes, I— *What??*"

"The family is calling it heart trouble," he said, "but that's what it was."

I stared at him.

Holmes stirred something noxious in the crock and kept talking. "Proprietary husband it seems, a constable in fact. Bit of an arms collector. Good man in his way. 'Wild West lead poisoning' they call it. Our Randall was in the habit of visiting other men's wives a mite profoundly. Matter of time, I should say. Tea?"

I sank into a chair. It caught and cradled me like the arms of an angel. "Tea. Yes, thank you," I said to my friend.

"Hold on," he said. Holmes was looking me over. He put a forefinger on my lower left eyelid and tugged it down a quarter inch. I blinked involuntarily. He took his hand away. "No tea for you. What is this I see in your eyes? Guilt, yes, but something— Hatred?"

"No." I sighed. "Yes. That is, I must see Madeline, but— It pains me hating a dead man."

"Why on Earth would one bother?"

I hesitated. "For the things he did while living, mostly," I said.

"Hmm, yes. And something else?"

"Well after—after—all that—well, he has his nerve creating a scandal with his death."

"I wouldn't worry. The man who put Randall down is rather well liked by the parties investigating."

Holmes's implication was: accidental death, no trial, no headlines.

"Well, there is that." I didn't feel much consoled by the facts, yet simply being in the flat relaxed me. A small expertly pitched fire was crackling at the hearth. I inhaled the fruity odour of fresh tobacco, then began coughing. "What in heaven is that stuff?" I pointed to the crock.

"Oh yes, this, I'm making ink." He seemed to be reminding himself. "Hydrochloric acid, hydrochlor— Ah!" He lunged across the room, grabbed something from a low shelf and poured liquid into a tiny beaker.

I closed my eyes, sighed and listened to him vigorously stirring his wretched admixture. When I opened my eyes, he'd covered the crock with sacking and gone to the door to relieve Mrs. Hudson of some burden. In moments he was facing me, setting down a vast tea-tray studded with fresh warm lozenge-shaped digestive biscuits. These looked rather fancy. On the tray sat two cups.

"I say, Holmes, were you expecting someone?" I picked up a biscuit and smelled its sweetness, then realized I should best leave it be. "I hardly wish to—"

"No intrusion, it is you I am expecting." So saying he began pouring the tea.

I had to laugh. "Well, this time your improbable prescience has somewhat abandoned you."

"How do you mean?" Holmes said mildly. He pulled a chair closer to myself and the tidy fire.

"Moments ago you decided I was in no condition for tea, yet I see you planned to serve me tea all along."

Holmes smiled obscurely, and passed me a full cup. I drank. "I say, what is this?"

"Chamomile. A mild herb to soothe the restless spirit, colicky babies and women's troubles."

I felt my cheeks colour slightly. "Yes, yes. I advise it all the time." Seeking to change the subject, I bit into a pale yellow biscuit.

Holmes was watching me. "Flavour remind you of something?"

"The scent alone reminds me of all that is pure," I said. "French, right?" I squinted at Holmes suspiciously. "I say, what are these called again?"

"Exactly, Watson," he murmured.

Madeleines, they were. Holmes had known hours before I had known that I would come here, and with Madeline Snow on my mind. As I was still comprehending this, the world's only consulting detective reached under the hassock, pulled out a beautiful slim leather-bound book and opened it past maroon marbled end-papers to an inscription writ in an oddly precise and familiar hand:

> For Watson, my Boswell, my friend, to herein record his most secret thoughts concerning outrageous events during the summer of Vittoria the Circus Belle. Write it all down, man, quick and now. Omit neither feeling nor fact, that the latter be understood, thus transmuted into Knowledge, to soothe the former. Doctor, sit now and write till you are well!
>
> Your admirer, S. Holmes

The book, in my hands now, was of smoothest vellum, all of the pages blank.

I was in fact quite overcome. Exhaustion and my many emotions of the night gone by had done naught to aid my concentration. For twelve hours I had lived in confusion and isolation almost worse than those of my bachelor days, for I felt my reluctance, or rather my inability to communicate with Mary acutely like a wall through the centre of my being. Now this show of concern—nay, complete understanding—on the part of my brilliant comrade was almost more than my nerves could endure. More than understanding: Holmes fully intended to restore my shaken heart, repair my soul. I doubted that this was possible, yet even so, I recognized that my doubts when it came to this man always proved groundless.

It's hard to recall what I said by way of thanks just then, in the way one cannot call to mind senseless dreams: I believe I began several sentences, and taken as a whole I said nothing coherent.

As a practical divertissement, I pulled a telescoping ebony and rose-gold dip-pen from my vest pocket, but Holmes said, "No, no, don't use that," and leapt from our embarrassing tête-à-tête toward his desk. He rapidly twisted open some fine mechanism. "Watson, quick!" I scurried over and handed him a curiously darkened glass hypodermic syringe, which he emptied into the vial in his hands, then set aside. With a deft motion he twisted an end-cap and reassembled the thing, which turned out to be an uncommonly beautiful writing instrument, overlaid with yellow gold in a barleycorn pattern. But instead of a nib, the pen too seemed to have a needle. "It's a McKinnon stylographic point," Holmes explained. "Cross is stealing the patent. The Reverend Franklin Dubiel presented me with this pen for 'the favour of exonerating him.' " Holmes shrugged, as if to say, Why do people credit me with the truth? (As ever, though sanguine of his very real powers, he lacked the arrogance to enjoy gratitude, which he often regarded as inaccurate praise.)

I stared at the wire-like nib. "Try it," he said. I did so. The narrow-nose pen seemed to skate across the vellum page, yet at the same time my handwriting took on the precise and even the look of Holmes's own.

"Quite satisfactory!" I declared.

Holmes leafed forward several pages. "You may set down your prefatory notes later. For now, write of the events concerning Vittoria the Circus Belle. And write of your cousin Madeline, setting down at length all you know of who she is, not neglecting why you feel that Lord Randall has been some harm to her."

"I say, Holmes!" I objected. "Such harm isn't something I feel, it's what I know! The deceased was a minor earl, true enough, but I assure you he was no gentleman!"

The voice that answered me was slow and deliberate. "His social standing is not at issue. Nor is your depth of feeling, my dear friend, which I assure you I respect for the honourable drive and empathic insight they impart to all your dealings, both medical and personal." Holmes drank some tea. "As you faithfully catalogue all the events to which you were witness, I shall smoke a few pipes and cogitate on various matters. Then with your emotion frozen in ink, we shall journey together to the earl's townhouse, and see for ourselves the impact of his villainy."

His plan caught me by surprise. "I appreciate your concern, Holmes, and wondered if alone I could will myself to go there, though I must. But haven't you better things to be about?"

"Many more pressing to the police, I'm sure," he chuckled, "but none better. Now write. No one need ever see what you shall scribble in that book. But if you will not do this, I fear for your nerves."

So saying, he began fussing with his slim flame-blackened clay pipe. I knew at once from this choice that all I'd hear from him would be the sigh of his smoking, interspersed perhaps with an occasional muttered revelatory expostulation, all in counterpoint to the ticking of the clock.

Once, indeed, in the ensuing moments, he cried, "Had they but recalled da Vinci invented the scissors, the forgery would have been plain!" and another time, "No precedent?! The Sanskrit word for 'war' means 'Desire for more cows,' " and yet a third time: ". . . much the same way that pressing one's thumbs into the eyeballs opens a crocodile's jaws." But no matter how intriguing or preposterous the outburst, I knew better than to interrupt him to ask elaboration.

Mostly, though, Holmes was quiet. His mind absorbed now with History, Legalities, Natural Science—the whole scope of other men's problems—he left me in a companionable silence to face my own.

The tea quieted my mind enough to work, and I began piecing together a mental scrapbook of Madeline.

Madeline. We were tiny children when we met. I'm not sure she noticed me then, for all were gazing upon her: the golden ringlets haloing her face, skin like a pale brown hen's egg but dimpled with a proud smile, and her eyes like the blue in a flame. 'Twas maybe Maddy's third or fifth Yuletide—I wasn't much older—and she'd been dressed in white, trimmed with lace and a crimson velvet sash. Much noise was made how like a frescoed Cathedral cupid she looked, all too precious for earthly use. I myself was quite invisible.

The next time I recall plainly seeing her half a decade later, no one raised any fuss: Indeed her hair had darkened to no real colour, her eyes had stoked down to palest blue, nearly white; her baby face had ovalled, and her smile when it visited seemed rueful. She wore a simple grey dress. Yet I knew Madeline immediately. To me her quality had if anything increased, and I knew though a child myself that I was witness to the formation of an uncredited elegance far superior to the gaudy infant.

When I spoke her name, she seemed surprised to hear it.

Another memory, likely late that night or the next. We were staying at Cousin Maddy's home, my brother and I in one bed. Noise jostled me out of a profound sleep. Half conscious, I drifted to the half-opened door and peered into the long floral-papered hall. There loomed my mother's brother railing at Madeline. She looked tiny in her muslin nightdress. She *was* tiny. The inconstant lamplight made her seem to flicker in and out of existence.

"But I didn't forget, Father!" she was protesting. "You never said!" Her voice had a calculated reasonableness to it, under which I sensed a disquieting hysteria.

I've not determined to this day what brought on the conflict, perhaps the lighting of the lamps, but suffice it to say I smelled strong spirits. By spirits, I don't mean to say kerosene. Far from making him merry, the spirits had the opposite effect.

"I'll teach you to forget!" he expostulated. The chance of learning anything else from such a beast seemed remote, so he set out to prove himself. "Where's my fishing pole? Where is it?"

"No, Father, please no! You'll wake the boys!"

This seemed to amuse him, for a semblance of a smile crossed his coarse features, like a small red wound. "Then fetch it quietly! Now!"

She returned to him nearly as soon as she'd left with a yard-long bamboo rod and a look of dread. Her large colourless eyes watched him seize the weapon in his right hand, and extend his left toward her, palm up. She placed her wrists into this huge hand and he made a fist around them, drawing them swiftly into the air high above her. Madeline lifted her head, looked at him and quietly said, "I've done what you wanted, haven't I?"

Rage twisted and darkened his face. Madeline swallowed her breath. The hate in his eyes dissolved her last hope. Her head dropped, and I could see the tracks of tears coursing down her face even before he began lashing her.

"Never!" he bellowed. "You've never pleased me, never!" The force of the beating intensified with his anger. "Hold still, child, will you? Stop making work!"

From where I stood in shadow I would guess she tried to obey. A glassy look stole over her streaked face with its ghostly eyes, and the fight, even the startle at the blows, seemed to wash from her being, as if she'd died and were only supported by her wrists in his hand.

The blows fell unaccompanied then. The rod whistled and smacked, whistled and smacked, and only the hem of her white gown responded, moved by the gusts of his fury like a floating apparition, but now and again revealing dark lines on her calves above tiny bare feet.

I, the coward behind the door, stood watching, sickened from eyes to gut, transfixed but, worst I confess, more afraid to move or breathe lest my mother's brother next turn his wrath on me.

Whistle, crack! The stick broke in two across her back. "Look what you've done!" the monster roared. "Broken a perfectly fine pole! They cost, you know, but of course you know!" He threw the useless end of the thing at the wall and stormed away.

Madeline then did something which stunned and embarrassed me. She ran into my room. Before I could explain my cowardice, expiate my shame, "I'm staying here," she said. "Come on. We're asleep." She climbed into the high bed, and I followed. We settled with me between herself and my brother, who mumbled, "What's all this?" then turned over into his dream. He slept curled as a foetus, taking more than his share of available space in the narrow bed, but I hesitated to force changes.

Madeline and I couldn't sleep at first, and though we were but children, whenever my body came into contact with hers in the slightest she pulled away in fear and pain. She lay on her stomach, breathing raggedly. I wondered if she were crying, or merely trying to catch her breath.

"I'm so sorry," I began.

"Hush," she gently commanded. "We're asleep."

She hiccuped awhile, then stretched her arms toward the headboard and arched her back until presently the convulsions subsided. That was interesting. (I believe now that this combination stretched the diaphragm, interrupting the rhythm of seizures.)

Meanwhile, I packed myself full hard against my brother's side and compressed myself as narrow as possible lest I further discomfit her. It was at this time, to the sounds of the child's pneumatic spasms, that I swore silently that if ever Madeline needed anything—any favour, any wish at all—that need would I fulfill instantaneously with all my powers and all my heart.

Becalmed by this vow, as if I'd arranged a mortgage against a troubling debt, I fell into a deep sleep.

Some hours later, I woke in that same board-like position, every muscle aching, head wretched. I lay quite alone.

Let us move away now from childhood's dreams and demons.

We'll take up our history years hence, flying to the balmy June which was not only a welcome break from the burdensome and dust-crested tomes of my medical studies, but also which began for me (and ended for her) the summer of Vittoria the Circus Belle.

All London was tantalized by the countless posted bills. Its tiny etching of the lightly dressed woman on horseback were but a hair's breadth from scandalous, yet the long broadsides were mounted everywhere, gummed with cheap paste to all surfaces flat or other-wise, and had indeed begun appearing in the dreariest days of March, months before the circus itself paraded jingling into our fair city. Little wonder then that I recall most of the wording verbatim, and even the relative size of the ornate lettering, wherein the longest lines of text were writ tiniest, and the shortest lines writ huge, like a bombastic performer speaking alternately in whispers and then in shouts:

J. P. Remson & Vincent Craswell Proudly Present
for your Edification and for your Amusement
An Authentic Continental Caravan
CIRCUS
at which shall appear before your astonished eyes
A Quality Array of the Best & Most Notable
Conjurers, Acrobats, Jugglers, Freaks,
Natural Wonders, Soothsayers & Wildmen,
Incomparable Feats of Strength & Dexterity,
Music, Confections, Amusements,
Diverse Gaming & Dangerous Beasts
from the Farthest Corners of Our Globe,
plus the ExtraOrdinary French Artistry of
the World-Renowned Rider & Dazzling Danseuse
VITTORIA
★ the Circus Belle ★

On Promenade With Her Parisian Prancing Ponies!
Come One, Come All to the Show of a Lifetime!
(Small Children & Ladies Welcomed at All Times)

Aside from these ubiquitous announcements and the bemusing reveries they inspired, the Times was all the show I foresaw as I made my way through streets ringing with commerce, festooned with brushes, boots and baskets; a world of merchandise hung in ever-various array a stone's throw from my door.

My ears had but adjusted to the morning hubbub of carriages, cabriolets, strident children and distant steam engines when I heard a woman's voice call out, "John! John!"

When one's Christian name is as commonly handed about as is mine, those who wear the moniker take small notice of its use. Indeed, I was very little more likely to respond to "John" than I was to take heed of a cry of "William!" or "George!" Additionally, I knew that the only lady I cared to hear from had returned so recently from a brief sea voyage that she was unlikely to be seen upon the street.

"John! John!"

Briskly, I kept walking.

"John! Watson!"

I stopped short. The man close behind me, bearing over his shoulder a great staff from which hung the limp cadavers of dressed brown rabbits ready for market, stumbled into my person, and in his mongering bellow performed for the benefit of those men within shooting distance (and unfortunately audible to the ladies as well) a vehement and elaborate oath concerning my shabby pedestrian comportment.

So I was already speechless and red-faced when Madeline approached, saying, "John, my word, could you not hear me?"

She let go her hold on her simple blue baise walking skirt, which she had hiked crucial inches that she might make haste and run. Unladylike as that activity was, she did not intend to publicly compound the error by allowing sight of her ankle-high boot-tops. Her face like mine was ripe with colour, but in her case from exertion rather than embarrassment. Beneath her ornate hat, strands of hair had dampened and come undone. Visibly she strained for breath, the whole region between her jacket's choker-like neck and her tightly cinched waist heaving mightily.

Do you remember? Corsets were so tightly laced when I was young that despite the myriad promised health benefits of such support, it seemed likely that at any moment Madeline would fall into a faint. Being a gentleman, it would be my pleasant duty to catch her in my arms. I'm not proud to say it, but for an instant I wished she would indeed swoon. My sole excuse is that I was young and never in my life immune to her loveliness.

Perhaps, Holmes, you don't see the beauty in her still, I wouldn't know. But I have looked at her longer, and for this knowledge I'm certain I could look at her forever.

So I nearly did as Madeline and I stepped aside from the foot traffic and paused for a time before a bric-a-brac shop, which specialized in distributing the homey goods and well-thumbed books of debtors. A commode set mirror caught my reflection, causing me to regret that I'd not put more efforts into the day's ablutions. Nor were my clothes the finest, though at the time I had no better. At last the girl seemed recovered enough to converse, and I, sufficiently collected now, spoke first.

"I am sorry I didn't stop. Really, Madeline, I could not imagine until you said 'Watson' that it was you. I felt sure that due to your recent voyage, you would be full in the grip of 'boat lag' at this time."

She smiled. "But John, Jane and I did not sail. The family has experienced—ah—reverses . . ." She took in a deep, satisfying breath, then explained what she required of me: my presence only, but immediately. Protection for herself and her cousin Jane, from Randall, whose motives she did not trust.

I accompanied Madeline to Jane's house in a hansom, and all

the hurried way she alternated between explaining, and exacting promises. The promises she needed of me were vague and open-ended, that I not do anything without her calling on me specifically, that I simply remain nearby for her to help however she wished, which as you may know I'd agreed to in silence so many years before.

Most of what she told me on that ride I knew or had guessed, but here are some of the facts which led Madeline to hide me in a parlour wood-closet: Madeline's mother and mine were sisters, Emily and Natalie, gentle ladies both. Emily died giving birth to Madeline, an event which no doubt worsened the father's temper. More recently, Madeline's father had at last succumbed to liver troubles, stemming chiefly (I would say in hindsight) from intemperance, vileness of disposition and notable imprudence. Thereafter her father's brother had taken in Madeline as a companion for his unmarried daughter Jane, a confident and sought-after creature who greatly enjoyed the girl's attentions as a respite both from boorishly eager suitors and from her father's incessant plans to see her well wed. Only recently had certain financial problems come to light. Madeline suspected these were compounded if not caused by her own dead father, whose pathetic estate her uncle still attempted to manage. Clearly she felt herself at the root of all the misery and ruin. "I always make work for everyone," she told me.

So now my cousin Madeline and I rode en route to *her* cousin (who was by blood no cousin to me) to forestall some ill-stated but apparent man-menace sort of doom. I made promises I did not understand, but she said I would. "You will soon see everything," Madeline promised.

Like any man who is no fool, I rode into battle quietly, but in the pit of my stomach I felt afraid.

It was an unusual structure, the wood-closet. Beside the ruddy and honey-hued stone hearth, it finished out the narrow parlour wall with the same solid masonry. Like the fireplace, it ran tall, wide and shallow. Most of the fuel logs had been considerately removed (some were stacked before the fire), but therein remained an odour of pitch and sap, and not a little debris—splinters, cobwebbing, birch bark.

I'm not a big man, and was less so as a student. Certainly in those days I was nimble, and eager to prove myself. (Even more so because, to my chagrin, Madeline had paid the driver with her own coin.) As I inspected this aperture, Maddy brought out a long green damask curtain of indeterminate age, which she hung deftly by means of some nails at top within that could not be seen. As if entreating to a waltz, hand to hand I helped the graceful girl down from the tiny footstool on which she'd been standing. She fitted it into the closet. Then smiling, she kept the curtain aside with a hand, elegantly gestured to me with the other and performed a half curtsy as if to say, "Your seat, sir."

Though not wholly surprised, I may well have looked alarmed at this strategy. If I were to act as a bodyguard, wasn't the principle to be a visible deterrent? If, however, due to an exaggerated faith in me, I'm expected to function as a sort of Trojan Horse (or the secreted contents of a poison ring), I had no wish to be revealed to the enemy whilst crouched on a microscopic stool in a cupboard, caught with both my side and my back flush against the wall.

Maddy looked at me, the stool, then did a terribly female thing. She rushed to the divan, snatched a fat fringed oval cushion, and set it atop the stool. *"Et voilà!"* she cried. "A throne fit for a king and a hero!"

Before I could stop laughing and enumerate my objections, a dog outside began barking and Jane called downstairs to us, "Maddy, you'd best be ready before he is here!"

Of Maddy I enquired, "She knows I am present?"

"Oh, she knew when I asked her for the curtain. It's Randall that she means."

"Randall is coming here now?"

She nodded. This was a problem. The young earl wasn't a man one would wish his daughters alone with. Or his cousins.

"Where's your uncle?" I asked, for I hadn't seen anyone about the house, or heard any movement's but Jane's.

"He's on a business errand. It's important, truly."

"Servants?"

She shook her head.

"Housekeeper?"

"We've been doing for ourselves since—"

A loud rap resounded on the door.

"Well, then, let me answer the door. You can be sure I know how to tell a man his presence is not required."

"Please." She looked at me with those pale eyes. "We've invited him. In secret. He's agreed to forgive part of a debt if we'd meet like this. Jane thinks—"

Another rap at the door. Then another.

Jane called, "I'm going to the door now!"

I said, "I can't say I like this, Madeline."

"No," she said, motioning me into the closet. "But I need you now, please, I'm scared!"

I wedged myself into the closet and sat down sideways, the only way I fit. "I said I'd do this and I will," I told her.

Social voices approached us.

"Don't forget your promise!" she implored.

I certainly recalled what she'd made me vow in the hansom: to stay put no matter what in the world occurred, even death. I was to listen, to watch if I could, but under *no* circumstance must I leave or call attention to my hiding place—not unless Madeline or Jane cried out the very words "John Watson!"

Plainly, nothing good could come of this.

I heard Jane's footsteps, and heavier ones beside her. Madeline dropped the curtain over my face.

Darkness.

Utter darkness.

Something was being said, in a man's low voice. It might have been, "Good day, Madeline," but I wasn't sure. A murmur came in reply.

Not only could I not see my hand before my face, I could not hear what transpired beyond the curtain. My luck worsened by the second, no doubt spoiling theirs. This tiny closet was no vantage point. Perhaps I should stand? Was that possible with this accursed stool in with me? Could I stand astride or atop it? And if so, could this be done soundlessly, or would the motion bring on discovery and discovery bring on attack? My heart pounded. Swiftly I commenced to experience a rather panicky sort of regret, the basic identifying emotion of Man in a Trap.

Yet, unless Randall, animal that I was told he was, could smell misery, I remained for the moment a less than public exhibit.

Then, like the dawn, I could see! Not well, but I could. My eyes drank in and adjusted to what illumination there was. I saw my knobbly hands resting on my dark trousers, and a definite pattern of light coming through the textured curtain. At the same time, I could hear even Maddy's soft, soft footsteps, and then the three arranging themselves on the divan facing the fire, facing me. Now that Maddy no longer stood before my cupboard with her back to it, matters had changed indeed.

"Well, Randall," said Jane, playing the proper hostess. "So good of you to come."

"Not so very good of me," Randall replied waggishly. "But here I am."

I leaned forward. Where the curtain ended, I could peer out and see the three of them on a worn divan long ago upholstered in crimson velvet. Jane, a dark-haired beauty, sat bolt upright in the middle, feigning to work on her stitchery, and in essence acting as the largest possible wall betwixt Madeline and Randall. I found that aspect agreeable.

The young Earl of Norris was the sort of man women liked and I didn't.

Although seated, Randall looked tall and proud. I saw at once he enjoyed to be looked at. He was clean-shaven, and meticulously combed, with the fair dimpled face and pursed rosy lips of a spoiled girl-child.

It was not simply his height, though, but his strapping girth which concerned me. While my complexion sallowed and my body dwindled from endless indoor study to someday save a life, Randall plainly spent mornings out in the fresh air, riding horseback in the shade of the forest, using an old musket against fox, beaver, pheasant and rabbit. Though larger than his typical prey, even altogether we three cousins made a poor match for his vigour.

"Yes, yes," Jane murmured, smiling. "Here you are; we're agreed on that." She performed a single stitch. "And you've arranged the favour we discussed?"

"You'd be surprised, my dear!"

"Do tell, Randall," Jane prompted. "How does this work?"

Randall made a show of examining his gold pocket watch. "When a half an hour has passed, Jane, your father will be shown into my office, outside which he waits even now. My trusted man Laurence will tell him I cannot see him today to take his mortgage payment, but will present him with a sealed envelope marked in my own hand with his Christian name.

"Within, he will find a receipt for today's payment, though no moneys will be accepted. For this I get two things, do I not?" He eyed the two women like a snake looking at a mouse.

"Two? I think not." Jane faced her cousin. "Maddy, give Randall the medicament we promised."

Madeline opened a paisley drawstring purse and brought to light a small cobalt glass bottle, ridged to denote poison.

Of a sudden, bright light fell on my face. For a split-second I feared I'd been discovered, but saw only an enormous scar-faced tom, switching its striped tail back and forth along the curtain, revealing me at intervals.

I leaned back and moved the curtain around the animal, which promptly jumped onto my lap. That tom weighed four stone if he weighed a feather.

Fortunately Randall was still transfixed by the poison bottle and snatched it from Madeline's hands. Ignoring the young lady's apparent shock, he demanded, "What is it? Will it work fast?"

Jane said, "I shouldn't expect you to ask if it's cruel or safe."

Randall waited.

"Although," Jane allowed, "any drug secretly administered which snuffs out an infant in the womb would be cruel."

Good God, I thought, what toxin are they providing him? Strychnine? Something more hideous? My questioning thoughts were drowned out by Randall's.

"But will it work? What is it? How long will it take? By what method is it given?"

Jane shook her head. "Our young physician friend said only to get this into her soon as can be. Injection is the most dependable method but—"

"That's well enough. I've a syringe on order from the apothecary."

Lady Jane interrupted. But as I was saying this is safest if given by spoon. Call it a digestive elixir if you like. If you care for Vittoria's—for the woman's—health—you won't allow her to exercise after, but let her rest for several . . ."

"Oh, she's strong enough—too strong, really—daughter of a filthy charwoman I don't doubt, or a hag who gathers fuel serenaded by Saint Clement's bells. An embarrassment now is all. The shop clerks say, 'Her smile is like the *Mona Lisa*.' A bad front tooth is all. I'll not allow her a fine FitzRandall for her travelling horse, freak and pickpocket show! Vittoria can overmaster a stallion fifteen hand high! Oh, how I worry after her precious health. All I do care to know is, why did this doctor not include a syringe for the injection? I mean, who is this doctor anyway, your cousin?"

"Something like that," said Jane, nodding. I came to the awful realization they meant me. I'd provided poison to no one!

"As for his name . . ." Jane smiled. I held my breath. Was she about to call me to her service, or was this just talk? "As for his name, you may learn it very shortly. For he is due here this very day, but if you leave now," she said, rising to her feet so that he must, too, "you'll miss him, and he'll never guess the medicine wasn't a purge for Madeline or myself."

He was standing now, sideways to me, wearing a false but handsome look of hurt. "But Jane, I thought you and I were friends! Why if you were half as plentifully endowed with money and moveables as you are with *womanly* charms, I should marry you myself. That is, in that case my uncle would permit me."

"Yes, Father told me of 'your uncle's' objection. Insufficient advantage, eh?"

Randall shrugged. "That is the other thing I gain in coming here, not having to again refuse your pathetic father's offer of a rather tempting arrangement, when in fact, being a man of normal appetites, I should certainly enjoy—"

Provoked by the threat of implications unsuited to mixed company, Jane smoothly interrupted. "I know that you imagine you fancy me, Randall . . ."

He gazed frankly at her. "More than imagining."

"Perhaps." Surprisingly, Jane smiled at the rogue, then blushed.

"No perhaps. In fact I intend to prove it!"

Jane must have meant to say "How?" when Randall made a grab at her skirts; the sound came out strangely. Jane fell back onto the seating, straightening her clothes, and said firmly, "Randall, you've told me you are busy of late, but coincidentally we are expecting guests; still it grieves us that you must depart so soon. Perhaps next time we can spend—"

He laughed. "Ah, no, I thank you both for your gracious hospitality, but I rather think it's best I stay." I was furious, and I knew the girls were thinking of using me. But would they? My heart beat loudly.

"However," he said, fingering his dear watch again, "if I leave now I just have time to meet your father and see his face as he tells me he cannot keep the house."

Appraisingly, he looked about the room and chuckled. "This is a grand old place. Not that I'd live here. Why should I? I'll just sell it to someone else." He leered at the girls. "Break the old bear's heart, it would, knowing he's not even man enough to give you two a home . . ."

Randall paused to let this sink in. "But I'll go . . . go to my meeting. Unless, my lovely Jane, you'd care to distract and delay me with some age-old satisfaction?"

She did her best to remain ladylike. "But what satisfaction canst thou have tonight?" With this, Juliet's balcony-scene question to Romeo, Jane meant to lighten matters, but Randall's response, being more physical than Romeo's, resulted in another skirmish. Jane shoved him off her, crying, "No! I can't! I can't!" and tugging down her skirts. "I—I have female troubles," she declared, "I cannot be of any use to you, sir!"

Beneath the huge cat my blood raced, I felt mobilized to fight, but the fight was ended.

"Really?" Randall said in patent disbelief. "Here I'd imagined your petty virginity was the obstacle to coming to your family's aid." Jane's face coloured, but she said nothing. "I'm going, then." Randall chuckled. "And still in time!" He took up his hat.

For the first time, Madeline spoke. "Wait, sir!"

"I told you, don't talk to him," Jane said.

"What's this, then?" Randall beamed with delight.

"Stay to tea," Maddy said.

"Tea!" Randall was outright laughing. "Marvellous!" he roared. "I thought my ears deceived me. The drab one has a voice!" Just when I thought he'd angered me to the limit, he said, "But I don't want tea. Just give me a few minutes, my dear."

"Out!" Jane said to Randall. Then she started, I could swear, to say my name. "Joh—"

But Maddy replied, "It's my home, too." Her voice resounded

against the masonry, clear and brave. Jane was furious, but said nothing. The same could be said of me.

There followed one of the strangest, most terrible scenes to which I've ever borne witness. I'd like to say I can't recall precisely what transpired, but truth is I cannot forget.

All right, Holmes, all right, I'll bloody tell it. I scarcely imagine any other person could believe so depraved a story, much less willingly consort with any person living or dead who had been in that room then, including myself. Yet I have little fear you will harbour ill-will against me for those events, though I myself do.

So, yes, I have feelings enough, but they're all a-jumble and herky-jerky. I will continue to outline for you (or is it me?) more of the facts.

He pulled Madeline's skirts up, right as she sat on the divan. No, that happened after—yes—Jane asked Maddy, "Are you sure?" and Maddy answered somehow by saying nothing. The room was so quiet I was sure they heard my heart beat. But who listened for mine? At once, Randall lifted Madeline's blue skirt, along with the white eyelet lace-edged ones that lined it. Then he lifted it more.

Above the plain well-worn and mended black wool stockings which were ribbon-tied just above the knees, her thighs looked rather brown against the bleached muslin of frilled long open-front · pantaloon-type drawers. Maddy's skin glowed like rosy pearls.

As if he'd some right, Randall parted her legs, stood between them. Her hair there, surely not meant to be seen like this, was tawny like clover honey.

He reached down, touched her in this citadel.

Her face contorted and she screeched in pain.

Then followed a moment of panic. I stood, with the obese mouser now digging its claws into my lap, and me holding onto him, biting my lip and remaining somehow silent . . .

Maddy meanwhile had contracted her knees toward her chest to kick at Randall, who reached out and caught her ankles and seemed quite amused with, nay, inflamed by, the show. I don't wish to make an indecent remark, so I'll just say that in addition to his interest in events, made evident by his own *déshabillé,* Randall's grin was monstrous. He moved in for the kill.

"Wait!" Jane had found her voice.

"But I don't *want* to wait." One wondered whether Randall knew how.

Jane's left leg shot out, and she pressed the shiny patent pointed toe of her black kid lace-up boot hard against Randall's belly, preventing him from finishing the job.

"A well-turned ankle," Randall rejoined.

(Holmes, you did tell me it is physically impossible for a pig to look up into the sky.)

Jane ignored the bait. Her foot remained in place.

"I'm not leaving *now.*" Randall was pouting.

"We shall see," Jane said coldly. "Maddy?"

Randall's hips pushed forward. Jane shoved the boot-point deeper into his belly, obscuring the patent leather toe-tip.

"Oof!"

"Wait," Jane repeated, then, "Maddy?" She petted the girl's neck. "My sweet dove, are you all right?"

"Bosh!" Randall expostulated. "She adores it!"

"Maddy??"

Madeline stared into the air somewhere, her hands over her lap. "I'm here," the girl said at last. She sounded smaller. "I'm sorry, Janie. I do mean to help . . . But must it hurt?"

"No, Maddy, no," Jane whispered . . .

Feeling weak and futile, I sat and felt my blood rising to fill the feline-inflicted wounds on my legs, even as the lead-footed animal leisurely readjusted itself on my lap. Which stung, but not as much as what happened later.

Jane stroked her cousin's mousy hair, pausing to swat Randall's hands away. "No, I won't let anything hurt you." So saying, Jane reached to her trembling cousin, into the girl's lap. With one hand she boldly took hold of both Madeline's wrists. Mind you, she kept her foot right where it had been. Firmly, Jane pulled Maddy's arms over the girl's head.

Maddy's eyes widened. Was it fear? alarm? For surely this was just how Maddy's father had grabbed her . . . I'd seen his fury, and doubtless Jane had, too, for she said quite clearly, "Hold still, child, will you? Stop making work!"

In recognition and terror, Maddy looked into her cousin's eyes. Jane stared back, not with malice but something else altogether. Clasping Maddy's wrist now to her own heart, Jane kissed the girl nearly imperceptibly on the cheek, whispering, "You've *ever* pleased me, ever!"

From where I stood in shadow, I saw Jane stroking Maddy's neck, throat and shoulders. Jane loosened and unbuttoned Madeline's shirt and corset-cover, and began kissing her cousin's shoulders and chest, whispering, "Such a good girl, so pretty, so dear . . ." and such. Then as first her mind and then slowly her heart understood what her cousin was trying to do, I saw Maddy throw her weight toward Jane, I heard Maddy gasp, a strange strangulated sound as if an ancient ghost were escaping the girl's soul through her throat.

Next came tears—from hope and gratitude—coursing from palest eyes down her be-kissed face, into her astonished mouth.

Jane continued her work, occasionally looking up to kick the fascinated Randall backward as needed, or slap his clumsily nearing hand and bark, "Wait!" close into his transfixed gaze.

But mostly she petted and kissed and undressed and in sum loved the girl in one enormous yet slow-shrinking spiral, effortlessly as if by implication alone conquering the untouched wilderness between. How to describe this steady, knowing approach? Holmes, fain to say it reminds me now only of that Japanese game of war you showed me—the one played with flat round black stones versus white shell disks on the cross points of a square wooden grid, owning whatever one's colour completely encircles. Here directness is of the lowest value, the least advantage. Over and over, while Randall

meant to plant a flag at territory's centre, and failed, Jane instead surveyed each border with intimate precision. Like the mountain to
Mouhamet, the girl, the Madeline, came now to the Prophet. New-
awakened flesh rose to Jane as simply as night-tides yearn up, up toward the heavens—then waves peak, tumble or relax, unfolding
themselves for the soft, brilliant moon.

Surely, as Inspector Lestrade likes to say, events had gone quite
a distance down Queer Street. But in truth I had no quarrel thus far.
In fact, Jane seemed to me a woman of genius just then, guessing
how to heal Madeline of a serious spiritual ailment, or else at least
how to get a bit of fresh air to the wound. I rather applauded the
pluck, the audacity: to transform Rape into Exorcism!

But I had (as I think had Madeline) forgot the reality of Randall's presence, the nature of some men to twist any advantage to a
greater one, to use with their every power what falls in their path—
no matter the cost to them in eternity—to grind the gentle in the
dust beneath their heels.

Jane, too, felt concern, for she enquired again of Madeline:
"Shall we send away our guest?"

The "guest" started to say something, but stopped when
Maddy said, "No." She insisted like a child. "I'm helping!"

"You are always helping me, Maddy."

"Not enough. I don't care what he does, but for the house, and
my life here with you. He doesn't matter."

For me, the analgaesia of Jane's devotion wore off fast when
she gave the nod to Randall, let him take what he wanted. She re-
tracted her foot from his belly—yes, she'd had to keep it there!—
measure by tiny measure. Jane held Madeline, and spoke to her;
Jane cherished the girl while Randall enjoyed the fruits of Jane's
labour. But Maddy looked all right with it. She didn't care now, so
far as I could tell, she didn't hurt, at least not too terribly. That day
she could likely endure Hades if within her cousin's arms.

I, on the contrary, had more than a little problem with developments, however foreshadowed. What was I here for, to lament the

hour of my birth? Yet there was at this point nowhere to go and less use in going.

Fuming with indignation, jealousy and rage, I tried to becalm myself by slowing my breath and involving myself in an inward recitation of the names of nerves and bones, yet watching Jane with Madeline with Randall, I hated to think of bodies (hers and hers) or cadavers (his).

Poor line of thought. I transferred my thoughts to: I'd never seen so much of ladies' underwear at once, save on a clothes-line. Odd how it bunched up now, her tiny becorsetted waist a-wash with layers of clothing from above and from below, enough for winter bedding . . . But all I could think was of her perfect skin peeking betwixt stockings and pantaloons, and of her sensibilities, which ought never face this plight, but be kept safe for that one wedding-night . . .

I pondered the dread consequences . . .

Next I transferred my thoughts to something neutral, I hoped: Randall's clothes, surely a subject of great disinterest. One item at a time, though I recognized what shop displays and clerks always point out as "Our Men's Best." Sure enough, garment for garment like a perfect catalogue of a fop, study made plain to me Randall wore "our men's best" silk neck scarf, our men's best shirt, collar, cuffs . . . I wondered if Randall adorned in men's best usually mistakes himself for the best man present.

Then I saw more of Maddy's flesh near his than I could stand the sight of, and, averting my eyes, lowered my gaze to the cat on my legs. Handsome he looked, quite self-assured. Desperate to put my mind onto something objective, I studied his head as any medical student might. The formations of his whiskers interested me. I noted that at each side of the nose leather, the whiskers were grouped into four short rows.

But unbearable sounds from the room still reached me. I closed my eyes hard, bent myself low over the scar-faced tomcat, wishing I could plug my ears, but unable to, lest my name at last be called, unlikely as that now seemed. No matter what, I would not abandon her.

Then as Heaven sought to comfort this poor captive in a closet, a rumbling came up, a distant engine muffling the grunts of the man I to this day have hated most. The sound grew louder, its rhythm building like a locomotive train, and when I suddenly knew what caused this sound, the sheer surprise of it nearly made me laugh aloud.

The cat. In my indignation I'd been puffing my breath hard on his fur, and this was his method of showing he rather enjoyed it. I stroked him. His back felt rather moist, too much so to have been wetted merely by my breathing. I put my head back down, onto my noisy, fuzzy companion.

I guess one might say I was crying.

After a silence I peered out again.

Randall fastened his pants, checked his watch, snatched up the tiny blue poison bottle, and made a hasty retreat. He banged the door on his way out.

"John Watson," Jane called gently. "Can I coax you out for a nice relaxing cup of tea?"

The mental image of we three fussing over little cups on that same divan sickened me. But just then, anything at all might have done so.

"I thank you," I said, my voice strange to me. "But I'd best be on my way."

"Come out now or cut a mail slot," said Jane, feigning high spirits. " 'Once, a philosopher. Twice, a pervert!' "

"Jane!" scolded Madeline.

"No," said Jane. "Voltaire!"

Stiff and aching I ventured from the closet, the old warhorse of a cat following at my side. Madeline looked nearly proper again, just more than a bit unkempt.

Volleys of daylight hurt my eyes.

"Look!" Jane gave a high-pitched laugh. "Old Curmudgeon's

made his first friend!" She chatted quickly now, too gaily, waving her hands, the way some women do when apprehensive or elsewise stirred. "Mudgy, you like him? Don't be aggrieved that he bit you, John. Curmudgeon bites everyone without exception. The remarkable thing is he stayed near you! Oh dear, oh my, I hope our mouser hasn't passed on his fleas to you, John!"

"I don't doubt it," I replied.

"I'm so sorry, John," Madeline said. She wasn't talking about old Curmudgeon.

"Please," I said, "Don't add that to it. Don't feel bad on my account to-day. I just couldn't bear it, Maddy. You mustn't deride yourself for any of this. Instead you shall rest. I've done all you have asked; now you must promise what I ask."

Madeline looked about her dreamily, as if she didn't know where she was. "John," she complained, "you're too good."

"Not by half. Now promise me."

After Maddy nodded her assent, I said, "Janie, see that she has a hot bath, will you? And bed rest after."

Jane looked relieved to know what to do. "I'll draw the bath this instant!"

"Mark me," I added. "Summon a physician if there's any unusual bleeding." Jane nodded. I felt awful. Madeline didn't look right at all. "And if she cries or blames herself, remind her of her promise." I coloured slightly. "You do seem to know what to say to her."

"I only wish I did, wish I could . . ." Regretfully, Jane shook her head.

I felt distinctly uncomfortable, a man-shaped reminder of all things vile. Additionally, I was to myself the embodiment of physical discomfiture: my arms needed to stretch and my back to twist. I needed to rub my neck and to eat something and to change my ripped trousers and to wash my cat-scratched legs and to quench my thirst with cool water and for a month to rest body and soul. But first I had to leave here, and before that I had to enquire: "Jane, Maddy, where might Randall be off to with that bottle?"

The ladies didn't know, but I had a definite notion.

"Promise me," I said to Jane, "You'll take care of Madeline."

"That," she said, "is what I will do."

Tenderly I kissed Madeline's hand, then departed.

I could not afford hansom cabs in my student days, yet for the second time that year and that day I rode in one. The first time was at Maddy's behest, as her guest; now if I exercised my quotidian prudence, a vigorous young woman's life might be forfeit. Plus, were Randall's tale true, an innocent babe was also imperilled. (When in 1666 the great fire of London burnt down half the city, only six people were injured. The deaths of *these* two persons then might be as great catastrophe, and through happenstance, no man was more likely able to avert that enormity than myself.)

All the same, I knew quite well I'd no idea of Randall's plans, his destination, or whether he travelled now by foot or cab or even by private carriage whose liveried driver stood outside the ladies' door while he performed his villainy. I still had no idea what the cobalt bottle contained.

What I did know was how to skip meals to offset this insane expenditure.

As the cabriolet jostled me thoroughly, I hung back beneath the tiny awning out of the sun, hoping not to be seen wasting my money. After sitting still in that cabinet afraid to make noise, the bumpy journey and the brisk pace exhilarated me. I'd have greatly enjoyed the sightseeing as London's work centres and monuments spun past, but I instead felt compelled to gain my fare's worth by examining each pedestrian, ever-vigilant in search of the evil earl. Indeed by the time I was near enough to the circus to hear the barrel-organ, I'd become so practiced looking for Randall that when we passed him I noticed his "men's best" white silk neck scarf. I might as easily have missed him: he was stepping from the door of a small pharmacy.

The hansom driver stopped after only a little urging, and as I paid out nine of my eleven pence, Randall walked right past us, untying a string-wrapped butcher-paper parcel about the size of this pen Holmes loaned me, but of slightly lesser length. In moments I was following Randall through the circus, down crowded paths between booths and carriages, pleased with the man's height now that I found it of use. Nor was his visibility solely of use to me. Behind and about him, a mob of talented street urchins crept and leapt, poised to relieve him of his valuables in the blink of a fool's eye. I wondered if he were clutching his pocket watch.

The crowd became denser as we moved toward the tents. In my way stood pale slender consumptive-looking women, donkeys and carts, people of every sort, booths that smelled of caramel and those which smelled of nefarious gaming. This last interested me, but not now.

I saw a pleasantly proportioned clean-shaven young man with shiny mahogany-colour hair coaching a tiny hairy-faced dog. Staring at his master, ears at attention, the dog stood upright on hind legs, forelegs folded, and whirled back and forth as if dancing. Just as I passed them, the young man yelled in a plain, harsh voice, "Good dog, Rocky!" right in my ear. The sound ricocheted within my head like pellets of shot. The man couldn't have meant this effect, though, for his sensitive hazel eyes met mine and an awkward smile tugged his mouth to one side when he said, "Sorry," or mouthed the word. I'm unsure: because suddenly the cacophony from innumerable "musical" bands nearly wiped my mind clean of the possibility of thought. Then my path cleared—I could see my man a dozen paces ahead, between us only a space of dirt and a stopped cart. I moved forward into that space, and a cartwheel gone loose hit me straight on in the abdomen.

When I looked up, Randall had vanished from sight.

I returned the wheel to its owner, who seemed unsurprised at his trouble, but glad to receive the wheel from myself, and not have to pay one of the wilier children to regain it. Before my eyes stretched a bewildering array of tents. Huge illustrated canvasses proclaimed unbelievable attractions:

WILD SAVAGE! The painting showed a patently insane, nearly naked bright red man scalping a yellow man.

WORLD'S LITTLEST GROWN MAN! The painting was of a man in a tea cup.

FROG LADY! A green frog with a woman's face afloat on a lily pad.

The preposterous canvasses continued as far as I could see. A bevy of gypsy girls hooded in showy handkerchiefs sallied forth offering to tell my fortune. One took my hand between hers and looked into my eyes. Her eyes were black, thickly fringed with matching lashes. Her hands were warm, her voice low.

"Your heart she is holding a question up for me," the girl said. Her voice had authority. She spoke as if she knew. That day my heart held a great many questions. I opened my mouth, but no words came out.

"Yes." She looked at me closer, smiling. "What is it you are wishing to know?"

"Where is Vittoria?"

"Vittoria." She nodded, and at once ceased to smile. "Vittoria Circus Belle." She disapproved, perhaps was insulted, but pointed a slender dark hand to a channel I'd not noticed between two huge yellow tents. "There."

I turned back to give thanks, but already she was lost to me in the throng. I hurried through the passage lest someone coming the other way question my presence. I found myself in a pleasant, more relaxed arena of caravans and cookery, where jugglers, ventriloquists and conjurers in silken vests rehearsed their arts, and circus children worked on tumbling and walked about on stilts. I watched one gentleman swallow a tuppence worth of halfpence seemingly for practice, while another hurried past carrying five puppets (including a dog and a devil) for a Punch and Judy show.

With so much entertainment at no cost, I doubted the public was allowed here. Fortunately, nobody seemed concerned at my presence. These were performers. It was not their job to police the fairgrounds. However, nobody present looked like they could be Vittoria. If I asked after her, might I be told to leave?

On the ground near a caravan lay a so-called "bonnet" from a gaming booth, dead asleep.

"Young man!" A woman's voice bellowed heartily from nowhere. "Look up, I say!"

"He's asleep," I said of the bonnet, looking around.

"Not him, you! Look up!"

I did, and saw the strangest woman perched on a tiny carved balcony high atop a wooden caravan. Somewhat portly, with large slightly bulgy green eyes, and a thick neck, she was decked out in a short, bright green sleeveless satin dress, which apparently fastened at the bottom to reveal her tiny suede boots, also green. Though her hands and feet were tiny and perfect, they grew at her shoulders and hips; that is, the woman had no arms and legs. She wore her thick dark hair piled on her head in an artful chignon. In one hand she held a well-cooked slab of breakfast bacon, in the other a hunk of bread. Beside her lay a tiny pair of green satin gloves with shell buttons.

She laughed at me when she saw me staring. "Hullo there, dearie," she said. "Fetch me an ale off the back stair, will you?" She pointed with the bacon.

I brought over a stone bottle, and opened it for her. "Have some if ye like," she told me. I thanked her. We shared some warm ale. I meant to ask about Vittoria, but didn't wish to insult her as I had the gypsy by asking too soon. The ale tasted good and I said so.

"Such a nice young man. What's your name?"

"I'm John Watson. Pleased to make your acquaintance."

She laughed, a quite engaging laugh. That combined with her smile made me smile a bit myself. "I'm Sadie," she said. "Sadie Book-binder. But there's nobody any more calls me that."

"Sadie's a fine name," I put in.

She laughed again. "Oh, they calls me Sadie, all right. But I'm an artist now: 'Sadie the Frog Lady.' "

I was reminded of the canvas poster of a frog with a woman's face.

"You don't look like any frog I've seen," I said. That can't have been the proper thing to say, but the ale may have loosened my tongue.

"Nor do I much resemble a lady, neither," she countered gleefully, wiggling her boots. "But nobody's demanded back his coin! I *am* a Frog Lady," she explained. "I know all there is about frogs! Like: A group of frogs is called an army. A fact, that is! True besides! I read it in a book. Did you know, there's all sorts of frogs. More than types of people. Some frogs will sing for you nicer than a bird! Me, I'm the best Frog Lady ever was. What's *your* trade, then, Mister John Watson?"

"I haven't any trade."

"No trade? A fine young man like you? Surely you do something."

"No, ma'am. That is, I'm at University."

"Well, a gent you are!" she said, finishing off the bottle.

I coloured at being called a gent, though the lady had me charmed.

"My family's Bookbinders," she continued, "all save me, that is, being as I am in Shows. My, my, University! What are you reading there?"

"Medicine," I said quietly.

"Medicine! Splendid! Just what I'm in need of! Fetch us another pint bottle, then, will you, Doctor?"

'Twas a relief to do so. Next, I would ask after Vittoria. But as I reached for the second stone bottle, another hand clasped it first. It was the largest hand I'd ever seen, and the darkest.

A voice above me growled, "Who might you be, eh?"

I looked up. And up. And up.

It became clear at once how Sadie had got herself so high on the caravan: that's where this huge young man kept her. He was wearing only a rough leather kilt sort of garment.

"Doctor! Frederick! Cannot one of you bring me that bottle?"

Frederick brought it around to her, but didn't open it. "What do you need with a doctor?"

I protested "I'm not yet a—"

"It's my wife I'm asking, Doc, not you."

"But Freddearheart," she protested, "You know as we're not marr—"

He grew impatient. "I asked you what you need with a doctor!"

"It's my knees again, dear." She began to laugh wildly. "Look—my elbows is swelled to twice their size! The young doctor cautioned me to quit the tumbling. But what can I be if not an acrobat? Look—here come my ponies now!"

Frederick sighed. "Oh, how Ale does make her merry! I say, Sadie, abstain, laughter's bad for the Show, but the wife likes her bottle, she does." He shrugged, then civilly shook my hand. "I am Fred Burke, the Wild Savage, World's Largest Man, World's Strongest, the Snake King, the African Giant . . ."

While he listed his impressive credentials, Sadie smiled, and a dozen horses and ponies, each bedecked with plumes, colourful livery and matching costumed riders, galloped past us to the largest tent, where they lined up outside a ten-foot-high entry-way.

On the last horse—a glistening chestnut gelding cantering slowly—rode the clear leader of the group, standing full upright yet relaxed on the saddle. As if this posture weren't enough, a yard of red (not orange) hair drew all eyes to her at once; huge brown oval eyes and full sensual lips conveyed a vivid, half-amused expression which drove one to keep looking, as if for clues to her remarkable thoughts.

All but for her corset, the rider's clothes looked to have been chosen for comfort and ease of movement, then as an after-thought decorated to suggest decency. For a blouse she wore a thin bias-cut long-sleeved garment of gleaming ivory, but spangled here and there with gold glass beads like a continuation of her glowing, delicately freckled skin. The sleeves were much fuller near the shoulder as was the style. Over the bodice of this blousing, a gold lace silk bolero had been tacked in place, guarding against complaint. Her matching skirt was not really a skirt at all, but a light nearly sheer ankle-length skirt-shaped pair of drawers or trousers, poorly disguised with the addition of a long panel in front and in back, also ivory with gold beading, trimmed in across the bottom with a lavish swath of silk lace to match the bolero. Bare feet completed the outfit, balancing her as she moved subtly to the horse's slow rhythm, undulating like a Turkish dancer.

"...and I surely am the World's Most Dullest Man for all you care," Frederick said amiably.

"Who's that?"

"What—the equestrienne with the smile and all the hair? That's Kay Dunn. A wonder, is she not?"

"Kay Dunn, I see ..."

"Well, you should see, for all your looking!"

"I came here to find Vittoria the Circus Belle."

"Yes?"

"Yes!"

"Well?" Frederick looked at me, puzzled.

"Well, how may I go about it?"

"You have no need of a formal introduction, not here."

"No, but how do I set about finding her?"

"Finding who then, sir?" He was shaking his head as if to dislodge nonsense from his ears.

"Why, finding Vittoria, of course!"

"You've found Vittoria," said the Savage. " 'Tis me you've quite lost."

I took his point all right.

Then of a sudden I espied Randall, walking apace toward Kay

Dunn, that is: Vittoria. I saw him address her. She nodded, still standing horseback, and headed in our direction at leisure, her expression filled with gladness like a child gliding atop a Magic Carpet. Randall, earthbound, and seemingly smaller, ambled alongside.

"My Lady Sadie named her last season," Frederick was telling me with pride. "She was a bit in her cups at the time, Sadie was (Miss Kay doesn't care for drink when she rides), and Sadie was watching the Show from the hay mow, announcing for all to hear that from that day forth Kay must be known as Vittoria the Circus Belle. From that show on she's been announced that way. We're allowed to see whatever shows we have time for, but only if we ourselves can't be seen by the audience. Not for free! Lowers the value, you know. Our Chief Showman says . . ."

I dislike recalling my own rudeness but I must report my faults as they are. Perhaps the habits of students, with the mind overserious and isolated, makes for poor manners. I should like to blame my youth, and the urgency of circumstance. But what redemption are excuses, for this action much less for my others? Without so much as a good-bye, I simply drifted away from this man who'd been kind and helpful to me; I wended my way purposefully toward Vittoria and Randall, hoping to speak with her in advance of him. I don't know what I, a stranger, expected to say which could lead her to distrust him, but it seemed important that I try to make some impression.

My face must have telegraphed the urge to speak with her, for at the sight of me she took the reins of the situation, signalling me back with a flick of the fingers, clearing a space before her horse. I obeyed. With no apparent effort she reached low as her ankles and grasped what I think is called the pommel of the saddle—a large fixed knob—on which she proceeded (doubtless for Randall's benefit) to perform a handstand. Lord, she was strong. She wavered not a tic, artfully folding her lower limbs this way and that. At last she pointed her toes to the sky. Her skirt-like trouser legs slid toward her face and one could see her striped stockings finished with bits of hanging jet beads just below the ankle where she'd cut off the feet of the stockings.

One could see more than that, too. I'd not known a woman could have such well-muscled—oh, I'll just say it! this is not for publication, anyway—I'd not known a woman could have such well-muscled *legs*. Vittoria was her own masterpiece (aside from the name perhaps), and my guess must be she knew it.

"Rajah!" she said, with a bold yet lovely voice. The horse's ears stiffened. "Rajah, bow!"

The gelding slid his front legs gradually forward in the dirt, and arched his back, lowering his front half to the ground, his mistress still atop him, feet to heaven. Then, quivering like a cat about to pounce, Vittoria's arms shivered and I don't know what she did, but she flew in an arc through the air and landed standing with her tanned feet on the ground at either side of Rajah's enormous and placid head. She somersaulted once more backward onto her feet, red hair plumping like a flag in a breeze, and then clapped, releasing the horse to stand.

Plainly it felt good to be Vittoria, her stance, even the look on her face gave proof to that, and like everyone who had the pleasure to see her, I wished I knew how it felt to have one's every limb and muscle co-ordinated for one's joyous living benefit.

Before the effect fully wore off me, she called her horse, fed him a nugget of something from a sack at her waist, and turned from me to Randall.

"Miss Vittoria!" I blurted. "May I have a word?"

"I regret," she said without any, "I've no patience for social calls before a Show."

"Please," I said. "It's important, urgent."

Randall averted his eyes from me. Vittoria looked bored.

"So I'm constantly given to understand."

I closed the distance between us. Rajah looked surprised.

"Miss Dunn," I said quietly, "I've reason to believe you may be in danger."

"Only daily. We thank you for your safety concerns; which I

shall not discuss. Perhaps the ringmaster will humour you. Good day to you, sir."

I wanted to tell her more, and was willing to be rude or fight Randall to do it, but the two of them hurried into the corridor between tents for a conference I was uninvited to attend, and besides, the horse Rajah stood blocking my way.

I lingered briefly, listening to the rhythms of their soft voices, but could not see much through the horse's chest. Randall expressed concern, maybe explained something, and Kay Dunn, Vittoria the Circus Belle, sounded grateful.

Then a brass band started playing, someone in a bright loose suit emblazoned with painted stars ran up and in a gruff voice yelled, "Vittoria!" and after she barked her answer, "Yes, Enzo, I know," I think perhaps she paused for some stolen kisses. That's just my supposition. It's unimportant. She did, however, seem a bit flushed when she came out. She put her arms up to the saddle, raised herself, and quickly rode the horse normally—that is, it would have been normal if she were a man.

I saw her join the queue of stallions, again dead last. She entered the big tent to applause I could not help but hear. I looked about for Randall, but he never came out from between the tents. I looked between them. Nothing. He must have exited the other way.

Gaining my bearings, I returned to the caravan where I'd conversed with Sadie and Frederick, but both were gone now. Even the stone bottles had been tucked away. They must have gone to the Show. Either that or were giving one. Seeing no use of remaining here, I decided to begin the long trek home, unless I happened upon a quill and ink on my way with which to make a note that the splendid Vittoria would probably dispose of without reading.

Tomorrow, perhaps, I would return and speak to the Ringmaster. Or the police. But how would I say I came upon this intelligence? For I could and would do nothing to sully the reputation of Miss Madeline Snow.

Lost in such thoughts, I headed from the caravan, feeling a

great deal older and more tired than I'd felt in recent years. Behind me I heard applause, and more applause, then a groan from the crowd. The show must be suspenseful, indeed.

Then I heard women screaming, and various shouts. I turned toward the big tent and saw someone running very fast. It was Frederick. "Doctor Watson! Doctor Watson! Vittoria has fallen from Rajah and hit her head. I shall bring you at once!"

I attempted to argue my credentials but this is not easy when a giant has hoisted you up, tossed you over his shoulder like a flour sack and, holding you by the legs, is with all his might speeding you away. We arrived quite soon, but even though I didn't walk a step, I was nevertheless out of breath: my diaphragm had lain across the giant's shoulder until he lifted me and dropped me onto a mound of hay, so though I wanted to say, "Where's Vittoria?" I couldn't.

Then I saw her being borne in our direction by a burly, smartly dressed man wearing the look of a pallbearer. "Doctor, help her," he cried out.

Her eyes were open, her mouth agape. One of her front teeth was ever-so-slightly chipped. I wondered if this had just happened, then recalled Randall's description: "A bad front tooth." Not very bad.

But what I saw next was bad, indeed: As they lay her beside me in the hay, I saw a gash on Vittoria's temple trimmed with blood like berry jam.

"Look, I'm not—" I began, but the giant glared at me. Vittoria's eyes, on the contrary, were non-responsive. I began again. "Look, I don't work alone. Surely there are other doctors in an audience so large!"

"We called for a doctor," said the dressed-up man. "We called and called, 'Is there a physician in the house? A healer of any kind?' Some sort of priest from Utah volunteered to pray, and then Frederick thought of you."

I looked at the wound again. Bits of grey matter, tiny as bread crumbs but to me most plain, oozed from the wound at centre.

I felt as if I'd been punched in the heart.

One of the first medical texts is an ancient Greek scroll, a copy of which was kept in the legendary library at Alexandria, which noted that when a patient's injury is such that the grey of the brain can be seen, nothing can be done. Always, the patient dies. It is that way still, Professor Bell lectured; likely this will never change.

"I don't believe this," I said, feeling at her neck for a pulse. Either there was none, or it was greatly reduced. "Fetch me a hand mirror!"

Sadie's voice came from the top of the hay mow: "Frederick, get mine from the caravan."

The enormous man returned nearly before he'd left, but we were none of us in time. I held the glass over Vittoria's parted lips but the mirror showed no fog, no breath, no life.

It was common knowledge what this meant. The group fell silent. I tried again. I fogged it myself, wiped it clean, and tried again. I left the mirror, still bright by her side. I pressed my hand onto her lower belly, palpating it quickly (it was notably firm), beneath the tightness with which her corset was laced. I closed her eyes and her jaw, folded her arms across her chest. Her arms were heavy, even for dead weight.

I felt then and I feel now that that was the worst day of my life.

A constable came to the group to ask what had happened. The Ringmaster reported that Vittoria had wobbled, begun gasping, then fainted while standing horseback.

The constable said, "Standing horseback? Well, that isn't what I'd call fitting behaviour for a woman, is it now?"

First she died, next this man spoke ill of what had made her so gloriously, enviably alive. None present had a word to say to him.

Sadie whispered something to Frederick, and then Frederick came over to Vittoria and gently arranged the dead woman's hair and clothing. The constable stared at the black giant in the leather kilt.

I moved aside to give Frederick more room, then stood and

walked out the tall back door I'd come through on Frederick's shoulder.

Behind me I heard footsteps. A tall (but not by any means giant) angular man was following me. He wore the vest and hat of a gaming bonnet, but hadn't the same weakness I'd seen in the faces of the others. "I say," he said when I turned round to look at him, "What's your name? Are you Watson?"

"Yes, exactly," I said. "They think I'm a doctor, but I'm not yet."

"Did you see anything?"

"Beg pardon?"

"What did you see today?"

"I saw a dead woman. I saw grief. Who are you?"

"Oh, me." He laughed, gestured at his outfit. "I work here and there, at this and that. I'm a clean-up man, really. Circuses are one of the most profitable places to observe animals, including people. I wonder oft-times why events happen, what caused them, what we can learn."

I nodded. "I'm a student. I suppose I do the same. I'm not much use, though," I said. "Certainly not today."

"Well, that's a conclusion, isn't it? But your facts aren't all in yet."

"How do you mean?"

"You say you're not much use today, but the day isn't over."

"Listen, sir, if you'd gone through the day I have so far, you wouldn't want to be the man telling me there's more to come."

He laughed, which seemed to sharpen his chin and cheek-bones. "Yes, I'm sure you're right to feel that. Still, you might be of use today. And before the facts are in, why, a conclusion is the place where you got tired of thinking."

"All right, all right, then! I dare you to make something use-ful of me now. And I'm not cleaning any tents for you."

The man laughed harder. And yet something in this conver-sation appealed to me, as if through reason the man was offering a simple yet genuine sort of redemption. It was impulses such as these which brought me to medicine in the first place, and events such as today's which made me feel my life—medicine included—was worth nothing.

I looked him in the eye and took his challenge. "You want to know did I see anything?"

"Yes."

"And who will you tell?"

"You."

"What?"

"You will decide what to do with the information. You will tell it all in writing to one person, the person you consider the most trustworthy. Include whatever medical data you have and whatever you saw, except, of course, me. In exchange for this, I will tell absolutely no one, on my word as a gentleman."

"As a gentleman?"

He patted his bonnet's vest and laughed aloud. "Well, on my word as a gentleman, if I am one, and if not, then on my word as a man. What do you say?"

I looked at him.

"You disbelieve me?" he asked.

"No."

I told him I'd seen a certain man (I did not say whom) leave an apothecary's shop. I showed him where Vittoria and Randall met. This interested him greatly. He wanted to know, to the foot, where they'd stood and I tried to clarify, but it wasn't easy looking through a horse. The direction of the conversation seemed to make him giddy. "Oh, you're being of use, yes-sirree!" he said. When he started to lecture, rambling about everything and nothing, I thought seriously that perhaps this bony, gibbering man was insane. I wasn't any more comfortable between tents with him, but he was on the far side of me, pulling up the tent-bottoms with his feet and bending low every foot or so to see the mud beneath. I had no alternative but to watch his progress, for I was far too fatigued to do anything. "Not easy, this," he commented, "but doubtless faster and easier to find such an implement here than if we'd needed to look through that haystack." He chuckled. "As the Tibetans say, 'No medicine better than patience.' They also say, 'Good men like to hear truth.' I intend to visit Tibet one day."

He kept looking, scrutinizing one small patch of dirt, then another. It seemed to me he was doing so as slowly as it could be done. Perhaps so he could complete his rather astonishing lecture. He had an awful lot to say, and I doubted every word. In later years, though, I happened to discover that more than several were true. As for the others I still don't know; I simply can't remember all of it.

"Babies have no kneecaps," he was saying. "They patiently wait two to four years to develop these. Our eyes, however, remain the same size from birth, but the ears and nose keep growing. Which might explain my face! Ah, look here; string from a small parcel. The pupil of an octopus's eye is rectangular, the same being true of a goat's. Other than human beings, black lemurs are the only primates which may have blue eyes. Blue eyes are more light-sensitive. An ostrich's eye is bigger than its brain. One might wonder if that's true of some people, based on their actions. The purple finch is always a crimson red. A Tasmanian devil's ears will turn pinkish-red when he's angered; a cat has thirty-two muscles in each of his ears, but these ears, however animated, don't much change colour. They do, however, redden in some people, and the pupil frequently dilates due to—Ah! What's this?!"

My companion saw something, but could not reach it without covering it again with tent canvas. He held the edge of the tent aloft on his foot and, gesturing to his find with his whole posture, he cried excitedly, "Quick, Watson, the needle!"

I reached down carefully and soon enough came up with a small glass hypodermic syringe, flecked with soil but perfect and unbroken. I laid the weapon onto his waiting palm. As daylight sparkled on the glass, I could discern a pale residue within. Immediately the man removed the plunger, sniffed at the aperture and smiled as if at the scent of a flower. He slipped the medical tool into a jacket pocket.

"Give me that!" I said. "Well, what does it smell of?"

"Oh, you don't want this," he said. "It'll prove worse than worthless, especially to the police. You saw which apothecary the villain went to, yes? That's far more valuable. Go there now and ask the man who's working if he recalls your man making this purchase."

At first, I thought the man was jesting, but he made no move to give me the tiny weapon. Instead, he led me out from the little tunnel, saying, "Now go to the apothecary's, and then write someone you trust about this tragedy."

It was the maddening end to an infuriating day: But I did what he'd said to do. After ascertaining that the young clerk at the apothecary did indeed remember Randall, I trudged home, images of violence and wildlife flying through my mind. Nothing made any sense. I wonder if it weren't for the water at a public fountain whether I'd have made it home that day at all.

As I neared my door, I discovered that circus pickpockets (sensitive perhaps to my state of mindlessness) had helped themselves to my last tuppence. I hadn't lost much, for I hadn't much to lose, but felt its loss all the more.

In my room, I poured water from the pitcher and ate some of yesterday's bread. Dinner finished, but too agitated to sleep, study or even enjoy the entertainment of a book, I gathered a few sheets of foolscap, dipped my pen in the well my father gave me and began my common practice of writing home.

Has wretchedness a sort of contagion? Just as I'd begun my letter in earnest (neglecting naturally enough to mention nearly all events of the day) my nib point cracked, shearing off the writing end entirely. Ink flew, sending drips which quickly expanded, forming ragged blotches on this affordable but too-absorbent paper. I had no other nibs. Careful not to stain my cuffs, I removed them, rolled my sleeves above my elbows and experimented with the stub in the margins. Not only was it rough, the tines were woefully uneven. So the pen, if one can call it that, skipped, dropped ink and did everything save write. I decided for the nonce I preferred to buy food, lodging and postage rather than nibs.

Discarding the soggy ruins of my letter home, I rummaged around in my drawer, found a quill which had seen better days, and with a pen knife trimmed it into fair working order. I began again, and found myself not writing home at all.

"*My dearest Madeline,*" I began—

> *I hope this letter finds you well and rested in Body and in Spirit. Kindly convey my respectful regards to your Jane, without whose caring presence I could not in conscience have left you today, so concerned was I, and am I still, for your Well-Being, which means the World to me. I will not refer more to matters best forgotten save to say that I am in possession of facts relating to Randall's whereabouts in the later hours of the day. He travelled next to a certain small Druggist (where he is well-remembered in his finery), and immediately thereafter he met with Vittoria privately at the circus, thereafter which I am sorry to say the Performer took a spill which cost her her Life. That Vittoria has lost her life is quite Public a matter, and shall likely be a topic of wide discussion throughout our City tomorrow. As for Randall's movements, I am sharing this Intelligence with you alone.*
>
> *Please take care to whom you speak about these matters, for your safety, my dear cousin, and that of your beloved Jane and even myself. However, irregardless of your Kindnesses to Him, I wonder now if your chances are not improved that the young Earl will keep to his new agreements concerning the usurious terms of the loan to your Uncle near the time of your father's Passing.*
>
> *I will not say that I failed you to-day, for I kept to my word as you exacted it. Yet my conscience does not rest easy, so*

*I ask you in this or any other matter to take Pity upon a man's
pride and to realize you will do me a grave Disservice if you
might ever require my Help or Assistance, my Efforts, Valuables
or Influence, yet neglect to call upon me to render unto you that
Service which painfully I feel owing.*

> *With a love that grows daily stronger,*
> *Your humble servant,*
> *John H. Watson*

I'd just written these lines when there came a gentle tap on my
shoulder.

"Come," said Holmes, softly. "You'll need to refill that pen in
a jot regardless. Let us go and pay our respects."

The word jolted me from my reverie. "Respects?"

"For the living, my man. We're going for the sake of the living! We'll talk as we walk."

So saying, he shut my notebook, took the pen from my hand,
closed it and installed it in my pocket as a gift. Before I could respond to this astonishing gesture, he put a coat and then his arm
about me, wrenched me to my feet, and marched me out the door.

We had travelled a ways down Baker Street when I stopped in
my tracks.

"When did the sun set?" I asked in wonderment.

"When it usually does," he replied drily. "At sundown, I believe. Come on."

"Yes, but—" I reached for my watch, forgetting that Mary had
recently left it with the watchmaker for cleaning and adjustment.
How long had I been in a trance, writing and before that fretting?
"Really Holmes, I need to know."

"You need to know when the sun sets? An age-old question,
my dear Watson. Walk and I will reveal all." At that moment we
turned onto Oxford Street, and I relaxed as Latimer's Bootery came
into view, knowing I could soon read the clock which stood like a

hydrocephalic street lamp before the Capital & Counties Bank.

Holmes continued talking. "Judaism is quite keen on the time of sunset—all their celebrations, indeed each new day begins at sundown. According to custom, it is officially sundown when one cannot tell the difference between a black thread and a red one. I rather admire the precision of that, don't you?"

I would have found this interesting, I imagine, for I do now when recalling it, but all I could do then was stare at the bank's impressive, free-standing clock. It said four. Could this be right? The clock must be broken, surely! But the gunmetal-blue second-hand swept freely round the pearly enamelled face. I checked the sky: black as ink. The street stood empty of citizens but for ourselves: the sole survivors of a man-eating eclipse.

"I say, Holmes, is it four A.M.?"

He nodded, and handed me as if from thin air a bundle made of a large, clean white handkerchief. The man was like a magician. I untied the cloth and found a slice of bread, a hunk of Cheshire cheese and three madeleines. The repast looked golden in the lamplight. As an after-thought, my stomach distinctly rumbled. It came to me that Holmes must become lost in thought as I had tonight, but far more often. Of course, he had no wife to worry over him. Before I was able to say, "But what of Mary?" Holmes answered my concern.

"You needn't run home just yet. I've sent word to Kensington some hours ago." I eyed him questioningly. "If you must know, I gave a note to Mrs. Hudson when she brought the tray. One of the Irregulars stood outside to collect it."

"You jest!"

"No, I sent Wiggins, who I'll wager sent Simpson in his place, who sent the new boy."

I hesitated to ask why he believed Mary received his note, and why I should suppose she wasn't worried again by now, and where on God's earth he expected we'd be welcome at his hour. Half-jokingly I said, "But that was an aeon ago . . . It is still May?"

"Yes, but now it's *next* May," he joked. From his jacket he pulled a cherrywood pipe and a slip of ivory paper. This last he handed to me. I recognized at once the narrow elegant penmanship of my dear wife's hand.

"Dear Mr. Holmes," I read. "Good of you to get word to me. Now that John is in your most excellent care, I feel at last assured and unburdened. Further, I shall expect him just as you say: in the morning, in need of rest but happily denying it. Tell him his watch is due back on the morrow. Cordially, Mary M. Watson."

"Now, Watson, this memorial vigil ends at sunrise," the consulting detective said. "There's no Hebrew ruling on sunrise, but Shakespeare notes specific birds which usher in the morning. So as we walk—for a lark, if you will—please tell me a few things."

I walked and ate, letting him formulate his questions. The Cheshire cheese was crumbly and sweet. The air just off the Thames felt moist and gusty, like many a damp Spring night, and I knew, were I alone making this journey to a dead man's house, it would seem more melancholy, indeed.

"I'm not sure how much you wrote in that notebook just now," Holmes said, "and, of course, I can't know *what* you wrote, but surely you are in more intimate rapport with the bases of your sentiments concerning that summer. In the fewest words, for what do you feel Randall is responsible?"

"For how sadly Madeline's life turned out."

"Hmm. Aren't you leaving out something?"

"By George, yes! He did kill Vittoria."

"Interesting. On what do you base this?"

"He gave her an injection of some poison, and shortly thereafter she died."

"I hadn't realized she died of poisoning. Didn't the newspaper say something else?"

"She died of a massive head wound."

"This Randall person bludgeoned her?"

"She fell from her horse."

"Ah. He trained the horse to drop her."

"You make the woman's death sound so silly." We were coming to a grand old gothic cathedral, whose bells chimed the hour.

"No one's death is silly," Holmes said. He had the cherry-wood pipe going well, and took a few extra puffs to prove it. "When these cathedrals were being built (and they were erected simultaneously all over Europe as well as here), many structures such as the cathedral at Rheims took well over a hundred years to complete. Think of it! Concurrent lifetimes, workers of all sorts jammed together. Naturally, there were a great many accidents. As sons and apprenticed workers learned the family trade—masonry, for example—by doing, really everything that could happen did. Scaffolds and materials fell. Tools were mishandled. Plenty of accidents happened, but very few of them mortal. It's like carriage drivers today: Our streets were designed for pedestrians and the occasional cart, and never meant to bear so much traffic. So collisions are not unheard of, far from it. But given the proximity of all these speeding vehicles, and the likelihood they might interact, it may be considered surprising there aren't *more* accidents and *more* deaths . . . Where was I?"

"Cathedrals."

"Yes. Accidents. All those workmen could be quite loud working at once over the long hard days, pounding and shouting to one another. But quite regularly one would hear the cry of a young man in pain and the pounding would go silent a minute, awaiting the news that the boy would live to bear some typical scar of his profession, often on the hands, of course, but it might be any place on his person. In these moments of silence, some philosopher would often announce as a warning, 'Ah, there's the sound of the Trade entering the body.' And so it was."

"Well, Holmes, what has this to do with Vittoria?"

"Just so: She was a most experienced horsewoman and acrobat, so say all accounts, yet she fell."

"She fainted."

"Fainted, say you?"

"Yes. The Ringmaster said she seemed to lose balance and her breath, then fell, and none of the innumerable witnesses disagree."

"Well, fainting! Tell me what causes that; you're knowledgeable in medical matters." (So was he, but I didn't wish to dispute while he was smoking his cherrywood and tearing up a conclusion.)

"A lot of things really . . . Palpitations, fainting and vertigo are all symptoms generally considered to be suggestive of cardiac arrhythmia. Any blockage of circulation can do the same. Then, of course, there's extreme heat or exertion, dehydration, starvation, excess bleeding or anaemia—even a serious fright might make one faint. Then there are matters related to expectant motherhood which could increase the patient's susceptibility to all the foregoing, and otherwise complicate matters, adding dizziness, nervousness, and in rare cases where toxemia is present, even raise the blood pressure."

"Pregnancy?" Holmes inquired. "That's what you mean?"

"Yes. It's been known to occur in women."

"Hardly ever in men."

"Exactly so."

"Blockage of circulation?"

"Yes, a prime cause of fainting."

"Could a blockage be caused by a corset tightly laced to disguise 'expectant motherhood'?"

"Yes, it might be caused by a corset tightly laced for any purpose. But such a cause would be ruling out poison."

"Indeed, poison. What sort of poison was used?"

"That I don't know. I only know it was injected."

"In large quantity?"

"No, I suspect not, as the syringe was small. Why?"

"Nutmeg is extremely poisonous if injected intravenously. Salt can be toxic. Ruling out all poisons if that could be done (and it cannot) would be time-consuming and ultimately valueless."

"Time-consuming, yes, but why valueless?"

"People don't go about injecting every household solution into others hoping to kill them."

"That is so."

Holmes said this next as if reciting to himself some private formula: "Everything should be made as simple as possible but no simpler."

"I don't follow."

"You said Vittoria died of injuries sustained during a faint, yet you know she was poisoned."

"Yes."

"I won't ask you how you know, as you are obviously taking care to hide the fact."

I looked at him. How much did he know?

"What I don't understand," he continued, "is why you never asked Madeline what poison it was."

"I meant to, yet I hated to bring up that day at all. Also, when I— Say, how did you know it was from Madeline?"

"Who else did you know then whom you would still be so anxious to protect, even from me?"

I coloured slightly, but in cover of darkness was not further embarrassed by obvious embarrassment.

"So why didn't you ask her?"

"Well, we exchanged a few polite letters, but I didn't wish to put the matter in writing. I assumed we would have the chance to speak in person."

"And didn't you?"

"We did, but not about that topic. Two months after Vittoria's death, Maddy wrote me that Jane's father had met with Randall's uncle. I was invited to 'the glad occasion' of Jane and Randall's imminent wedding! Well, I was appalled but relieved at once, you can understand, and called upon Madeline to, uh, inquire after her future plans. I was astonished to hear that not only was she pleased with the match, but she was leaving with the newlyweds the week after their wedding to 'help them settle' in their country home! I pleaded with her to stay in London; I was sure with the financial pressure thus relieved by the marriage that Jane's father would willingly provide her with a home until a suitable marriage could be found for her. Madeline is, as you know, a lovely gentlewoman. She took my hand, looked me sweetly in the eye and said, 'Whither Jane goest, I shall go.' The shame of it! The waste! But for Randall traumatizing her with his selfish, loutish ways, my cousin would have had a home and a family of her own!"

"Like you have."

"Yes! Well, Mary and I haven't any children, but we hope to. The point is, look how her life turned out because of one weak and loathsome man!"

"How did her life turn out, then?"

"Sadly, as far as I can see."

"Why do you say that?"

"From that meeting onward, I barely saw Madeline. It was as if Jane's life plans had simply swallowed Madeline's. First there was the wedding to be arranged, and quickly so that they need not travel at the height of winter. Jane's mother was no longer living, so Jane's father thought it appropriate that Madeline take on those tasks. Then actually moving to the country with them, helping them 'settle in'—you'd never know Maddy wasn't Jane's lady's maid! I wrote Madeline often, and after several months began beseeching her to come to London if only for a visit. I could not leave London due to my studies, I explained, but I certainly had time to see her, and knew a number of fine gentlemen who were anxious to make her acquaintance. I would be more than happy to chaperone if she liked. Moreover, even if she did *not* wish to explore her social possibilities just yet, I suggested it was high time she let the newlyweds get acquainted in privacy. This much was only their due . . ."

"And the result?" Holmes asked.

"The result surprised me. The newlyweds were already quite well acquainted, she wrote, a child was in fact expected, and she would not leave Jane's side. There the matter ended. I ceased writing eloquent entreaties, and the four of them, Madeline, Jane, Randall and the child moved together to London after the child was walking."

"Ah, so she did return to London, then."

"Not she, Holmes, they. I tried to arrange to see her, to speak with her. She tried to arrange for me to 'meet the baby.' I saw her and the baby, little Randall. They were in preposterously good health and good cheer. She seemed to do nearly all the work associated with the child, although Jane, of course, and Randall doted on him. They did have someone to do the washing, and a cook and so forth . . ."

"Doesn't sound like life turned out so sadly for her. Sounds as though you're the one who's sad."

"You're not listening!"

"Really? Are you?"

"I'm saying without the least concern for her, they let her live with them as a nanny, when rightfully by birth her social station is just the same as Jane's."

"But not Randall's," Holmes put in.

"Oh, what's the use in talking about it!" I cried. We were nearing the House of Norris then, and it was plain to me we would not reach an understanding before we reached the door. "Holmes," I said, placatingly, "you've always been a man of Science, not of Society. There is no earthly reason why you would comprehend that treasure known as family life of which Randall has deprived her."

"Let me ask you two more things, then," Holmes said. "First, can you repeat to me that saying about self-aggrandizing speech which begins 'As we say in medicine'?"

I laughed and obliged him. "Of course. It goes: 'As we say in medicine, if you've seen one instance of a malady, you say, "In my experience . . ." If you see two, you say, "In case after case . . ." And if you see three, you say, "In my series . . ." ' "

We laughed together at that.

The door bore a carved letter N, surrounded for the occasion by a black-ribbon wreath. I rapped with the griffin-shaped knocker.

Then Holmes asked, "How many people have you met who are really like Madeline?"

"Just the one."

"So 'in your experience,' then, the lives of Madelines turn out sadly. Yet all the evidence isn't in. Talk to her, Watson. 'He who is too shy to ask questions will never learn.' "

"Who said that, Confucius?"

"Rabbi Theodor Klein."

The door opened and we went in.

We were shown into an enormous parlour hung with black draping. A dozen weary men and women of what had obviously been a larger crowd earlier sat in armchairs waiting for the rosy fingers of dawn to release them from their vigil.

Against the far wall, a raised funeral bier had been erected, surrounded by numerous small tables which held enormous displays of white lilies, and carnations twisted into the shape of the cross, and such-like. I stepped up to the bier which held the mortal remains of Lord Randall, Earl of Norris. The carved mahogany casket was the most elaborate I had ever seen. The funeral home's "men's best" casket, I supposed. He looked good, even better than before; he was clean and tidy (somebody had got all the blood off him), and at last he finally wasn't doing anything, the sight of which came as a relief to me. He had, surprisingly, the same expression on his face which had bothered me so much before—a look of eminent self-satisfaction. Perhaps this was just an accident of the shape of his mouth. I would ask a phrenologist.

"John! John Watson!"

I turned toward Madeline like a flower turns towards the sun.

She wore black, of course, but the intervening years had rounded and ripened her so that black became her, for the same reason that black can make the very young and thin look pinched and angular.

Behind her, trying to affix a necklace around Madeline's neck was Jane, so that all I could see of her at first was her hands around Maddy's throat.

"Well, John, what do you think?"

It was a grey pearl choker, and went well with Madeline's eyes.

"It looks exactly as it should," I said.

"Young Randall found that today," Jane told me, "when he was going through a deed box. As soon as he saw it he said, 'is for Lady Madeline' "

"Randall," Madeline said to the child, "this is your cousin, Dr. John Watson, but you may as well call him Uncle. You're the man of the house now, so it's your job to welcome him and introduce him to those who are here."

"Hello, Dr.—Uncle John!" the boy said, and shook my hand manfully. A beautiful boy he was; he looked to be about eleven, with amber curls and eyes like the blue in a flame. "Welcome. Of course you already know my mothers (your cousins), and these gentlemen are my father's friends and hunting companions." Young Randall introduced each by name, and told of the biggest animal each had shot. We all shook hands and Randall Junior seemed pleased with our progress. After he had introduced all the well-dressed gentleman, he turned to the houseman. "This is Gregory," Randall Junior continued. "Gregory's family has been in service to this family for seventy-two years." Gregory nodded. Then a smile stole across the lad's face as he came to the good part: "Every Saturday morning, all of us—all of us men, that is—go hunting. And of course they go with us."

He was pointing to a trio of sizeable dogs who had set up shop beneath the bier and so were able to guard their still master and rest at the same time. "The black and tan dog is called Sammy. Sammy is fast and never quits. The fawn-color dog is Topaz. Topaz is Sammy's mother." As the child mentioned the dogs' names, each pricked up its ears, but otherwise lay very still. "Father said that Topaz was too old for the hunt and probably wouldn't come back with us one of these weeks. So I said just leave her here in the house. He said no. But now *he's* not going on the hunt . . . So I'm not going on the hunt. Lady Madeline and Mother say a young man can learn to do other things besides read and hunt. But I like to hunt! I also like Science. I'm going to be a famous inventor one day like Thomas Edison and Jules Verne. O! I forgot to say we have a retriever, too. A Labrador. She's the stout black one. We named her Little Doris after the Dickens play."

One of the hunters turned to us. "I say, don't you mean Little Dorrit?"

"No," young Randall said firmly, "she isn't."

The gentleman looked away and began adjusting his watch-fob.

"Dr. Watson, Uncle! Madeline tells me you know everything there is to know about science, and that you might be able to explain some of it, too."

I spied Holmes in a corner of the room near a pianoforte and an enormous harp. My friend seemed to be enjoying a pipe near an open window, and some amusement at our conversation as well.

The hunters were putting on their coats. "Randall dear," Maddy said to the child, "please find my cloak and your mother's and meet us by the front door, would you? Then the three of us may take a morning stroll together."

The child bolted into action and was seen no more.

Madeline took my hand, and walked me to the funeral bier.

"Maddy, I've worried about you my whole life," I told her.

"I've noticed that, John, and I've never understood why."

"Well, you could have married and had a family, but these people just made a nanny out of you."

"Oh, John, that's what all your beautiful letters said, but that isn't what happened."

"What did happen?"

"With this marriage, each of us got what we wanted, that's

what. Jane wanted Randall. Jane's father wanted to see Jane well
wed. Randall married a beautiful woman, has a well-brought-up
heir, and he hunted in the forest every Saturday morning, and visited women Tuesdays and every Saturday night. Randall's uncle
wanted Randall to marry for advantage. Maybe if Randall hadn't
extorted huge interest on a loan he made to Jane's father when my
father died, maybe we wouldn't have thought to extort Randall's
proposal. But as I said, everyone got what he wanted."

"I notice," I said, "that you never said what *you* wanted."

Madeline grinned. "I've never had to say what I wanted. It
simply came to me: your friendship, the chance to spend my life
with the woman I love, seeing her happy, our boy . . ."

Which reminded me: "He has very unusual eyes, doesn't he?"
I said, looking right at her. "I've only seen eyes like that once before."

If she understood me, she pretended not to. "Judging from the
company you keep, I can only hope the eyes you speak of aren't
floating in a jar somewhere."

"And now he's the new earl," I persisted.

"A minor earl," Madeline said. "And you know better than
anyone he is his father's son. The earlship is uncontested. Young
Randall is the sole heir. It would simply revert to the Crown, elsewise. Let's not speak of such a thing. I brought you here to ask two
favours of you."

"Anything."

"You always say that."

"I always mean that."

"I suspect you do. But to what purpose?"

"Since childhood it's been plain to me that one or two bad
men ruined your life."

"John! What a romantic notion! Short of killing me, how
could anyone ruin my life? Even then, my life would only be
stopped; the parts gone by wouldn't be ruined." Madeline looked at
me determinedly. "Believe me, nobody can ruin my life for me."

I believed her.

"Now that I've made clear I'm not owed anything, may I still ask you for two favours?"

"Three wishes."

"Only have two right now. The first is—Randall Junior needs something to do on Saturdays. What he doesn't know is you are the closest thing he has to a father. He needs someone who'll show him some manly arts other than simply taking aim . . ."

"I'm sure it isn't that bad, but I know Mary will be pleased to have company, and the lad might go on some of my rounds with me, if he's interested."

"He is!"

"Done, then. I am honoured. How else might I help?"

"Well, this last favour is rather more complicated. It has to do with paying a debt of sorts. Money isn't the problem."

I raised my eyebrows until she spoke again. "I fibbed when I said everyone got the result they wanted. I left someone out. Can you guess who? Come on, you know. Vittoria."

The mention of her name startled me. "You feel responsible for Vittoria's death?"

"Of course! I don't know exactly what happened, but we shouldn't have encouraged Randall. We were selfish. We should have warned him to stay away from her."

"That would have been ruinous for your family."

"No," Madeline said. "We had already achieved ruin. If anyone paid a price, it was Vittoria. Which is so very unfair."

This discussion was beginning to worry me. There were things I might rather not know. Perhaps that explained why I never asked her certain questions. "Well, to be practical," I said, "What could you possibly give Vittoria now that she would want?"

Maddy looked at me, astonished. "Why, what did Vittoria ever want? Fame. Immortality. To be acknowledged. You know when Jane and I were expecting the baby, we hoped we'd have a girl so we could name her Vittoria. Randall would have been livid, but there are two of us . . . Of course, we had a son, and Randall named him. Did you guess? You did?

"So as soon as our boy started sleeping through the night, we began a second plan to make amends to Vittoria. Many highly skilled riders are women, yet in the parks, the horseback statues are ever paying homage to men, men of war. Maybe there's a statue of the maid of Orleans, Jeanne d'Arc, on horseback, but I've never seen one. I'd be surprised if Coventry has a statue for Lady Godiva; I'd like to see that! Jane and I want to erect a life-size monument to Vittoria the Circus Belle, in a public park, square or garden. We've worked very hard on this. We have collected two portraits, some sketches by a sculptor and we have three tinted albumen print photographs of Vittoria herself, one in full costume! Her hair can't have been that red, can it? No! But since we've already let her down once, we're terrified we'll compromise something else: her costume, her pose, her smile, the plaque. So there are problems. Once word gets out about the costume, unless this is established as a favoured theme by distinguished gentlemen, Jane and I fear all our plans will be for nought, and that Vittoria will be as unremembered as she is dead. But you, John, you and your friend Holmes who's hiding between the harp and the window, you know a lot of people.

"What do you say, John Watson? Will you support us? Don't you think Vittoria deserves a statue in the city of London?"

I thought of Vittoria as I'd seen her first, standing horseback when Frederick told me she was Kay Dunn. How thrilling, how self-contained, how perfectly balanced and alive she was, muscled and practiced to do just as she liked, till all London was enamoured of the mere idea of her. I wished I had seen her show. I felt poorer knowing I'd go to my grave never witnessing all she lived for.

I also felt poorer that she'd gone to *her* grave with me doubly in attendance. I fancied myself a humanitarian and a healer, but given my performance on the day of her death, I may as well have shot the poor woman at close range.

"Madeline," I said to her. "I swear you and Jane shall get your statue raised, even if I must speak with every London horsewoman and every patron of the arts and every member of Parliament."

Maddy gave out a whoop of joy. In her delirium, she grabbed and kissed me on the face and neck, and then sped downstairs to tell Jane the news. I doubt that Madeline knew she was kissing me, but I knew she had been, and I felt dizzy and weak like an expectant mother in a cinched whalebone corset.

I staggered over to Holmes, my face doubtless purple from recent intrigue. Holmes gestured, at me or at the dead man, I'm not sure which, saying, "A sage can learn from a fool; a fool cannot learn even from a sage."

I tried to keep pace. "Rabbi Klein tell you that?"

"It's a Buddhist precept."

"Aha. What else have you been pondering?"

"I've decided to obtain some camel's milk. Not much, maybe a pint."

"Whatever for?"

"To try with my tea."

"But why the devil *camel's* milk?"

"In four thousand years, no new animal has been domesticated, so I won't wait, I'll choose among the milks of those mammals already tamed. I read that camel's milk won't curdle, which seems a fine quality."

"But gad, Holmes, what can camel's milk taste like?"

"Precisely why I must obtain some," Holmes said. "I will let you know next week."

We stood for a time staring out the window. "Did you see the man from Surrey?"

"Surrey? I didn't notice."

"The man who let us in, their driver, I should think. Did you note the hair-loss pattern?"

"Yes. Smallpox I'd say." From across the room I could easily see the rough area where it had started on the neck, and without wanting to, I visualized the small red lesions boiling relentlessly across one side of his head and half his face over the course of days. It was the sort of thing one waited out at a respectful distance, hoping first it wasn't deadly in this instance, and second that the disfigurement wouldn't be too great. "Must have been dreadful," I noted.

"Tends to be," Holmes remarked. We walked to the window and looked out as the first wan rays of light seeped into the night sky. "Speaking of medical matters," Holmes said, reaching into a pocket, "do you know what this is?"

I opened a tiny Chinese box of carved red resin. Inside was a glass tube marked with gradations. It was the vial of the syringe implicated in Vittoria's death!

"The clean-up man at the circus! That was you?"

"The same."

"May I?"

"Sniff as you please."

"Chamomile!" My dear cousin had given Randall chamomile tea, and told him it was a deadly abortifacient toxin. Thanks in part to her unwillingness to harm anyone (and to the vanity of women, and to the sturdiness of corsets), Madeline's bastard son became a landed earl, while she lives out her days married in all but name to her cousin, her closest female friend.

I, too, got what I'd wanted: a wife, a family, Madeline's happiness and even, in the way she chose to bestow it, her earthly love. Consider: This boy whose conception I witnessed, which event took in large measure not Madeline's innocence, after all, but mine (for that day I learned to hate), this boy whose mother I have always loved will now be like a son to me. My sweet Mary will welcome a child's presence, if only a day a week. Perhaps the contact will help her to conceive. One hears of such things happening.

After seeing Madeline so happy today, I believed anything could happen!

I watched the three of them now out on the lawn in front of the house, less Lord Randall's victims at this late date, than his survivors: Madeline and Jane in long cloaks walked side by side, conversing, the boy in the lead as the sun rose. One needn't drink camel's milk, I was fairly sure, to have a surprise with one's breakfast. What could be less exotic than one's own cousin? Yet all this time I imagined her as some put-upon Cinderella while she was living the life she dared to imagine.

Perhaps camel's milk is tasty. Surely, worth a try.

The light intensified as it usually does—another perfectly ordinary English morning. The women and the child heard a singing in the sky and looked up. Overhead flew an exaltation of larks.

Contributors Notes

HENRY SLESAR won the Mystery Writers of America's Edgar for *The Gray Flannel Shroud* and television's Emmy award for his former position as head writer of the long-running daytime drama *The Edge of Night*. His prolific writing career includes over five hundred short stories, of which approximately one-third are science-fantasy, a novel adapted into film as *Twenty Million Miles to Earth*, and scripts for the TV classic series *The Man from U.N.C.L.E.* Another Sherlock Holmes story, "The Case of the Notorious Canary Trainer," appears in *The Resurrected Holmes.*

H. PAUL JEFFERS is the author of more than thirty books of fiction and nonfiction, including the Sergeant John Bogdanovic mysteries, *A Grand Night for Murder* and *Readers Guide to Murder,* and a pair of Sherlock Holmes novels, *The Adventure of the Stalwart Companions* and *Murder Most Irregular.*

PETER CANNON's literary parodies include *Scream for Jeeves,* a combination of the styles and themes of P. G. Wodehouse and H. P. Lovecraft; *Pulptime,* a novel about Lovecraft and Sherlock Holmes, and "Holmes and the Loss of the British Barque *Sophy Anderson,*" a Holmes story in the style of C. S. Forester, published in *The Resurrected Holmes.* A native Californian, Mr. Cannon grew up in Massachusetts and now divides his time as a freelance writer between London and New York.

PAT MULLEN is a New York University theatre teacher and author of *The Stone Movers* (Warner Aspect Novels). Her stories,

"Lydia's Season," "The Curse of the Wandering Gypsy" and "Don't Open That Book!" have appeared, respectively, in Marvin Kaye's GuildAmerica anthologies *Angels of Darkness, Witches and Warlocks* and *Don't Open This Book.*

KATHLEEN BRADY is the author of *Ida Tarbell: Portrait of a Muckraker* (University of Pittsburgh Press), *Lucille: The Life of Lucille Ball* (Hyperion) and a novel, *Inside Out* (W. W. Norton). She has appeared on the A&E Biography program *The Rockefellers,* and the PBS series *The Prize.* She is a resident of New York City.

TERRY MCGARRY works for *The New Yorker,* has written dark fantasy tales such as "Cadenza," "Loophole" and "Red Heart," and was a 1992 runner-up for the Gryphon Award. Another Sherlock Holmes story that she "edited" is "Victor Lynch the Forger" in *The Resurrected Holmes.*

EDWARD D. HOCH, a former president of the Mystery Writers of America, is one of the most prolific writers in the history of mystery fiction. His bibliography numbers more short stories than Ed can remember; the current tally is somewhere over eight hundred. He "edited" "The Manor House Case" for *The Resurrected Holmes.*

CAROLE BUGGÉ has "edited" several nigh-perfect Sherlock Holmes pastiches for St. Martin's Press, which soon will publish her first Holmesian novel, *The Star of India.* She wears many hats: improvisational comedy teacher and performer, playwright-composer, poet, writing instructor. She has written several excellent fantasy stories and two earlier Holmes short stories, "The Case of the Tongue-Tied Tenor" (in *The Game Is Afoot*) and "The Madness of Colonel Warburton" (in *The Resurrected Holmes*).

CRAIG SHAW GARDNER writes both horror and slapstick fantasy, notably a series of *Arabian Nights* spoofs and the hilarious Ebenezum sorcery novels. His earlier Sherlock Holmes forays include "The Politician, the Lighthouse and the Trained Cormorant" (in *The Resurrected Holmes*) and "The Sinister Cheesecake" (in *The Game Is Afoot*).

ALINE MYETTE-VOLSKY is a resident of Fanwood, New Jersey, and mother of the esteemed fantasy novelist Paula Volsky. Her genteel horror story "The Bear Garden" appears in Marvin Kaye's GuildAmerica anthology *Don't Open This Book.*

PATRICK LOBRUTTO is cofounder of the Foundation science-fiction imprint, and is now an editorial director at Bantam Doubleday Dell. He is the recipient of the coveted Best Editor Award at the World Fantasy Convention. His comic stories "Vision Quest" and "Genesis for Dummies" appear, respectively, in the Guild-America anthologies *Masterpieces of Terror and the Unknown* and *Don't Open This Book.*

P. C. HODGELL has written several well-regarded fantasy novels, including *Godstalk, Dark of the Moon,* and *Seeker's Mask,* as well as a collection of short fiction, *Blood and Ivory.* She is currently working on a fantasy sequel to Walter Scott's *Ivanhoe.* A teacher at the University of Wisconsin, she lives in a wind-swept mansion with her mother, three cats and 1,600 balls of yarn, "because I'm an art knitter."

ROBERTA ROGOW is a New Jersey children's librarian who contributes to science-fantasy periodicals, the *Merovingen Nights* anthologies and three collections of new Sherlock Holmes tales published by St. Martin's Press, which is also slated to publish her first mystery novel. Paragon published her study *Futurespeak: A Fan's Guide to the Language of Science Fiction.*

SHARIANN LEWITT is usually a hard-science-fiction writer with eight books to her credit, the most recent being *Interface Masque* from Tor. She is originally from New York, studied in France before completing graduate work at Yale, and then spent two years working with a group of Saudis. When not on the road she lives in Washington, D.C., in a mixed human-avian flock.

JAY SHECKLEY has worked as a newspaper editor, mistletoe distributor, writing instructor, hot-tub (women only) hypnotherapist, book publicist, artist and designer of humorous bumper stickers ("Gefilte" and forty other fish), was top earner at the 1992 San

Francisco AIDS Dance-A-Thon and is co-owner of the Dark Carnival Bookstore in Berkeley, California. Her work has appeared in *Gallery, Heavy Metal, National Lampoon, Night Cry, Pulpsmith, Twilight Zone, Weird Tales* and the anthologies *Devils and Demons, Don't Open This Book, Fantasy and Terror* and *Total Abandon*.

Acknowledgments